About the aut

The author was born in Scotland and, after serving in the Army, embarked on a career in industry.

He has worked in several different sectors in senior roles and was latterly CEO of a large international data capture company.

He retired for the first time in 1995 to take on a consultancy designed to help new businesses become established.

In 2018, he finally retired from business life to become a full-time author.

John lives in Scotland and Portugal with his wife, and they have two grown-up sons.

THE NORWICH MURDERS

The sixth DCI Burt murder mystery

JOHN REID

THE NORWICH MURDERS
The sixth DCI Burt murder mystery

Vanguard Press

VANGUARD PAPERBACK

© Copyright 2022
John Reid

The right of John Reid to be identified as author of
this work has been asserted by him in accordance with the
Copyright, Designs and Patents Act 1988.

All Rights Reserved

No reproduction, copy or transmission of this publication
may be made without written permission.
No paragraph of this publication may be reproduced,
copied or transmitted save with the written permission of the publisher, or in
accordance with the provisions
of the Copyright Act 1956 (as amended).

Any person who commits any unauthorised act in relation to
this publication may be liable to criminal
prosecution and civil claims for damages.

A CIP catalogue record for this title is
available from the British Library.

ISBN 978 1 80016 463 5

Vanguard Press is an imprint of
Pegasus Elliot MacKenzie Publishers Ltd
www.pegasuspublishers.com

First Published in 2022

Vanguard Press
Sheraton House Castle Park
Cambridge England

Printed & Bound in Great Britain

Dedication

To my wife for her continued support and assistance in writing this novel and also to my reading forum for their sometimes humorous but always constructive comments.

Also, from the DCI Steve Burt Series by John Reid

The Forgotten Gun
The Auction
The Disciples
The Watchers
The Voice

Coming soon in the same series

The Abduction

Acknowledgements

For Richard at Kaya Consult for his invaluable help and advice.

This is a work of fiction. Names, characters, businesses, places, events and incidents are either the products of the author's imagination or used in a fictitious manner. Any resemblance to actual persons, living or dead, or actual events is purely coincidental.

Chapter One

Detective Sergeant Elsie Brown sat in the living room of her two-bedroom semi-detached house. The clock on her wall showed it was 09.02 a.m. She had bought her house, located in the village of Stone just outside Norwich, when she'd been promoted to CID. As she sat, she looked back to the day twenty-five years ago when she excitedly moved into her brand-new home on what the builder had advertised as luxury living for young families.

Elsie had never had a family and after she left school, she had joined the Norwich Constabulary as a young cadet. She had had very few boyfriends but didn't know why her love life had been so spartan. She'd been told that she was a pretty girl, and she knew she enjoyed boys' company, but somehow her career always put budding husbands off. She realised she was now fifty-three years old and had been a police officer for thirty-five years. She smiled to herself as she remembered the phrase 'married to the job'. She sighed, wondering where the years had gone.

This burst of nostalgia she knew had been brought on by her new Deputy Chief Constable's suggestion she might like to consider retiring and to take a week's leave to think about it. She admitted to herself that lately she hadn't been enjoying her work, mainly because she'd been removed from frontline cases, and put in a room full of musty old files that needed to be computerised. The work was boring, and Elsie wasn't really good with computers.

Her mind went back thirty years and she saw herself as the keen young woman determined to make her mark in a man's world. She'd enjoyed everything about being a police officer right from the start. The training, the friendship and even the uniform. Her school friends thought she was mad. She had had a string of good A levels and could have gone on to university, but Elsie had made up her mind and joined the Force.

As she contemplated retirement, she thought back to the cases she had helped solve. She had hoped her career would take off when she was promoted to detective sergeant, but it seemed the fates were against her. For reasons she didn't understand, and which no one had ever explained to her, the glittering career she sought had failed to materialise. She'd been a good and willing assistant throughout her career and had been instrumental in obtaining many convictions.

Other officers who had retired always said there was one unsolved case they took with them and as Elsie sat in her comfortable leather chair thinking about it, she knew this was a truism. She thought back to a murder case she had worked hard on, one that had baffled the team. The case still haunted her, and she had continued working it on her own time even after it had been classified as a cold case.

She sat and closed her eyes seeing the events of 2009. Elsie had been a member of Inspector Jack Ralph's murder team. They had been called to an incident at Manor Court, an expensive block of flats, fairly central to Norwich's main railway station. The victim was identified as a Mrs Tracy Nelson. She was an air hostess working on European routes. Her husband Philip Nelson was an insurance executive with the city's main employer. Elsie remembered him as a small weedy looking individual who never looked her straight in the eyes. His wife, on the other hand, was the opposite; she was a good-looking blonde woman with all her assets in the correct proportions.

Philip Nelson had discovered Tracy when he got back from work. Her naked body was laid out on their bed, and she had been strangled. The pathologist reported that she was either raped or had had consensual sex, but despite the presence of large quantities of semen, the murder squad had been unable to find a single suspect. Elsie was convinced that the victim had a lover, and something had gone wrong between them. However, DI Ralph didn't think much of Elsie's theory and dismissed it.

Recently she'd had more time and had found new evidence and missing reports that hopefully would lead to her boss re-opening the case. The file was permanently on her desk in the closet she called her office back at Force HQ.

Elsie shook herself out of her daydream. This was a sign she was worried. She had come to realise that her whole life was her job. She had few friends and despite the fact that she lived on an estate, most of her neighbours were young families struggling to pay their mortgages. They were, in the main, pleasant enough but would never make a friend of Elsie. She had acquaintances on the job but no real friends. All she had was her black tabby cat. Elsie was beginning to realise retirement would be very lonely.

A knock at her front door brought the detective sergeant back to the present. She wasn't expecting anyone. She rarely had visitors, so she was curious to find out who was calling. As she walked to open her front door, she grumbled under her breath, "I bet it's either someone selling something or it's the Mormons again."

***

Elsie Brown's bloodstained body was found lying on her living room floor when a neighbour noticed her black tabby cat scratching at the front door. The neighbour, a young mother who had only recently moved into the area, rang Elsie's front doorbell. Getting no reply and seeing Elsie's old Ford Fiesta sitting in the road she banged hard on the door. Still getting no reply, she called the police.

A patrol officer gained entry to Elsie's house at 11.07 a.m. on Monday September the 11th. Norwich City Police had a murder to solve. Detective Sergeant Elsie Brown had been beaten to death.

Chapter Two

As the Norfolk Force were gaining entry to Elsie Brown's house, DCI Steve Burt was enjoying the last official day of his week's leave, playing with his baby daughter Rosie. He enjoyed these quiet moments holding her and listening to the little noises he knew all babies made but somehow the noises Rosie made were special.

His leave had passed quickly but he'd loved being a full-time dad, even for such a short period. It was now Sunday September the 17th and Steve realised he hadn't missed being away from the office at all this week. The last occasion he'd taken time off was earlier in the year when the family had enjoyed a two-week break in Italy. That was all the leave the DCI had taken since January.

Dr Alison Mills, his wife, was downstairs in her surgery seeing a patient who could only come on Sunday mornings. Alison had found combining a full-time career and motherhood difficult at first, especially as Steve worked irregular hours, but slowly she'd adjusted and had settled into a routine. Fortunately, before his leave, his caseload had been normal with nothing requiring his individual attention.

As Rosie smiled and blew bubbles, Steve reflected on his year. It had been six months since his last serious case, and he recalled his team had performed well. His notional second in command, Inspector Peter Jones, was gaining in confidence although as a graduate entrant he was young for his rank. The DCI mused that a few more years of working with him in his Special Resolutions Unit would see Peter Jones become a very competent police officer.

Alison arrived just as Rosie dropped off to sleep. "You haven't let her fall asleep, Steve?" Alison took their daughter and whispered, "She'll wake up hungry and then not want to go to bed when she should."

Alison smiled at her husband and theatrically threw her head back. "Men, I ask you!"

After laying Rosie in her cot, Alison returned to put the kettle on for a cup of tea. As she turned away from the kettle, Steve was standing behind her and wrapped his arms around his wife and kissed her sweetly on the lips. The couple stood wrapped in each other for a full minute before Alison pushed Steve away.

"Sit down and I'll bring the tea. I need to talk to you about something." The DCI did as he was told and sat in his comfortable armchair.

With their cups in hand Alison began. "You know Flo is trying to tie Terry down to setting a date for the wedding?"

"Er, no." Steve was wondering where this conversation was going. Inspector Terry Harvey, Head of Technical Support at the Met, and a good friend of Steve's, had become engaged to Steve's colleague, Florance Rough. Florance would always be known to the DCI as Twiggy. She had been one of the first people assigned to Steve's unit known as Special Resolutions.

As his wife talked, Steve thought about his first meeting with Twiggy. She had been made a detective constable in CID only because the Metropolitan Police didn't have a uniform large enough to fit her. Her line manager at the time had solved the problem by arranging her transfer to CID, so she could wear her own clothes. During their first case, Twiggy had proven her ability with figures and had been instrumental in solving a case no one wanted solved. As a result, she had been transferred as a civil servant to the Treasury and permanently seconded as a civilian to the Met's Financial Crimes Unit.

The DCI heard his wife talking and shook himself back to the present.

"Are you listening?"

"Sorry darling. I was thinking of Twiggy and Terry. What were you saying?"

Alison gave a loud sigh and smiled at her husband. "I was saying they've been looking at houses and Flo isn't sure Terry is as keen as she is."

Alison and Twiggy had become good friends since Alison had treated her as a patient. Under Alison's guidance, Twiggy had reduced her weight considerably, although she was still a little overweight.

"Well, Terry is older than Twiggy. Maybe he's thinking that he's giving up his freedom."

Alison sipped her tea. "Mm. Maybe but Flo says he's making all the right noises, but he won't commit to any properties they've seen."

"Maybe he didn't like them. It can happen you know."

"Yes, I know but Flo's worried."

Steve knew the tone of voice his wife was using meant he was about to be given a job. "Go on, what do you want me to do?"

Alison looked over her cup. "Well… we thought maybe you could ask Terry about their house hunting. Try to find out what he's thinking. Flo's really worried."

Steve laughed out loud. "You women are devious. I'm supposed to go up to my mate and ask why he hasn't bought a house with his fiancée who, by the way, thinks he might be having second thoughts."

Alison smiled demurely. "That's about it."

The DCI continued to laugh while he finished his tea. "You know I think I'm running a dating agency. Think back to Andy Miller. He married that Samantha we brought in as a profiler on one of our cases. Now we have Terry and Twiggy and before I left to go on leave, I heard a rumour that Matt Conway was dating Poppy."

"Well, they're all young and single so why not?" Alison took the teacups into the kitchen and went to check on Rosie.

Steve drifted comfortably into a light sleep and thought about his present and previous team. Andy Miller was the one who stood out. Originally very shy he had developed into a first-class thinker and almost single-handedly had solved one of Steve's most difficult cases. His reward was a transfer to the National Crime Agency where he was now an inspector.

Detective Sergeant Matt Conway was a career cop and still young enough to climb through the ranks. He was ambitious but resented graduate entry officers being promoted above him, especially when the direct entrant was younger than him and still wet behind the ears. He'd proven himself a good number two to Peter Jones when asked to act as his bagman and seemed to have come to terms at least with Peter as his senior officer.

Detective Constable Mary Dougan was a graduate entrant also on his team, but she would be moving on, soon to be replaced no doubt by another direct entrant. Not for the first time, Steve considered that his role was more to run a mentoring school than a CID unit.

As his eyes began to close, he thought about Amelia Cooper, AKA Poppy. He realised that despite her young outlook on life she was a very competent officer who was wasted as Steve's admin assistant. She clearly was a good-time girl when not on duty and liked to spend money on clothes, but in the office, apart from her dress sense, she was a real asset to the team.

Sleep took over as Steve visualised his team hard at work and his return tomorrow.

***

Monday morning, September the 18th, arrived with bright sunshine and a light southerly wind. After his usual morning routine of breakfast, Steve stepped out of the apartment above Alison's surgery and started his walk to the office. Not knowing how many of his team would be in, he decided not to buy coffees from his usual coffee shop. He was trying to cut down on his caffeine intake anyway.

Poppy was at her desk and Steve was pleased to note she was paying lip service at least to his request that she dress down in the office.

"Where is everyone?"

Poppy gave a lopsided grin. "Well, Peter Jones and Matt are out on enquiries and Mary has the day off."

"Right. So things have been quiet?"

"You could say that. Peter went trawling other departments to see if he could take over some of their caseload. He got a series of burglaries from the burglary squad, a hit-and-run from traffic and a GBH from general crimes." Poppy pulled a face. "Nothing too exciting. I guess all the serious criminals have been waiting for you to get back."

"If only, Poppy." Steve produced a ten-pound note. "Put that in the coffee fund and get us two coffees please. I'll have a look through what's on my desk, unless you already know?" Steve was referring to Poppy's habit of listening in on his conversations.

With an exaggerated '*would I?*' look, Poppy smiled demurely and went to get the coffees. She reappeared seconds later. "Oh! I almost forgot. Commander Brooks asked if you could see him this morning at your earliest convenience and to remind you there's a case review session this afternoon at two o'clock." Poppy disappeared having delivered her message.

Steve looked at his desk. It was neatly stacked with buff-coloured files and the yellow internal envelopes. With a groan he set to work opening each file and envelope. After his second cup of coffee, he'd cleared everything and handed the necessary paperwork over to Poppy who was busy inputting data into the files and then filing the hard copies.

She groaned, thinking it would take her all day.

***

At 11.23 a.m., Steve walked into Commander Alfie Brooks' office. Alfie was pleased to see the DCI and immediately stood from behind his desk to warmly shake Steve's hand. "Good to see you back Steve. Coffee?"

"Er. No thanks, sir, but I'll have a tea."

Alfie, knowing the DCI's reputation as a coffee drinker, was surprised but he nodded to his secretary and both men seated themselves in Alfie's comfortable leather chairs.

"How was your leave?"

"It was great. A whole week of doing nothing except playing with Rosie, walks in the park and relaxing evenings in front of the TV."

"I envy you in a way, but Mrs Brooks is well past having another child." Alfie laughed "Still, at least you got a week off with no interruptions."

The tea arrived for the DCI and a coffee for the Commander. They made small talk for a while with Alfie telling Steve about the recent staff movements, the gossip and eventually the subject of Superintendent Blackstone came up.

Blackstone had been at the centre of Steve's last big case. The DCI had put a case together showing he was corrupt and involved in some high-end criminal activities. In order to get him to talk, Internal Affairs had agreed a deal that meant he could resign on full pension in exchange for what he knew. The case was over six months ago, and Steve had all but forgotten about Blackstone.

"What's Blackstone been up to now?" Steve was curious.

"He's dead. Seems he drowned at his villa in Spain. The Spanish police have read it as an accident. But…"

"You think it's Sir Patrick tidying up?"

"Wouldn't you? After that spy case he liquidated everyone with anything to say. I'm surprised you're still breathing and that's what I wanted to talk to you about."

The DCI sat back. He could see Alfie wasn't comfortable and that meant something serious was on its way.

"I was horrified by that spy case and the double murder you handled six months ago. I couldn't believe that our Deputy Commissioner and a guy from the DPP's office would be party to murdering people we should have locked up. At the time I'd had enough and seriously thought about quitting. What went on in this office wasn't the type of police work I want to be involved in."

Alfie was sipping his by now cold coffee, but he didn't seem to notice. "It's taken me a while, but I've decided to hand in my papers. I'm retiring. I told the Commissioner I'd do three years, but she'll get two and a half. I'm fed up with political expediency over good old-fashioned thief taking."

"Wow. I didn't expect that, Alfie. I'll miss you."

"Yeah! And I'll miss the job but not your insubordination and lone-wolf tactics. They have given me more grey hairs over the years than I should have." Alfie was laughing. He felt a great load had been lifted from his shoulders now he had told someone of his plans. "I've not told anyone else so keep it to yourself until it's announced officially but I'll tell the department heads at this afternoon's case review meeting."

"No problem. When are you off?"

"Once they find my replacement, but the Commissioner wants me to stay on for a few months. I reckon I'll be away by Christmas."

"Well. I suppose that'll call for a big party but seriously, Alfie, I will be sorry to see you go. I know I've caused you a few problems and we've had our differences but despite it all I like to think we are friends."

Alfie was blushing. "You're right, we have argued over the years, but we got through that as only friends can." He gave a deep sigh that said, 'it's over'.

Alfie stared at Steve in a not unfriendly matter and was obviously building himself up to make another announcement.

He started slowly. "Steve, you recall last year I suggested you take promotion?"

Steve was cautious in his reply. He simply offered a bland "Yes."

"If I recall, you didn't want to go to Vice as the department head."

"No, Alfie, I didn't want to be deskbound." The DCI wasn't sure where this conversation was going.

"Ah! Yes, I remember now."

Alfie was lying. He knew exactly why Steve had turned down the offer of promotion to Superintendent responsible for the Vice Unit within the Metropolitan Police Force. "You didn't want to be office bound. You see yourself as a man of action."

Steve knew Alfie was up to something, so he persisted. "No Alfie, not a man of action; I told you I was happy at operational level looking after Special Resources but felt I wasn't suited to the politics senior officers seem to spend all their time playing."

Alfie sat back and remained silent for a few moments. "But the idea of promotion doesn't frighten you?"

"No, of course not, but I'm not suited to all the paperwork. I'm an operations man and with respect, I'm no pen pusher."

If Alfie Brooks took Steve's comment as a slur on himself, he didn't react to it.

As the two men sat there in silence, Steve blurted out. "Look Alfie, sir, can you get to the point and stop all this sparring?"

"Right. As my farewell I'd like to put you up for a Chief Superintendent's job with the Norfolk Constabulary. You'd be Head of CID and as such could be as operational as you want to be. An old mate of mine has just been appointed Deputy Chief Constable and the current head of CID is retiring. He says he's looked at the talent he has in his senior ranks and there's no one he'd want to appoint."

Steve opened his mouth, but Alfie raised his hand to stop him and carried on. "It's a great opportunity, Steve. You'd skip a rank and go straight to Chief Super. You'd run your own show and the money's a lot better."

The DCI was in a state of mild shock. He had thought Alfie was lining him up for a desk job, but certainly nothing like this.

"What can I say?" Steve, having digested the Commander's words, was now very excited by the offer.

"You can say yes, but I know you'll have to discuss it with Alison. It would mean a relocation but Norfolk's a nice part of the world. You'd have to meet my buddy but I'm sure with your record and my recommendation it's a formality." Alfie stopped talking and visibly relaxed now he had got this news over to Steve. After a moment's silence he went on, "Talk it over with your wife and let me know by the end of the week but I hope you say yes. The job's got your name written all over it."

An excited Steve was ready to say yes straight away but knew he'd have to talk it through at home. "Well thanks Alfie, I'm flattered by your faith in me."

The Commander stood, indicating the meeting was over. "Just give it careful thought and let me know."

A lightheaded DCI Steve Burt walked down the stairs to his eighth-floor office practising his potential new title. He repeated to himself a few times, "Chief Superintendent Steve Burt." He liked the sound of it as he continued his descent to his office.

***

Ex-Detective Inspector Jack Ralph of the Norfolk Constabulary had retired to the pretty Suffolk village of Long Melford. He'd retired three years previously and he and his wife had bought a simple detached thatched cottage on the outskirts of the village. Long Melford, with its wide main street and numerous antique shops, suited the couple. Jack liked to walk and visit the local pub for a beer each lunchtime while his wife, Patricia, loved visiting the antique emporiums and trying to spot a bargain.

Jack hadn't looked forward to retiring but having accepted that his powers of deduction as a detective inspector were not what they used to be, he'd accepted the inevitable.

Retirement had welcomed Jack and he'd settled into his new life. He had his garden and he'd bought a vintage MG TD to tinker with and to drive around the country roads with the hood down. His wife Patricia had joined the WI and the local ladies' sewing circle.

The couple had no children, so they just had themselves to think about and retired life for Mr and Mrs Jack Ralph had developed into the happiest times of their forty years of marriage.

Every Monday Jack and his wife drove out in the MG and visited one of the many good pubs in the surrounding villages for lunch. They found Monday a good day to eat out realising the pubs weren't as busy as they were at the weekends. On this particular Monday, September the 18th, Jack had decided on a very nice pub in the small village of Clare. The Three Feathers was a smart privately owned hostelry run by a stout publican called John. The building had originally been a stable but was now a comfortable place to eat and drink.

The couple ordered their food and with a pint of best bitter in his hand, Jack selected a table by the window. His wife followed clasping a glass of soda water. Patricia Ralph didn't drink and really didn't approve of her husband's liking for beer. The couple talked and sipped their respective drinks until their food arrived on large round plates, piled high with plenty of meat and vegetables.

As he always did, Jack commented on the amount of food he'd eaten and how his waistband would have to be eased. As part of their Monday lunch ritual, Mrs Ralph joked she'd have to remove her corset when they got home. The fact she didn't wear such a garment didn't spoil the story. The landlord John had heard these expressions every time the couple ate at his pub but played along and said he was glad they had enjoyed their meal.

They ordered coffee and while it was being brewed, Jack decided his bladder was full of ale and left the table to visit the outside toilet. His wife sat contentedly. She was enjoying the sun streaming through the window and her feeling of well-being only got better the more she thought about their present life.

The coffee was served and as she drank hers, Patricia Ralph realised she'd been daydreaming for over five minutes and her husband's coffee was getting cold. She was uneasy about setting off to the outside gents' toilet so asked the landlord to go and make sure her husband was all right.

Suddenly John, the landlord of the Three Feathers, ran out from the small toilet block and was sick over his newly laid block-paved path. He'd found Jack Ralph, but the man wasn't breathing. His days of gardening and tinkering with his MG TD were over.

Retired Detective Inspector Jack Ralph had been murdered. Someone had battered him over the head multiple times leaving him on the toilet floor. Jack Ralph's death had not been easy. It looked like a frenzied attack by someone who didn't like the retired police officer. Suffolk Constabulary now had a murder to deal with.

At 1.55 p.m. on Monday September the 18th, just as DCI Steve Burt of the Metropolitan Police was entering Commander Alfie Brooks' office, Suffolk Police were heading to a crime scene.

Chapter Three

As Steve entered the Commander's office, he saw the usual bunch of senior officers. Tea and coffee were on offer and the waitress who always handed out refreshments at these meetings was taken aback when Steve asked for a tea. The usual mingling went on with officers nodding greetings, shaking hands and a few going into a huddle in a corner.

Alfie called the meeting to order and those present took their seats around Alfie's boardroom-style table. The six officers present all reported directly to the Commander, but Steve noted a seventh member was seated next to Alfie. The DCI had no idea who this new face belonged to nor what it was doing at the meeting.

In his opening remarks Alfie explained. "Ladies and gentlemen, the detectives among you might have spotted we have a guest." Pointing to the new face, Alfie continued, "This is Superintendent Charles Grover. Superintendent Grover has been appointed to a new post, that of Director of Internal Communications and Document Support."

Steve was sure he heard a collective groan from his colleagues. Such an appointment meant more paperwork and form filling.

Alfie handed over to the new man. "Good afternoon, all. As the Commander has stated, my name is Charles Grover. If we are using first names, I prefer Charles and certainly not Charlie."

As Charles rambled on, the DCI was struck by this man's lack of stature and presence. He looked like a filing clerk who worked in a solicitors' office. His dark suit, white shirt and neutral tie identified him as a shuffler of paper, rather than a frontline police officer.

Steve returned to the present when he heard his name being mentioned. Superintendent paper pusher was still droning on. "The quality of reporting I have witnessed to date is shocking. Special Resolutions is the only unit that completes its weekly reports on time and updates its case files immediately anything is reported." Charles was looking at Steve who became very embarrassed and avoided eye contact with everyone.

"DCI Burt's admin assistant would appear to be the only competent officer in this building. If your admin officer isn't up to scratch, you should replace them." Charles was in full flow but glancing around the table, Steve got an impression no one was listening, and he was talking to himself.

"Your budgets are based on the crime figures and the reports you present. The Force is underfunded and unless your record-keeping and reporting improves, I fear you will all see reductions in next year's budgets." He was drawing to a conclusion which Steve for one was pleased about. Charles' voice was high-pitched and nasal. It was not a voice of authority and certainly not one the DCI wanted to listen to.

"So there you have it. Please gee up your admin assistants to file every document correctly completed on time and please make sure your crime files are updated as soon as an event occurs. Both the CPS and the DPP set great store by accurate up-to-date crime files."

Charles stopped talking and appeared to be waiting for a round of applause that he didn't get. Silence descended until Alfie took control again.

"Thank you, Charles; I'm sure this team have taken on board your remarks. Thank you for coming. No doubt we'll be in touch."

Alfie made it obvious that the new face was dismissed but he didn't appear to get the message. Everyone present expected him to leave but he continued to sit. Alfie let a few seconds go by before saying, "Charles, we wish continue our meeting now and your presence isn't required."

"Oh! I see, I thought I was invited to sit in." Alfie's blunt message was at last understood. A rather embarrassed Superintendent Charles (don't call me Charlie) pushed back his chair and left. Once the door was closed, the room erupted with laughter. One old time chief superintendent even asked, "Where the hell did the Met get him?"

Alfie obviously shared the views of those present so allowed a few minutes of character assassination to take place at the expense of the recently departed superintendent. The Commander eventually called the meeting to order, and the case reviews began.

Steve found such meetings boring. His department had initially been established to take over serious crime cases other units within the Met either couldn't or didn't want to handle. No unit chief ever wanted to admit defeat on a case, but his colleagues found Steve's Special Resolutions Unit a convenient dumping ground for their more difficult cases. It meant the DCI's caseload was up and down and at this moment he wasn't dealing with anything of interest to this forum.

Alfie controlled the meeting by interrogating each department head in turn by asking questions, making observations and suggestions, referring to the time each serious case had been open and generally offering assistance.

The meeting had been going on for over an hour when Alfie turned his attentions to DCI Cathy Melrose. Steve knew Cathy was mid-forties, married with a little boy and was a high-flyer destined for more senior rank. She was currently head of the second murder squad that reported to Alfie. As Alfie was finishing her interrogation and congratulating her, Cathy spoke up.

"There's just one other thing, sir; my headless body case. I told you we were working on it but to be truthful we're getting nowhere. It's been three weeks now and we have nothing." She glanced at Steve. "I have the file here and wondered if Special Resolutions might take a look."

Alfie turned to Steve. "Well Steve, how's your caseload?"

The DCI smiled inwardly. Alfie knew Steve didn't have a major case on at the moment. "It's fairly light, sir. I'd be happy to look at Cathy's case."

Steve saw relief pass over DCI Cathy Melrose's face as she pushed the file towards him. "It's all in there, Steve, or should I say there's nothing in there except a few photographs and the pathologist's report."

Steve opened the thin file and was horrified by the pictures. He immediately closed it telling himself he'd get to it later.

The DCI was always last to be interrogated by the Commander and on this occasion the interrogation lasted less than thirty seconds.

Alfie called the meeting to a close with the announcement of his impending retirement from the Force. The news was greeted with genuine shock and sadness. Alfie was popular and treated everyone the same. During his time as Commander, he'd kept police politics away from his frontline officers and had coaxed results from the most difficult of cases. Everyone wished him well, said he'd be missed, and left to get on with their own careers wondering who might replace Alfie.

***

It was three thirty p.m. when Steve, clutching the thin file, arrived back in his own office. Poppy was at her desk and Inspector Peter Jones was sitting talking to Matt Conway. As Steve entered, silence descended and an air of expectation filled the outer office. Steve knew when caseloads were light his team often expected the case review meetings to throw up the type of case Steve's unit was designed to handle.

The DCI knew the signs so held up the thin file above his head. "If somebody gets the coffees, I'll share this with you all."

Immediately the atmosphere changed and became electrified. With coffee in front of them and seated around Steve's small conference table, Steve opened the file and, using magnets, secured the horrific pictures to his whiteboard. He sat down and read aloud from the remaining contents of the file.

"The headless body of a woman, age estimated as no more than thirty, was pulled from the Thames beside Putney Bridge on Friday September 1 this year at 09.44 a.m. The post-mortem was inconclusive and did not state cause of death due to the absence of the head. The police pathologist confirmed there were no obvious reasons he could identify on the torso that would have caused death. His conclusion was that some form of head trauma was most likely the cause of death. Forensics could not get any trace evidence due to the time the torso had been in the water. The lady had a tattoo on her left forearm resembling a small bird and had painted fingernails and toes. She had been sexually active before her death."

Steve closed the file and pointed to his whiteboard. "That's it. All we have is a headless body, a tattoo, painted nails and no forensic evidence. As you can see, what's left of the body isn't pretty due to the time in the water." He reopened the file and scanned the post-mortem report again before adding, "The pathologist estimates the body had been in the water no more than seventy-two hours." Steve went to the whiteboard and using a black felt marker wrote TUESDAY 29 AUGUST. "That's the best estimate of when the killing took place."

He returned to his seat, looked at the expectant faces and asked. "Any thoughts?"

From the silence that followed the DCI knew this was going to be a tough case.

Peter Jones in his lilting Welsh voice asked, "Do we know where the body went into the river?"

"No but it's a good point, Peter. Get on to the River Police. They should be able to give us a handle based on tides and currents where the body went in."

Peter made a note, and as he wrote Poppy chipped in. "Do we have any idea of who she is?"

"There's nothing in the file, and it doesn't look as though the cadaver was fingerprinted."

"If you get me a set of prints, I can do a search. You never know she might be on file somewhere."

Steve examined Poppy closely. He realised she'd slipped back into wearing her tight-fitting dresses but decided to say nothing.

"Good, Poppy, get onto the mortuary. Ask one of the technicians to fingerprint our Jane Doe and tell him it's urgent and you need them sent to you electronically."

Poppy smiled, pleased to be given a part to play in the investigation, and scribbled a note to herself.

Steve stood up taking control. "Right. Peter, you contact the River Police. Poppy, you get onto the mortuary about the prints. Matt, I want another post-mortem but carried out by a Home Office pathologist. Get onto the Home Office liaison team and set it up for tomorrow morning, say ten o'clock. You and I will attend. I'm not saying the first PM was sloppy but the lack of fingerprints in the file is a bit of a concern."

Matt nodded and Steve asked if anyone had anything else to add, but nobody did. The team from Special Resolutions left reenergised as they set off to solve another apparently impossible murder case.

***

At the same time DCI Steve Burt was being handed the headless body case, two men were sitting in a far corner of the British Airways executive lounge at Heathrow Airport. They were enjoying their champagne while waiting for a flight to Amsterdam to be called. The names on their boarding passes were Andrew Clark and David Grove and the same names were on their new forged passports.

Their police files identified them as Andrew and David Black. They headed up a London gang involved in drugs, prostitution, money laundering and extortion. They were also known to the police as being two of the most dangerous men in London who killed anyone who got in their way. Andrew was the older of the two and the dominant force in what their father, before he died, often referred to as the family business.

Andrew Black was a few months short of his sixtieth birthday. He was a stout man with enormous hands. At a fraction of an inch under six foot, he was a fearsome character especially when roused to anger. He and his brother had known nothing except a life of crime and Andrew took pride in devising ways to thwart the police in their efforts to charge and imprison the pair.

David Black was five years younger than his brother and smaller at five foot nine inches. He was also slimmer and of lighter build and appeared to have the family characteristic that specified overly large and powerful hands. The younger brother was more fearsome than his older sibling. It was David Black who liked to inflict pain on his victims. It was said he had no feelings and took killing people in his stride.

Both men still had good mops of dark hair neatly cut and groomed. They had been arrested many times but each time the police put a case together, something happened to stop the trials and the brothers walked. A combination of expensive lawyers, bribery and, if necessary, murder had worked to keep them out of prison and avoid a criminal record. To the outside world, they were legitimate businessmen as pure as the driven snow. To the police, they were dangerous thugs who enjoyed torture and murder especially when protecting their empire.

They were also known to Interpol and for this reason didn't travel as themselves but under false identities. Their trip to Amsterdam was all about business. As they sat talking in low whispers, anyone glancing in their direction saw exactly the image the brothers wanted to portray, just two men waiting for a flight. The truth was that if their contact in the Netherlands could fulfil the promises he'd made, then the brothers would be stronger, richer and would control almost all of the illegal activity in the capital and beyond. The brothers were moving up.

As they finished their champagne, their 4.10 p.m. flight to Amsterdam was called. They excitedly walked towards their departure gate confident of a successful trip and looking forward to sampling the delights of night-time Amsterdam.

***

Steve had put off meeting Inspector Terry Harvey to the point where he couldn't put it off any longer. The DCI, despite his work as a detective, didn't like getting involved in other peoples' private affairs. Marriage to Alison had changed that and he realised all the stories about nosey women were probably true although he'd never say so to his wife. Her request to quiz Terry Harvey about his relationship with Florance Rough didn't sit well with Steve. Terry was a friend but so was Twiggy. He knew Alison was trying to help Twiggy better understand Terry's plans, but Steve thought the couple should talk things through themselves.

Having set his team loose on the headless body case, Steve sought out Terry. He found him in his little office tucked away in the corner of a large open-plan area that comprised the Met's Technical Support Unit. As the head of this unit, Terry had helped Steve solve many of his most difficult cases by applying technology but also using his devious, almost criminal mind. The DCI often thought that if his friend hadn't become a police officer, he could have had a career as a master criminal.

As Steve entered the office, Terry looked up and closed the file he had been studying. Steve knew Terry had a way of manipulating budgets to ensure his department always had the most up-to-date facilities and equipment. He suspected the inspector, by the way he hurriedly placed the file in the top drawer of his desk, was working on something devious.

"What can I do for you Steve? Not another rush job I hope?"

"No, nothing like that. I just came over for a chat."

Terry was suspicious. "It's nothing to do with Poppy is it?"

Terry was DC Amelia Cooper's uncle. Amelia preferred to be called Poppy and was Steve's admin assistant. This family connection had been useful in the past as Terry had gone the extra mile to support his niece's role in some of Steve's cases.

"No, don't worry, she's fine. I just wanted to see you after my leave. See how things were going. You know, see how the wedding plans were going."

Terry laughed. "You can't fool me, Steve. The women have put you up to this visit. I bet your wife told you to see how Flo and I were getting on. Am I right?"

"Well… Yes, in a way. It seems Flo's getting nervous about the house hunt and the wedding."

"Mm. I sensed she wasn't happy with me." Terry paused to gather his thoughts. He felt a heart to heart with Steve might help especially as Steve's wife would undoubtedly hear what Terry said from her husband.

"It's the house, Steve. I'm a good bit older than Flo and she wants a big house in the suburbs, somewhere in the country. We've been looking in places like Surbiton, Epsom and Walton-on-Thames but the prices are huge. Even if we both sell our flats we would need a large mortgage and at my age I'm not sure I need a mortgage at all. You know I think the world of Flo and I'd do anything to make her happy, but I don't think she realises what she's asking." Terry sat back in his chair.

"Oh! I see. So that's all it is. You're not having second thoughts?"

"Christ no, look at me. I'm lucky to have Flo and I really want to get hitched. It's just the age difference that worries me about the house. We can buy a large new apartment in a nice part of London by selling our own places and not need a mortgage, but Flo has her heart set on a house."

Steve thought of his own upcoming conversation with Alison about a move to Norfolk. He could sympathise with his friend.

"Have you explained houses come with gardens and gardens have grass that doesn't cut itself?"

"That's the point. She wants a garden. Says we'll both enjoy pottering around and growing flowers and vegetables. I think she's gone a little Mills and Boon."

"You'll work it out. I think she thinks you've gone off her."

"Don't be daft. She's the best thing to happen to me." With a grin he cheekily added, "Unless you discount the new upgrades to the facial recognition software of course."

Steve stood laughing. "If you're not careful, I might tell her you said that."

The DCI left to return to his own office and his walk home. He wasn't sure how Alison would take his news nor how he would introduce the topic.

Chapter Four

Steve arrived home after his first day back after his week's leave, in good time to play with his daughter before she was put to bed. A warning from Alison not to get Rosie too excited fell on deaf ears. Rosie was now seven months old and developing her own personality. Steve was convinced she had said "Dada" a few days ago but Alison told him it was only noises, and he was interpreting them for his own ends. As he tickled Rosie's chin she made giggling noises and clearly enjoyed the attention.

Alison having finished preparing the evening meal of chicken supreme, handed Steve a glass of white wine and took charge of their daughter. As the pair headed for Rosie's bedroom, Alison called over her shoulder, "Turn the oven off in five minutes."

Steve sipped his wine and thought about his upcoming conversation with his wife. He knew she was ambitious for him, and he had practised his speech highlighting the advantages of country living for Rosie, but still, it might be a hard sell.

With Rosie asleep, the couple finished their evening meal. They discussed Steve's first day back and Steve told Alison that Alfie had handed in his papers and would likely be gone by Christmas. Alison said she'd had a relatively easy day with only straightforward cases. Slowly the topic turned to Terry and Twiggy.

Steve relayed Terry's comments about not getting cold feet and that he desperately wanted to get married to Flo. He explained Terry's concern about the age difference and his reluctance to take on a large mortgage.

"So Flo's got herself upset over a house?"

"Seems that way although I don't know if Terry has explained it to her."

"Silly pair." Alison smiled a telling smile. "I'll have a word. I don't think Flo's aware of any of this."

"Probably not. Now my darling, I want to discuss something with you when you're nice and relaxed."

Alison looked quizzically at her policeman husband. In a childlike voice and fluttering her eyelids she said, "Well officer, I'm not doing handcuffs."

The couple relaxed on their large sofa. Alison sat with her feet under her, and Steve lounged comfortably allowing his own feet to stretch out in front of him.

He took a deep breath and started. "Alfie asked me today to consider putting myself forward for a Chief Super's job in Norfolk. It would be as Head of CID."

"That's wonderful, darling, it's what you've always wanted."

Steve was shocked. He had his speech about being better for Rosie all prepared, but his wife had taken the wind out of his sails. "Really, you don't mind?"

"No. I think it's wonderful but it's a very long commute."

Steve thought it had been too easy and knew Alison wasn't that naive. "No darling, we'd have to move. Relocate, maybe to a Norfolk village, buy a house with a bit of land. Rosie could have a pony." Steve carried on with his pre-prepared speech. Alison listened and the DCI thought his words sounded convincing.

"But Steve." Alison was clearly a little taken aback by his news. "Our lives are in London. I've got my medical practice. I've got patients. I can't just up sticks, and move."

Steve didn't want an argument, but he knew this was his chance to persuade Alison of the merits of moving. "We wouldn't suddenly up sticks. It would take time to move. You could sell your practice and buy into another one in Norfolk. We might even find a retiring GP who'd happily to sell to you and pass on his patient list or you could start a new practice. Maybe do some hospital work. You've often said you miss working in the NHS."

"But Steve, it's not that simple. All our friends are here. We'd never see them."

Alison was running out of arguments but still needed convincing.

"Yes, we would, but I'd have more free time. We could come down at least once a month and we'd make new friends up there. We could take our time and find the right house in the right place. Rosie will be ready for nursery in a year or so. It gives us plenty of time to find just the right place."

"Oh, it's a big decision and a lot to take in. When does Alfie need to have your answer?"

Steve decided to bend the truth. "Well, it's an old friend of Alfie's who is handling the recruitment. Alfie wants me to go up and meet him as soon as I can, but I won't go until we've decided it's the right thing for us as a family."

"That's not fair. You're putting all the pressure on me. I suppose I need time to come to terms with it. You know I'll support you whatever you want to do." Alison was clearly upset at the thought of upping sticks and moving to a part of the country she didn't know.

"Why don't you go and meet Alfie's pal, anyway? If you like what they are offering and you want to take the job, we'll have another chat and it'll give me more time to think about it. If we decide it's for us then we'll take a long weekend and go look at some areas."

Steve knew his wife had only heard the news now and would need time to consider the options. While he'd hoped for an immediate yes, he realised this was as good a compromise as he was going to get. He lent over towards his wife and gathered her in his arms. "I love you Doctor Mills. It's a deal. I'll go and have a look but if the job isn't right, I won't take it. If it is, I'll get an estate agent to start sending us property details so you can see what's on offer and look at the prices. If we can't settle on anything, or if you feel uneasy then the deal's off and we can stay as we are."

Alison kissed her husband. "Agreed, but no high-pressure selling tactics to make me say yes. We both have to want this."

At that moment, the baby alarm sounded. Rosie was stirring looking for her late-night feed.

***

The two brothers were met at Amsterdam's Schiphol Airport by a weedy looking individual holding a piece of cardboard with the brothers' false names written on it in thick felt tip pen. He had been sent to firstly take them to their hotel and then onwards to a members-only club to meet the man they'd come to see.

After checking in and a quick wash and brush up, the man drove them to the club that from the outside looked like a brothel with its flashing bright red lights and a bouncer at the door. On either side of the club were the usual Amsterdam storefront windows where prostitutes showed their wares and looked for business.

Andrew and David Black were met at the door by a lady who clearly didn't feel the cold even though this September evening was a little chilly. Her body was only partially covered by a light see-through fabric that hid nothing. The younger brother admired her shape and looked forward to perhaps seeing even more of her later in the evening.

She wiggled her way in front of the brothers balancing on what looked like six-inch stiletto heels. The room was large, and the low lighting gave it an intimate atmosphere. A red glow was everywhere and because it was later in Amsterdam due to the one-hour time difference, the room was fairly full. She guided them past tables where men were being entertained with cheap champagne at €100 a bottle that normally would sell for €5, and the promise of better things to come. At the far end of the dimly lit floor, a heavy red velvet curtain was open showing what looked like a private booth. The brothers entered to find a figure sitting at a table. Behind him were two large men the brothers took to be bodyguards. The man was a dark-skinned individual dressed in a black t-shirt and jeans. David Black noticed he wasn't wearing socks and that each of his fingers on both hands were adorned by a ring. This was the man who could be their passport to greater riches and power.

The man remained seated and with a wave dismissed the hostess who had guided the brothers to this booth. The brothers knew he was called Jean Franco, that he was part American and part French, and he controlled the biggest criminal syndicate in Europe.

Jean Franco indicated the brothers should sit and dismissed his bodyguards who took up station on the other side of the velvet curtains. No one spoke and without asking, another scantily clad girl appeared with a tray of drinks which she placed on the table and, without looking directly at any of the men, left.

Jean Franco poured three large whiskies and held up his glass. "Here's to a new dawn, gentlemen." The brothers quickly picked up their drinks and echoed the toast.

"Now to business." Jean Franco had a decidedly American accent. It somehow added to his sinister appearance and caused the brothers to drink more quickly than they might normally.

Their host continued. "You don't know it, but you have been working for me for a number of years. All the best Colombian white powder you sell to your clients comes from me. You see, I operate a kind of franchise scheme. The guy you get your stuff from was my main English distributor. He also handles the girls, and I wasn't pleased to learn you were recruiting home-grown tarts. If we reach an agreement, that has to stop. You only use girls I supply."

Andrew Black thought *so far so good*. He said aloud, "Of course Jean, we are happy to abide by your rules."

Jean Franco looked directly at Andrew. "The only reason you're here is because the previous franchise owner didn't obey my rules. He's now feeding the fishes somewhere in the North Sea."

Both brothers swallowed hard. Despite their own use of violence, this stark statement frightened them.

"My accountants tell me you've always paid on time, and we've had no problems with you as a distributor. I also like the fact you've kept one step ahead of the cops and dealt with your problems yourselves."

Jean Franco drank his whisky and topped up all three glasses. "That's very good but if you are to take over my distribution business in England, you'll have to convince me you can do it. I already have a network of secondary guys like you, any one of whom would jump at the chance you're being given. How will you deal with them?"

It was a good question and Andrew as the oldest chose to answer. "Jean, we already control most of London. That's where most of your business is done. If your other people in the provinces don't like your decision to use us then we'll deal with them."

"It's not that simple. I have regular shipments of high-grade Colombian going into England. I have a factory that cuts it with chalk powder and bags it up. This part of the supply chain has nothing to do with you but if you can't distribute it, it'll pile up and I don't want that." Jean Franco sat back, waiting.

Andrew answered again. "Jean, we have everything ready. As I said, we're the biggest outfit in London plus we run a few County Lines operations. I know you have an existing distribution set up and we can improve it. We're on the ground and we know what we're doing."

Jean was clearly thinking. "Yeah. I hear all that, but you'd also have to get the girls earning. I spend money on them. I bring them over from further east; I dress them and make them look respectable, but they are no good to me unless they're on their backs three or four times a night.

"I'm not talking your local prostitute, the kind you've been running. I'm talking high-class hookers. They get a minimum of a thousand an hour and to be honest that's the future of our business. Drugs are beginning to be less profitable but high-class call girls are in demand."

Jean's American accent was getting to David Black. He felt it was intimidating and he didn't like the way Jean Franco looked at him.

"Look Jean, I hear what you say, and I agree we don't as yet deal in high-end hookers. But we know people who do and with your organisation behind us, we can take them over, no problem." Andrew Black was winging it and hoped it sounded convincing.

"They'll need to be put up in nice places to stay."

Andrew for the first time felt relaxed He opened his arms and with a broad grin said, "Goes without saying, Jean."

Jean Franco smiled an evil smile that did nothing for his features. He was clearly arriving at a decision.

"OK. I'll have one of my guys work with you for the first couple of months. Hold your hands until you settle down. I'll put the word out to my existing distributors that you two are now the go-to guys." He paused and glared at the brothers. "But remember, if you don't play straight with me, you'll end up feeding the fishes, just like the last guy."

"You can trust us, Jean." Andrew was over the moon but decided he had one last question. "I presume our percentage take will be the same on the total business even though we're dealing with the whole of England?"

"Yeah. But it needs to be earned. Do we have a deal?"

The brothers stood to shake Jean Franco's had but the French/American remained seated.

"I only shake hands before a killing."

Once more the brothers feared what they had just agreed to, but the lure of the extra power and almost unlimited income helped them overcome their trepidation, at least for now.

Jean Franco called to someone and as if by magic a huge spread of food was placed on the table. The brothers weren't food buffs but recognised some exotic foods on display including lobster and caviar. Two hostesses appeared wearing elegant long evening dresses and carrying two bottles each of chilled champagne, but not quite the same as that being served to other customers and sat down beside the brothers.

Jean Franco stood after making the introductions and made to leave. As his bodyguards opened the curtain for him, he stopped. "Come here tomorrow morning at eleven. We'll sort everything out then. Help yourself to the food and order any booze you want." He swept a hand over the tables. "The girls are yours unless you prefer something else."

The biggest crime boss in Europe left having agreed to give the brothers control of his empire in England.

***

Alison was bedding down Rosie for what she hoped was the final time when Steve's mobile rang. It was Matt Conway.

"Sorry to bother you so late, Steve, but I thought you'd want to know the new post-mortem is set for eleven o'clock tomorrow morning. We've got the new top man so we should get anything that's going."

"Right, thanks Matt. I'll see you in the office tomorrow first thing. We'll have a look at what we've got and then get over to the post."

Matt hung up and Steve's mind turned to the headless body in the river. He shuddered as he thought of the pictures taken by the scene of crime photographer. For some strange reason, his resolve to find the killer suddenly became stronger and he became aware of his desire to get the poor headless girl justice. This killer would be caught.

Chapter Five

Steve was up early the next morning. The thought of promotion to Norfolk and his now overwhelming desire to solve the headless torso case had contrived to keep him awake. He woke his wife with a cup of tea in bed and sat on the side of the bed as she drank it.

"Is this a bribe to persuade me to say yes to Norfolk because if it is, it's working."

"Not really." Steve teased. "Am I that obvious?"

"Sometimes, but I guess you've got things on your mind." Alison put her cup on the bedside table. "Steve, I'm not against a move to Norfolk especially if it's for your career. I just need time to come to terms with such a big move."

The DCI stretched out and pulled his wife towards him. "I know darling, just give it time and you never know, you might love it."

Before she could answer and right on time, Rosie could be heard through the baby alarm making noises that said she was awake and needed feeding.

Steve happily went to the nursery and collected his daughter. A new day had begun.

This Tuesday morning wasn't as pleasant as yesterday but was fine for a brisk walk to New Scotland Yard. The DCI arrived before eight a.m. to an empty office. He'd bought three coffees on his way in thinking at least two of his team would be at their desks. He realised it was a bit early so settled behind his desk and started to drink his first coffee of the day, remembering he was cutting down on his caffeine intake.

He stared at the whiteboard showing the photographs and notes the team had studied yesterday. He couldn't believe anyone could do such a thing but knew from his previous murder cases that human beings were capable of anything. His mind turned to how they might solve this murder but all he could tell himself was by solid police work and maybe a few lucky breaks.

Steve decided to leave his meeting with Alfie till later in the day. Despite the certainty he'd exuded with Alison, he knew another few hours would give him more time to consider such a major move before saying he'd go to Norwich and meet the new Deputy Chief Constable.

Poppy and Matt Conway arrived at the same time. Steve chuckled to himself as he thought of his comments to his wife about him running a dating agency. Both detectives took the cups of coffee on offer with thanks and retreated to the outer office and their own desks.

Poppy was first to tap on the door frame and enter Steve's office.

"I got the fingerprints from the headless girl through last night from the mortuary. I started to put them into the system, then I realised it would take me ages so, I asked Uncle Terry to run them against all the national databases. After all, he has all those computers, and he can access things I can't."

The DCI was always amazed at Poppy's lack of regard for protocol. "It's just as well Inspector Harvey's your uncle." Steve knew this was a smart move and he couldn't be annoyed with Poppy for long. "When did he say we might get a result?"

Poppy was halfway out the door. "You mean after he moaned and groaned and told me this was the last time?" Poppy didn't wait for an answer. With an impish smile she said, "Sometime this morning." She skipped through the door into the outer office. Steve noticed she had definitely reverted to her previous dress sense and was showing off her figure. With a groan he realised he'd have to have another word.

Inspector Peter Jones was next to arrive bearing coffees for everyone. After handing them out, he entered Steve's office.

"I had a word with the River Police as you asked."

The DCI asked Peter to wait while he called in Matt and Poppy to hear Peter's report. All four sat at Steve's table and sipped their coffee.

"I spoke with an Inspector Lightburn. He's been on the river all of his career so knows it like the back of his hand. I explained our corpse had been found beside Putney Bridge and we think she was killed around the August 29. He had some charts he looked up and said if it was found on the first day of September and that meant it had been in the water for three days, then it probably went in close to where it was found."

"How is that possible?" Matt Conway was making notes and asking questions.

"He gave me a whole load of technical maritime speak about ebbing tides and flood tides but bottom line and based on the state of the river over the three days the body was in the water, Inspector Lightburn thinks it would have been pulled up and pushed down by the tide. Given the conditions, it wouldn't have moved much."

Steve steepled his fingers in front of his face as he considered Peter's news. "So she was murdered but we don't know where and dumped in the river close to Putney Bridge?"

"That's it. Sorry I couldn't get more."

Poppy was bubbling for reasons best known to her. "What side of the bridge was the body found?"

Peter Jones looked up his notes. "Oh, yes, I forgot. The River Police guy said the body was found on the north side. If she'd been dumped on the south side, she'd be miles away. Seems there's a sand bank that splits the river there and the south side is very fast and very tidal. The north's slower and doesn't move much so definitely the north side."

"I could do a search of missing girls aged between say twenty and thirty, starting half a mile out but focusing on the north side. If I get nothing, I could go to one mile and so on in half-mile increments up to say three miles." Poppy was sucking her pen.

"Good thinking, Poppy. It's worth a shot but make sure you don't get a family member to help you. Make this all your own work." Steve made his point to Poppy without having to be serious. She smiled a smile that had mischief written all over it.

Matt had been studying the whiteboard from his seat. "What about the tattoo? It's fairly distinctive. Maybe we could use Poppy's plan and canvas all the tattoo parlours. See if any of them recognised the bird."

Steve mentally kicked himself. "I should have thought about that. Peter, can you do that? Poppy, get Peter a list of all tattoo places to coincide with your missing persons' areas."

As Steve was finishing, Detective Constable Mary Dougan appeared at Steve's office door. She saw her colleagues looking at her in horror. She put her hand out in a gesture that said 'stay away' but said, "Don't worry, I'm not as bad as I look and I'm not infectious. It's only hay fever but it's bad just now. Sorry I was missing yesterday boss, but I felt dreadful."

"Christ Mary, you look awful. Are you sure you should be at work?"

Mary giggled. "You should have seen me yesterday before the tablets began to kick in. But no, I'm all right. I just need to stay away from trees and closed spaces."

Mary sat down and Steve considered what had been said over the past hour or so.

"Right, here's what we have." The DCI pointed to the whiteboard. "A headless body of a girl aged less than thirty for now. We have no forensics but we do have another post-mortem this morning so we might get lucky. We have a tattoo of a bird.

"Peter, take Mary out in the fresh air with you and check all tattoo parlours north of Putney Bridge. Poppy will give you a list to match the areas she's doing a missing persons sweep on. We have Tech Services looking for a fingerprint match to see if she's in the system. I think that's it for now unless anyone has any other bright ideas to share?"

No one did. Mary sniffed and blew her very red nose.

"You sure you're OK?"

"Yes sir. As I said, it's hay fever. I'll be fine."

The DCI thought she looked anything but fine but allowed her to carry on.

"Matt. We'll leave at ten thirty a.m. and head over to the morgue."

***

Poppy was initiating her missing persons search and drawing down names of tattoo parlours in the areas north of Putney Bridge at the same time Andrew and David Black were ordering more coffee in the breakfast room of their four-star hotel. Both had thumping hangovers as a result of Jean Franco's overly generous hospitality. They'd stayed in the club enjoying its attractions until after midnight and then taken two of the hostesses back to their hotel rooms. Neither man had much recollection of the final part of the evening, but both agreed they must have enjoyed it. The girls had been beside them when they woke and were still upstairs in their bedrooms. It was obvious that they weren't early risers.

The coffee supplemented by a few headache pills was beginning to ease the drumming inside the brothers' heads. The weedy driver was hovering around the entrance to the dining room ready to take them to their eleven-a.m. meeting with Jean Franco and a bright future. Or so they hoped.

***

As Steve and Matt entered the mortuary, the smell of formaldehyde immediately entered their nasal cavities. Steve had attended more post-mortems than he could remember but had never got used to the smell. They rang a bell screwed to a tall shelf-like desk and immediately a short girl dressed in green surgical scrubs appeared. Matt explained why they were there, and that they were expected at eleven a.m. A glance at the utility government-issue wall clock confirmed it was 10.56 a.m.

"Yes gentlemen, you are expected. Can I ask you please to go into the male locker room, over there?" The girl pointed to an off-white scruffy looking door that needed fresh paint. "You'll find scrubs, masks and wellington boots. Please change into them and leave by the door at the far end of the room. I'll meet you there."

The name badge pinned to this efficient person's green top said *Samantha Grey, Senior Technician.*

Steve and Matt did as instructed, and suitably dressed, they were met by Samantha who escorted them into the main part of the mortuary where the grisly work of seeking answers from the dead was done. This morgue was a standard affair with two stainless steel tables in the centre, white sterile looking tiled walls, white floor tiles, and several sinks located around the perimeter of the room. The smell of death and formaldehyde was everywhere but the senior technician Samantha, and the imposing figure of the Home Office pathologist didn't appear to notice.

"Ah, there you are." Steve knew the tall and well-rounded pathologist was Dr Ian Evans. He was one of the country's leading pathologists and feared by defence lawyers. He stood over six foot tall and had a huge girth that made him look like a Russian babushka doll. Dressed in his green scrubs and plastic disposable apron, he was a fearsome figure especially as he was also wearing a surgical mask covering the lower part of his face.

"I won't shake hands for obvious reasons. I've been having a preliminary rummage around." His voice had a Scottish lilt, and his gloved hands were already covered in blood and gore.

Steve saw the headless body on the stainless-steel table had been re-opened by cutting into the stiches holding the skin together following the first post-mortem.

"I rather gather you're not overly content with the first post, Chief Inspector?" The question was directed at Steve.

"It's nothing specific, sir. We only got the case yesterday and there seemed to be a few gaps in the PM report."

"And you thought I might find something my colleague missed. Is that it, Chief Inspector?" Dr Evans sounded jolly enough, and Steve didn't take his comments as a criticism.

"Well, I suppose so." The use of his rank told the DCI that Dr Evans knew exactly who his two visitors were.

"Right you are. We're not perfect you know, but I think I can say the first post didn't miss much. Truth is, without the head there's not a lot to go on."

Dr Evans leant over the cadaver and started prodding with what looked like a dentist's toothpick. He was concentrating and the DCI could see that behind his face mask, had a pained expression. After a few minutes he looked up.

"As you know the organs from the first post were removed." He waved his arm to a sink in the far corner. "That's them over there. I've had a look, but I couldn't see anything out of the ordinary." The doctor waved Steve and Matt nearer to the table. Using his dentist-looking tool, he pointed inside the empty chest and lower body cavity. "See there, that discolouring. I'd say this girl has had an abortion at some point in her life. I checked her organs and there's evidence of medical intervention. It looks professional so probably done by a doctor. If so, Chief Inspector, it could be your lucky day. All abortions must be reported so you may be lucky."

Steve tried to assimilate this news. "Any idea how long ago she had the abortion?"

"Difficult to say." Dr Evans rose to his full height as he stretched his back. "But no more than a year ago based on the scar tissue."

Steve saw Matt make a note. "Anything else, Doctor?"

"Yes. You're not looking for a killer with any medical knowledge. The severing of the head was very amateurish and was messy. I'd say your killer started with a knife and finished with something like an axe or at least a heavy, sharp object. Anyone with medical knowledge wouldn't have needed so many attempts to get the head off. I only hope the poor girl was either dead or unconscious when your perpetrator carried out the beheading."

Steve took on board the doctor's remark and visibly shook. He couldn't imagine anyone doing such a thing but knew someone had.

Like a stuck record the DCI asked in a lower voice. "Anything else?"

"Yes. I'd say she wasn't British. Her skin tone suggests southern Europe possibly Spanish or Italian, somewhere warmer. Might be Spanish but she's not from our fair isles. I've had a good look but I've nothing much more to add except the tattoo. It's fairly old and small. It could have been done when she was a child and I've seen it before."

Steve jumped in. "You have?"

"Yes. I had a cadaver about six months ago. Another young girl as I remember, but she did have her head on." The pathologist laughed at his own joke. "I'm certain the tattoo was the same. I'll dig out the file and send it over."

"Thank you, sir. Can you remember the name of the victim?"

"No but I'll find it. I can't remember if they ever got an ID."

Steve's heart sank. If this other tattooed victim had been identified he'd have a start point to try to trace the name of the body on the table.

"I understand you've now got fingerprints and I'm re-sampling the stomach contents. The tox screen results should be back by tomorrow. The previous pathologist seemed to have skimmed over the laboratory work. Probably worried about budgets." Again, Dr Ian Evans laughed at his own joke. Steve and Matt smiled politely.

"Well, that's it, gentlemen. I'll get that file over to you, assuming my secretary can find it, and I'll let you have my report tomorrow once the tox screen information is to hand. Samantha will show you out. I'm sorry I couldn't provide the silver bullet."

Steve and Matt followed Samantha as they both thanked the pathologist. Having reversed the procedure, the pair met the Senior Technician outside the main mortuary area. She gave Matt a card. "In case you need me for anything. It has all our numbers; mine is the last one." As she turned away, Steve noticed Samantha smiling sweetly at his detective sergeant and that Matt was smiling back. Steve smiled to himself and thought, *Here we go again. I'm running a bloody dating agency.*

Chapter Six

Just as Steve and Matt were being escorted by Samantha, the flirty senior technician, into the mortuary, Andrew and David Black were sitting opposite Jean Franco in the same curtained-off booth in his sleazy nightclub as they had last night.

Another man was seated next to him. He didn't look like a gangster. He was short and slim, wore a three-piece business suit and his fair hair was well-groomed and combed with a left-side parting. The impression of an accountant was completed by the gold-rimmed specs that he seemed to push up to the bridge of his nose every ten seconds.

The club was quiet with the only noise coming from the cleaning crew as they vacuumed the carpets and removed any stains from the soft furnishings. Andrew Black noticed Jean had several buff-coloured folders in front of him and a calculator.

Jean Franco's Americanised voice seemed particularly powerful this morning at least to the brothers who hadn't quite recovered from last night's extravagances.

"This is my colleague, Antonio." Jean waved an arm in Antonio's direction. Antonio nodded but said nothing. Jean Franco carried on. "Now, to business. Our business is split into different activities and runs on military lines but first, and most important, it is a money-making business. I like to think of the business in two parts."

David Black felt this gangster had made this speech before.

"First there's your side. The dark, black sleazy side that makes the money. Then there's the light side, the honest side where your dark and sleazy activities get washed clean and we live without fear of the law." Jean leant forward in his chair, "But remember," — the brothers both felt pure evil coming from this man — "you're on the dark side just like your predecessor. He tried to betray us and move to the light side. Make sure you don't. The fish have had a meal of one guy who made a mistake; they'd have no problem feeding on another two. Are we clear?"

Both brothers nodded their understanding.

Suddenly Jean Franco brightened up. The sinister and evil Jean disappeared to be replaced by a more jovial and relaxed big boss.

"OK, lecture over. I know you boys will do a great job working for us and," Jean paused, "you'll make a lot of money for yourselves if you stay honest."

David Black felt the last comment held a threat and concluded that, no matter how happy or jovial this man appeared, violence was never far from the surface.

"Right, let's get down to business. Always remember boys, we are a business." Jean fingered the files in front of him.

"First we have the drugs business. This is an area of change and you two will be at the front of it." Jean lifted a file from the top of the ones in front of him. "You know the drugs game; you are, after all, my biggest distributor in London and that's why you're here." Jean glanced at Antonio. "But you must also know the business isn't the same any more. Too many Ma and Pa operations being run from home garages. Other gangs setting up and undercutting prices to buy market share and they're cutting the pure stuff with rubbish to make it go further. The poor addicts don't know what they're getting. As part of our new business plan, you're going to do something about it."

The brothers nodded, afraid to speak, wondering what they were expected to do.

"We all know powder these days is on the way out. It's still an important part of our business but let's be truthful. Most addicts would rather take a pill than mix up stuff to shoot up their arm or ruin their nasal passages by sniffing powder up their noses. Christ, good quality Colombian is selling for less than half what it did six months ago." Jean was getting worked up but stopped to draw a deep breath. "So as a business we're having to adapt. We have a new business plan and a new strategy." Jean saw the brothers were suffering from last night. He turned to Antonio. "Tony, go get the boys some medicine. A couple of vodkas should do it and bring me a coffee."

Looking at his new UK managers, he said with some sympathy. "I hear you had a good night last night?"

David answered feeling he was the more awake of the two. "Yes, thanks, Jean, your hospitality was great."

"Yeah, I heard."

As Antonio reappeared with the drinks, Jean Franco continued his briefing. "As I was saying, the margin on powder has gone. All the kids want now is tablets. So like any business we're adapting. Tony here has set up a production plant somewhere near a place called Norwich to produce tabs. At the moment it's running on a small scale but when you get back and start working, we'll crank up production to 40,000 tabs a day. See, we're cutting our Colombian with more chalk and powder. It means for a real high the kids have got to buy two tabs. We know the poor-quality Ma and Pa rubbish is selling in the clubs for four pounds each. Our new line will retail at the same, four quid, but we know the user's going to need two, so each sale should be eight pounds retail."

Jean paused to drink his coffee and examine the brothers' faces to see if they understood. They didn't. Jean Franco moved on regardless. "You see, gentlemen, we're going into the wholesale business. We'll wholesale our stuff to the main dealers and the street guys at two quid a tab. They can sell them on at nearer the four quid that seems to be the going rate. Your job is to get our product circulating so nobody will have any need to buy from small-time operators. I know you have existing contacts but from now on there will be no independent operators. Anybody selling tabs or powder will be contracted to us. You'll set up wholesalers who'll buy in bulk and pay two pounds for each tab. They, in turn, will sell onto the street dealers at say three pounds a tab and the street guys will sell to their users at four pounds a tab. If you get any resistance then you deal with it.

"You're already the biggest supplier in London so it shouldn't be hard, but we need to be in Manchester and Birmingham. You need to get this form of distribution up and running and get our product on these streets and as I said, it's up to you to sort any problems."

Both brothers were feeling more like themselves as a result of drinking the neat vodka and tried to understand what Jean had just said. Before either of them could question him, he picked up the calculator and tapped the keys as he spoke.

"You've got eight weeks to get the operation in place. Then we'll be making 40,000 tabs a day. That's eighty grand a day. Remember you'll be selling in bulk so this should be no problem. Now you only have to deal with a few wholesalers."

David Black understood this part as Jean carried on. "You'll see this makes expansion easier. You don't get down and dirty dealing with the individual dealers looking for a few ounces of crack or half a dozen tabs; you deal in bulk. Once the wholesaler has his order, we don't care where or how he shifts it. We only have to make sure he does and places a regular order. Now do you understand?"

"Yes, I see that, Jean." Andrew Black liked the idea. "Very clever."

Not impressed by flattery, Jean continued punching keys on his calculator. "From the tabs that's 2.22 million pounds every four weeks. Got it?"

The brothers were shocked at the number. Reluctantly David spoke. "So we have to sell and collect 2.22 million pounds worth of tabs every four weeks?"

"That's it." Jean cleared the screen on his calculator and punched in more numbers as he spoke. "Plus, the powder. It's a dying trade but it's a market we are in, so let's make the most of it. I reckon we're currently selling upwards of fifteen kilos a week in the UK. We'll ship the powder on the same basis as the pills. Every wholesaler will also buy powder at a discounted wholesale rate." Jean finished hitting keys.

"So now, that makes 2.22 million from the pills and a further 1.4 million for the powder." He laid down his calculator with a flourish. "That's a grand total of £3.62 million you'll deliver to us every four weeks less your commission. Your take will be 10% so you'll make £362,000 every four weeks. Forget your previous deal, this is better for you. I presume this is a satisfactory arrangement?"

David Black was calculating the annual amount they would make but couldn't hold all the zeros in his head. All he knew was that this was a bonanza payday if they could gear up as Jean was requesting.

Jean Franco allowed a few minutes for the numbers to be absorbed.

Andrew Black couldn't work the numbers out but knew it meant bumper paydays ahead if they could get things in place within the next eight weeks.

He asked. "And you have similar operations throughout Europe?"

"Yes. The European Union kindly opened the door to customs-free cross-border trading. We have similar operations in every European Union member state."

Andrew thought about the numbers and was overawed by the amount of money Jean Franco must be making.

Jean turned to Antonio who had remained silent throughout the briefing. Antonio nodded as a sign that Jean should carry on.

"Are you both clear on our drugs set-up and what you have to do? I'll discuss how you get the money to us when we're finished."

The brothers stumbled over each other to answer. Both spoke at the same time. "Oh! Yes Jean."

As Jean Franco passed the drug file over the table, he knew greed was a wonderful weapon but wondered how long these two would last. If he had had time, he would have found better calibre people but the previous manager of his business in the UK had had to be dealt with swiftly leaving a hole that he hoped these two could fill.

"That's the file. All you need is in there. The name of the guy running the Norwich operation and so on, plus existing dealers you don't know. Make sure they know you before the end of the week." A sly grin spread across his face. "Remember, you're wholesalers of product now, and it's cash and carry. If anybody can't pay on delivery, they don't get the product and you get rid of them. Replace them with people who can pay. We don't give credit."

Jean Franco was smiling but his eyes were cold and penetrating. "Now gents, as I said, this is a business. We run on profit and loss, margins, business plans and cash flows. You don't have to worry about any of that. Just do your job." Jean was thinking how simply he could explain the next part of his briefing.

"The drug business is in decline and that's going to affect all our future earnings, but when something goes down, something else goes up. I know you two have tried the flesh business and you've dabbled but you set your sights too low. The money is in high-end, high-class hookers. Not your young thing from a council estate trying to make a few pounds."

The brothers didn't know what Jean was talking about. They ran a few prostitutes but admitted they were low rent.

"Take the girls you had last night. They're smart, clean, well-dressed and know their way around a man's anatomy. Do you agree?"

David Black was jumping in his seat as he recalled the girl called Primrose and how she had made him feel. He regretted having drunk so much earlier on and couldn't remember how his encounter had ended. All he knew was, he enjoyed it. He stammered "Y-yes Jean, I agree."

Jean took on the air of a CEO of a large corporation. "Right. So you see that's now our growth market. Your predecessor did a good job setting up the London flesh operation a while ago, so all you have to do is take it over and expand it." Jean noticed David was looking excited, probably thinking he'd enjoy more girls.

"We have sixteen high-end escorts set up in London. They bring in good money and that's why you are going to expand the whole operation. Each tart gets through two punters a night at 2000 pounds a roll. That's 4000 pounds each. If a John wants all night she charges four grand, so her contribution is the same."

Andrew was astonished. "You mean men pay two grand for a bird?" He couldn't believe it.

"Oh yes, but only if you know where to market their wares. We've got that sorted and Antonio here will assist. We invest heavily in the girls. Thanks to the EU we bring them here from all over Europe, train them a little, dress them and when they're ready, we'll send them to you.

"This is where our corporate growth is coming from. The deal is you get 10% of their earnings but you pay for their accommodation. That comes out of your 10%. We pay the girls from here including the fee for their minder, but remember, they need to be living in high-end places, not dumps. Their clients are paying good money for the best, including a comfortable bed in a nice place."

Andrew Black was nervous. "You mean you send us girls like the ones last night and we find them somewhere to live?"

"Almost. The present sixteen are controlled by their minders. We run two girls to one minder. So for every two girls we send you've got to find a minder. You'll have to get the minders under contract."

Andrew was beginning to see the plan. He was nodding as though deep in thought.

"Right." Andrew Black was scratching the bridge of his nose as he often did when under pressure. "So, you send us the girls, we find them somewhere to stay and we pay for it. We have to find a minder for each two girls and maybe employ someone to market their services."

"Got it in one my friend although the marketing is taken care of, but you have to pay for it."

Andrew wasn't convinced. "But you said we would only get 10%. I don't think that's enough."

Jean once more glanced at Antonio who actually smiled. Jean reached for his calculator and like a teacher explaining a theory to a backward child, started to explain. He again punched keys as he spoke.

"We now have sixteen girls each earning four grand a night and they work six nights a week. That's sixty-four thousand pounds a night and £384,000 a week which is £1,536,000 every four weeks. I'm going to send you another sixteen girls over the next eight weeks so the take should double." Looking directly at Andrew, Jean's eyes seem to burn into Andrew's brain. "That means we take over three million every four weeks and you get £300,000 as your share. Apart from paying for the accommodation and the marketing, you've no other overhead. I think it's a sweet deal."

Both brothers hadn't calculated the enormity of what was being proposed and their earning power from both the drugs and now the girls. Slowly Andrew looked at the piece of paper he'd written the numbers on. said. "So we get £362,000 from the drugs and £300,000 from the girls?"

Jean was pleased to see at least Andrew understood. "That's £662,000 you'll be earning every four weeks if, in eight weeks' time, you have everything sorted. Our corporate plan shows drug income falling but flesh income rising over the next year." Jean Franco had resumed his CEO air. "You'll quickly have forty girls in the stable and flesh is easier to sell. You'll expand, as with the drugs, into more northern cities." Jean sat back and placed both hands on the table. "Well boys, that's it. You have your future and are now part of our organisation."

David Black was churning the numbers over and lost count due to the number of zeros. He was trying to calculate Jean Franco's earnings over twenty-seven European countries. All he could tell himself was it was that it was a fortune.

Andrew, always the diplomat, stood and shook Jean Franco's hand. "You won't regret this, Mr Franco. We're your men."

Jean Franco politely stood, and this time accepted the handshake but was far from convinced the brothers were anything other than a stopgap.

"Now sit down." Jean pointed to Andrew. "I believe my associate Antonio wants to say a few words."

Antonio sat forward and unsmilingly started his speech. "I look after the company's money so here's how you'll operate."

Antonio's English was accented. David Black thought he sounded Italian and quickly made the leap that he must be Mafia.

Antonio continued. "First the drug money. You will receive daily shipments of pills from Norwich. With each delivery will be an invoice for the number in each batch. You will wholesale these pills and as Jean said, no credit, so you'll have cash coming in daily. Set up a supply contract with your wholesalers. I will give you the contracts but each wholesaler commits to a minimum number of tabs each week. Every Monday someone will call, balance your books and after paying you your commission, he will take the excess cash away. You will balance the books at the same time for the powder and receive your commission. Is that clear?"

Antonio, although not a big man, had an air of menace about him and Andrew felt this Italian was even more dangerous than Jean.

Both brothers nodded.

"Good. As for the flesh. You will visit the girls' handlers each morning before ten a.m. and collect the previous night's earnings. This will be four thousand pounds from each girl. If any minder is short, you will discover why and replace him if necessary. How you do it is your affair. Every Monday, Wednesday and Friday someone else will call and balance your account. If it is correct, you will receive your commission and this collector will take the rest of the money."

Antonio looked at the brothers with eyes that didn't look friendly. "Is that clear?"

Again, the brothers nodded. They were excited by the income, but seeing these two men close up, wondered if greed was in fact a good thing.

Antonio carried on in his accented English. "Remember the girls are the growth. You need to market them properly or they won't have enough work and that's bad for you and for business. We have a guy who takes care of making sure the people who need the service know about our girls. You'll meet him next week and sort out his fees." Antonio sat back and looked at Jean. "That's it. Good luck boys. I'll meet you next week."

The brothers were about to stand when Jean took a sheet of A4 paper from the remaining file in front of him and pushed the paper across the table. "That's a loan note for one hundred thousand pounds. We know how important working capital is so that's a loan to help you settle the new girls in and recruit their minders. You'll see we're only charging 8% compound interest weekly so the sooner you pay this off the better off you'll be." Jean pointed to two dotted lines at the foot of the page and handed Andrew a pen. Both brothers, too scared to talk, signed the agreement.

Jean Franco pulled the last item from the remaining file. It was a sealed envelope. He held it by its corners with something approaching reverence.

"Inside this envelope are three names and contact details. You will not open this envelope unless it is a real emergency, and you need help. The names in here are of people who are important to our entire business so don't screw with them and as I said, only contact them if something serious happens. One is a senior policeman; one is a captain of industry and a big noise in the City of London and the third is a government minister. Guard this envelope with your lives. Do you understand?"

Andrew took the envelope plus the two files. As he did so, he noted one file said 'drugs', the other 'flesh'. The brothers stood and shook hands. "Good luck boys and remember, we're trusting you to make a lot of money for all of us."

Clutching the files and the envelope, David told Jean Franco he could rely on them.

"Your flight back isn't until seven tonight. You'll be collected from your hotel at five p.m." Jean looked at his watch. "It's 2.15 p.m. The girls are still in your rooms so go back and have a good time. Everything's paid for. Just be in the foyer at five p.m."

With a satisfied grin on their faces, the brothers left to be driven by the weedy guy with no name back to their hotel and more pleasure.

Once they'd gone, Antonio said, "I give them six months before they really screw things up."

"Doesn't matter. We've started looking around. A couple of names have been recommended. If we get three months out of them, we'll be in good shape."

Jean Franco left to return to his large corporate office in the business section of Amsterdam, leaving Antonio to wonder how his association with Jean Franco would finally work out.

Antonio Conti was a numbers man. He'd been Mafia all his life. He'd even married a senior Mafia don's daughter. He sat back daydreaming about his past. When he first met his wife, he thought her a pleasant but plain girl. She had given him two children, a boy also called Antonio and a girl called Maria. Over the years as his wife became fatter, she had also become more domineering, insisting he climb the ranks of her beloved Mafiosi. He thought about his children. His son would be thirty now and Maria twenty-eight. For a peaceful domestic life, he'd gone along with his wife's demands and had risen quickly through the ranks.

As the mob's chief bookkeeper, he'd learned that sometimes violence was necessary to achieve the results you sought. He learned how to launder vast sums of money and deal with the necessarily sleazy world that brought enormous wealth and influence. Although small in stature he had in the past been forced to put his naturally gentle nature behind him and participate in some brutal events on the orders of his Mafia bosses. Slowly he'd rebelled against the sickening violence and the assassinations that were becoming everyday events in his life. He saw himself becoming hardened to this routine violence that he thought unnecessary. Slowly he realised that this life was not for him and when he had refused to take part in a planned horrific act against a town mayor, he knew his days were numbered.

On a visit to the mainland and supposedly overseeing the assassination of a prominent politician, he had fled Italy for good, leaving his family behind. He loved his children and was sorry to have abandoned them but his wife he knew he wouldn't miss. He was convinced he was doing the right thing and had been happy to escape his Mafia roots. As an insurance policy he had escaped carrying incriminating files on his Mafia bosses, both financial and criminal. As the keeper of their financial records, Antonio Paulo knew where the real Mafia wealth was and believed that while he held this data, he was safe from reprisals.

Having changed his name to Antonio Conti, he knew he would need to set up an arrangement with some other criminal organisation as a way of making a living but also trying to keep himself safe. His former colleagues had long memories.

After three years of being employed by several low-grade gangsters throughout Europe, he'd met Jean Franco in Berlin one afternoon a few years ago.

As he sat looking at the ceiling, Antonio recalled this first meeting. Jean was a large man with little intelligence and a tendency towards violence. At that time Jean was running a largely unstructured mob of drug dealers and pimps. His organisation although large, profitable and violent was low rent and unsophisticated. Antonio saw his opportunity when Jean asked him to help improve what Jean saw as an empire.

He'd now been working with Jean Franco for about two years during which time his business acumen plus his mixture of financial and political skills coupled with his propensity for violence when the occasion arose, had made him invaluable to Jean Franco. He smiled to himself as he recalled explaining to Jean Franco how money-laundering schemes worked and Jean's inability to grasp even the basics.

Antonio had worked hard setting up Jean's present legal and illegal empire, or what Jean, with his limited understanding, preferred to call light and dark. He'd established a chain of legitimate businesses as a front for cleaning the vast sums of money coming from drugs and prostitution. He had borrowed on Mafia models for such things and with a little massaging he had quickly established Jean Franco as an apparently legitimate business tycoon.

Unfortunately, Antonio knew that Jean Franco was becoming dangerous as he had begun to believe his own press. Having set up Jean's empire, Antonio knew how it functioned and he congratulated himself on being responsible for lifting the middle-level gangster from just another thug to what he was today at least to the outside world: a captain of industry running what looked to be a multimillion-dollar European business empire. Antonio smiled; he knew he was the real power behind the business and was working on a plan to eliminate Jean Franco when the time was right. He was planning even greater things for the business but not with Jean Franco. He told himself. "Once a Mafioso, always a Mafioso."

Chapter Seven

Steve returned from the mortuary with Matt Conway at 1.06 p.m. to find Terry Harvey, Head of Technical Support, sitting on Poppy's desk talking to her. As Terry was Poppy's uncle, Steve guessed they weren't discussing work.

Steve asked Terry into his office and Terry perched himself on the chair opposite the DCI's desk and opened a folder he had been carrying.

"Just give me some good news Terry." Steve was feeling deflated after his trip to the morgue and still had the smell of death in his nose.

"I've run the prints from the headless girl. Sorry Steve, nothing, she's not in the system. I checked every database I could think of but came up empty."

Steve saw Terry was disappointed. "Don't worry Terry, it was a long shot." Steve opened the files on his desk expecting his friend to take the hint and leave but Inspector Terry Harvey sat still. Steve knew the signs and allowed a slight grin to appear. "Go on, you've got something else, haven't you?"

Terry pulled a photograph of the bird tattoo found on the headless torso from a file. He pushed it across Steve's desk towards him. "I ran it through every database known to man and got nothing, but when I put it through as a symbol it seems a company in Italy use it as their corporate badge. The company is called Italian Resources with headquarters in Rome but that's all I've got. Could just be a coincidence."

"You know Terry, sometimes you amaze me. The pathologist said he thought our Jane Doe was from a warm climate and actually said it could be Italy. Without realising it, you've maybe just confirmed it." Steve sat back. "Come on, I'll buy you a tea in the canteen."

Terry knew Steve as a coffee drinker and was surprised at the invitation. Nonetheless he readily accepted the offer as a reward for his hard work.

Steve ordered their drinks, and they found a table away from the door. Just as their drinks were being delivered, Steve, who had his back to the entrance, realised that all the male and a few of the female officers suddenly stopped talking and drinking to stare open-mouthed towards the entrance. Within seconds, Poppy was standing behind her boss conscious of the looks she was attracting especially from the male members in the canteen.

Steve looked at Terry who had also noticed a change in atmosphere the moment Poppy appeared in her all-too-revealing attire. Poppy took a seat without being invited.

"The Commander wants to see you urgently, sir, he just called through." Poppy, although aware of the longing glances from some of the male officers seated at their tables, carried on as though such occurrences were normal. "I told him I'd come here and tell you."

Steve arrived at a decision he'd long been putting off. "Thanks Poppy, you can stay with Terry and have my tea, I haven't touched it."

Steve stood to go, and as he did, he tensed himself to deliver the comment to Poppy he knew he should have done weeks ago. He leant in to talk quietly to Poppy. "You've been told about dress codes before. If you don't start to wear more suitable office clothes, I'll put you back into uniform. That way at least you'll be covered up and the males in the canteen can enjoy their lunch."

The DCI walked away hoping Poppy would heed his warning, however, deep-down, Steve felt it was a lost cause, Poppy was Poppy.

***

The DCI entered Commander Alfie Brooks' office at exactly 1.44 p.m. on this Tuesday September the 19th. He didn't know it, but this meeting would change his life forever.

"You wanted me, sir?"

Alfie was behind his desk dressed in his uniform shirt and tie. Steve noted Alfie's uniform jacket was slung casually over a chair by his conference table. Alfie acknowledged his arrival and indicated he should sit at the table and joined him. The two men sat opposite each other.

Alfie leaned forward in his chair. "You'll think this is a put-up job, but honestly it's just a coincidence. Norfolk Constabulary have asked for the Met's assistance with a murder case. Your Special Resolutions Unit is first call when outside forces ask for help—"

Before Alfie could continue, Steve interrupted. "So I'm going to Norfolk whether I want to or not. Is that it?"

"Yes. It's just a coincidence but it will let you see what you'd be taking on if you decided to apply and you'll meet the Deputy Chief."

Steve knew such coincidences happened so made no protest. "What's the case?"

Alfie rose and returned with a file. He slid it over the table towards the DCI. "Seems one of their own, a DS Elsie Brown, was found murdered on the 9th of this month, that's ten days ago. The murder squad up there have made no progress at all, that's why they've asked us for help. She was found in her house beaten around the head. There's no apparent motive and so far they have no leads and no forensics."

Alfie smiled. "I'd say it's right up your street."

"Yeah, thanks Alfie."

"You're to meet a Chief Superintendent Emily Channel, Head of Norfolk CID. If you took the job, she's the one you'd be replacing. Apparently, she's a bit of a dragon and has been forced into early retirement so I don't think you'll get much help." Alfie sat more upright in his chair. "Seems the victim was in the same boat. Past her sell-by date but didn't know when to leave so forced early retirement was necessary. Apart from that and what little is in the file, it's all yours."

The DCI sighed. "I was at a post-mortem this morning. Young girl fished out of the Thames. Her head had been chopped off. So far, we have nothing plus I've got a few other cases going on. Do you really want me to go to Norwich for this case or is this you trying to force my hand?"

Alfie acted hurt and threw his arms up. "Steve, how could you suggest such a thing!" He was smiling. "But no, seriously. As I said, you know your unit is first call on for something like this, but I agree it will give you a chance to look around."

Alfie stood and Steve followed. As they walked towards the office door, Alfie placed a hand on Steve's shoulder. "You're to get there tomorrow morning around ten. Sort your team out and take a bagman.

I've been told by the Deputy Chief that you'll get full-time assistance, but you never know." Alfie hesitated and in a low voice asked. "I don't suppose you reached a decision about the Norfolk offer?"

Steve knew he and Alison had but decided to keep that information to himself still believing this assignment was of Alfie's making. "We'll never know now, sir as I'm off up there anyway."

The two men parted, and the DCI headed to his office.

***

In Amsterdam, the brothers didn't go straight to their hotel rooms, denying themselves the pleasures that awaited them. Instead, they went to the bar and ordered drinks and sandwiches. Seated at a corner table they discussed the files they had been given and tried to analyse the morning's events.

"I don't know if we can do this, Andrew." David Black was the worrier of the two brothers. "I think we're in over our heads. These guys are real mobsters and what do we know about business plans and crap like margins and cash flow?"

Andrew, as the older brother, always saw himself as the leader, and the one with the better brain. "Look David, it's simple. Everything's in these files. Names, addresses, contact numbers, everything we need. All we have to do is follow what's in the files and we'll learn as we go."

The drinks and sandwiches arrived, and Andrew took a great bite out of his sandwich.

"But what about the girls? We don't know how to get high rollers to pay four grand a night." David was pleading and hadn't started his drink or his food.

"Don't worry." Andrew tapped the top file he'd laid on their table. "In here it says a geezer called Ramos has already set things up. Seems he knows what to do. All we have to do is make sure he knows he's working for us now. You heard what Jean said about getting more girls? All we have to do is find some cheap upmarket pads and recruit a few pimps."

Andrew finished his sandwich and downed his whisky in one swallow. He sat back patting his stomach and looked at his brother.

David was not convinced but had no real argument to throw back at his elder brother. Limply he said, "I suppose so but what if it all goes wrong?"

"Relax, it won't. We've got the protection racket, don't we?" Andrew didn't wait for an answer. "And who do we protect?" Andrew's voice was light and almost singing as he waited for David to respond.

The pair stared at each other, Andrew willing David to catch on. Eventually he saw a glimmer of recognition on his brother's face and a broad smile appeared. "Archie McLaren."

"Got it. We protect Archie's string of less than desirable low-end joints that he uses for his illegal immigrants' business, but we know he has a few high-end pads he uses for other purposes, and he has a legitimate buy-to-rent business. We put the screw on Archie, force him to vacate his top-end properties for a while and we'll take over the flats."

Andrew was amazed at his own brilliance. "See, no problems." Andrew was eyeing up David's untouched food. "Are you going to eat that?" He pointed to the sandwich. "You'll need all your strength this afternoon. Let's have another drink and go and see the girls. The car is coming at five, so we'll have a couple of hours' fun." He raised his arm and snapped his fingers. "Two more of the same." He pointed to his empty glass and David's still untouched one. As the waiter was retreating, he called out and instructed that two bottles of champagne be delivered to their respective rooms.

David picked at his sandwich and started to drink his whisky still feeling they were in over their heads, but Andrew's confidence was catching and as he finished his whisky and the second one arrived, he told himself everything would be OK. He ate his sandwich, finished his second drink and followed his brother upstairs.

***

At the same time as the brothers were embarking on their afternoon of pleasure, Steve was in his office deciding on his next course of action. He looked at his watch. It said 3.44 p.m.

He called Matt Conway in. "Matt, you'll have to pack a bag. We're off to Norwich tomorrow. We've been called in on a murder case. I've no idea how long we'll be away but better pack for say five days. Sign out a pool car and pick me up at five tomorrow morning. I want to miss the traffic and we've got a meeting with their Head of CID at eleven."

"Right you are, boss. I've never been to Norwich."

"What have you done about tracking down the abortions the pathologist told us about?"

Matt was about to answer when Poppy appeared. "I've started tracking down abortions within the M25 for the last twelve months." Poppy had an A4 pad that she was studying as she spoke. "I'm merging all the data into one file and then we can cross reference against non-UK girls, but specifically southern European. I'll only take a few hours, so we'll have something tomorrow."

Steve had to admit Poppy was good, but she was not only dressing inappropriately, she was still listening in on the DCI's conversations. Steve's jaw dropped when Poppy announced. "I don't suppose I could come to Norwich with you, sir. Unlike Matt, I've been there several times and I know my way around. I could be a big help."

The DCI admired Poppy's never-say-die spirit and her ability not to see when she was on thin ice. It wasn't possible to stay angry with her for long. She was like a puppy dog that had chewed a piece of furniture but looked at its owner with an innocent expression not knowing what it had done to deserve a reprimand.

Steve simply smiled.

"Thanks Poppy, but I need you here. No doubt we'll need backup and you're better placed here with access to Terry." Steve noticed Matt was struggling to keep a straight face.

"Stick with the abortion thing. It's probably the best lead we have on that case and contact Norwich. Make sure they're expecting two of us and that we're checked into a decent hotel."

Poppy disappeared and within a few minutes, Peter Jones and Mary Dougan arrived at Steve's door looking windswept. Without ceremony, Peter sat in the chair opposite Steve. Mary, looking better for having been out in the fresh air, stood by the door leaning on the door frame.

"We've been to every tattoo parlour on the list Poppy gave us." Peter didn't look happy. "We got nothing, absolute zilch. Sorry Steve, but it looks like a dead end."

The DCI decided on his action plan. "Peter, we've been given an out of area murder case in Norfolk. I'm heading up there tomorrow with Matt. I've no idea how long we'll be gone but you are now Senior Investigating Officer on the headless corpse case."

Steve explained that the pathologist, Dr Ian Evans, thought he'd seen the tattoo of the bird that was on the cadaver's arm before, and that he felt that, from her skin tone, she was probably from southern Europe possibly Spain or Italy.

"He is going to track it down and send over the details. Get onto Interpol and get them to check the tattoo and do a search of missing girls aged between twenty and thirty from the bottom end of Europe. Also, Terry Harvey has found the tattoo could also be corporate logo for a company called Italian Resources. It's another Italian connection if nothing else."

"Right Steve, but that could be a lot of names."

"Yes, I know, but it's all we have. Also, Dr Evans said our victim had had an abortion within the past twelve months. Poppy's on that now so you might get something from that."

"Peter Jones was ambitious and relished the thought of being SIO on a murder case, but also realised he'd probably have to rely on his DCI's experience.

"Right, I've got all that. Do you want to be kept up to speed?"

"Yes. Call me each day. I'm not taking over. You are the SIO, it's just I want to be kept up-to-date and I might be able to help, even from Norfolk."

"Got it, Steve."

Mary Dougan was still standing by the door. "I presume I'm with the DI on the headless case sir?"

"Yes Mary. It's a difficult one and needs all our talents if we're to get a result."

She nodded and lifted herself off the door frame she'd been leaning on and returned to the outer office.

Peter stood, and after a few words with the DCI, also went back to his desk in the outer office.

Steve cleared the pending files on his desk and passed them to Poppy for filing. He then called around various colleagues including

Commander Alfie Brooks to tell them that Peter was now SIO on the headless case and he would be away for a while. Alfie Brooks knew Steve would have to rearrange his affairs and was happy to note Peter Jones was being given more responsibility.

With all his loose ends tied up, Steve packed his briefcase and left the Yard at 5.22 p.m. He rehearsed what he'd say to his wife about the coincidence of the case in Norwich and his potential job offer. As he walked, he role played both sides of the conversation, and smiled. He was sure Alison would smell an Alfie Brooks set-up and Steve knew he had no answer other than she could be right.

Chapter Eight

Matt Conway collected Steve from his home at exactly five a.m. Wednesday September the 20th was promising to be a fine day although the weather forecast said it might rain in Norfolk in the late afternoon. The pair made good time with Matt driving, and they stopped for breakfast at a roadside burger bar just off the A12 north of Chelmsford. Having polished off a greasy burger and two cups of coffee, the two detectives completed their journey arriving at Norfolk Constabulary Headquarters in Horwich at 10.23 a.m.

Having parked in a visitor's parking space, Steve and Matt found themselves in a reception area and confronted by a civilian receptionist. She was a pretty girl in her mid-twenties and appeared to be extremely efficient. It was obvious that the detectives from the Met were expected but the pretty receptionist insisted on seeing their IDs and had them complete a visitor registration card. Eventually she produced two cards inside plastic wallets with lanyards that said 'Police' every few inches along their length. It reminded Steve of the seaside rock he used to get as a kid with the resort name repeated along its length.

As they were being cleared to enter, a uniformed constable arrived who introduced himself as PC Forster, and asked the pair to follow him to Chief Superintendent Emily Channel's office. Steve noted that PC Forster was nearing retirement age and given the size of his belly would struggle to pass a police medical board.

DCS Emily Channel sat behind a large desk in a well-appointed office. Steve cheekily saw himself behind the desk and was impressed by the size of the office. It was bigger than Alfie's back at the Yard and Steve noted by counting the chairs that the conference table could accommodate twelve people. There was a fireplace on the far wall with an ornate stone carved fire surround and the red coloured carpet was thick and showed no signs of wear. Steve thought Norfolk Constabulary knew how to look after themselves.

"Good morning gentlemen, pleased to meet you." DCS Channel stood and walked around her desk holding her hand to be shaken in turn by Steve and Matt. DCS Emily Channel was a large woman by any standards. She wasn't overly fat nor overweight, but what Steve's mother would have called big-boned. She stood an inch taller than the DCI at six foot and wore dark-rimmed glasses that were on a string around her neck. On initial examination Steve felt the lady gave off an air of efficiency but from her body language he thought she might not be too friendly.

After introductions, the three sat at the long conference table. The DCS sat at the head while Steve and Matt sat opposite each other. Emily Channel ordered coffee without asking if her guests wanted any. She sat with her arms folded staring at the new arrivals and letting the silence cloud the room. Matt looked at his boss and shook his head slightly. The Metropolitan Police detectives played the silence game.

The coffee was delivered and as Emily Channel sipped hers, she spoke. "So Mr Burt, you're the great hope of policing are you? Come to show us country bumpkins how to catch a killer."

Steve was taken aback by the obvious hostility. He wondered if the DCS knew he was her potential successor. He made a note to test the waters before he left.

"Well Ma'am, I've been on similar secondments before, and I've always worked well with the local officers." Steve gave what he hoped was a reassuring smile. "I'm sure this won't be any different. We're only here to help and maybe look at things from a different perspective."

"Yes, well, we'll see," she said as she drank her coffee.

Steve noticed she wasn't wearing a wedding ring. The carefully tailored jacket and blouse she wore looked expensive, but Steve felt she had been more a working frontline copper during her career.

"We have a problem, Mr Burt—"

Steve interrupted. "Steve, please."

The DCI received a withering look from the senior officer. "Yes, as I was saying DCI Burt, we have a problem."

Steve realised this was not going to be friendly.

"The SIO on the case, Inspector Dave Peddie, is at home sick. He's due to retire next week so I'm not pushing him to come back. It means you'll have to assume the SIO role as a direct command rather than the consultative one I'm sure you'd hoped for. In other words, Mr Burt, you'll have to get your hands dirty." This remark had a sarcastic ring to it that Steve took exception to.

"Superintendent Channel, I resent the slur that my colleague and I have travelled up here on some sort of holiday. We are here to help and I'm quite happy to assume a command role within your force until we find your colleague's killer. May I also add that if a fellow officer in the Met had been murdered, every detective would be volunteering for unpaid overtime until the killer were caught. From what I've seen and heard since arriving here, you and your team have not given this case the priority it deserves."

Emily Channel's face got redder and redder the longer Steve sounded off. When he'd finished, she was obviously angry.

"Just remember who you are talking to, Inspector. You may get away with such insubordination in the Met, but you bloody well won't in Norfolk!"

Steve sat in silence as Emily Channel fidgeted with the buttons on her jacket. The tense silence lasted several long seconds before the DCS spoke again.

"You clearly don't understand our position, Steve."

The DCI was visibly shocked that she had now chosen to use his Christian name.

"Poor Elsie Brown and I were beat constables years ago and despite what you think, I'm keener than anyone to find her killer. Our problem is we're very under-resourced. For some reason, all our CID officers, with a few exceptions, are due to retire soon, and to be honest even for one of their own I don't think they are capable of running a major murder enquiry. That's why you're here, but if you say anything about this outside this room, I'll have you both shipped back to the Met before you can sit down. We're proud of our Force and I won't hear anything derogatory said about it, even if it is true."

Steve saw the senior officer, although still angry and hostile, was calming down. Her outburst didn't bother him, but it gave Steve the opening he was looking for.

With an innocent expression Steve calmy asked, "I hear you too might be retiring soon, Ma'am?"

Emily Channel suddenly looked very tired. Her big-boned frame suddenly seemed to shrink, and Steve thought he saw a tear in the corner of her left eye. As she quickly and casually brushed the back of her hand over her eyes in order to hide her tear, she sat more upright.

"I don't know where you get your information, but yes, I am retiring soon." There was an air of finality in her statement.

Steve carried on fishing to try to discover if she knew about his interest in her job. "I suppose your successor has already been appointed?"

"Not that I'm aware, no."

"If, as you say most of your CID officers are retiring, I don't suppose there'll be many internal candidates?"

Emily Channel looked quizzically at Steve through narrowly slotted eyes. "Are you just curious or do you have another agenda?"

"No Ma'am, just trying to get a picture."

Before Emily could respond, a tap at the door was heard and what Steve took to be another elderly looking CID officer appeared.

"Ah!" The DCS turned to welcome the new arrival with a warm smile. "Sit down Geoff; these are the officers from the Met." Emily made the introductions.

The new arrival was Detective Sergeant Geoff Cummings. Steve thought Geoff looked more like a farmer than a police officer. He was short by present standards and his cheeks were red, matching his bulbous nose that was a clear sign of a heavy drinker. He wore a checked tweed suit that looked as though it had been worn by his father and his stocky appearance rounded off the agricultural effect. The DCI took an instant liking to DS Cummings.

"Geoff will be your liaison while you're here. He's worked the case so you should find him a great help." Emily Channel looked fondly at her sergeant. "Almost time Geoff; any plans?"

Steve felt the two were entering another dimension and discussing nothing to do with the case. His earlier misgivings about a lack of urgency returned.

The pair continued their conversation as Emily turned to Steve. "Geoff and I are retiring on the same day." She looked kindly at Geoff. "It was Elsie, Geoff and me all those years ago on the beat." The Head of Norfolk CID seemed to allow herself a few seconds of nostalgia time before standing up.

"Right. I'll leave you to get started. Geoff, show the DCI and his sergeant to the office we've set aside for them, and you'll be full-time with them at least for the next six weeks." Detective Chief Superintendent Channel was once again all business and less than friendly as she fired a final remark at Steve. "That is if you've solved the case in six weeks."

Steve bit his tongue and followed Geoff out the door.

***

As the trio made their way through the corridors of Norfolk Police HQ, Steve had a sudden thought. "Geoff, can we see where Elsie Brown worked?"

"Sure, it's a bit of a broom cupboard." As they followed, Geoff he spoke candidly. "You know she was being forced to retire? She could have carried on, but the Chief Constable brought in a new Deputy a few months back. He's determined to get rid of us old wood. Me, I'm retiring anyway, but Elsie didn't want to, the Force was her life."

They arrived at an office whose door was firmly shut. Geoff hadn't exaggerated. It really was the size of a small broom cupboard. A small desk and chair almost filled the room and apart from a small two-drawer filing cabinet the office was empty. There was only room for two people to be inside at the same time, so Geoff stood in the corridor. Elsie Brown had obviously been a tidy person. Her desk was neat with only a few office essentials and a computer obvious but what caught Steve's eye was a buff-coloured file marked 'CLOSED'.

Curious he picked it up and said to Matt, "Have a rummage in the drawers and the cabinet. See if there's anything of interest."

As Matt started to search, Steve joined Geoff in the corridor. He held up the file. "Why would Elsie have a closed file on her desk?"

Geoff laughed. "Oh, that was Elsie's pet project. She was given permission to work on it in her spare time but to be honest the past few months I think she's been working it full-time."

Steve opened the file to see the front page gave the name of Mrs Tracy Nelson, murdered on the 10th of October 2009.

Steve looked at Geoff. "Who was Tracy Nelson?"

Geoff released a sigh, and his face took on a faraway look. "It was the case Elsie wouldn't let go. Tracy Nelson was discovered by her husband, strangled and laid out on the marital bed. She was naked and according to Forensics, had recently had sex but not with her husband. We worked the case for months. We had enough forensics but couldn't match anything. Elsie was convinced we'd missed something but our DI at the time, a bloke called Jack Ralph, pulled the shutters down and it's remained unsolved."

"You mean Elsie was working on this for eleven years?"

"Yes. On and off. She'd occasionally tell me something about the case but to be truthful, she was wasting her time. If there was anything, Jack Ralph would never have pulled the plug."

Steve thanked Geoff and placed the file inside his briefcase. Matt Conway reappeared dusting his arms. "There's nothing, sir. The filing cabinets are full of old memos and an empty whisky bottle. There's nothing in the drawers of the desk except a map of East Anglia and a few pens." Matt held up the map. "I brought the map in case it's relevant later on."

The three detectives made their way to the office assigned to Steve and Matt. It was a pleasant open space with six standard police issue desks neatly spaced around the room. The atmosphere smelt fresh, and Steve detected a whiff of fresh paint. There was a large whiteboard on one wall and a bank of windows facing the car park. Looking out the window, the DCI estimated they were on the fifth floor but after travelling down to Elsie's broom cupboard and up again he was slightly disorientated. The three took a desk, each thinking about the next step.

Steve and Matt set about emptying their briefcases and Matt set up the laptop. At Steve's request, Geoff left to get three coffees. Once they had their coffee Steve, as the new SIO, opened the discussion.

"Geoff, these files you have…" Steve pointed to the case files that were stacked on another desk. "Are they digitised?"

"Of course they are. We may be a county force but we're not totally backward."

"Sorry Geoff, I should have known." The DCI regretted his choice of words. Looking at Matt Conway, Steve continued. "Matt, get the electronic versions and have them sent to Poppy. I'll call her now." Turning to Geoff, Steve asked him to show Matt to the computer section in order he could get the electronic version of the files on a memory stick.

As the two left, Steve phoned his office. Poppy answered on the first ring. "How's the country, sir?"

"I don't know yet Poppy, we've only recently arrived. Listen, Matt's going to send you a series of files on the case here. The victim is called Detective Sergeant Elsie Brown. I want you to set up the files and do your crosschecking thing. See if anything's been missed or doesn't make sense." Not wishing to enter into a long conversation with his admin assistant, Steve asked, "Is Peter in?"

"Yes, hold on." Poppy recognised her boss' tone and realised he wasn't in the mood for small talk. Steve heard various muffled voices before Peter arrived on the other end of the phone.

Without any preamble Steve asked, "Anything on the case, Peter?"

The Welsh DI was young for his rank and was always nervous when asked direct questions although he knew his DCI was sympathetic to his need to learn. "Not much Steve, the file arrived from the pathologist. Dr Evans says the other victim died from being beaten and probably tortured. There's a photo of her tattoo and I'd say it's identical to the one on our headless victim. The body Dr Evans is referring to was found in a rubbish skip behind some shops in Newham six months ago. Girl about the same age as our victim, sexually active and wearing cheap chain-store clothes." Peter paused. "Sorry Steve, but that's all we've got except the case is still open. There was no ID, and the victim is still in cold storage."

Steve was disappointed but not surprised. "OK Peter, don't worry." He was about to say something will turn up when he heard a commotion on the other end of the line. He could tell Peter Jones had his hand over the receiver and was talking to someone in the room. After a few seconds Peter was back. "Sorry sir, Poppy's got something I think you should hear."

Steve was disappointed by Peter's willingness to let him hear any news from Poppy. Since Peter was the SIO, Poppy should have given him any news so that he could decide its relevance to the case.

"Sir!" An excited Poppy replaced Peter on the line. "I've just had a call from the Italian police, an Inspector Alfonso." Poppy's enthusiasm suddenly disappeared as Steve heard a sigh and silence before she resumed in her usual bubbly manner, "He sounded rather dishy, you know, the accent and everything."

As Poppy paused again, Steve smiled. This was typical Poppy.

"Anyway, Alfonso said he was based in Palermo on Sicily. He'd seen the all-station e-mail with the copy of the tattoo. He said it's a Mafia tattoo. It seems when a Mafia member has a little girl, it's usual for them to tattoo a little bird onto the forearm of the girl when she's about ten. It's supposed to say the girl is pure and sweet and will marry into their society when she's old enough. Alfonso said over the past thirty years or so it has only been done to the girls of senior Mafia bosses. If our two bodies have the tattoo it means their fathers are or were senior Mafia men."

"Interesting, thank you Poppy. Did he say anything else?"

"Not really, only that it was unusual for girls of Mafia bosses to turn up dead."

Steve sat in Norwich trying to analyse what this meant. "Put Peter back on, Poppy."

Peter came back on.

"What do you make of it, Peter?"

"I'm not sure Steve. I've asked Poppy to do a search of all criminal activity that has Mafia links in London, see if we get anything."

"Good start. Has Poppy come up with anything on missing persons?"

"She says it's still running but I'm looking at her now and she's saying she's changing the parameters to look for any Italian connections on the missing persons files."

"Right, stay at it, Peter. Keep me posted."

Matt Conway and Geoff Cummings returned as Steve finished his call to the office. "Right, Geoff, we should go and look at the crime scene. I don't suppose we'll learn anything after a fortnight, but we should get a feel for your colleague." Steve stood to go as did Matt.

Geoff Cummings stayed seated and looked at his watch. "It's 12.35 sir, it's my lunch hour."

Steve and Matt looked at each other in disbelief. Steve knew things were different in the County Forces but a fixed lunch hour in CID was unheard of. The DCI decided not to become the heavy. He knew Geoff only had a few weeks till he retired and that he might be useful to the investigation. "OK, Geoff, you pop off and have your lunch. We'll see you back here at one thirty."

Geoff levered himself off his chair and as he was leaving said, "Oh, you're both booked into the Royal Oak. It's just around the corner and is a nice comfortable pub. They serve the best real ale in the area. The landlord's a friend of mine so you'll be well looked after." With a wave Geoff was gone, heard saying, "See you in an hour."

Steve and Matt sat and laughed. "Bloody hell sir, an hour for lunch? We're lucky to eat at all when we've a case on."

Steve, conscious of his future plans, was beginning to see the job ahead if he became DCS Emily Channel's successor. Trying to be diplomatic, Steve looked at Matt. "Yes, it's a bit unusual."

"A *bit*! Come on sir! Everyone we've met, with the exception of the receptionist, is a geriatric. They're all retiring. Christ, it's like an old folks' home and now an hour for lunch." Matt was saying what Steve was thinking. "What's the bet that CID start at nine and finish at five Monday to Friday with an hour for lunch with weekends free for social and recreational pursuits." Matt's tone was sarcastic, but the DCI suspected he was right.

"Let's go find our digs. Geoff said the place was around the corner. We'll get our rooms and settle in, have a coffee and a sandwich and get back here by one thirty p.m. no problem."

The pair set off to find the Royal Oak before immersing themselves in the Elsie Brown murder.

Chapter Nine

The three detectives arrived outside Elsie Brown's house at two p.m. exactly. Steve saw the blue-and-white police tape had not lasted and was flapping from its one remaining fixing over the front door. He took a 360-degree view of the area and saw nothing out of the ordinary.

Geoff, already wearing overshoes and blue latex gloves, opened the door while the two Scotland Yard detectives put on their forensic-proof attire. Geoff stood back as Steve entered first. He saw blood on the wooden floor just inside the front door.

"In the file Forensics say she was probably hit as soon as she opened the door."

"That's right. The blood spatter and the blood pool confirm that."

Steve took a further step in. "Forensics then say she was dragged into her living room and beaten about the head."

"Yes." Geoff looked sick and pale just being here. "They say she was dragged and beaten again. You'll see the blood on the carpet in front of the sofa."

Steve examined the area. "You can both come in."

Matt was holding one of the files open. "The post-mortem report says the blows that killed her were from a blunt instrument. Something like a baseball bat but the killer also used a brass candlestick to inflict one final blow." Matt was silent and looking thoughtful. "Why would the killer use say a baseball bat that he clearly brought with him and then use a brass candlestick that was on the victim's mantlepiece?"

"I'm not sure. It's an inconsistency we need to consider, but I don't buy a baseball bat as the weapon, not if the first blow was delivered when she opened the door." Steve was talking to himself. "A baseball bat is an obvious item. I don't buy our killer walking up to the front door in broad daylight carrying the thing. It's too much of a giveaway and when Elsie answered the door our killer would have to swing the bat from behind his head. Surely someone would see it happen." The DCI returned to normal behaviour. "It's just not possible. The weapon has to be something else and maybe he used the candlestick to disguise the shape of the wounds his weapon choice had left."

"You mean he's killed before using the same weapon?" Geoff Cummings was impressed by the DCI's reasoning.

"It's possible, Geoff." Steve strode towards the dining area of the open-plan room. The entire outside wall was made up of sliding patio doors. Outside was a neat but small lawned garden that backed onto the rear garden of the house opposite.

"Geoff. What house to house did you do?"

"Just the usual. We did the houses in this row and most opposite but as it says in the reports, nobody saw anything."

"What about the houses at the rear?" Steve motioned Geoff to join him. "Those houses in the parallel street might have seen something. This room has these big windows so anyone looking over here might have seen something. Certainly, the one directly opposite and the two either side of it."

"Christ sir, we didn't think of that."

"Right. Get onto whoever and do a house to house again and include those houses at the back."

DS Cummings looked a bit sheepish as he went outside to make a call.

Meanwhile Matt Conway had searched the other rooms but unsurprisingly he returned to the living room saying there was nothing obvious.

"I didn't think there would be, but Matt, why would someone smash in the scull of an unmarried female police officer starting right on her front doorstep? Then drag her into the living room and apparently keep hitting her with his own weapon? Then for a finale hit her after she was dead with her own brass candlestick?"

Steve looked around the room. "In the report it says the search team found the candlestick beside the body, but the real murder weapon wasn't found. Also, as I said, I don't buy a baseball bat. It had to be something else that was small enough to be easily hidden but fierce enough to kill using a short backswing. Remember the first blow occurred as soon as our victim opened the door." Steve demonstrated the difference in swinging a baseball bat and swinging something else using a shorter swing.

Having seen the demonstration, Matt spoke up. "Er, could it have been a cosh? Same shape as the end of a baseball bat and easier to swing without drawing attention to yourself."

"Good point Matt; I don't suppose there's anything in the file about an alternate weapon theory?"

Matt examined the file as he stood next to Steve. "No sir, nothing. Looks like they held onto the baseball bat as the weapon."

Steve and Matt stood outside the front door as Geoff Cummings finished his call. "There'll be a squad redoing the house to house tomorrow and they'll do the adjoining street."

Steve nodded as something caught his eye. There was a small line of shops on the far corner of the street that joined Elsie's road, at right angles. Steve spotted a post office sign.

"Did anyone question the shopkeepers or the postmaster over there?" Steve pointed to the row of shops. He noted that, apart from the post office, there was a hairdressers, a newsagents and a Chinese takeaway.

"I don't think so sir. They're a bit far away and it's unlikely that anyone from there would be looking this way."

"You may be right Sergeant, but I spy a CCTV camera." The DCI pointed.

For the second time in ten minutes, Detective Sergeant Geoff Cummings said, "Oh, we didn't think of that!"

Steve was beginning to see why the investigation into the killing of Elsie Brown had stalled. The three officers walked towards the small parade of shops. The DCI was calculating the distance to Elsie's house and trying to work out if the CCTV would have the range to capture anything useful. As he approached and saw the rust-coloured marks on the camera, his heart sank. Geoff remained outside which suited him. He was a smoker and was glad of the opportunity to fill his lungs with smoke.

Steve and Matt entered the post office. It was a small space and not very tidy. The usual post office desk with its wire grille was located in one corner. The rest of the shop was a cluttered mixture of envelopes, superglue and a range of similar small office paraphernalia. The air in the shop was musty with a faint paraffin smell as though the place was heated by paraffin heater in the winter. There were no customers, and a small middle-aged woman was behind the post office counter.

Steve and Matt showed their warrant cards. "We're looking into the murder of Elsie Brown who lived just over the way from your shop." Steve pointed to indicate Elsie's house.

The woman who was dressed for comfort rather than fashion took a sudden interest. "Yes. It was a terrible thing. Poor Elsie; she was a regular you know; every Saturday rain or shine. She'd put her savings into her account."

Steve thought Elsie's saving habits probably had no bearing on her murder so moved on. "I see you have CCTV. Is it working?"

"Oh goodness me yes, the post office insists on it. Why do you ask?"

The DCI ignored the question. "How long do you keep the discs?"

"Oh no. We don't have discs. Oh no, we have the old tried and tested VCR system. The cost of having a new digital system installed was ridiculously high so we just have the old tape. What are you asking for?"

Again, Steve ignored the question. "How long do you keep the tapes?"

"The post office says six months, but we don't bother. I'd say we have maybe two months. We only have so many tapes and over-record them. We use the same tape for a week."

"So you'll have the tape for the 11th of this month?"

"I should think so. I suppose you want to see it."

"No. We'd like to take it with us. You'll get it back when we're finished with it."

The woman looked sceptical. "I'll need a receipt."

Steve wrote a receipt in his notebook and tore it out, handing it to the woman in exchange for a VCR cassette that had *W/C Monday 11th September* written on its edge. This was the date of Elsie's murder. As Steve and Matt exited the post office, they saw Geoff stamp on the cigarette he had been smoking.

"Any joy?"

"Maybe but we'll have to view this tape." Steve held it up.

Matt Conway started to walk towards the other shops. "Think it's worth an ask, boss?"

"Yes. You and Geoff take the other shops, I'll be in the car. I need some thinking time." Steve set off leaving his two colleagues to visit the other shops and ask their questions.

In the car, Steve allowed his mind to drift between this current Norfolk case, the headless body case in London and what his initial thoughts were on the possibility of taking over Norfolk CID. He knew the investigation into Elsie Brown's murder had been poor. If one of their own in London had been murdered at least a thorough investigation would have been carried out and everyone would have gone the extra mile, but not here in Norwich. So far the people involved hadn't shown any real concern or urgency plus most people he'd met were heading for their pensions. Steve wondered if the whole of Norfolk CID was retiring soon. He allowed himself a smile and envisaged himself taking the job only to find he had no detectives. They were all away on Saga holidays.

He forced himself to consider the current case. Elsie, a long-standing CID officer, had been bludgeoned to death starting on her doorstep. Steve asked himself, *Why and for what reason?* The DCI was aware that some criminals carried grudges against the officers who sent them down but rarely carried out their often-outlandish threats. *No,* he thought, *there's something more behind this killing.* Steve considered the brutal manner of the murder. Why so violent? And the choice of murder weapon was odd. He'd dismissed the pathologist's idea of a baseball bat, but Matt's suggestion of a cosh held up. He made a mental note to check out known villains who favoured a cosh as a weapon. Steve sighed as he thought of the lack of leads. He looked at the VCR cassette and hoped it might give them something.

As he allowed his mind to turn towards the London case, his mobile rang. It was Poppy.

"Afternoon sir, everything going OK?" Poppy was bubbling and Steve knew the signs. She'd found something. He was torn, hoping her news concerned Elsie's murder, but at the same time a break in the headless torso case would be welcome.

"Yes Poppy, everything's fine. What have you got?"

Poppy was coy and dragged out her tale. She enjoyed playing the little girl but knew herself it was an act. "We-e-ll…" Poppy began slowly holding onto each syllable too long. "I've checked all the abortions inside the M25 for the past twelve months." She deviated from her prepared narrative. "Do you know sir, getting medical information is almost impossible. Luckily, there aren't many abortion clinics but no one at any of them was prepared to help even when they knew I was investigating a murder case."

The DCI smiled at the assumption Poppy was investigating the case. He gave her full marks for initiative as she returned to her script.

"Well basically, I got nowhere. The last one I tried was the one closest to the north end of Putney Bridge, but I didn't realise it. I got the usual run around but persuaded some snotty receptionist to put me through to someone in authority. She eventually put me through to some guy in the office. He was like all the others, until I mentioned murder and added that we were looking for an Italian or Spanish connection. It took a bit of doing and the use of all my womanly talents." She giggled. "But I got one name. He wouldn't give an address or anything else and said he really shouldn't have even given me the name. He said he remembered an Italian girl from around a year ago because she was very pretty, and he took a fancy to her." Again, Poppy left her script. "Do you know, sir, if you want access to an individual's medical records you need a court order for each one?"

"Yes Poppy, I did." Steve had decided to let Poppy ramble. He felt he needed cheering up and eventually Poppy would get to the point.

"So all I had was a name. It was a long shot, but I ran the name against the missing persons database I created and bingo, I got a match."

Steve stopped Poppy. This was beginning to sound important, and he knew Poppy should be reporting her findings to Peter Jones. "Poppy, you know you should be saying this to DI Jones. He's the SIO."

Poppy puffed a great sigh and in an impish voice said, "Yes I know but he's not in and I thought you'd like to know we're making progress."

Steve gave in for the moment and in order to satisfy his curiosity told Poppy to carry on.

"Right, so with the names matching, I had an address from the missing persons' report. I got Uncle Terry to use his computers to get me a phone number. Turns out there's no private phone at the address but there was a payphone in the building. I thought it can't do any harm, so I called the number and a female answered. Said her name was Jill. She sounded either half asleep or high on drugs."

"Poppy can you please get to the point?"

Poppy allowed an annoyed tone to enter her voice. "Don't be in so much of a rush, sir, I'm getting to the good bit." As always Poppy thought the use of "sir" when showing annoyance would get her out of trouble and again, she was correct. The DCI sat and listened.

"This Jill told me that two Italian girls used to share a room in the building. One disappeared about seven months ago and the other around six weeks ago. One of the neighbours reported both girls missing at the time. She confirmed that the girl called Sophia Paulo was the name of the girl who vanished six weeks earlier." With a vocal flourish Poppy happily announced. "That's the name I got from the abortion clinic. It has to be our headless body."

"It might seem that way Poppy, but we'll have to go slowly." Steve could feel Poppy's enthusiasm.

With a coy tone, Poppy shot back. "No, we don't sir; this Jill also told me Sophia Paulo had a small bird tattoo on the inside of her left arm. It has to be her."

Steve agreed but knew proper checks had to be made. "Good work Poppy. So you're saying this girl Sophia Paulo had an abortion about a year ago, she's Italian and has our tattoo on the inside of her left arm?"

"Yes sir, and there's more," Poppy ploughed on. "The other girl, the one the pathologist Dr Evans told us about, she also had the same tattoo. Her name was Mariola Scala, and she disappeared just before the date on Dr Evans' post-mortem report. She *has* to be the other victim."

Before Steve could gather his thoughts, Poppy was enthusiastically rattling down the airwaves at him. "I got onto Immigration and the Italian embassy. They sent over passport details and the passport photograph of Dr Evans' victim matches the post-mortem picture. For sure Mariola Scala is the body locked away in cold storage. It also means we can put a face to our headless corpse."

"Bloody hell, Poppy, that's great work!" Steve felt elated by this breakthrough. As he laughed, he told Poppy, "We'll make a detective of you yet."

Both Steve and Poppy were now laughing with each other. Steve saw Matt and Geoff approach the car. On seeing them he returned to his formal self. He held up a hand indicating they should wait outside the car.

"Poppy, great work, but listen, you must report this to Peter. As I said, he's the SIO. Don't tell him you've told me. Peter will call me tonight and I'll pretend I'm hearing it for the first time. You do know why I'm telling you to do this, don't you?"

"Yes." Poppy sounded slightly deflated. "There's a chain of command and Peter's in charge. I just want to prove to you that I'm better than an admin assistant, sir. I want to be operational."

"Poppy, this is very good detective work. Look, we're in the middle of two murder cases. When things settle down, I'll see what we can do. OK?"

A reluctant Poppy agreed. "Yeah, fine."

"And you'll give the information to Peter?"

"Yes, and I won't say we've had this call."

"Good. Now how are you doing looking for Mafia connections?"

"Give me a chance, sir. I'm good but not that good. I've got something searching but it'll take a while." Poppy was off on one of her rants that verged on insubordination. "When I know something, sir, you'll know."

Steve accepted Poppy was busy and noted the use of "sir" in her rant again. He would have a word with his feisty admin assistant, but later. Steve congratulated Poppy once more and hung up. He understood Poppy's frustration at being stuck in the office, but the DCI believed when admin assistants were junior serving officers as opposed to civilian staff, they learned more about CID procedures more quickly and became better officers. He allowed himself to visualise himself as head of Norfolk CID and putting in place an order that all admin assistants should be serving officers. He exited the car to stand with his colleagues allowing Geoff Cummings to smoke.

"We checked the other two shops, sir, but they saw nothing." Matt looked disappointed.

"Well, we've got another house to house tomorrow. You've come up with the idea that the weapon might have been a cosh, and we've maybe got some CCTV. It's progress, Matt." The DCI was trying to remain positive. "We've only been at it since after lunch." He cast a glance at Geoff who seemed oblivious that the lunch reference was a sarcastic comment meant for him. "Check out all known violent offenders known to favour a cosh as their weapon of choice. Let's see what that throws up."

The three detectives left the murder scene at 4.24 p.m. to return to Norfolk Force Headquarters.

***

At 4.24 p.m., Andrew and David Black were seated in their less than palatial office in East London, having their first whisky of the day. They'd spent most of the morning recovering once more from the excesses of Dutch hospitality and had enjoyed their time yesterday afternoon with the hostesses from Jean Franco's club. They had drunk heavily on the flight back and as the time difference between Amsterdam and London bought them an extra hour, they'd finished up in their local until last orders.

David Black was the more concerned of the brothers. In his more lucid moments during the morning, he'd restated his worries over the deal they'd struck with Jean Franco. During the morning, Andrew the elder brother had agreed with him but after a heavy lunch, a few drinks and an hour's sleep he now appeared to be back to his bullish self.

As David restated his concerns, his older brother once more overrode his younger brother's view.

"Look, it's dead simple. We've got the files. On the drugs we just get a few of the boys to visit our main outlets and get them to sign those contracts. All this wholesale crap is nonsense. When did you ever hear of a gang like ours having signed contracts? I'm telling you, give it a few months and we'll hear no more about margins and cash flows; that's for big companies not for the likes of us. Jean Franco's one of us. All he wants is the money."

David Black wasn't convinced but he knew his elder brother was probably right.

Andrew sat with a glint in his eye. "You know little brother, that envelope Jean Franco gave us, I'm wondering whose names are in it."

"Steady on, Andy, we were told to keep it safe and not open it unless we were in trouble. Leave it."

The glint in Andrew's eyes became even more pronounced. "Yeah. But if we opened it who would know? And if the people are as important as Jean Franco was suggesting, there might be a few extra bob in it for us. After all, anybody mixed up with Jean Franco can't be legit."

"You mean *blackmail*?" David was even more worried. "Don't be daft. Look you said yourself, we've got a good thing going now not only with the drugs but these high-class hookers. Don't spoil it by being too greedy."

"You could be right, but I'd like to know whose names are in that envelope."

The brothers returned to their discussion on how to sign up the drug runners they currently used. As always, Andrew wanted everything done in a hurry and felt they needed a statement to let people know of their new status.

"Get Shorty and Lurch to get round the pushers and the like. Make sure they know they only buy from us and put a minimum weekly amount on each contract just like Jean said but up their present purchases by 10% and make sure they all know it's cash up front. They're dealing with a big firm now."

David dealt with the dealers and pushers and knew most of the bigger players. Shorty and Lurch were David's bodyguards. As with most underworld nicknames, they did not represent their owners. Shorty was over six foot four and weighed almost two hundred pounds. Lurch's nickname was more accurate. He was tall and skinny and walked with long strides. Despite his appearance, he was deadly and had dispatched more than twenty souls to their final resting places for fairly trivial reasons and that was people other than those David had ordered him to get rid of.

"OK, I'll get started but what about the girls?"

"We'll pay Archie McLaren a visit tomorrow. With a bit of persuasion, I'm sure he'll see what's best for him."

David Black stood up to go find Shorty and Lurch. "I hope you're right, brother, because if you're not, we are in big trouble."

***

When they returned to their office, Geoff once again surprised the officers from the Yard. "Right gents, that's me, I'm off, I'll see you tomorrow at nine."

Steve looked at his watch. It was just a few minutes until five p.m. He decided to test the waters thinking ahead to any decision he might have to make about his future.

"Geoff, we're in the middle of a murder case. The victim was one of your own and our only lead may be on this videotape. We need to see this tonight and I don't think it appropriate for our liaison officer to knock off at five."

"Well, I'd love to stay but see there's no overtime any more, and we have got used to the nine-to-five lifestyle. I've an appointment about my feet at half past five so I couldn't stay anyway. Oh, and you won't get that tape played tonight either. The video suite locks down at four and doesn't open till ten tomorrow. The inspector in charge of technical has been off on sick leave for months and his assistant has to take her grandchildren to school in the morning and pick them up at night. The DCS agreed the opening hours of ten till four so she can cope."

Steve was amazed as was Matt Conway, who for something to say blurted out, "Does this grandmother get an hour for lunch?"

With a serious expression, Detective Sergeant Geoff Cummings stared directly at Matt. "We *all* get an hour for lunch, and we need to recharge our batteries ready for the afternoon."

With a wave, the local detective sergeant left to have his feet attended to.

In disbelief, Steve and Matt looked at each other. Matt broke the silence. "Is this a wind-up, Steve? Tell me we haven't fallen through a black hole and we're back in the sixties."

"No Matt, I almost wish we had. At least that would explain things, but not everyone in Norfolk can be like that, there must be some young blood around."

"I'm not sure I'd bet on it. What do you want to do?"

"Let's get out of here and get back to our digs. See if the pub has a VCR machine and hopefully, we can see what's on this tape."

As Matt and Steve walked Matt dialled Poppy and asked her to search all felons who had used a cosh during their criminal career, starting within Norfolk Constabulary. As usual, Poppy wanted to know why Matt needed to know. He told her enough to keep her curiosity at bay.

Chapter Ten

After a few attempts, the owner of the hotel put together an old VCR machine with an even older TV. The equipment was set up in Steve's room and rested on an old wooden-backed chair. Recognising it wasn't perfect, Steve agreed it was the best they could do.

"This is ridiculous, Steve. Look at us, trying to solve a murder and having to sit in this crappy bedroom looking at a tape on an antiquated TV when we know not more than half a mile away there's a perfectly good technical suite we should be using, but it's closed because granny has to collect the kids from school." Matt was clearly upset and annoyed.

"Don't worry Matt. Let's see if there's anything before you blow a fuse." Steve inserted the tape and pressed play on the dusty VCR machine.

It took a few minutes of black-and-white dots chasing each other on the screen before the image settled down. The CCTV camera was a model that was fixed and should have been facing the front door of the post office, but the DCI surmised that over the years it had worked loose and was now pointing towards the road. Although not exactly lined up with Elsie's house, the clearing image showed the road that Elsie's little two-bedroom property fronted onto. It was slightly blurred but the detectives could make out her car parked just outside the house. It was obviously dark, and the image was time and date stamped 04.10 a.m., on the 11th of September. Steve noticed the system wasn't continuous but took a picture every minute.

"It's not very clear." Matt was standing close to the TV hoping to get a better view.

"Let's see. Hang on, I'll fast forward till nine a.m. and we'll let it roll."

The detectives watched as each frame clicked into place. The picture quality was poor probably because the tape had been over-recorded too many times. As they watched, a frame appeared showing a white Land

Rover Discovery in the centre of the screen. When the next frame appeared, it was gone. Steve used the remote control to back up to the frame showing the Land Rover. It was time stamped 08.41 a.m. Both men now approached the TV. "It's too grainy Matt, I can't make out the registration."

"No but it may have nothing to do with the case."

"True. But it's an expensive car. I didn't see many like it this afternoon even driving through."

"I'll make a note of the frame number just in case." Matt had noted that each frame was sequentially numbered. He wrote the number in his notebook as Steve pressed resume.

Each frame continued to click into place until Matt shouted, "Stop!"

Steve pushed pause on the remote control. Both men once more approached the TV screen. In the centre of the picture, the same white Land Rover Discovery was seen once more but approaching from the opposite direction. The time stamp was 08.49 a.m.

"That has to be more than a coincidence."

Steve agreed but cautioned, "It could be someone looking for an address. It might be innocent so let's not jump to conclusions."

"Right." Matt stared at the screen. "The quality's so bad I can't make out the registration number either."

Steve pressed resume again and once more, images started to click into view. As they watched, it was Steve this time who called out, "What's that?" as he hit pause on the remote control. Once more both men peered at the TV for a closer look. At first Matt couldn't see anything but Steve pointed at the screen. "Look, beside Elsie's car, looks like a man, and see there," Steve pointed. "That's the end of the path leading to Elsie's house and our mystery man seems to have turned onto it. I'd say he was headed to Elsie's front door."

"You think that's our killer?"

"Well. The time stamp says 08.59 a.m. The pathology put time of death no more than two hours before she was found."

Matt opened the file. "Says she was found at 11.07 a.m., so it fits."

Both Yard men sat back considering what they had seen. Steve left the image frozen on the screen.

"What do you think, sir?"

"I think we're looking at our killer but all we have is his lower legs. Not a great start if we want to identify him. The quality's so bad I'm not even sure it's a man but I'll bet whoever belongs to those legs came from the white Land Rover."

Matt sat forward in his high-backed wooden chair. "Pity the quality's so bad. Do you think we can get it cleaned up tomorrow?"

"Yes, but not here. I want Terry Harvey to look at this, but I suppose they won't have a motorbike to spare." The detectives laughed without humour.

"We'll leave this for now; it's six thirty. Let's meet up in the bar at seven and have a drink before we eat." The DCI stood and stretched. "I'm whacked. A drink, a meal and an early night, I think."

Steve was washing his face, freshening himself up when his mobile rang. It was Detective Inspector Peter Jones. As soon as Steve answered, Peter's Welsh tones sounded just as Poppy did when she had something of interest to report. Peter was clearly excited, and Steve knew why.

As the DCI listened to Peter's explanation as to how Poppy had unearthed the identities of the two corpses, Steve was pleased to hear Peter giving credit to Poppy. He knew many officers who would have claimed the credit.

Once Peter had finished with Poppy's news, he recalled his and DC Mary Dougan's afternoon activity for his boss. "We got a list of Italian businesses spreading out from the north end of Putney Bridge. We thought given the Italian connection, especially Mafia, we might get something."

From the tone of Peter's voice, Steve suspected they'd not achieved much.

Peter went on, "We interviewed dozens of Italians, and none would open up. No one recognised the girl Dr Evans told us about and when we showed them the picture of the tattoo, they either didn't recognise it or when they did, they clammed up. We met one guy called Luigi. He runs a bakery, and he was the only one who'd open up. He said he recognised the tattoo but warned us off. He said asking questions about the daughters of Mafia high rollers wasn't good for our health even if we were police. He didn't know the girl and told us the tattoo was dangerous."

Peter sounded both elated at Poppy's news but disappointed by his own efforts.

"OK, Peter." Steve assumed the role of mentor. "What's your next move?"

"I've already alerted a forensic and search team for tomorrow morning. I want them to go over the flat the two girls shared. You never know. We might get something."

This is an action Steve would have taken but it didn't go far enough. He asked. "Anything else?"

"Poppy's still waiting for missing persons from Interpol. I'll canvass the area around the girls' flat. See if anybody saw anything, but we need a break."

The DCI considered Peter's course of action and was satisfied it was enough. "Right, Peter. Keep on the Mafia connection and missing persons from Italy. Poppy's looking at any Mafia connections in London. We can discount anything from Spain. We now know for sure the victims are Italian. Get onto Immigration and see when they arrived here. Terry Harvey gave us the tattoo as a corporate logo. Leave that side to me. I'll speak with someone and try to get a handle on this Italian Resources group. See if it's important to the case."

Both men hung up and Steve immediately dialled his home. His daughter, Rosie, hadn't gone to sleep, and he heard her gurgling at the other end of the phone. He talked about his day and Alison was curious about Norfolk. Steve explained he hadn't seen much of the county, but he'd call tomorrow earlier, and they'd have a longer talk.

It was 7.11 p.m. when Steve met Matt in the bar. Carrying their beer to a table set in the middle of a pleasant old-worlde looking room, the officers ordered just a main course. They suddenly realised they were hungry and were looking forward to their meal.

Both detectives had brought the case files to the table knowing they would be discussing the case over their meal. As Matt cut a piece of gammon he asked, "Why did they ask us in on this case do you think?"

Steve had almost finished his steak pie. "Not sure, Matt but, looking at the files, they don't seem to have made much progress. It's probably someone higher up covering their back. After all, the victim was a serving officer."

"I see that." Matt spoke with his mouth full. "So have we made progress?"

"I think so. We've discounted the murder weapon theory; we've got a bit of CCTV." The DCI pulled the VCR cassette from his folder. "We think our killer is male judging by his lower body and his footwear and he most likely drives a white Land Rover Discovery. I'd say that's not bad for our first few hours on the case."

"Yeah, I suppose so."

"We'll go over and see Elsie Brown's old boss, this DI Jack Ralph, tomorrow. Seems he retired to Suffolk so it's not far."

Matt noticed Steve's mind was wandering. He sat waiting for his boss to return. After a few seconds Steve refocussed on his colleague. "You know, Matt, I still don't understand why Elsie was so keen to keep the Tracy Nelson case alive. I've scanned the file but can't see anything of interest."

"Maybe she just wanted something to do in her last few months on the job."

"Mm. I can't see her wasting her time. She'd been in the job a long time. There's nothing in her record to suggest she put away any major criminals who might have held a grudge, but anyway, threats from convicts are usually made against the SIOs, not their staff." Steve again drifted off and spoke out loud while thinking. "No, Matt, we've got something else going on here and the only anomaly we have is Elsie's pursuit of the Tracy Nelson case." Steve pulled himself together as a waitress served them tea and coffee. "Let's find time tomorrow to go over that case. We might find something."

As the two detectives were finishing their drinks, a tall slim figure dressed casually in sports jacket and jeans appeared beside their table. He took a chair from an adjoining table and sat down. Neither Steve nor Matt knew the man who immediately held out his hand. "I'm Callum Robertson, Deputy Chief Constable and I know you are DCI Burt."

Steve took the outstretched hand. "And you must be DS Conway." Matt followed suit and shook the Deputy Chief's hand.

"I'm sorry I couldn't meet you when you arrived, but I was called away to yet another meeting. Believe it or not it was to talk about the amount of money the Force is spending on tyres for our patrol cars."

Callum Robertson laughed. "I ask you, bloody tyres. Anyway, I hope you were well looked after."

Steve, realising this must be Alfie Brooks' mate, was diplomatic. "Yes fine, thank you sir."

"And how do you find Norfolk Constabulary?"

The question was directed at Matt. "Well sir, everyone seems a bit old and getting ready to retire."

The Deputy Chief smiled. "Ah, of course, you were directed towards our DCS Channel and her Saga group. Emily's been fighting retirement for years and has surrounded herself with her old-time pals. She's found jobs for anybody who served with her way back, jobs that keep them on the active list, hoping to squeeze a few more years for them to boost their pensions." Callum looked at the officers from the Yard. "I should have realised but please don't base your judgement of us on Emily Channel's crew. We have some very good and capable officers within Norfolk and hopefully you'll meet a few of them before you go."

Steve noticed Callum Robertson hadn't ordered a drink as a silence descended over the table. It was broken when the Deputy Chief asked, "DS Conway, I need to talk with DCI Burt in private. I'm sorry but would you excuse us? The pub has a nice residents' lounge that's always empty. Steve, perhaps we can have a few words in there and leave Matt to order a drink."

The residents' lounge was empty, as predicted. En route, the Deputy Chief ordered two pints of real ale and waited for them to be delivered before opening the discussion he wanted to have with Steve.

"Again Steve, I'm sorry your introduction to our Force was a bit haphazard. Emily Channel is old school, you know, married to the job and very protective of her staff. Believe it or not, a few years ago she was being touted for command rank in Kent, but nothing happened. I think it was that disappointment that may have soured her. At least you've witnessed one of the reasons I spoke to Alfie."

Steve was curious. "How do you know the Commander, sir?"

"Forget the sir when it's just us. It's Callum." The Deputy Chief took a long pull of his beer. "I came down from Aberdeen about twenty years ago as a CID sergeant. Alfie Brooks was a CID Inspector but was in a different squad. As he was promoted, I seemed to keep pace and eventually I got to be his bagman when he made Chief Inspector."

"So how did you finish up here?"

"It's a long but normal story. Alfie and I got on pretty well and I had a couple of good years with him. I got a posting to Birmingham with Alfie's blessing as a DI on a promise of a DCI's job within a year. I spent a few years there, then onwards and upwards, a move to Manchester, then Kent and now here."

Steve simply nodded allowing Callum to carry on. He took Steve by surprise by changing the subject and asking. "What are you doing with a VCR cassette?"

Steve explained how the post office camera had been pointing towards Elsie Brown's house and they had some grainy images that should help the case.

"Unfortunately, your technical support unit closes at four so the grandmother who runs it can collect her grandchildren from school."

Callum looked annoyed. "Ah, another one of DCS' Channel's retirees. I'm sorry about that. What do you want us to do with it?"

"Well sir…eh, Callum. I'd liked to have biked it to the Met and let our own technical guy examine it, but I'd like something by tomorrow."

"Give it to me." The Deputy Chief took out his notebook and passed it to Steve. "Write the details there and I'll get it biked to the Met tonight. Your man will have it when he gets in tomorrow."

A relieved Steve did as instructed, and handed over the tape.

"You see Steve, although Emily Channel isn't the problem, her attitude to the job is. I know it's funny and we call her clique of old timers the Saga brigade but it's an example of why I want new blood. Our CID force has an unacceptably high average age. Since I got here three months ago, I've been trying to call time on those officers who frankly should have gone a few years ago. It's taken some persuading, but I've now got my way and by Christmas we should see a good clean-out. Don't get me wrong. Although they're old for the job, they have all been good officers in their day. We owe them a lot, but you'll appreciate that so many officers with years of experience all going at once will leave a hole."

Steve understood Callum's concerns. "At least CID won't close down for their lunch hour once they've gone." As soon as he'd made this remark, Steve saw it wasn't appropriate.

Callum smiled a weak smile. "Yes, that's true." The Deputy Chief sat back. "Historically, Norfolk have promoted from within where possible. I'm an exception but they didn't have a choice. Command-rank candidates were thin on the ground." Callum paused to study Steve. "It was the same when we started looking for Emily Channel's replacement. Internal candidates are either too old or too young. I'm afraid Norfolk hasn't been very good at succession planning. Also, the whole of CID needs wakening up. We need to be more dynamic. We need a head of CID who is a real thief catcher, not a paper and desk man."

Steve saw how passionate his prospective new boss was. "So you asked Alfie for a recommendation?"

"Yes. And he recommended you. I've looked over your record and there's no doubt you are the real thing. You're a very good thief catcher but you do have your faults."

Steve wasn't enjoying this conversation but satisfied himself with a mouthful of real ale.

Callum carried on. "Your record suggests you're a bit stubborn and are happy to bend the rules to get a result. Alfie says you can be insubordinate and on occasions you've behaved like a vigilante."

Steve shrugged his shoulders, deliberately staying quiet.

"All these things I'm sure you won't deny, but in a funny sort of way, Steve, those faults that others see in you are exactly the attitude I want you to bring here. We need a hard-hitting DCS to shake things up and get our detective squad away from always going by the book." Callum drained his glass. He laughed. "Of course we don't want the book thrown away all the time."

Steve had been nursing his beer. "So you're looking for someone to come in and shake things up?"

"Exactly."

"And if it were me, I'd have a free hand?"

"Most of the time. Obviously, there's a chain of command but Alfie thinks you'll cope."

Both men sat looking at their beer glasses. Steve thought Callum was on the point of ordering another beer when he announced, "Callum, if you don't mind, I'd like to get to bed. We were on the road early this morning and I'm really knackered. Can I think about what you've said and maybe we can talk about it later?"

"Yes, no problem, Steve. You know there will have to be an interview process and other candidates have to be considered but as head of the selection committee I'm fairly sure you'd be a shoo-in if you applied."

"When would you want me to start?"

"As soon as. Emily Channel will be away by Christmas and to be honest there's no point in you shadowing her for a month or so. Best to get a clean start once she's gone, so first of January next year sounds good to me."

The DCI acknowledged this was a reasonable time scale. As both men stood to leave the Deputy Chief stopped at the door. "Steve, find whoever killed poor Elsie Brown and you will arrive here with your reputation preceding you."

Steve thought easier said than done but told Callum he'd do his best. It was 10.37 p.m. when DCI Steve Burt's head hit the pillow. He was sound asleep by 10.40 p.m.

Chapter Eleven

Antonio Paulo, or Conti as he was now known, hadn't slept well. As dawn arrived on a cold Thursday morning in Amsterdam, he sat looking over the canal outside his terraced office, drinking his second coffee of the day. There was an apartment attached to the office and Antonio preferred to sleep there. His own palatial home was outside Amsterdam, but he felt it was too big and despite having several servants, the place didn't feel comfortable. He'd had a broken night's sleep largely of his own making. He'd allowed himself to think too much about how he would unseat Jean Franco. This led him to remember the meeting with the brothers from London. Antonio knew the parts of Jean Franco's operation in other EU countries were reasonably stable. Over the years, Jean Franco had killed anyone who represented a threat to him so now everyone in the organisation was completely subservient.

He'd spent what seemed like hours considering what he'd do with the business once Jean Franco had been removed. The EU operations were not very dynamic largely because the people running them were second-rate. Antonio realised this didn't matter. Jean Franco had culled anyone who spoke up leaving yes-men behind. Such men did their jobs and returned a steady income without too much interference from the centre. When he took over, Antonio told himself he'd leave this well alone. He knew the UK was the big prize. If they got it right this was their big expansion opportunity. Everything was set up. It just needed someone to run it, but Antonio knew it wouldn't be the idiot brothers Jean Franco had insisted would do for now.

He picked up his diary and turned to today's events. On the page headed Thursday 21st September he had written BOARD MEETING LONDON. 12 NOON LOCAL TIME. He looked at the wall clock. It said 06.01 a.m. Antonio was being collected at ten to be taken to the airport to the company's private Lear jet for his trip to London, so the time difference between the two cities gave him an extra hour in

Amsterdam. His secretary would be in soon fussing around and ensuring he had everything he needed for his meeting. Marcel, Antonio's secretary, was a willing worker who knew nothing about the company's criminal activities. He'd proven to be efficient, hardworking and good at his job. He'd been Antonio's secretary for three years and was proving to be indispensable.

Still in his dressing gown, Antonio poured another coffee. He sat daydreaming and probably due to his broken night's sleep found himself dozing off, and as he slept, he saw his wife and children as he'd left them. He wondered how his son, Antonio, was faring. Before running, Antonio had confided in his long-term friend, Luigi. Luigi was a foot soldier and not too bright, but he'd been a loyal friend since school. Luigi was the only person he could trust and had given him a mobile number for emergency contact.

Luigi had promised to keep Antonio informed about his family, so he knew Antonio junior was progressing within the organisation and working for one of the Mafia dons in Sicily. He could only surmise that his fleeing the family hadn't be held against his son. His mind turned to his wife but quickly moved on to his daughter, Sophia, a pretty girl, his little bird, and he hoped she would marry well. He'd often thought of visiting his children in some faraway spot but knew it was impossible. As he dreamt, he saw men dressed in black coming for him with guns and knives. He knew he was a wanted man as Antonio Paulo. He hoped Antonio Conti would be safer.

He had been concerned for Sophia after Luigi sent him a message saying she'd gone to London to find her father. Antonio knew the ways of the Mafia and was convinced she'd have been followed in the hope she would lead them to their one-time bookkeeper. Luigi's last contact said he'd lost touch with Sophia, but she hadn't returned from London. As Antonio drifted further into a light doze, he vowed to seek out his daughter. The next thing he knew, his secretary Marcel was gently waking him saying the car would be arriving in forty-five minutes.

***

As Antonio Conti was drifting into a deeper snooze, Steve and Matt Conway entered the breakfast room of the pub. Matt was curious to learn what the Deputy Chief Constable had had to say the previous evening. "He seemed like a decent bloke."

Steve couldn't say too much. "Yeah, he is, he just wanted to know if we needed any help with the case. He arranged to get the CCTV tape down to Terry Harvey." Steve looked at his watch. It was 07.55 a.m. "It should be on Terry's desk by now."

Both detectives ordered and were not disappointed by their full English breakfast and unlimited cups of strong tea. They avoided talking about the case and at 08.43 a.m., they set out on their hour and a half drive to Long Melford, and an interview with Elsie's old boss, DI Jack Ralph.

***

Terry Harvey had arrived in his office at 08.10 a.m. on Thursday the 21st of September to find a package on his desk. This wasn't unusual but Terry noticed the wrapping wasn't internal. This package had been wrapped outside, not within Scotland Yard. He was suspicious of unsolicited packages and had the parcel scanned before unwrapping it. Inside a box was a VCR cassette and a handwritten note from Steve Burt.

Terry and Steve had become friends over the years and Terry knew Steve wouldn't ask him to do something without good reason. The note simply asked if Terry could tidy up the images. Looking at his desk and having talked with his team of technical wizards, Terry decided he'd work on the old-fashioned tape himself. His desk was clear, and everyone seemed to be busy.

The request to clean the tape up was vague but Inspector Terry Harvey had worked with vaguer instructions in the past. He pushed the cassette into an older style VCR machine and saw what Steve and Matt had watched the previous evening. It was clearly a single-frame system and each frame clicked into place having rested on the screen for a minute. Terry was tempted to fast forward but contented himself by examining each frame before using his remote control to simply move onto the next frame. He saw the images were almost cloudy due to the fact the tape had been overwritten many times.

Terry's first task was to transfer the grainy images onto a new and unused VCR tape. He set the machines in motion and returned to his office knowing the transfer operation would take a few hours. As he sat at his desk his phone rang. It was Steve Burt.

"OK Steve. What's with the old tape?"

Steve knew Terry too well to be fooled by his casual questioning. He knew Terry liked a mystery and enjoyed helping to solve Steve's cases.

The DCI explained about the murder and the CCTV camera that had luckily swung towards the victim's house. "We looked at it last night but it's too grainy. I'm hoping you can clean it up. There's a white Land Rover Discovery that passes a few times and what I'm sure is the lower body of a man walking towards the victim's front door." Steve decided to ask for the impossible. "If you could get a reg number and a picture of the driver it would be a great help."

Terry didn't rise to the bait. "From what I've seen so far it would be a bloody miracle if we get anything."

"Yeah, but you'll try?"

"Of course. So what's this case that's taken you to Norfolk?"

"Steve explained the case and that he and Matt were now investigating the murder of a Norfolk Constabulary CID officer. "We're on our way to interview her old boss. See if he can shed some light but we're not hopeful. We need a break and maybe that cassette holds the break we need."

Terry Harvey knew when to be serious and when to be flippant. He could tell from his friend's voice that flippancy wouldn't go down well now.

"Leave it with me, Steve. It'll take a few hours, but I'll do what we can and let you know when I'm done."

Steve hung up as Matt was navigating the narrow country roads that led from Norfolk into Suffolk. It was 10.37 a.m. when Steve and Matt arrived in the pretty village of Long Melford. Steve knew it was famous for antique shops and its wide main street gave it an old-fashioned air as though time had stood still. After a long and according to Matt, arduous drive, the pair stopped at the Bull Hotel for a coffee and to ask directions to Jack Ralph's cottage.

Suitably refreshed the detectives knocked on the front door of an old cottage that looked like the picture on a chocolate box. It was exactly 11.07 a.m.

The door was answered by a sad-looking lady dressed in black. Her eyes were puffed, and she looked as though she had been crying. Her nose was red from blowing it too often and she held a cotton handkerchief in her hand.

"Yes?" the woman croaked, not opening the door all the way.

Steve introduced himself and Matt and they both showed their warrant cards. "We'd like a word with Inspector Ralph, if we can."

At this, the woman started crying almost uncontrollably. She tried to speak but the words wouldn't come. Another woman appeared behind the first and took control. "Forgive my sister but she's still in shock. Come in, I'm Jane, Patricia's sister."

The elder sister ushered her sibling away from the door and sat her down in the pretty but small living room. Steve and Matt were invited to sit down, and Jane left the three together as she went into the kitchen to put the kettle on. Steve thought back to the number of times the simple act of boiling a kettle for tea helped calm things down.

Matt looked at Steve with a confused look. Neither officer wanted to say anything in case it set Patricia Ralph off on another crying bout.

Steve was also confused but concluded that perhaps Jack Ralph had died. Jane returned with a tray of mugs and a pot of tea. "We've no milk so you'll have to have it black."

Steve and Matt smiled and said in unison that it was OK, they preferred it black.

Once the ceremony of pouring the tea was over, Steve ventured a comment. "Is the Inspector out?"

Patricia once more collapsed into a fit of tears. Jane left her to sit there sobbing while shaking her head at her sister as if to say, 'pull yourself together'. She turned to the detectives, "It's obvious you haven't heard. Jack was murdered on Monday."

Steve and Matt were shocked, but Steve's brain immediately wondered if the two killings were connected. To him it was too much of a coincidence. Jane went on to explain the circumstances of how Jack Ralph had been found in the outside toilet of the pub in Clare.

"I presume Suffolk police are investigating?"

Jane gave her sister a withering look. "Yes, but they told us yesterday they were stumped. An Inspector Rory Gillen is in charge. Nice man but I don't think he's very bright."

Steve turned to Patricia Ralph. "Mrs Ralph, I'm sorry for your loss. We're investigating the killing of one of your husband's colleagues, Detective Sergeant Elsie Brown."

Patricia screwed up her handkerchief even tighter, but the news of Elsie's death seemed to revive her. She was clearly shocked. "*Elsie*. Elsie Brown's dead?"

"Yes. Ten days ago, on September 11. We were hoping your husband could give us some background on Elsie."

Patricia seemed alert and had stopped crying. Steve had witnessed such behaviour before, when a sorrowful individual heard of another serious event, they concentrated on the second occurrence almost forgetting their own situation. He knew the shrinks had a name for it, but it wasn't his job to remember. He was only aware of the condition.

"Jack always liked Elsie. She was a kind woman and a good detective. Jack…" Steve saw Patricia Ralph was struggling to keep herself together as she mentioned her late husband's name. "Jack always said the reason she had got stuck at sergeant was her inability to let things go. If a case were unsolved, she would try to keep it alive. The higher-ups didn't like that, and poor old Elsie was stuck. I only met her a few times, so I didn't really know her. I'm sorry I'm not much help."

Steve saw this was a great strain on Mrs Ralph and thanked her for her time and once more said how sorry he was.

Outside Steve and Matt stood by the car.

"What are the chances two colleagues get murdered within days of each other? Especially CID officers."

"Fairly slim I'd say."

"Get onto Poppy. I want Elsie's phone records over the last six months. I'll get onto Commander Brooks. My gut tells me these cases are connected and we need to get Suffolk's authority to take the Ralph murder case over."

"Right, but why not use Norfolk's resources?"

Steve didn't answer right away. "I don't know Matt. I think I'm more comfortable using our own people. Besides, we don't know their procedures. Let's keep this in our own house as best we can."

Matt shrugged and walked away from the car to call Poppy. Steve called Alfie Brooks. After the usual pleasantries, the DCI told Alfie about the two murders.

"I'd like to investigate both murders. It's too much of a coincidence but I need you to smooth things with Suffolk Constabulary."

"Leave it with me. Have you met Callum Robertson yet?"

"Yes. He came to our pub last night. Seems a good sort."

"He is but he's ambitious. Wants to be head of the Met one day or at least Chief Constable of a regional force." Alfie paused. "Any thoughts on the job offer?"

Steve could visualise Alfie plotting his future. "No Alfie, I haven't had time, but when I know, you'll know. Let me know about Suffolk. I've a feeling it's important."

Matt walked back. "All done, Steve. She'll get on to it."

Matt, as the driver, had realised that if he drove from Long Melford to Bury St Edmunds there was a good dual carriageway that would save them at least thirty minutes on their way back. The pool car didn't have any navigation system, so he'd taken what looked like the most direct route from Norwich to Jack Ralph's house not realising how slow and winding the back roads were in this part of the country. The drive back to Norfolk Police Headquarters was easier and both detectives had time to think.

***

Just as Steve and Matt were pulling onto the A14 dual carriageway, DI Peter Jones and DC Mary Dougan were standing outside the apartment block where Sophia Paulo and Mariola Scala had lived. The building wasn't modern but a 1960s cheaply put together flat-roofed structure now suffering from its poor-quality construction and lack of external maintenance. Other parts of this up-and-coming area of London had already had a makeover and from what Peter had seen, this was the last block to be treated.

He and Mary had discussed the case again and summarised their conclusions without arriving at a clear path forward. The forensic and search teams were going over the girls' flat with a fine-tooth comb in the hope of finding something that would move the case forward. The neighbours had been interviewed and couldn't help except one girl who lived in the adjoining flat. She reported hearing men's voices coming from the flat but only after Mariola Scala had left. The neighbour thought Sophia Paulo had turned to prostitution to make a living. She also said a large foreign-looking man had been hanging around the street just before Sophia had disappeared. Peter had arranged to have the girl collected in the early afternoon to sit with a facial software technician from Inspector Terry Harvey's squad in the hope she could accurately remember what this foreign-looking bloke actually looked like.

"Let's get a coffee. The CSIs will be a while yet."

Peter knew they could add nothing to what was going on inside the flat but also knew they had to be present in case the search turned something up.

***

Inspector Terry Harvey was looking at his computer screen. It was now 11.33 a.m. and he'd spent the last three hours or so cleaning up the images from Steve's VCR tape. He'd found an ingenious way of pixelating the old images onto into a new format that allowed him to sharpen the edges of each image before intensifying the remainder of the image. Because the original was made up of one-minute fixed images, Terry was able to scan each frame into his new sophisticated software. He then created a disc of all the images allowing each to flow one after the other just like a slow-motion film.

He sat back pleased with his efforts. As he pressed play, he was anxious to learn if his efforts had paid off and to see if anything or anyone was obvious.

As the frames clicked on, the Inspector stopped the CD as the white Land Rover Discovery appeared in the shot. He rolled the images on until he got the second image of the car coming in the opposite direction, this time towards the camera. With mounting excitement, he allowed the images to continue until the lower half of a figure could be seen approaching the victim's path leading to her front door.

Inspector Terry Harvey was a thorough man and took pride in his work. He'd noted as the white Land Rover returned not only was the registration number readable, but the image of the driver was now clearer although not recognisable with the naked eye.

Terry was known to get first use of all experimental hardware and software as it was developed. He'd used such experimental kit in the past to help solve several high-profile crimes, some of which involved his friend, Steve Burt. Terry knew they were experimenting with deep facial recognition software that could identify an individual even when their face was misted or clouded over. The software probed beneath the image and sought out the identifying features needed for a match. Terry knew it hadn't been tried so collected together a few of his senior software technicians and they set to, using the experimental software on the clouded image Terry had retrieved from the VCR tape.

As the group discussed the implications of this new innovation, the screen linked to the mainframe computer started to flicker and slowly, pixel by pixel, an image appeared. It looked clean and the image was clearly recognisable as a man in his late forties with long dark hair and a scar above his left eyebrow. The image suddenly stopped, and the computer continued to work. Within seconds of the image freezing, another screen appeared showing a police photograph of the individual, his name and other details plus a summary of his criminal record.

Terry and his team were overjoyed. This new system obviously worked and if the identification was correct then the Metropolitan Police Service had another tool in its armoury. The ability to identify criminals from poor pictures was a major boost.

Back in his office, Terry worked at producing a video of the relevant images including those produced by the experimental system and e-mailed it to the DCI. He then lifted his phone and called Steve. It was 12.06 on Thursday the 21st of September. Just over twenty-four hours since Steve and Matt Conway had met the head of Norfolk CID and started their investigation into the killing of Elsie Brown.

Chapter Twelve

As Steve and Matt made their way back to Norfolk Force Headquarters, Steve's mobile rang. It was Commander Alfie Brooks.

"I've got clearance from Suffolk for you to investigate this other killing. Their SIO is an Inspector Rory Gillen. The ACC at Suffolk says he'll be expecting your call and says thanks. Even though it's only been a few days, they've not made any headway."

"Thank you, sir. I'll call DI Gillen when we get back to Norwich."

The line went dead as Alfie realised Steve was on hands-free and Matt Conway was in the car. Steve had no sooner hung up than Poppy called. She'd checked out Elsie's phone records for the past six months.

"I've scanned and e-mailed them to you. I've looked for patterns but couldn't see any. Without knowing who belongs to each number she dialled it's a bit of a waste of time so I'm running all the numbers against the national directory. I should be able to give you names and numbers before close of play today."

Steve was pleased to hear Poppy sounding so efficient and clearly happy. Perhaps promising her he'd talk to her about a move to operations had at last convinced her she had a future other than as an admin assistant.

"Good work, Poppy, keep at it. We've just picked up another murder case that may be linked to the one we came to investigate. Let me have the list of names and numbers and if I need more, I'll call you."

Even a very serious sounding Poppy couldn't resist a quick comment as she said, just as she hung up. "I'm here to serve."

As Steve and Matt drove on Steve's phone rang again. Matt looked across. "Bloody hell, sir. You're popular today."

"Steve, it's Terry. You sound as though you're driving?"

"No, Matt's driving. I'm just a passenger. I hope you've got good news. We've just picked up another murder." Steve explained how they had gone to meet Jack Ralph only to learn he'd been murdered a few days earlier. "It's too much of a coincidence. Our victim worked for Inspector Jack Ralph and now he's dead."

Terry thought this through and agreed. "Right. I may have something for you."

When Terry said that Steve knew it was good news.

Terry went on, "First, the good news. I've got a registration number for the white Land Rover Discovery. The bad news is the plates are false. They were stolen off a Ford Ka in Ipswich the day before your first killing."

Steve's heart sank but he said nothing allowing Terry to carry on. "However, due to a new piece of software…" Steve laughed out loud. He'd heard Terry start so many revealing discussions with just this opening. "I have an ID for the driver."

"Bloody hell, Terry, that's fantastic. Who is it?"

"Not so fast Steve. The image was very blurred, and the new system hasn't been approved as being admissible in court. It's highly experimental so it may have thrown up the wrong suspect." Terry went on to explain how the deep facial recognition software worked. "So you see, there's room for error."

"Yes, I see that Terry, but if it's thrown up someone with a record at least it's a start."

"Your man is called Neil Furlong. He's a career criminal. Bit of a brute with convictions for GBH, wounding with intent, drugs and manslaughter. He's got mob connections and got out of the Scrubs just under a year ago. The interesting thing is he lives in Ipswich and that's where the number plate on the Discovery was nicked."

"Well done, Terry. Can you get the data over to me?"

"Already done and I've sent a copy to Poppy to update her case file. Thought I'd save you a job as you're on holiday in Norfolk."

Steve smiled but decided not to respond. Terry went on and explained how he'd made a video showing what was on the VCR. "It's easy to follow. If you need any more just shout."

"Thanks, Terry." Steve had another thought. "You're not doing anything for your niece are you?"

"Well, you know Poppy. She's asked me to run some phone numbers against the national registry. Shouldn't take too long, we're a bit quiet. Why do you ask?"

"Oh, no reason, just curious." As Steve hung up he explained to Matt how Poppy was manipulating her Uncle Terry again.

Matt laughed. "That's Poppy, she'll always find a way."

As the pool car approached Norfolk Headquarters, the laughter had subsided, and Steve had explained everything to Matt. The pair found their way to their office. It was 2.47 p.m. On the journey back they had spotted a roadside diner and Steve had stumped up the cash for two hamburgers and Coke. As they walked in, DS Geoff Cummings was at his desk reading a newspaper.

"Did you enjoy your lunch, DS Cummings?" There was more than a hint of annoyance in the DCI's voice which was lost on the old-time detective.

"Very pleasant, thank you sir. How did you get on in Suffolk?"

"Well. Not that too many people around here seem to care, but DI Jack Ralph has also been murdered. His body was found in a pub toilet in a place called Clare."

"That's not very fair, sir. Geoff Ralph was a mate of mine. I'd not heard he was dead."

"Fair or not, Sergeant, this means we've got another killing on our hands." Steve explained to DS Cummings that he had authority to investigate both murders.

All three detectives sat at their desks while Steve contemplated their next move. He stood and approached the whiteboard and wrote as he talked.

"Let's see where we are. Elsie Brown, murdered, on the 11th of September, that's eleven days ago. Jack Ralph murdered on the 18th of September, that's four days ago. We have two colleagues murdered within seven days of each other." Steve looked at the board. "We know Elsie Brown was bludgeoned to death. Matt, get onto this SIO in Suffolk. As him to forward the PM report and the case file to Poppy and to us here but ask him how Jack Ralph was murdered."

Matt left the room to call DI Rory Gillen of the Suffolk Constabulary.

Steve stood staring at the board while Geoff Cummings just sat, staring at the wall. After a few minutes Matt returned with a grin on his face. "DI Gillen seems like a nice guy. He'll get the files over and guess what?" Matt didn't wait for an answer. "Jack Ralph was bludgeoned to death just like Elsie Brown. We could have the same MO for both cases."

"Good. That gives us a link." Steve wrote this latest information on the board. "Right. We also have the CCTV."

As Steve said this, he realised Geoff Cummings hadn't asked about the CCTV images. Steve decided to write off their liaison officer as a waste of space. He'd clearly nothing to contribute and was simply going through the motions. "We have the white Land Rover Discovery and a name." Steve wrote the name of Neil Furlong on the board. "Matt, we need to know everything we can about Mr Furlong. Get Poppy to chase it up."

As if wakening from a deep sleep, Geoff Cummings looked up. "He's a bad one sir. We've had him in here a few times over the years but he's slippery. Always has a high-price lawyer trying to run circles round us. I reckon he's got away with murder a few times."

"Would Elsie have had any dealings with him?"

"No, not really. She'd have known who he was, but I don't think she was responsible for arresting him or anything."

"Mm. So we've got two killings with the same MO and a name of a known hard man." Looking at Matt, Steve made to leave. "I'm off to see DCS Channel. I promised to keep her up to date. Matt, pull up the stuff Terry Harvey sent. Have a look, you might spot something else."

Steve left the two detectives. One sitting doing nothing and one setting up his laptop. As he left, he called over his shoulder. "Geoff, make yourself useful, get some coffee for Matt."

As the DCI went to find the head of Norfolk CID, he allowed his mind to wander. He felt the Norfolk and Suffolk cases were definitely linked but no matter how hard he tried to isolate the cases, his mind wandered back to the headless torso. He found himself constantly being drawn back to London and wondered how Peter Jones was doing as SIO.

Then he had the whole new job offer to consider. When he arrived yesterday, he'd told himself he was excited and was looking forward to seeing where his future lay. But now after only one day he found himself being mentally pulled in different directions and he hadn't yet focused on living and working in Norwich. He told himself, not for the first time, that he had to concentrate on one thing at a time and right now it had to be the killings of Elsie Brown and Jack Ralph. He tapped on the office door of Detective Chief Superintendent Emily Channel.

"Got a minute, Ma'am?"

Emily Channel looked up. "Oh! It's you, I suppose so." This wasn't the warmest welcome Steve could have wished for.

"I promised to keep you up to speed on the case, Ma'am."

With thinly disguised annoyance, the DCS pointed to a chair and nodded. Steve explained about the CCTV and Terry Harvey's work cleaning up the images. He told her about the killing of her former inspector and that a career criminal called Neil Furlong had been identified as possibly having something to do with the killings.

"So you've come to tell me how brilliant you are and how poorly run my CID unit is."

The ferocity of Emily Channel's response to his report threw Steve momentarily off balance. He allowed himself to think this senior CID officer was a real cow. He knew he'd achieved more in twenty-four hours than she had in eleven days. He knew he hadn't been triumphant in his report, but the DCS seemed incapable of acknowledging how fast he had moved the case along. Steve was angry but fought to keep his emotions under control.

"No, Ma'am, I told you I'd keep you up to date and that's what I have just done. Clearly you don't want me around, but I've been sent to do a job. In future, I'll report directly to the Deputy Chief." Steve stood to leave.

"Hold on, sit down." The DCI detected a thawing by the Head of Norfolk CID. "I'm sorry. That was unnecessary; you didn't deserve that. Please forgive me?"

Steve remained silent his anger still near the top of the scale. He nodded as Emily carried on.

"I'm being forced to retire by the end of the year as are a lot of my most loyal and dedicated officers. Morale especially among CID has gone through the floor since Callum Robertson arrived. I suppose I see you as an extension of him and I'm naturally hostile to a man who told me I'm past it."

The DCI's anger level subsided as he listened to this woman begin to unburden herself to him.

"I've been here a long time and worked my way up from constable to where I am now. Most of the officers I started with are still around and have a few good years left in them. You've met Geoff Cummings. Geoff's a good example. He's not due to retire for another two years but when a senior officer suggests you'd be more use running an allotment it tends to demotivate you. Geoff's a first-rate officer but the Geoff you're seeing isn't the real DS Geoffrey Cummings. He's just so fed up he's only filling in time until he can escape."

Steve was beginning to have a change of heart. "But I understand the Force hasn't done any succession planning and a lot of CID officers are nearing retirement age?"

"Ah! You've been nobbled to take my job." Emily Channel became animated. "Bloody hell. I knew there was more to just calling in the Yard. That bloody man Robertson, he's a slimy underhand sod. You're not interested in the case. You're here to spy and look us over." Emily's anger was real.

Steve realised he'd shown his hand but needed to bring the DCS back to his way of thinking. "I'm sorry Ma'am but you're way off beam. Yes, I admit the Deputy Chief has asked if I am interested in taking over Norfolk CID, but please believe me I am here first and foremost to solve the murder of Elsie Brown and now Jack Ralph. I'm not here to spy and I'm certainly not here to show anybody in a bad light. Yes, I'm interested in looking around but only to gauge if my wife and family would be happy in Norwich."

"Yes, sorry again. I can understand as a Chief Inspector the jumping in rank to Chief Super is appealing and I suppose I'd have done the same thing in your position. So what do you think of us… unofficially?"

Steve tried to pick his words carefully. He explained his shock at CID having a lunch break and technical support closing at four p.m. in order that the grandmother running it could collect her grandchildren from school. He told Emily that he felt no one cared about Elsie's murder and there was a general air of lethargy within the officers he'd met.

"I understand, Steve." This was the second time Emily Channel had used Steve's Christian name. "But up until three months ago the whole team were on the ball. There was no such thing as an hour for lunch or picking kids up from school. We were a damned good CID force. As I said, since Callum Robertson got here, he has done nothing but undermine morale to the extent that those officers being forced out are giving him the finger. The older detectives see what's going on and their enthusiasm for the job isn't what it was."

Emily Channel was clearly passionate about her unit and her job. "I suppose I'm to blame because like everyone else I was hurt by Robertson's remarks. Like Geoff Cummings, I'm not interested any more, just happy to mark time and wait for the inevitable. But if you do take over, I can tell you there's a great bunch of officers ready to be re-energised. You'll go a long way to find a better bunch if you can successfully manage them." Emily sat back. She looked tired.

"Thank you for your candour, Ma'am."

"Yes, well. It's not your fault. It sounds like good work so far and I believe you about looking to solve the case, rather than spying on us." The DCS smiled. "I'll have a word with Geoff. Tell him you're one of the good guys and not to bugger you around. You'll find he can help. Tell him to come and see me." Emily Channel picked up a pen and opened a file indicating that the meeting was over.

Steve left Emily's office, and on his way back to his own office, he found a quiet corner and called Alfie Brooks. After exchanging pleasantries and once more telling Alfie he hadn't decided on the job, Steve got to the point of his call.

"Can you check out Callum Robertson? He was ACC with Kent before he came here. I'm looking for background, you know... how he was perceived by the Force. Do people there think he did a good job? Was he liked... that sort of thing?"

Steve explained to Alfie that he was experiencing a morale problem in Norfolk and that Callum Robertson seemed to be responsible.

"Steve, command rank officers didn't get where they are by being popular. I'm sure Callum's been given a brief and he's only carrying it out, but I'll check. Remember, I told you he was ambitious. If you pitch up as his man you could be carried along with him. I'm sure he's looking to be the Met Commissioner one day. He could be a good friend."

Steve listened and kept his thoughts to himself. "Thanks, Alfie." He returned to his temporary office and told Geoff Cummings the DCS wanted to see him.

As he sat down Matt looked up. "Poppy's been on. She wants you to call her back." Matt was examining the case file on the Jack Ralph murder. He carried on. "Oh! And the SIO on this Ralph killing wants to know if you want a meeting. He's suggested tomorrow morning at the crime scene."

Steve considered this. He didn't have his thoughts in order, but it seemed like a good idea to meet the SIO and view the crime scene. Matt Conway continued talking. "I've checked the map. The murder was in a village called Clare. It's not far from where we were this morning. Should take about two hours if we take the A14 most of the way."

"Tell him we'll see him at eleven tomorrow." Steve dialled Poppy's number. She picked up on the first ring.

"Are you sitting down, sir?"

Steve knew the signs. Poppy had something and was excited. The DCI knew the best thing to do was to let Poppy tell her story her way.

"Yes, I am Poppy, fire away." Steve gave out an involuntary sigh.

Poppy began. "Well. You know we got the first victim's telephone records and then I ran the numbers she called against the national directory."

"Yes." The DCI knew that Poppy had persuaded Terry Harvey to do the work but said nothing.

"Right. Well, all I got was names and numbers. I got the file Uncle Terry put together from the CCTV. He told me it was to go in the case file as if I didn't know." Poppy was allowing a degree of annoyance to enter her voice and sounded as though she were about to deviate from her script.

"Get to the point, Poppy."

"Yeah. Sorry. It's just that I know what I'm doing. I don't need anyone to tell me what to put in a case file." Poppy paused gathering her thoughts and returning to her script. "Right. Well, I noted Uncle Terry had given you a name, Neil Furlong. I checked Elsie Brown's calls and she called him three times the week before she died."

The DCI sat back trying to understand the significance of this information. His brain suddenly clicked into gear. "What dates did she call and how long were the calls?"

Steve heard Poppy clicking keys on her keyboard. "The first was on Friday September the 8th. The call lasted twenty-two minutes. The second was on Saturday, September the 9th; that call lasted eleven minutes and the last call was on Sunday September the 10th but that call only lasted four minutes."

Steve was thinking hard. Matt Conway stopped reading the second murder file sensing something important was happening. "So she called the bloke we suspect might be her killer on three consecutive days before her murder and the last time was Sunday and she was killed on Monday? From the length of the calls, it sounds like they had a lot to talk about the first time but less the second and probably only said hello and goodbye the last time."

Steve was still deep in thought before Poppy broke his concentration. "That was the only private number she phoned three times in the last six months. The other multiple calls were to her office, a few friends and the local takeaway. But I got another suspicious one. She only called the number twice but again just before she was killed."

Steve was totally alert. "Go on."

"We-e-e-ll…" Poppy dragged out each letter creating an air of mystery that she loved. "She called a London number on Friday September the 8th just before she called this Neil Furlong. The London call lasted six minutes. Then she called again on Sunday September the 10th, but this time after she'd spoken with Furlong."

Steve knew Poppy had a punchline so asked, "Who does the London number belong to?"

"It's registered to an Andrew Black."

"Never heard of him. Poppy do a—"

Poppy interrupted. "Do a background check, sir. Is that what you were about to say? I'm not a dummy, you know. I did a search. Turns out Andrew Black is a big noise in London's underworld. He's served time for violence but seems to have been clean for the past ten years. I checked with the intelligence unit, and they said he runs his operation with his brother. Seems he's the main drugs man and also runs a few prostitutes. They've had word he's trying to move up in the world, but they did say they've no ongoing investigation into these brothers' activities."

"Bloody hell Poppy, that's great work." Steve decided to test his admin assistant's deductive skills. "What does it all mean though, Poppy?"

The excitement in Poppy's voice was palpable down the telephone line.

"What if Elsie Brown was investigating something and had tied Neil Furlong to the crime? And what if Furlong worked for these London brothers and what if they didn't like Elsie's investigation and decided to order Furlong to do away with her?"

The DCI considered Poppy's analysis and admitted he couldn't fault her logic.

"Thanks Poppy. That makes sense but we've no idea what Elsie was looking into." Steve suddenly stopped talking as a flash passed across his conscious brain. "Bloody hell Poppy, that's it! Elsie was looking into an old murder case that hasn't been solved. From what we know she wouldn't let it go and was probably the only case she was looking into. What if she got too close to solving it, and that's what got her killed?"

Poppy was ecstatic at being in the middle of these revelations. "Sounds good to me, Steve." The DCI noted Poppy called him Steve. He didn't mind and had encouraged a degree of informality among his team. Poppy had earned the right to call him what she wanted.

"Good work Poppy. Leave this with us; I'll call tomorrow. Oh! Before you go, any news from Peter?"

"He's on his way back from the two girls' flat. Forensics have finished but I don't know if they found anything."

"Ask Peter to call me later." The line went dead, and Matt stared at Steve expecting to learn what Poppy had just passed on.

Chapter Thirteen

Inspector Peter Conway and Detective Constable Mary Dougan arrived back at New Scotland Yard just as Poppy finished her call to Steve. Both looked exhausted having spent most of the day hanging around waiting to learn if the CSI team had unearthed anything that might help the case.

Mary sat at her desk and set about the task of writing up witness statements that Poppy could transpose into the electronic case file. Matt had a few words with Poppy before sitting down to re-evaluate what they knew about the headless torso case and the killing from six months ago that now appeared to be linked. He took his large pad and scribbled doodles rather than make concise notes. He found it easier to let his thoughts wander. This was a technique the DCI had taught him when he first started, and he found it worked. He shut his ears to everything around him and concentrated.

First, he sketched a body without a head. Against this, he wrote the name *Sophia Paulo*. Immigration had confirmed she'd arrived from Italy, approximately eighteen months ago, from Sicily. As an EU citizen, she had free movement and was never questioned by the UK Border Force.

Peter sketched the second known victim that the pathologist Dr Evans had notified them about. Mariola Scala was also from Sicily and arrived at the same time as Sophia Paulo. Peter thought they must have arrived together. He then drew a large question mark and wrote 'WHY'.

He drew a clear evidence bag from the inner pocket of his jacket. It contained the few items he'd taken from the girls' flat. He arranged the contents on his desk. There was a photograph of a family, mother, father, son and daughter. From this photograph, Peter assumed that this was Sophia's family in Italy. She looked to be in her late teens in the photograph but based on other photographs and descriptions of her from her neighbours, Peter thought this was the girl without the head. The forensic team had found staining on bed sheets that suggested Sophia had entertained male visitors just as one of her neighbour's statements had suggested. Peter wrote on his pad the word 'prostitute'.

Other items included a postcard with an Italian scene from someone called Luigi. It seemed a short message and was written in Italian. Peter made a note to get it translated. Also on his desk was a mobile phone with a flat battery. Again, he made a note to ask Terry Harvey to look at it.

Just as he finished writing Terry's name, the man himself appeared and sat in front of Peter's desk. He was holding a buff folder. Terry said, "We've had your witness since two o'clock. She's had a lot of attempts at this photofit but how accurate it is I'm not sure. She says it looks like the man she saw but I don't know. Anyway, there it is." Terry handed over the file.

Peter studied it and saw a fattish round face with fashionable stubble on its chin. The eyes were close together but wide and the nose was slightly crooked. The face had a full head of hair that the witness had obviously thought was black. The face had the swarthy look of a southern European and had an unsmiling and not very friendly persona.

"Terry, I don't know if this is accurate but it's bloody good." Peter was impressed.

"Yes, but it only helps if you can identify him."

"Yes. Of course you're right."

Terry sat in silence, smiling. He was waiting for the DI to ask him to do something. Terry knew that if Steve were the SIO he would already have asked Terry to run his facial recognition software to try to identify the face. He knew the image that had been produced using the latest technology was good enough for a match if the sketch was accurate. As Terry waited, hoping Peter would work out for himself what use could be made of the identikit, the DI asked instead, "We got the victim's phone. The battery's dead, but I wondered if you could do anything with it, maybe get her call records?"

"Leave it with me." Terry took the phone and realised Peter wasn't his boss. "Look, Peter, if Steve Burt was here, he'd have asked me to run that image," Terry pointed to the file on Peter's desk. "Through our facial recognition protocols. See if we can identify him." Terry let the silence hang before carrying on. "Would you like me to do that?"

DI Peter Jones, as the SIO, realised he should have asked already. He felt deflated as he said he would.

Terry removed the file and as he left turned to Peter and in a low whisper. "Don't worry lad, you'll learn. Just stick with the DCI."

Peter, feeling embarrassed, didn't look up at either Poppy or Mary who had heard the conversation. Instead, he wrote on his pad that Terry was dealing with the phone and the image of the man seen hanging about the block of flats just before Sophia Paulo vanished.

Feeling stronger and telling himself he was learning, Peter looked up in Poppy's direction.

"Do we have any Italian speakers in the place?"

"Sure. We have an International division. Someone there must speak Italian. They're on the seventh floor."

"Right. Mary, if you keep on the witness statements, I'll take this down and hopefully get it translated."

Peter had just left as Poppy and Mary shared a giggle at the DI's expense. All Poppy said was "Bless him, he tries hard."

As the laughter subsided, Poppy's phone rang. When she realised who was calling, she subconsciously fluffed up her hair and assumed her little-girl-lost persona. "Oh! Inspector, how nice to hear from you again."

Mary looked on, not believing that anyone could change so quickly. Her voice was an octave higher and her body language exuded sex. Poppy continued to listen and gave an occasional giggle.

"Alfonso… are you sure?" Mary was only listening to one side of the conversation.

"Well thank you, I'll pass it on. Alfonso, do you ever get to London?"

Mary realised Poppy was talking to the Italian Police Inspector she'd previously described as sounding dishy.

"Yes. Well, you know where to find me. I'd love to show you the sights." After a few more minutes of long-range flirting, Poppy hung up with a beaming smile spread across her face. She started to write up notes on her conversation with the dishy Inspector Alfonso.

The two women detectives spent the next ten minutes discussing Poppy's less than subtle approach to Italian men. Mary marvelled at Poppy's ability to say what she wanted without reservation. Mary confided she wasn't into men but even with her friends she was more circumspect.

Peter Jones reappeared, and they got back to work. Poppy picked up her notes.

"Inspector, I've just heard from the Italian police. Remember we asked for a missing persons search? Well, they've confirmed both your victims left Sicily on a commercial flight but haven't been seen since. But get this..." Poppy loved suspense. "Both are the daughters of Mafia gang members, but Sophia Paulo's father — one Antonio Conti — is on the run from the Mafia. He was a senior member and was the accountant. Inspector Alfonso told me that no matter where he runs, the gang bosses will eventually get him. They'll use any means including killing his family."

Peter sat and thought. His mind was logical but worked slowly analysing all the data. "So you're saying there may be a link between our killings and the Sicilian Mafia?"

Poppy shrugged. "Could be."

Peter looked at his watch. It was 5.43 p.m. and time to go home. He decided he'd call the DCI with an update once he was home and had more opportunity to consider everything that had happened.

***

The brothers had taken a leaf out of Jean Franco's book and arranged to meet Archie McClean in a sleazy strip club in the worst part of Soho. The area around had been cleaned up over the years due to a variety of reasons. Mainly the police closing down the clubs and brothels but also by greedy property developers looking for a quick profit. However, a few of the less salubrious clubs had survived only because their location wasn't right, or the building wasn't worth saving. The Erotica Club was one such place. The brothers didn't own it but did provide protection. Andrew Black was considering emulating Jean Franco and buying the place. He saw himself lording it over the staff, especially the hostesses and allowed himself to dream of one day interviewing tall, slim educated girls who of course would have to prove to him how much they really wanted a job.

David Black sat next to his brother in the booth they had chosen for their meeting. He surveyed the inside of The Erotica Club and, unlike his brother, thought the place a dump. The red velvet drapes were either heavily stained or had holes in them; the carpet on the floor had once been a quality multipatterned Axminster but was now part of a sticky assault course designed to stop any fleeing punter dead in their tracks. Although it was early, a few of the girls were sitting around. David wasn't impressed and told himself he'd pay them money to keep their clothes on.

After waiting for around ten minutes, the brother saw Archie McClean saunter in as though he didn't have a care in the world. David Black looked at his watch. It was exactly 5.43 p.m. Unknown to David it was the same time that DI Peter Jones was leaving New Scotland Yard.

Andrew Black, as the elder, assumed the chair of the meeting. After looking up the meaning of the word 'conglomerate', he had explained to his younger brother that as they were now part of an international conglomerate, things had to be done properly; also, that meant he was the chairman.

"Now Archie, we only have one agenda item for this meeting." David Black assumed his brother had also looked up the word 'agenda'.

"Oh aye, and what would that agenda be?" Archie still retained his Scottish accent and was clearly suspicious of Andrew, placing undue stress on the word 'agenda'.

"We provide you a service, do we not?"

"Aye. If you call collecting a hundred quid a week for doing bugger all a service."

Andrew was unfazed. "But we don't provide the same service to your other property interests. The places where you keep your better tarts. Do we?"

Archie dressed in his usual t-shirt and jeans moved uncomfortably in his seat. He wrongly thought the brothers were putting the squeeze on him for more protection money. "I don't need you to protect my other places. They're in upmarket parts of town. Some of them even have doormen to keep out the rough elements."

Andrew smiled a lukewarm smile and stared at Archie. The little Scotsman was fidgeting and pushed back the few strands of long grey hair that remained on the top of his head as Andrew carried on. "You don't understand Archie." There was real menace in Andrew's voice. "We're giving you a deal. We won't charge you any more for the services we supply to you at your... let's say, *lower end* establishments. In return you'll vacate the top end flats, and we'll take them over. We'll pay the rents, the rates, everything. We might even do a bit of decorating."

Archie was both relieved and shocked. He was relieved he wasn't having to pay more protection money but shocked that the brothers even knew about his upper-class escort ring. "Nothing doing. I make good money out of those girls. Where else would I put them?"

"That would be your problem, Archie. I do hope you're not going to make an issue of this. We want those six flats."

"But why; you're not into prostitutes in a big way?"

"Not yet but we soon will be. We need those flats but don't worry, you have two weeks to move out."

Andrew, playing the part of the chairman, pulled a diary from the pocket of his jacket and with a flourish opened it. "Yes, that'll do. Be out by the 5th of October, that's two weeks today."

"Get lost. You can't just tell me to get my girls out of their homes."

David recognised it was his time. He stood and moved round to stand behind Archie McClean. He put his oversized hands heavily on the Scotsman's shoulders and squeezed.

"Now Archie. You know what my brother can do, so please make this easy on yourself. Just do what we ask."

The pressure on Archie's shoulders was becoming painful. He knew that if he didn't agree, David Black had other ways of hurting people, even killing them. Archie held out until Andrew told David, "That's enough, take him out the back. It's time he felt real pain."

Archie screamed as David gave one last squeeze. "OK. OK, I'll do what you want." David resumed his seat as Archie tried to move his bruised shoulders.

"There now, Archie. You see we're reasonable people." Andrew was back acting as chairman. "That's how we do things in business. We don't charge you any more for our services and in return you give us the keys to the flats you're renting. It's called a quid pro quo."

David rolled his eyes at this further evidence that his brother had somehow discovered a dictionary.

"Bring the keys to our other office in two weeks and our deal is done. You may leave now."

David had never known his brother to be so polite and this new Andrew also took Archie McClean by surprise. In a daze of uncertainty, the Scotsman stumbled away from the table still exercising his shoulder muscles.

"There we are, brother, I told you it would be a piece of cake. Tomorrow we'll go see the guy who's organising the existing girls. See how the land lies and maybe get a free sample." Andrew nudged his brother in the ribs. "What do you say?"

David nodded his agreement. "Yeah. Sounds like a plan Mr Chairman."

***

Steve and Matt had freshened up and were now sitting in the residents' lounge of their pub/hotel. Before joining Matt, Steve had called home and spoken to his wife. They'd talked for ten minutes, and Alison had told Steve his daughter Rosie had almost taken her first step earlier in the evening. He promised to get back as soon as the case allowed, but confessed he'd been handed another case that could be linked. Alison knew what she was marrying into when she agreed to become the DCI's wife and accepted the current situation with good grace. All she said as they hung up was, "Look after yourself and hurry home."

Steve had given Matt the Tracy Nelson file that may have caused Elsie Brown's death. He felt a fresh pair of eyes might shed more light on the case. Steve had read it through several times and couldn't see anything that might have led to Elsie being murdered.

Each armed with a beer, they stared at the file now lying open on a small coffee table between their chairs.

"I can't see anything, Steve. The case was well investigated. The husband found his wife naked on the marital bed, dead. There was some forensics especially semen, but they didn't get a DNA match. Neighbours saw nothing; Mrs Nelson was an air hostess and travelled a lot. The husband worked in insurance and had a watertight alibi. There were no other suspects, so they kept the file open but dormant."

"That's how I read it but somewhere, either in there or at Elsie's house, she found something and that something got her killed."

The door to the residents' lounge opened and Geoff Cummings entered dressed as he had been earlier in the day. He'd brought his own beer. "Couple of beers behind the bar when you're ready." Without being invited, Geoff pulled another chair closer to the Scotland Yard detectives. After a long pull of his beer followed by an appreciative burp, Geoff placed his drink on the coffee table next to Elsie's file.

Steve was almost shocked to see the sergeant who took an hour for lunch and finished at five sitting here apparently willing to help with the case.

"Detective Chief Superintendent Channel had a word. She said you two were straight and I should give up on the bullshit I've been shovelling in your direction. So here I am gents, yours to use."

Matt had not been privy to Steve's conversation with Emily Channel, so this new Geoff was a revelation. Steve now understood what the head of CID had meant by "having a word."

"Good to know, Geoff." Matt wasn't convinced. "So all that hour for lunch crap was exactly that, crap?"

"Yes. Sorry Matt. We've got a few issues up here with our new Deputy Chief and those of us in his sights have… well… decided to work to rule so to speak but it's not really us. We're just like all coppers. We want to catch the bad guys no matter what the clock says."

Steve was pleased to hear Geoff's explanation. "Right Geoff, here's what we've got. A white Land Rover Discovery passing Elsie's door minutes before she was killed. We've identified the driver as one Neil Furlong; lives in Ipswich. Also, we know Elsie phoned Furlong on each of the three days before her death. We also know she called some gangland boss in London on two occasions before her death. We're putting Furlong firmly in the frame, but we can't work out the connection to this old case and Elsie's murder."

Steve lifted his beer as his phone sounded. It was Poppy again. The DCI looked at his watch. It was 7.11 p.m. "Poppy, are you still in the office?"

Poppy obviously excited replied in a fake American voice. "Sure am, sir."

"Good for you. I hope the overtime is worth it?"

"Depends. Uncle Terry's here as well."

"I see. The whole family's ganging up on me now." Steve laughed and he heard Terry Harvey in the background encouraging his niece to get on with it.

"After we spoke, I got to thinking. We know our victim called the two numbers we've identified but we don't know who this Furlong person or who the London gang boss called. So I got Uncle Terry to do a bit of digging. It seems every time Elsie Brown called Furlong, he called London immediately afterwards. The only time London called Furlong was the night before Elsie Brown was murdered."

Steve interrupted. "And you think this London boss sanctioned the murder of our victim the night before it happened?"

"Well. If Elsie had something on Furlong and was putting the squeeze on him and he was taking his orders from London, and Elsie obviously knew of the London connection and was getting ready to expose the killer, it's just possible Furlong was ordered to kill Elsie."

Steve considered this theory. It made sense. "What does Terry think?"

Terry Harvey was on the line. "It all stacks up for me, Steve. Your girl Elsie must have found proof but instead of reporting her findings she went off grid and got herself killed."

"You could be right. Good work, Terry. Tell that niece of yours to get off home. Norfolk CID don't have an unlimited overtime budget. And Terry, tell her, well done."

"Hold on Steve. This London boss, Andrew Black and his brother are big-time gangsters involved in almost every criminal activity in London, but they've never been convicted."

"Interesting. Thanks Terry. Now you both get off home." Steve addressed his colleagues.

"That was Poppy." He explained what Poppy had discovered about the sequencing of the phone calls. "It all helps but doesn't throw any light on an eleven-year-old case."

Geoff Cummings sat back, having finished his beer. He looked at the two London detectives. "Drugs. That case was always about drugs." He spoke with the conviction of a man who knew he was right. "We had a bit of a drugs problem here in Norfolk around 2010. London gangs were coming up here, taking advantage of us country bumpkins. We set up a drugs squad and they did a good job of limiting the spread, but we always suspected there was a delivery line into Norwich. We could never prove anything, and customs never caught anybody, but drugs were getting here, and a lot of them.

"Elsie was sure that Tracy Nelson was involved in smuggling drugs into the country. She was an air hostess and most of her schedule involved flying from Norwich Airport to Amsterdam. She also had a record for soliciting and being drunk and disorderly. Elsie thought Tracy was a good-time girl. We tipped off customs and she was often stopped coming in, but they never found anything."

Steve and Matt said in unison, "I think I'll have that other beer."

While Matt went to get three more pints, Steve quizzed Geoff. "Were there any heavies around at that time?"

"Oh, there were plenty but no one we could pin the murder on. I know Elsie fancied one of two London brothers for the killing. I can't remember their names, but they would come up from the Smoke once a week, usually at the weekends. We had surveillance on Tracy Nelson at the time and caught her with them in the Grand Hotel a few times. Elsie was convinced one of these London lads did for her but her DI at the time, poor old Jack Ralph, said there wasn't enough evidence. Elsie thought there was, and the more Jack said they didn't have enough, the more Elsie suspected Jack was on the take."

Matt arrived carrying a tray containing three pints of real ale. Steve brought his DS up to speed paraphrasing what Geoff had just said.

Geoff was, as Emily Channel predicted, turning out to be very useful.

"Jack Ralph retired over three years ago. Why didn't Elsie go to her new DI?"

"Simple. She'd been banging on about it for years, but no one took her seriously and when she let it be known she thought Jack Ralph was on the take, the whole force more or less cut her off. I don't know if Jack was bent. He retired in some style after all, but he was generally well-liked around here. Elsie didn't make many friends by her antics."

Matt chipped in. "So when she was murdered, her death wasn't exactly top of anyone's task for the day list. Her case wasn't vigorously investigated?"

"No. Not until you two turned up at the behest of our new Deputy Chief Constable, Callum Robertson."

All three detectives drank their beer and thought deeply. Steve was the first to speak.

"So we have Elsie Brown, obsessed by an eleven-year-old murder she thinks is drug-related. The victim has the type of job that could allow her to act as a courier or mule bringing in drugs from Amsterdam. Elsie knows from surveillance that the victim is friendly with a couple of heavies from London that she thinks might be involved in drugs. It's her working theory that one of these heavies killed Tracy Nelson in some sort of lovers' tiff or in a fit of rage, but one of them killed her after having sex with her in her own bed. Elsie took her evidence to her DI who doesn't want to know, and Elsie starts to think he must be on the take, getting backhanders from this drugs gang. The case is shut down, but Elsie keeps at it. Is that about it?"

Both Geoff and Matt agreed that was a fair summary.

"But what did she find out that got her killed and where the hell is it?" Steve pulled his hand through his hair. "Matt, tomorrow get Poppy to pull DI Jack Ralph's bank records going back as far as eleven years if she can. Let's have a look and see if Elsie was right. Geoff take a team and go over Elsie's house again. She must have written something down. It might be your search teams weren't in the mood trying to solve the murder of someone who wasn't liked."

"Will do, sir. Glad to see we have a real detective on this now."

Steve took a chance. "But if Mr Robertson hadn't asked for help from the Yard none of this would be happening."

Geoff Cummings looked sheepish. "You're right of course. I suppose we're acting like school kids, but he has an ability to piss people off big time."

Steve nodded, understanding the detective sergeant's point of view. "Oh, and Matt, while you're on to Poppy, get her to call up the post-mortem for Tracy Nelson. Let's see if anything else was missed."

The three settled down to have a general get-to-know-you chat when Peter Jones called Steve. The DCI left the lounge taking his beer with him. Standing in the connecting hall between the bar and the dining room, he listened to his DI.

"Peter, what have you got?" Steve tried to sound upbeat, but in reality, the headless torso case worried him.

"I think we're making progress, Steve. We spent most of the day at the girls' flat. The CSIs pulled it apart and found a few things. I think it's obvious our latest victim Sophia Paulo was definitely on the game. She wasn't too fussy about clearing up. We found stained sheets and wrappings from condoms all over the place. Forensic have samples of everything so we'll get DNA but unless it was one of her punters, I'm not sure it will lead us to our killer."

Steve detected that Peter, despite his lilting Welsh accent was getting depressed. "All you can do, Peter, is work the case. Don't look to solve it yesterday, it takes time. Follow the clues, you'll get there."

"Yeah. Thanks Steve. We got confirmation from Italy that both girls left Sicily at the same time and as we suspected both were the daughters of Mafia gang members, but Sophia Paulo was the daughter of a high-ranking member who was the gang's accountant. Seems he did a runner a few years ago. No one in Sicily seems to know where he is, but Poppy's dishy Italian policeman told her the Mafia never forget and they'll try to get to their accountant through his family."

"So you think the killing could be Mafia related?"

"I don't think we can rule it out." Peter Jones rushed on. "We also found a few items in the flat including a postcard from Sicily addressed to our victim. It was postmarked four months ago." Steve could almost feel Peter preparing to read the card.

"'YOUR FATHER IS DOING FINE BUT SAYS IT IS TOO DANGEROUS TO MEET YOU.

HE WILL SEE YOU FROM AFAR BUT ONE DAY YOU WILL BE TOGETHER.

YOUR BROTHER AND MOTHER ARE FINE.

LUIGI.'

"That's it. It doesn't say much."

Peter again sounded despondent.

"No but it tells us her father knows where she lived. If this Luigi knows it may be that others do as well."

"Good point."

"We've no idea where the father lives?"

"No, nothing." Peter went on to explain how Terry had suggested running the identikit picture against his facial recognition database. "It seems one of the neighbours saw this man hanging around the building. Terry thinks his new software might get a match if the bloke is in the system. You never know."

"Good work, Peter. Sounds like progress and you've got a few things to work on. Get that postcard fingerprinted and get any usable prints scanned into our database but include Interpol and Italy. We may get nothing but if Luigi's prints are on the card, and if he's in the system, then at least we'll know who he is."

Steve had another thought. "If our victim was working full-time as a prostitute, she must have had a pimp. Get Mary to dig out known pimps around the area of the flat. Visit a few and pull their chains. One of them had to be controlling our Italian girl. Let's find out who and what they know."

"Will do Steve. I'll call you tomorrow with another update."

***

Antonio Conti had arrived safely by private jet at Biggin Hill Airport in Kent from Amsterdam and had been whisked away to his office in central London where he chaired the first of several meetings planned over the next few days.

The meeting had been ordinary with nothing to do except sign a few papers and discuss forecasted revenues. Antonio knew the whole exercise was a sham. Half of the businesses he had set up were a front for his money laundering scheme turning Jean Franco's dirty money into respectable, clean, useable funds. The other half were legitimate businesses that Antonio enjoyed seeing making honest profits. His task was to remember which business was supposed to do what.

The meeting had achieved one thing and that was to further distance Jean Franco from the real business affairs of his empire. Antonio knew that even businesses set up as fronts could be run as legitimate organisations and be profitable in their own right. He also knew this was a concept beyond Jean Franco's grasp. The day when Antonio would rule the vast Pan European empire wasn't too far away.

Antonio now rested in his hotel suite. It was, in his opinion, the best hotel in London. After all, the company owned it and he was the only guest occupying the entire top floor. It was located off Buckingham Palace Road. Antonio had bought the struggling hotel eighteen months ago and immediately introduced it to Jean Franco as another money laundering investment. Officially it ran twenty bedrooms renting out at two thousand pounds a night. According to the accounts and the bank statements, it was full seven days a week and all the guests paid cash. The truth was that Antonio was, as always, the only guest and the staff consisted of people Antonio had recruited, unknown to Jean Franco.

As Antonio relaxed in the sumptuous surroundings of the only suite in the hotel, the room telephone rang to announce Antonio's guest had arrived. Antonio smiled looking at his watch. It was exactly eight p.m.; his visitor was on time. Dressed in an old-style smoking jacket and wearing leather slippers, the ex-Mafia man enjoyed the walk over the deep-piled carpet in anticipation of welcoming his guest.

A polite knock at the double doors that opened into the suite announced the arrival of Mr Thomas Lesson. Thomas or Tommy to his friends was one of the three names inside the envelope Jean Franco had given Andrew Black at their Amsterdam meeting. Tommy was CEO and Chairman of The Hazel Group, a large multinational business that Antonio — unknown to Jean Franco but using his money — had invested in and was now their biggest shareholder. Tommy Lesson was a dapper little man who always looked as though he had just stepped from a Bond Street tailor's shop window. He was in his early fifties and walked with a slight limp as a result of a car accident several years earlier. Today, his trademark rimless glasses were perched on the end of his nose, as usual. Tommy Lesson was a self-made man who had supported the correct political party with lavish donations that now gave him influence in the corridors of power at Westminster.

Antonio knew Lesson was consulted on many political decisions and was expected to be given a peerage in the next honours list. Antonio's steward relieved Tommy of his coat while Antonio motioned his guest towards two very large and comfortable armchairs that stood in an alcove of the suite. Antonio nodded to his steward who acknowledged the unspoken command to bring drinks for the pair.

Antonio didn't like Tommy Lesson, but he was useful. He was well connected politically, and his company dealt all over the world in various commodities and industries. Tommy had a gambling habit, and it was this that had first brought Tommy to Antonio's attention. Realising that men who gambled usually had other habits, he first approached Tommy with an outlandish scheme that the city gent baulked at. He had firmly stated such schemes were beneath his dignity and made it clear he was not interested in such things, especially if they were illegal.

Antonio remembered how this very prim and proper gent had changed his mind when he realised how much Antonio knew of his private life and the sums of money involved. It hadn't taken much to persuade Tommy Lesson to fall in line. Once he had received his first payment for services rendered, Lesson belonged to Antonio. Antonio knew greedy men always wanted more of everything and now Tommy Lesson would do anything Antonio asked of him.

As the two men talked about the traffic, the weather, the cost of living and so on, Antonio brought the conversation around to the reason Tommy Lesson was seated opposite him.

"There are going to be some changes, Tommy. Our UK operation is about to be expanded so you'll have more sterling to deal with but fewer euros." Antonio was beginning to put in place his plan to oust Jean Franco. "I presume that will not give you a problem?"

Tommy Lesson looked to be considering this statement although Antonio knew it was all an act. This greedy man would do anything Antonio asked him provided he continued to receive his commissions and free access to the string of high-end hostesses provided by Antonio.

"It shouldn't be difficult." Tommy was savouring his vintage brandy. "We've just been awarded a new government contract to build ten Fisheries Protection boats, so lots of lovely pounds sterling will be swilling around the place." Tommy suddenly stopped talking and his expression changed to one of concern. "I will get my usual commission rate, won't I?"

"Yes, of course, but as I said we are concentrating on the UK market. The EU will be dealt with separately in the future, so you'll see fewer euros." Antonio was not about to divulge anything to this little man, but this was the start of Antonio's plans for the future. He realised the UK was a growth market and a much steadier jurisdiction to operate in. Europe was, in Antonio's opinion, simply a mish-mash of different countries with their different attitudes to the type of commodities he was dealing in. Some of the European countries were still poor, but in the UK, he would have no problem. There was real wealth generation here and it was ready for his smarter way of working.

"So when are you setting up this expanded business?"

"Soon but keep this quiet. Remember we need security. Not a word to anyone until I tell you we have started."

"Eh… how much cash will I be required to handle?" Antonio knew Tommy wanted this figure to calculate his likely commission.

"Don't worry, Tommy. It will be enough. I may need your political contacts to help get us going." Antonio looked seriously at Tommy and slowly asked, "I presume that won't be a problem?"

"No, I shouldn't think so. Just tell me what you need."

"Good. Now, something else. I want you to attend our board meeting tomorrow. I'll need a board resolution signing. I'll propose you onto the board just before we vote. You will of course know how to vote."

"Which company is it?"

"East Asian Ventures." This was another of Antonio's companies set up to launder money. He was running sixteen separate businesses for the purpose of cleaning up Jean Franco's dirty money, but he knew that soon it would be his money.

"No problem at all, Antonio. I'll get a director's fee and other benefits?"

"Of course."

Both men sat in silence. The reason for the meeting was over. All they had to do was finish their drinks and for Antonio to give Tommy the time and place for tomorrow's meeting.

"We have some new ladies arriving in a couple of weeks. Quentin will no doubt call you."

"Ah! Splendid." Antonio's servant appeared as if by magic and aided Tommy Lesson in putting on his topcoat.

After Tommy left, Antonio reflected on a satisfactory meeting and was pleased he had launched his takeover plan although it still needed finessing.

Chapter Fourteen

Friday the 22nd of September dawned blustery and wet. Steve had risen early and phoned home around seven thirty a.m. to have a long chat with Alison. He'd promised to try to get home for the weekend subject to progress with the case. They discussed Norfolk and the job. Alison could tell her husband was fired up by the prospect of becoming head of CID within a county Force, but she also detected a slight hesitance. Steve explained the effect Callum Robertson had had since arriving and how he was not universally liked. Once more Alison said she would support her husband no matter what he decided. She finished the conversation with a plea for him to try to get home sometime over the weekend.

Steve had taken Elsie Brown's case file to bed and had again read it from cover to cover. He had analysed her notes scribbled in the margins with difficulty. Elsie clearly wrote like a doctor. After rereading the file, he felt he was no nearer to understanding what Elsie had discovered that had led to her murder. All night he'd tossed and turned thinking about Elsie's murder and consequently hadn't slept well.

Over breakfast, Matt asked Steve if they were going to talk with their prime suspect in the Elsie Brown murder, Neil Furlong.

"Let's leave him for now. We'll meet DI Rory Gillen at the pub in Clare this morning. See how the land lies and then decide. We've got a few things to come in that might help."

As Matt finished his full English breakfast, Steve had a sudden thought. He knew he was struggling to keep focused on the cases here because he kept allowing himself to drift back to the Italian girls in London.

"Look Matt, I've got a call to make. I'll see you by the car in ten minutes."

The DCI finished his coffee and went back to his room.

He dialled Honorary Inspector Florance Rough, known to Steve as Twiggy. Twiggy was getting set to marry Terry Harvey and Steve knew from his wife she was near to breaking point with having to make most of the arrangements. When he'd first met Twiggy, she was a large lady but had worked hard at slimming down with the help of the DCI's wife and although not thin, she had lost a lot of weight. Steve knew he wasn't being unkind. Twiggy had always wanted to be smaller and hated herself in her previous state. Terry had originally met Twiggy before her transformation, and he had been captivated by her character and charm. Her size was not a factor in his proposal.

"Yes, I'm just leaving."

"That's a nice welcome I must say."

"Oh. It's you Steve. Look I'm sorry but I'm behind. Is it important?"

Steve wasn't sure whether it was or not but ploughed on. "Twiggy, I need you to do what you do best. Get inside the figures of a company for me."

A great sigh came down the line. "Is this company bent?"

"Could be; that's why I need you."

"Give me the name."

Steve checked his notebook. "It's called Italian Resources."

"What do you suspect?"

"Not sure but there may be a Mafia connection. That's all I know. If you're in a hurry I'll fill you in on the case later. It's just the logo for this company matches a little bird that the Mafia tattoo onto their daughters."

Twiggy laughed. "And you want me to look at this company just because its logo is a little bird?"

Steve felt embarrassed but held his ground. "Yes, you'll soon know if there's anything to it or if this company is completely legitimate."

"Look I have to go. Leave it with me. I'll be in touch." The line went dead.

As Steve put his phone in his pocket he thought back to when Twiggy had transferred out of Special Resources and had become a Civil Servant. Since then, she'd developed into one of the best forensic accountancy technicians in the country. Deep down he was so proud of the way Twiggy had worked hard and found success.

***

The journey to the Three Feathers pub in Clare Suffolk took just under two hours allowing Steve and Matt to arrive exactly at eleven a.m. as planned. They were surprised to see a patrol car parked in the pub car park and a tall, slim, not very well-dressed man leaning against the door. As the two detectives exited their car, the tall figure prised himself off the police car and walked towards them.

"DCI Burt? I'm DI Gillen, Suffolk Constabulary."

The two men shook hands and Steve introduced Matt. Steve noticed DI Gillen was carrying a buff-coloured case file.

"The landlord — he's called John — is inside waiting for us. He's put coffee on. I guessed after your journey from Norwich you could do with some caffeine."

Steve took an instant liking to this tall DI. Anyone who had enough sense to order coffee in advance must be all right.

As the three detectives entered, they spotted John sitting by a window at a table with four cups and a steaming coffee pot resting on the table. All three had to duck to avoid hitting their heads on the old, low 18th century beams that held the pub up. After introductions and coffee cups filled, Steve began by going over the events as he'd read them in the file.

John nodded. "That's about it, Inspector. The lady asked me to go and make sure her husband was all right. She said he was in the toilet. I'm an ex-soldier, saw service in the Gulf but the sight of that poor bloke beaten to death like that turned my stomach."

"Can you think back to that time? I think you said it was around lunchtime."

"Yes. The couple had just finished their lunch so it would have been after one o'clock."

"Was the pub busy?"

"We had been, but the crowd was thinning out, so I suppose it might have been nearer a quarter to two."

Steve knew from the police and pathology reports that the time of death was between one thirty and two o'clock. He went on, "Did you see any unusual characters hanging around that day?"

John sipped his coffee, reminding Steve that he hadn't started his. He noticed Matt had finished his. Steve tried the coffee and admitted it tasted perfect.

"Not really. We get a lot of passing trade at lunchtimes, so we occasionally get a weirdo but not last Monday."

"And the toilet is outside adjacent to the car park? I presume anybody could park up and walk into the toilet without coming into the pub?"

"Yes."

"Do you have any CCTV?"

"Yes, but it only covers inside the pub and the door from to the car park. I gave it to your man there." John pointed towards DI Gillen.

Rory Gillen spoke up. "We analysed it sir, but as John says, it didn't cover the crime scene nor the car park."

Everything the landlord had told Steve exactly tallied with his statement.

"Well thanks for your time, John." Steve drained his coffee and stood, signalling to his colleagues they were leaving. "We'll just take a look at the toilet and leave you in peace. Thanks for the coffee, it was excellent."

Outside in the toilet there was nothing to see. Steve realised the killer could have come by car and parked in the car park. "He must have got lucky. This is a pretty popular spot in a pub, but it seems no one was caught short at the time of the killing."

Matt looked at Steve. "Except our victim."

"Is there anything you need from me, sir? I've brought the file. We carried out a door to door, interviewed the pub customers who were left but got nothing. It seems the killer came from the car park, and I was wondering if the victim was known to his killer. Maybe he staked the toilet out waiting for the victim to come out." Rory Gillen stopped and looked quizzically at the DCI. "Or it could have been a random killing. Maybe Inspector Jack Ralph was in the wrong place at the wrong time. It certainly wasn't robbery. His wallet and watch were still on him."

Steve saw where the inspector was coming from.

"I think I'd agree with you except for the choice of weapon. The pathologist stated he was bludgeoned with something like a baseball bat, just like the killing in Norwich. We think it may have been a cosh, not a baseball bat. It looks like the same killer."

Rory Gillen understood. "But who and why, sir?"

"That's what we have to find out, Inspector. Let's take a turn round the village."

Rory handed Steve the file he had prepared and after locking it in the boot of the pool car the three set off to explore Clare Village.

Steve didn't know what he was looking for but felt someone in this small quaint village must have seen something. Rory Gillen confirmed that a thorough house to house had been carried out. "I went through each report, sir. It was a properly conducted house to house. Nothing was missed."

The DCI was satisfied, and the trio continued to walk up the main and only street. After about a hundred yards, Steve called a halt. "There's nothing here. Let's head back."

As they started back towards the pub car park, Matt Conway stopped. He pointed to what appeared to be a newly refurbished block of apartments. "Is that a CCTV camera?"

"Bloody hell Matt, you're right." Steve quickly crossed the road to get a closer look. His companions followed but not with such gusto. "It's one of the latest 180-degree jobs. We might get something from it. Rory, what do you know about this place?"

"Nothing sir." He peered in the glass panel of the entrance door to the flats. "There's a sign on the wall. It says security is provided by A.J. Cook and is by 24-hour surveillance cameras."

"Do we know who A.J. Cook is?"

Matt, who was standing back from the door, gave a cough and as Steve turned to face him, he pointed. Almost directly opposite, was an estate agents, and the name over the shop said A&J COOK ESTATE AGENTS.

The DCI rolled his eyes indicating how stupid he had been not to spot the shop. All three entered to find a small open office with the usual glossy pictures of overpriced country properties on the walls. There were two desks both facing towards the door.

At one desk a middle-aged matronly looking woman was busy talking on the phone. The other desk was occupied by a man in his late fifties; his nameplate, showing 'Alfred J Cook' was at the front of his desk. The proprietor of the establishment looked like the estate agent he was. He wore a tweed sports jacket together with a bright yellow waistcoat and what looked like, but probably wasn't, a regimental tie. He sported a small neatly trimmed moustache, and his appearance was rounded off by the small gold rimmed glasses he wore. His hair was cut in the 1940s style of short back and sides.

Alfred looked up and smiled. In a high-pitched voice he said, "Good morning, gentlemen. How can I help you?"

All three produced their warrant cards and Steve made the introductions. Alfred confirmed he was the man identified by the plaque screwed to the front of his desk.

"We understand you provide CCTV security for the building opposite?"

Alfred Cook beamed. "Oh yes. It's state-of-the-art you know. Clare hasn't seen anything like it. It operates on a 180-degree arc covering the front of the building. When anyone presses the intercom to gain access or a resident approaches the front door to enter, the sensors on the camera immediately stop the camera rotating and it goes back to a fixed position directly above the door. No one enters that block of flats without us knowing about it."

The estate agent was obviously proud of his CCTV system.

"Do you have the images from Monday of this week? That would be the 18th?"

"Oh, you must be investigating that awful murder at the pub?" Alfred put his hands to his mouth, reliving the shock.

"Yes, we are, sir. Do you have the images?"

"Yes. Yes of course. Would you like to view them?"

A quick glance at Matt and Rory confirmed they couldn't believe their luck. "That would be most kind sir. We only need to view images from, say, twelve noon and two p.m."

Alfred Cook led his guests into a back room and set up the system to play back the day and time requested. Matt sat in front of the screen and thumbed through the sharp, coloured images. The period between twelve noon and two p.m. revealed nothing. "Nothing here, sir. The angle only covers the edge of the pavement and the first yard or so of the pavement. We can't see the cars nor any people walking to or from the pub. Sorry."

"It was a long shot, Matt." Steve turned to Alfred Cook. "Thank you, Mr Cook. We didn't see anything that helped but we tried."

Mr Cook escorted the detectives out of the back room into his office. As Matt pulled the door open to leave, Alfred Cook spoke up. "That murder really spooked the village you know. I think I may have been the last person to see the poor man alive."

Matt let the door close on itself and stood back. All three detectives turned to look at the estate agent.

"You think you saw the victim before he was killed?" Steve couldn't believe his luck.

"Yes. I know it was him because the local paper splashed his face all over its front page."

Alfred Cook sat down behind his desk obviously settling in for a good yarn.

"You see I always take my lunch between one and two. A bar lunch at The Feathers is enough for me these days. Miss Truman," — Alfred smiled in the direction of the woman seated at the other desk — "she takes twelve till one. That way we don't leave the office unmanned." The estate agent was warming to his tale. Steve decided not to interrupt.

"Well, I'd finished my salad and decided I needed a Jimmy Riddle, so I paid and went outside to the toilet. As I was finishing, your murder victim came in and stood at the opposite end of the trough. I washed my hands—do you know they only have cold water?" Getting no response Alfred carried on. "Well, that's it."

"What time was this?"

"It must have been ten to two or maybe just before." The DCI considered the time. It matched the pathologist's estimated time of death.

"Did you see anyone else?"

"Well yes. A very rude individual. As I was leaving, this brute of a man rushed past me. Not even an 'excuse me', nothing. Normally I'd have taken him to task, but he was such a big brute I thought discretion was the better part of valour."

"Did you get a good look at his face? Did you notice anything unusual?"

Alfred Cook grinned. "Detective Chief Inspector I am blessed with a photographic memory for faces. I'd recognise that man anywhere. As to unusual, well yes. He was carrying what looked like a pipe in his hand. I thought it unusual. After all men don't usually light up a pipe in a toilet. Do they"

Steve's entire system suddenly jolted into action as he thought they do if the pipe is a cosh. He realised this could be the break the case needed but he had one final question.

"Did you not tell this to the police before?"

"Well no. No one asked."

Steve looked quizzically at Rory Gillen, raising his left eyebrow to say, "I thought you'd checked the house to house?"

Before Rory could answer Miss Truman spoke up. "When the constable called to ask if I'd seen anything, Mr Cook was out on an appointment."

Not wishing to upset his new star witness, Steve said nothing in response. "Mr Cook, if we put together a gallery of faces would you be able to spot this fellow if his picture were there?"

"Oh, most certainly."

Steve was on a high. "Thank you, Mr Cook. My colleague DI Gillen here will call back later and ask you to review the gallery. He'll bring a colleague who will also take your statement."

The detectives left and walked quickly back to the pub car park.

"Right Rory, get along to your nearest nick. Pull a few files and make up a standard ten-shot gallery and include Neil Furlong's face. You should be able to call up mugshots centrally. If you have a problem, call Inspector Terry Harvey at the Yard. He'll help. Also, when you go back to Mr Cook take a uniform to take his statement and leave him there. I want you up at Norfolk HQ once you finish with Cook. Sorry to drag you up there but we all need to debrief especially if Cook picks out Furlong."

"Will do, sir and it's no problem to get to Norwich."

As Matt drove the pool car out of the pub car park, Steve noted the time on the car clock. It was 12.49

Chapter Fifteen

As the pool car approached the A14 at Bury St Edmunds, Steve's mobile sounded. He saw it was Geoff Cummings. As soon as Steve answered, Geoff was rattling words as fast as he could. "Slow down Geoff, I can't hear you properly."

"Sorry, sir. It's just I've got something you should see and it's not good."

"OK Geoff. What is it?"

"We searched Elsie's house again. I got a couple of mates from the search team to help out. Luckily, I was upstairs on my own when I found something stuffed behind a dressing table in Elsie's bedroom."

"Yes. What is it?"

"I'd rather not say over the phone sir. What time will you be back?"

"Should be sometime after two. Is this thing you have crucial to the case?"

"Yes, sir, I think it is."

"OK. We'll see you when we get there."

As Steve and Matt drove on, Steve updated Matt on his strange conversation with Geoff Cummings.

***

Poppy was in the office by herself, enjoying a few quiet moments. She looked at her watch. It was 12.50. She knew the DCI was going to Clare with Matt and was judging how soon she could call him. Her desk was full of little bits of information concerning both the Norfolk and London cases that she needed to pass on.

Poppy opened her plastic lunch box and started to eat an apple. She'd decided to go on a diet after reading in a newspaper that puppy fat could become permanent if you didn't diet it off before you reached the age of twenty-five. The article told the reader how to calculate their Body Mass

Index. Poppy had and realised she needed to lose six pounds. She didn't mind. She liked apples and anyway, working for Steve Burt, she rarely had a lunch.

As Poppy crunched into her apple, she realised how much she enjoyed her job and how she liked being in the centre of the cases Steve seemed to attract. She knew she was good at her job and conceded that on occasions she pushed her luck with the DCI. Her mind turned to Steve's promise to talk to her about the possibility of her becoming operational. She thought about how she would love to crack difficult cases and speed up the promotion ladder. She determined to hold the DCI to his promise to at least consider moving her away from admin to frontline duties.

She recalled her conversation with her uncle, Inspector Terry Harvey, about her dress code. Terry had pointed out that her chances of going operational wouldn't be helped by her appearance. She knew he was right and remembered the embarrassment on Steve's face when he tried to tell her about her appearance. Poppy vowed to dress more sensibly and knew she was pushing it with her designer dresses and provocative necklines. Her phone shattered the peace and brought her back to reality.

"Special Resolutions, DC Amelia Cooper speaking."

"Ah! My pretty voice."

Poppy immediately blushed as she recognised the beautiful Italian voice of Inspector Alfonso from Italy.

"My pretty voice, I have something for you." Poppy was swooning at the lilting Italian-accented English. She visualised Inspector Alfonso as an Italian waiter she had once had a crush on. She saw a handsome man in his early thirties with a mop of black hair and the body of an Adonis.

"Yes Alfonso. What is it?"

"I have a match to a fingerprint you took from a postcard. Your DI Jones sent it over."

Poppy, keen to impress, interrupted. "Well actually, Alfonso, it was me who sent the request."

"Ah! You are also efficient, and I am sure you are as pretty as your voice."

Poppy was swooning. The accent from Italy was still having an effect. She told herself to pull herself together and not behave like a teenager.

"The print we matched belongs to a Mafia foot soldier called Luigi Repucci. He is a dangerous man so my pretty voice, if you ever meet him, be careful. I have sent you his file. He is really a nobody within the family but was known to be loyal to Antonio Paulo, the bookkeeper who ran off."

Poppy was recovering and in a professional voice thanked Alfonso for the information and promised to keep him informed of developments. She accessed her computer and found the Italian's e-mail with Luigi Repucci's file attached. It took her several minutes to get things in order before calling the DCI.

As she dialled Steve's number, Poppy was still a little flushed. The sexy Italian voice was overwhelming. She promised herself that one day she would meet Inspector Alfonso.

At 1.21 p.m., Steve's mobile rang again. He saw it was Poppy. "Yes Poppy. What do you have?"

"Well sir, I've got lots. I think I'll give all of it to you although some of it is for DI Jones, but I think you'd better know about everything."

Steve sighed. Poppy was at it again. For some reason she didn't like dealing with Peter Jones, but Steve was secretly thankful he was being kept apprised of the headless girl case, although he couldn't be seen to undermine Peter. He'd have another word with Poppy.

"Poppy." The DCI's voice held a warning. "I've told you before. Peter is the SIO on the two Italian girls' murders."

"Yes, I know, sir, but everything is coming to a head on both yours and Peter's case at the same time. You're the senior so if I tell you everything, I won't forget to tell Peter."

Steve gave up. "All right Poppy, let's have it." He put his phone on speaker so Matt could hear the conversation. From her voice Steve could tell Poppy was happy.

"Right. I got the bank records for the murder victim in Suffolk, Jack Ralph. I had to get a court order, but Commander Brooks signed it off." Poppy digressed from her narrative. "You should have seen his face when I went to ask him to approve the order. That cow of a secretary of his wasn't keen to let me in but when I mentioned your name, she gave in. The Commander's really quite sweet."

"Yes Poppy. You were telling me about the bank records."

"Oh! Yes. I've sent them to your laptop but looking at them it seems he was receiving a fixed payment of one thousand pounds a month starting in 2009. This doubled in 2016 and there's a dodgy looking reference number for the payments. They were made from a London bank."

"So Elsie may have been right. Jack Ralph was on the take."

"Don't know, sir, but you'll see these payments didn't come from his salary."

Steve considered this information before asking Poppy to carry on.

"I got the post-mortem report for your cold-case victim, Tracy Nelson. I ran it against the programme, you know, the one my predecessor Andy Miller wrote. The one that checks for inconsistencies in PM reports. Well, there are none. It confirmed the victim had high levels of alcohol and cocaine in her system and she'd enjoyed male company before she died. Cause of death was strangulation. The only strange thing was the pathologist reported her attacker had large hands."

"Was there any reference to some kind of frenzied attack?"

"No, nothing. Only strangled by someone with big hands."

Steve realised this probably meant her killer was the man she'd had sex with just before he killed her. If they could identify the man, then they'd have their killer. But how?

"Lastly for your case, I've trawled the databases for criminals who use coshes." Once more Poppy deviated from her script. "I was amazed how many there are. Do you know how many different things constitute a cosh under the law? An old sock filled with sand is a cosh, a lead pipe is a cosh, a piece of—"

Steve interrupted. "Poppy, can you get to the point?"

"Yes. I drew a blank. It was just a list of names and there were too many to narrow the list down, so I did a manual search and only looked for one name."

Steve jumped ahead. "Tell me the name was Neil Furlong."

"You got it in one. Every time he's gone down for assault or GBH, he's used a cosh."

Steve felt his case was coming together. "Good work, Poppy."

"Thank you, sir. You won't forget we're to talk about me becoming operational?"

In truth and with so much going on, the DCI *had* forgotten. "Of course not, Poppy," he lied. "What's next?" Steve had been writing in his notebook and turned to a fresh page realising Poppy's next burst of information would be about Peter's cases.

"Now to the two Italian girls. Inspector Alfonso called. Remember the postcard Peter found in the girls' flat and you asked him to circulate all the usable prints?" Poppy carried on without an answer. "Well, I did it and Alfonso got a match on one of the sets of prints. They belong to a Luigi Repucci. Not surprising because the card was from a Luigi, probably the same man." Poppy went on to recall her conversation with the Italian policeman and Luigi's closeness to the Mafia's accountant. "He is the one who vanished and is the father of one of the dead girls."

Steve was puzzled. He hadn't been full-time on this case and needed time to assimilate this information. "Poppy. Read out what it says on the card."

After hearing the words, Steve made the connection. "Our headless girl is the daughter of a senior Mafia figure who was the accountant in Sicily and who took off and is now in hiding. Your Italian policeman said the Mafia never forgot and would get to anyone the needed to through their family." Steve stared straight ahead at the road. "Are we looking at a Mafia gang killing trying to force their accountant out of hiding, or a revenge killing?"

"Surely if it was to force her father out of hiding, they would have left her head on to make her easily identifiable."

"Yes. Good point, Poppy. We'll have to think about this."

"That's it. Mary and Peter are out canvassing pimps and before you say anything sir, I'll give Peter the information without telling him I've already told you."

Steve smiled. There she was again. Being slightly insubordinate but the use of the word "sir" meant she'd not be taken to task. Steve admitted, Poppy was one of a kind and he wouldn't be without her.

Matt had heard the conversation and was able to discuss the implications of Poppy's information. The pair talked animatedly most of the way back to Norfolk HQ but as they drew nearer to Norwich both retrenched into their own thoughts. Steve knew he was intrigued by the headless murder but acknowledged to himself he had to concentrate on Elsie Brown and Jack Ralph.

The London detectives walked into their temporary offices at 2.21 p.m. to find Geoff Cunnings pacing the floor holding a clear plastic evidence bag that seemed to contain handwritten pages.

The DCI sat at his usual desk before studying Geoff who seemed to be flushed and agitated.

"Right Geoff. Let's hear it from the top."

Geoff sat at his usual desk but drew his chair nearer his colleagues.

"You remember you told me to revisit Elsie's place and do another search?"

"Yes."

"I took a couple of uniforms to help, both good lads and sensible. When we got there, we just scratched around not knowing what we were looking for. After about ten minutes, I left them downstairs and went to look in the bedrooms. I started in the main bedroom and after finding nothing, I noticed the dressing table had been moved. There were grooves in the carpet where it had been moved in and out. I pulled it out and this fell to the floor." Geoff tossed the evidence bag to Steve who caught it.

"What is it?"

Geoff Cummings looked behind him as though he were in an old Ealing comedy, but his face was deadly serious. "It's a missing witness statement from the Tracy Nelson killing. It's been properly processed but wasn't in the file. It must have been removed during the investigation."

Steve was confused. "Who removed it?"

"Well! That's the thing. I took it to our fingerprint boys. A mate works there, and I got him to do an unofficial job. He got a match. The only prints belong to Jack Ralph. There are a few smudges, but DI Ralph definitely handled it."

"Bloody hell Geoff, that confirms what we got from his bank statements." Steve explained about the regular payments into Jack Ralph's bank account starting at more or less the time of Tracy Nelson's murder.

"Have you read this statement?"

"Yes. It's from the neighbour who lived directly opposite the Nelsons. She said she heard a commotion on the stairs outside of her door and went to look. She saw Mrs Nelson and a large man kissing as they tried to climb the stairs. She said they were obviously drunk. When they saw the neighbour they laughed, called her a nosey old cow and Mrs Nelson apparently said, 'Sort her out Andy'. The neighbour closed her door and locked it. The next thing she knew Tracy Nelson was dead and the police were all over the scene."

"Is this witness still living at the same address?"

"Ah! No. She died three years or so ago."

"So we have a missing statement that should have been in the file, and it appears to identify Tracy Nelson's killer as a big man called Andy. This was eleven years ago. It seems Elsie was right about DI Ralph being on the take and from this we have to assume he was bribed to lose that statement but somehow Elsie found it. Maybe that's what got her killed." Steve looked at Matt for confirmation of this new theory.

Steve told Geoff about the estate agent in Clare bumping into DI Ralph's probable killer and that Rory Gillen was putting together a photo line-up board, but that the description appeared to match that of Neil Furlong. "Our admin assistant back at the Yard ran a search on all criminals known to favour a cosh as a weapon. She found Neil Furlong had served time for coshing his victims."

Geoff looked impressed as Steve continued with his analysis. "We know from our colleagues in Tech Support at the Met that Neil Furlong was outside Elsie's house at the time of the murder and that Elsie called him on each of the three days before her murder. We also know, thanks to some clever technical support, that Neil Furlong spoke to someone in London immediately after Elsie's calls to him."

The DCI stopped talking and slapped his forehead with the palm of his right hand. "Bloody hell, I'm an idiot." He fished out his notebook and started flicking through pages. "There it is, I'm a real plonker. The London number is registered to an Andrew Black. Andy!"

Matt took up the narrative. "So Elsie finds this witness statement that DI Ralph suppressed. She somehow links Furlong to the killing of Tracy Nelson, calls him out and Furlong calls this Andrew Black in

London who's a bit of a gangster. He has a brother so it's likely the Black brothers were the ones involved in the drug scene eleven years ago and we know they knew the victim. The missing statement puts an Andy with the victim and the number Furlong called is registered to an Andy, probably the same one who was with Mrs Nelson the day she was killed." Matt paused trying to understand a part of the puzzle. "But how did Elsie get onto Furlong?"

"Easy. He was on the scene back then as a heavy for hire. We gave him a tug over the Nelson murders, but he was alibied. He couldn't have done it, but he was close to these brothers. Elsie would have seen the link. Looks like that's what got her killed." Geoff Cummings looked sad, despite having probably just solved the case. He said he needed a break and volunteered to get coffee. As he left, Steve's phone rang.

"Steve. It's Callum Robertson. Got time for a chat?"

"Not just now, sir. We're right in the middle of a case review."

The Deputy Chief Constable was not a man to be put off. "No problem. It's 3.44 p.m. I'll see you in my office at five. That should give you enough time to finish your review." The DCC didn't wait for confirmation. He simply hung up.

Steve's phone immediately rang again. This time it was DI Rory Gillen. "I'm just on the outskirts of Norwich, sir. I don't know how long I'll be but not too long." Almost as an afterthought Rory added, "Oh, by the way, Mr Cook picked out Neil Furlong, no hesitation. His statement should be on your e-mail and with your girl at the Met."

"Good work, Rory. See you shortly."

Steve told Matt and the pair sat thinking. They both thought they had enough circumstantial evidence to arrest Neil Furlong for the murders of Elsie Brown and Jack Ralph, but both knew neither would be satisfied until they had this Andy from London if he had ordered the hits.

Geoff reappeared with the coffee and the three continued to discuss the ever-mounting evidence against Neil Furlong.

Chapter Sixteen

Rory Gillen arrived at four p.m. and after another round of coffees and a tea for Steve, they once more reviewed the evidence against Neil Furlong. Before they began, Steve called Poppy.

"I need you to do a couple of things, Poppy. First, I want you to pull the complete file of evidence we have against Neil Furlong. The DI from Suffolk has sent you his statement on the identification of Furlong in Clare. You'll also have a statement from a Mr Alfred Cook confirming that he saw Furlong on the day of the murder of Jack Ralph."

"Yes. I've got all that."

"Good. So, a complete file ready to go to the CPS when I tell you. Got it?"

"Yes." Poppy sounded ready for anything. Without saying anything to the DCI she felt her part in solving this case was crucial and she somehow had ownership of the outcome. This was her case.

"Second, get onto Terry. I need a search of all traffic CCTV cameras on the roads in and out of Clare at the day of the murder, that's Monday the 18th, between twelve noon and two p.m. I'm looking for a white Land Rover Discovery."

"Will do. I've been onto DVLA and confirmed Neil Furlong drives the same vehicle."

"Well done, Poppy. It's another piece of evidence. I'll call you later." Steve hung up.

With all four detectives now fully briefed on the case, the debate turned to how best to proceed against Furlong.

"We need to be careful. I don't want him spooked before we're ready. Similarly, I don't want this London Andy warned off. I'm convinced he gave the order to kill both Elsie and Jack Ralph and it looks like he may be the killer from eleven years ago." Steve was talking out loud but not to his audience.

"So what do you want to do, boss?" Matt knew the signs and tried to bring the DCI back to the discussion in hand.

Steve slowly looked at his colleagues. "Right, I want the CPS' blessing before we arrest Neil Furlong, and I don't want Furlong talking to anyone once we have him. Rory, he lives on your patch. Can you arrange to arrest him first thing Monday morning and get a forensics team into his place? We need more physical evidence and the best place to find it is in his house."

"Sir, is there a jurisdiction thing here? My governor won't like us arresting him if you're taking the lead."

"Good point. I've checked and because the first killing was in Norfolk Constabulary's patch, they have first call on Furlong, but they called us in, so it's the Mets' first call. Your Chief Constable agreed to let us in on the Jack Ralph killing and, given it's the same killer, the cases are linked. I'm afraid your governor will have to be unhappy but if we're right about Furlong he'll have a murder in his clear-up rate statistics to boast about."

Rory Gillen smiled. "Sounds like you know my DCI, sir." No one spoke and Steve continued to look at the Suffolk DI. "Oh, yes." Rory was flustered. "Sorry, yes I can lift Furlong Monday morning and get a CSI team into his house."

"Good. Once you've arrested him, I want him transported to the Met. Matt, unless you have any objection, I want you to stay in Norwich over the weekend and be with Rory when he arrests Furlong. You can bring him to the Yard."

Matt looked shocked. "You mean I get a weekend's holiday on expenses?"

"Almost, liaise with Rory setting up the raid. Better go in at six a.m."

"Right. Where will you be?" Matt wasn't sure what delights Norwich held for a single copper over the weekend, but he vowed to find out.

"I'll be in London. Rank has its privileges you know. I'll be in the office tomorrow morning if you need me. We'll tackle Furlong when you get him down there. I'm hoping he'll put this London gang boss in the frame but I'm not holding my breath."

Steve's phone rang. It was Terry Harvey. "You don't half expect a lot. A traffic CCTV search on a Friday afternoon!" The DCI knew Terry wasn't annoyed. This was his game, and he played the hard-pressed technocrat very well.

"OK. I'm sorry but what do you have?"

"You are one lucky policeman DCI Burt. We've got a white Land Rover Discovery entering and leaving Clare. It entered at 12.55 p.m. and left again at 1.53 p.m. The good part is this time the plate is real, and it's registered to Neil Furlong."

Steve gave a delighted laugh. "Well done, Terry. Has Poppy got this?"

"Yes. I'm calling from your office. She looks like the cat who got the cream and says she has the submission for the CPS. She just needs your covering report."

After hanging up, Steve turned to his audience and passed on the news from Terry Harvey. "It's all coming together. So that's it. We'll get a CPS decision tomorrow. Assuming it's a go, then Rory, you and Matt lift Furlong and rip the fabric out of his house if you have to. We need physical evidence. Matt, you'll have the CPS's decision tomorrow so liaise with Rory so he can get his troops organised. Any questions?"

Geoff Cummings who had sat in silence raised his hand. "What happens if the CPS say we don't have enough?"

"Geoff, I've taken weaker cases to them before, and we went ahead. Believe me, we have enough. I just want to be sure they're on side. I have a feeling this case won't be over just because we arrest the killer."

Steve opened his laptop and keyed in his report to accompany the file to the CPS. He looked at his watch. It was 4.44 p.m. He calculated he had time before his meeting with the DCC. He e-mailed his document to Poppy with an instruction to get everything over to the CPS and to mark everything 'URGENT'. She should insist on an opinion before twelve noon tomorrow even though it was a Saturday.

At five p.m. exactly, Steve was shown into the palatial office of DCC Callum Robertson. Steve was immediately impressed by the DCC's appearance. He was standing by a large panoramic window looking out. This was only the second time they had met, and the first time Steve had seen him in uniform. Not only was Callum Robertson tall, but he was also muscular. His tailored uniform let everyone see he had a flat stomach and a well-developed physique. Such a vision would normally be derided by the DCI as an officer who looked as though he'd just stepped out of a tailor's window, but Steve admitted he looked every inch the senior police officer he was.

Seeing Steve, the DCC walked towards him and the pair shook hands before settling into comfortably padded red leather tub chairs that looked and smelt new. Almost on cue, a secretary arrived to take an order for drinks, tea for Steve and a coffee for the DCC.

"Well Steve. How's the case going?"

Steve was reluctant to say too much until he had a CPS opinion, but Callum Robertson gave off an air of a man he could trust. "We're hoping to make an arrest on Monday morning, sir."

The DCC pulled a theatrical hurt expression. "Callum please Steve, when it's just us."

Steve nodded. "Sorry, er, Callum."

"That's great news. After only three days you've got someone in the frame. You'll arrive here with a reputation second to none Steve. Everyone in CID will do anything you ask of them. Great work."

Steve felt it necessary to point out the contribution made by DS Geoff Cummings and DI Rory Gillen, not forgetting his own bagman, Matt Conway.

"Yes, but it's your name on the docket. You are the SIO. You get all the plaudits."

Steve noted that the DCC hadn't asked about how they had put Neil Furlong in the frame and suspected the reference to plaudits wouldn't stop with Steve. Callum Robertson would take the credit and the plaudits for bringing the Met in in the first place.

"Now Steve. Have you decided to apply for head of CID here?"

In truth Steve hadn't. He'd been too busy trying to sort out his caseload and had really not thought about it, except he was alarmed by the present head of CID's comments concerning the new DCC.

"Not really, Callum. I'm obviously interested and flattered but with the case here and another ongoing investigation in London, I haven't had time to think about it."

Callum Robertson suddenly looked less than friendly. He quickly covered up his anger as the drinks were delivered.

After his secretary had left the DCC spoke. "This is a one-of-a-kind opportunity, Steve. You may never get another chance like this. Your application has to be in one week today and as I told you, with me on the selection panel, you'd be certain to be appointed." The DCC smiled still disguising his anger at not being given a positive answer from Steve. "With this murder solved in three days there's no one who can stop you getting the job."

Steve knew everything Callum was saying was true and he was tempted.

"Have you spoken to your wife about the move?"

"Yes, but only briefly. She's more concerned about her medical practice and schooling for our daughter plus of course somewhere to live."

"I know it's not easy and you haven't had much time. Tell you what I'll do. Suzy my secretary was brilliant when we moved from Kent. She put everything in place with estate agents, schools and so on. I'll ask her to put something together. Maybe call your wife and start the ball rolling so she can see we're not stuck in the Dark Ages up here."

Steve wasn't sure Alison would appreciate such assistance but thought it couldn't do any harm. The pair swapped stories and Steve found himself explaining how Geoff Cummings had found the missing witness statement. Callum Robertson seemed interested and understood the significance of the find but cautioned against any action being taken against Jack Ralph.

"The poor man's dead. No point dragging up old skeletons. We need to look forward."

After another ten minutes of general chat, the DCC called an end to the meeting. Steve left and was exiting Norfolk Police Headquarters underground car park at exactly 5.53 p.m.

***

Peter Jones had arrived back in the New Scotland Offices of the Special Resolutions Unit accompanied by Mary Dougan at four thirty p.m. just as their boss, sitting in front of his laptop in Norwich, was writing his summary sheet for the CPS.

Poppy was ready to update Peter on recent events and, under instructions from the DCI, knew not to say she had already briefed her boss. "I have a few things for you, sir."

"Good. Let's hear them, Poppy."

Poppy explained about her conversation with the dishy sounding Inspector Alfonso. She explained about the fingerprints and that Alfonso had traced them to Luigi Repucci. "He's a small-time Mafia gang member in Sicily but was friendly with a bloke called Antonio Paulo. Antonio Paulo skipped Sicily with a load of supposedly incriminating documents leaving his family behind. This Antonio was a senior bloke and the mob's accountant. He's also Sophia Paulo's father."

Peter and Mary stared at Poppy. Mary was the first to realise the significance of this information. "You're saying our murder victim's father is a man wanted by the Mafia?"

Poppy assumed an air of self-importance. "Looks like it. Also, the dishy sounding Italian policeman said the Mafia never forget and would try to get to the father through his family."

Mary was sharper than Peter. "So the postcard saying it was too dangerous for her father to make contact might have been correct. This Luigi is the go-between. He didn't tell our victim where her father was but presumably the father knows where his daughter lives."

No one spoke but Poppy thought Mary was probably correct.

"Right." Peter Jones had caught up. "So we're thinking the Mafia killed both girls, but why?"

No one had an answer and as Peter struggled to make sense of the case, Terry Harvey appeared. He was carrying his usual buff-coloured file. Sensing the atmosphere in the office, he stood in the doorway. "Is this a bad time?"

"No, Terry, we've just had some new information and we're trying to digest it." Peter had taken a seat behind his desk.

"OK. Remember the photofit of the guy seen hanging around?" Terry was speaking to Peter.

"Yes. You were hoping to use your computer magic and get us a name."

Terry tossed the file he was holding to Peter. "His name is Gunther Schmitt. A German who can be contracted out to the highest bidder. He's some kind of private detective. At least that's how he fashions himself. From his record, he seems to be more of a hired gun. He's been linked to several gangland killings all over Europe. Seems he's been spotted just before a killing, just like this time. I can't find any Mafia connection so maybe Poppy could speak to her Italian heart throb. Get his take on it."

Although Terry was following protocol by giving this data to the SIO he knew he could also suggest ways forward and how to best use this information.

Without being asked, Poppy rushed into Steve's office and closed the door saying she'd better do it now because Italy was an hour ahead in time to the UK.

Terry stood awaiting a response from Peter. "Thanks, Terry. If this German is working for the Mafia, we have another connection. We've just learned that the second girl was the daughter of a senior Mafia guy on Sicily. Seems he was their accountant and he's done a runner. I'm thinking his daughter left Sicily to come to London to look for her father who's clearly in hiding. The Italian police told Poppy the Mafia have long memories and would try to get to their accountant through his daughter. If this Gunther character was hired to kill her, what have they achieved and why cut her head off? It only made identification more difficult and really doesn't send a message to the accountant."

Terry was impressed by Peter's summary, but he knew Steve Burt would have to be on the case to move it forward.

"Hold on Terry. I'll report in, let the DCI know." Peter hit keys on his mobile and was connected to Steve who had just got onto the ring road around Norwich that had been designed to ease traffic. Steve thought as a road it was failing in its purpose based on his crawling speed stuck as he was nose to tail in traffic.

"Sir. It's Peter. Can you talk?"

"Yes Peter, I'm stuck in traffic."

"Oh! Right. It seems the postcard found in the dead girls' flat that came from Italy was sent by a bloke called Luigi Repucci." Peter went on to tell Steve everything Poppy had previously divulged to him about Luigi.

Steve made encouraging noises as Peter told his tale. "Then Terry Harvey has tracked down the guy seen hanging about the girls' flat."

Steve was suddenly all ears. This was new to him. Peter explained in great detail about the German and retold the summary that had so impressed Terry.

"Sounds promising Peter but you're right. We need—" Peter cut Steve off.

"Hold on a minute, sir. Poppy may have something else." As Steve held on, he heard mumbled voices and a high degree of excitement coming over the airwaves.

Peter was back. "Sorry Steve, but Poppy's just finished talking to the police in Sicily. Seems our Gunther Schmitt is known on Sicily. They told her he's known to do research work for the mob. That means finding people who don't want to be found. Poppy's contact says that although Gunther is believed to have killed many times, his contract with the Mafia would be solely to find people. The Mafia always do their own killing."

Steve was still crawling so had time to consider this information. "Put me on speaker, Peter."

The DCI could now be heard by everyone present. Terry looked at Mary Dougan who didn't seem to be taking part in the discussion. Her head was down, and she seemed to be flicking pages of her notebook.

"So Peter, do you think this German is our killer?"

Steve had deliberately, and he realised unwittingly, put the DI on the spot. Peter didn't speak for a long ten seconds.

"If what Poppy was told is true, it seems unlikely. Most probable explanation is he was hired to find the daughter but not to kill her."

"Yes. I agree it sounds the most likely explanation. Nonetheless you need to find Gunther and interview him. If he was hired to find the daughter, he must know something. You might have to sweat him, but I bet he has information we need."

"Will do, Steve."

Just as Steve was about to congratulate Terry on another impossible task well done, he heard a screech coming from his office. Mary Dougan jumped up shouting. "I knew it, it's him!"

Those in the room just stared. It was only Steve's remoteness that allowed him not to be shocked by Mary's outburst.

"What is it Mary?" The DCI's voice filled the now silent room.

"Sorry sir. It's just that we may have something on this German. The DI and I have been out all day tracking down pimps to see if any of them was our victim's handler. One of them said he'd had a bit of trouble with a German. He wanted a specific girl but the guy we interviewed didn't know the girl and couldn't help. He said he'd heard the same bloke was hassling other pimps looking for this one girl. The description matched Inspector Harvey's photofit."

"Good work, Mary. Are you thinking Gunther knew the accountant's daughter was a working girl and he was using the pimps to get to her?"

"Yes sir, I do."

"Well, that's positive enough. Did you get anywhere with the pimps?"

Peter Jones answered, "Not really. None of those we spoke to knew our victim."

The traffic on the Norwich bypass was starting to move more freely. "Well done everyone. Poppy, I'll be in the office tomorrow. I need you in to take care of any queries from the CPS."

"No problem, boss."

The call was ended and as Steve picked up speed, he called his wife.

"I'll be home later. I'll call you when I'm about half an hour away."

They briefly exchanged gossip and Steve heard his daughter trying to form words but only succeeding in blowing noisy bubbles he could hear down the phone. The DCI was content but still didn't know if he would take the job in Norwich.

He had a long journey ahead of him but reasoned it would be worth it to see his wife and daughter and to sleep in his own bed tonight.

***

It was 7.55 p.m., just as DCI Burt was turning onto the M11 motorway on his journey south, when the Black brothers entered a fancy restaurant in London's west end. The Pelican Restaurant was full of diners who seemed to be mostly couples. Andrew Black had called the person listed in the file he'd been handed by Jean Franco as being the marketing man for the girls. His name was Quentin Somersby, and it was he who had suggested they meet at The Pelican.

The brothers were dressed as 1930s American gangsters and were stared at by most of the diners. Both wore dark pinstriped suits, black shirts with white ties, and the image was completed by the large white hat each brother wore. Quentin had reserved a booth and a waiter showed them to their seats explaining that Mr Somersby had not yet arrived.

"Did you see the looks we got when we walked in, brother?" Andrew Black or 'the Chairman' as he'd started calling himself, removed his hat as he settled into the booth. "These people here recognise important people when they see them. I told you if we dress to look important, people will give us respect."

"You're right, brother, but I feel such a fool wearing the hat." David Black looked around the restaurant. He knew he was smarter than his elder sibling but all his life he had let Andrew control his every move. As he gazed at the diners, he noticed that at almost every table the male companion was significantly older than his female dinner guest. David mentioned this to Andrew who joked it might be an upmarket dating service.

David continued to watch until the main door opened, and a character appeared dressed in the most outrageous clothes. The new arrival spoke to the head waiter before heading in the direction of the brothers. As he approached, the brothers noticed he was wearing a purple corded jacket, a bright-yellow shirt with a matching tie that had been tied with an impossibly large knot, extremely tight purple trousers at least around the crotch and purple suede shoes. The whole image was rounded off by a fur-collared coat draped over the man's shoulders. His hair was salt-and-pepper coloured and had been styled to stand up on top of his head.

"Gentlemen, I'm Quentin Somersby." The statement was made as Quentin prepared to sit while simultaneously offering a hand for the brothers to shake. Andrew and David Black looked at each other not knowing what or who had just joined them. Quentin fussed with his coat, carefully folding it onto an adjoining chair. Once he was satisfied his coat was safe from unwanted creases, he turned to the brothers.

"Well now, this is nice. I do like your outfits boys, very intimidating, very 1930s!" Quentin flapped a hand in the direction of the brothers. "Now, I believe you wanted to see me to discuss our mutually beneficial business arrangements." Quentin was fluffing up his silk handkerchief protruding from his breast pocket.

Andrew as the self-proclaimed chairman decided to take charge.

"Yes. Well, Quentin, thanks for coming. You know what's going on. We've been appointed by Jean Franco to run his UK operation and we understand you have a part to play in supplying punters for our new upmarket escort business."

Quentin smiled and continued to fluff up his handkerchief. He didn't comment on Andrew's statement. Instead, he turned away from the brothers and called a waiter. The waiter appeared and Quentin took hold of his wrist.

"Isn't he a sweet boy? He's gorgeous." Quentin winked at the brothers. Speaking to the waiter, he said, "I'll have a large single malt with just a tiny drop of water."

The brothers ordered beer, large ones.

Andrew continued. "We're just setting things up but within a few weeks, we'll need you to up your game. We demand total loyalty from our employees and anyone stepping out of line will be sorry. Do you understand, er… Quentin?"

The drinks arrived and Quentin once more took no notice of Andrew's statement.

"Thank you, dear boy." Quentin made a great show of fishing a ten-pound note from his trouser pocket and handing it to the waiter. "For you. Now hurry off and let me talk to these gentlemen." Quentin leered at the departing waiter.

Andrew was becoming embarrassed and frustrated by Quentin's antics.

"Look Quentin, we're here to talk business, not to watch you try to pick up a waiter."

Quentin, to the brothers' continued annoyance, once more fluffed up his handkerchief. His head was bowed so that he could see his top pocket.

As he raised his head he stared directly at the brothers. The look on his face scared David. This wasn't the man they had been sitting with moments before; this was an evil-looking man whose eyes bored right into David's brain.

"Listen you pair of idiots, get it straight. You work for Antonio Conti and me."

The brothers just stared, and David's jaw dropped trying to understand how Quentin could change so quickly.

Quentin leaned forward. "All you have to do is meet the girls and take them to their accommodations. You pick the flats…" Quentin pointed a finger at Andrew. "But no dumps, only high-end places. Got it?"

The brothers said nothing. Andrew Black was trying to understand what was being said. He told himself he was the chairman and should be in charge.

"You pay the rent, rates and so on and remember each flat must have two bedrooms, because the girls share. You got your orders in Amsterdam and remember it's one manager to two girls. We don't call them pimps. I'm the only pimp they'll ever need. One of my men will collect the money each morning from each manager and bring it to me. I'll sort it out and someone will deliver it to you each Monday, Wednesday and Friday. I'll give you a bank account number that you're to pay the money into. Remember you pay in the day we deliver to you. You keep 10% for your troubles. That's it."

Andrew in his role as chairman had now found some courage. "Just a minute, Quentin, or whoever you are. That's not the deal we signed up for. Jean Franco told us we were in charge and all you did was find the punters."

Quentin sat back looking sadly at Andrew. "Forget what you were told in Amsterdam. I'm telling you how this works here. Antonio Conti is the main man and I work for him. You in turn work for me. Do as you're told, play nice and all the riches you were promised will be yours." Quentin leaned even further over the table. "But screw anything up and you'll be feeding the fishes."

This last statement was said with an underlying threat and the brothers knew this man was not to be crossed. Quentin flipped a business card over the table.

"You can get me on these numbers. Phone me when you've sorted out the first accommodations. I need addresses, phone numbers and nearest tube stations. I think we're done here." Quentin stood and carefully draped his fur-trimmed coat over his shoulders. He leaned over the brothers and said, "Get rid of the Al Capone gear, you look ridiculous. All you're doing is drawing attention to yourselves when you don't have to. And another thing, no fooling with the girls. If you fancy any of them it's two grand a time. Nothing is for nothing, and you can pay for the drinks."

Andrew was determined to have the last word. "Excuse me but you don't exactly blend in."

Quentin smiled and immediately resumed the role he was playing when he arrived. "Well dear, when you're dealing with tarts and punters, someone who looks and sounds like me is never seen as a threat." Quentin turned to leave. "Bye, bye, darlings, remember to give me call."

The brothers sat watching this chameleon mince his way towards the exit. They were stunned. Finishing his beer, Andrew wasn't happy. "I think we'll have to get rid of that person who has just left, brother. He doesn't know who we are."

David despaired sometimes of his brother's lack of foresight. "Listen brother, it's no big deal, in fact it's a better deal for us. We do less but get our money. Don't go looking for trouble. We'll be good."

David finished his beer and spotted a few tables were now empty and a few of the girls were sitting by themselves. All the solo girls were looking in the direction of the booth. David pointed this out to his brother who instantly forgot about the past thirty minutes. Andrew was always a sucker for a pretty face. Two girls approached the booth and the brothers realised they were in the country's only restaurant/brothel.

As David asked the girls to join them, he wondered if his elder brother really would knuckle down and accept things as they were. He doubted it.

Chapter Seventeen

Having arrived home after ten the previous evening, Steve's wife left him to sleep until he woke. Saturday morning, September the 23rd was a bright dry day and Alison had made plans for the family to have a picnic in the park. Steve had explained he had to go to work this morning but promised to be home by one p.m.

After a leisurely breakfast and spending some quality time playing with his daughter Steve set out for the Yard at 09.22 a.m. He decided to walk as it was a nice morning and the walk allowed him to clear his head and concentrate on the Norfolk murders. He stopped at his usual coffee shop and despite having decided to give up coffee, bought two takeaways. One for him and one for Poppy.

When he walked into his office, Poppy was hard at it typing away furiously into her computer. She looked up, saw the coffee and without being offered one, put her hand out and mumbled, "Thank you."

Steve grinned.

Poppy was obviously busy and as she typed away, she said, "Nothing from the CPS yet sir?"

The DCI entered his inner office and sat behind his desk enjoying the coffee. Having been away for three days, his desk was covered with reusable internal mail envelopes. He opened a few and finding nothing of immediate interest, he placed the remaining unopened envelopes in one of the trays on his desk. He told himself he'd catch up with everything on Monday.

The phone on his desk burst into life. "DCI Burt."

"Good morning, Chief Inspector. This is Cedric Spindle with the CPS. I was just checking you were in. I was handed a file late last night and told it was urgent. I'm fairly new and wondered if I could come round and discuss the case."

Steve sat back and rolled his eyes. He thought *Another bloody child*. He told himself he was getting fed up with nursing green rookie kids. He knew it wasn't this lad's fault he was new and conceded everyone had to start somewhere, but why did a lot of them finish up on his doorstep?

"Of course, Mr Spindle but I'm not here for long. I just want your opinion on the evidence and I'm off to enjoy my weekend."

"I'll be there in twenty minutes."

Poppy, as usual, had been listening in. She called through, "Was that the CPS?"

Steve couldn't be annoyed with his admin assistant so simply said yes.

Poppy appeared at Steve's office door. She was dressed in jeans, a blouse and a pink sweater. Steve was tempted to say she should dress like this all the time she was at work, although he knew he would never say this to Poppy.

His assistant had obviously finished whatever she was inputting and sat in front of Steve sipping her coffee. She was about to start her campaign for frontline duties when the large figure of Commander Alfie Brooks appeared. Knowing she had been thwarted, she withdrew gracefully allowing the commander to take her seat. She closed Steve's office door behind her giving the two senior officers some privacy.

"I'm surprised to see you here today, sir."

Alfie looked quizzically at Steve. "And you don't think commanding officers work weekends?"

"Actually, no." Steve smiled. "I thought anyone above DCI only worked Monday to Friday."

"Well, here I am, living proof that you are wrong." Alfie Brooks chuckled. "Actually, Mrs Brooks is shopping, and I brought her in. I'm at a loose end for the next couple of hours so I thought I'd pop in on the off-chance someone might be in."

Steve nodded an all-knowing nod.

"But I'm glad you're here. I checked with Kent about Callum Robertson."

Steve shifted forward in his chair. "Yes… and?"

"Seems he's a real high-flyer. The comment was he was like a whirlwind when he first arrived in Kent as an ACC. He has his sights set on being Commissioner of the Met one day soon. Norwich is a stepping-stone, but with the Chief Constable up there due to retire in two years

I'm sure Callum Robertson has his eye on that job and then on to the Met."

"What about his style of management? It seems he's got a lot of people's backs up in Norfolk."

"Look Steve, he's obviously a political animal. I've known Callum for a while, and he's always been the same. He's a good cop but looks out for himself and his career. If you're one of his chosen few then you'll have a fast ride to the top, but word is if you don't give him what he wants, he'll drop you like a stone."

Alfie became fatherly towards the DCI. In a soft voice, he said, "Steve, I know you have a decision to make but this is a once-in-a-lifetime opportunity. I believe you would work well with Callum; I hear Norwich isn't such a bad place, and Alison and Rosie will have cleaner air. London's getting as bad for pollution as it was forty years ago."

"Thanks Alfie. I know all these things, but I just get a feeling about Callum. Nothing tangible, it's just the way he's ridden roughshod over some very good, experienced officers. I'm not sure I could work for him."

"Steve, with an arrest in those murder cases three days after your arrival, you'll be well in with the rank and file. Callum's not a bad bloke, he just gets things done, but the decision has to be yours. You know there's a superintendent's job around the corner if you stay here but it's not Head of CID."

Steve was about to answer when Poppy knocked on and opened the office door.

"Sorry sir, there's a Mr Cedric Spindle from the CPS to see you."

Poppy left the door open and as she turned Steve saw she was giggling to herself.

"That's my cue to leave. Think things over, Steve, applications close next Friday."

Commander Alfie Brooks left saying he'd have the canteen send down coffee as Steve had a guest.

Poppy ushered Cedric Spindle into Steve's office. After formal introductions and handshakes, Steve invited Cedric to take a seat. The DCI recalled Poppy's giggles and saw why she might think Cedric a comic character. It wasn't his fault, but Steve had to admit he'd welcomed more imposing characters into his office. The DCI had expected a young recently qualified solicitor based on Cedric's comment that he was new. This solicitor was far from new. He was short at around five foot seven inches and plump. He clearly didn't work out. He was wearing his business suit complete with tie making no allowance for a more relaxed dress code at the weekends. On closer examination, Steve put his age at mid to late thirties. His hair was thinning, and he'd obviously shaved in a hurry as his face showed razor nicks, one of which was still seeping blood and only just beginning to close up. Cedric dabbed at his wound with a paper tissue. The DCI noted the man from the CPS had entered carrying the government-issue soft leather brown briefcase which looked brand new.

The CPS lawyer sat examining and adjusting the file he'd brought with him in his new briefcase. He didn't look at Steve and seemed lost in the paper he was rearranging. Steve knew this was the file Poppy had prepared so he called her in. While Steve and Cedric sat opposite each other, Poppy took the chair at the head of the table sitting between the two men. She looked pleased to be involved and had brought her laptop which she set up.

No one spoke until Cedric Spindle had finished fussing with his file. He looked up and smiled a shy smile at both the DCI and his admin assistant.

"Now DCI Burt, about this Neil Furlong arrest. I understand you are seeking a CPS opinion before proceeding?"

"Yes. I just need to be sure the CPS will take the case forward. I realise we've built our case on circumstantial evidence but I'm sure it'll stand up. I just need confirmation from yourselves."

"Yes, I see. I notice you intend to charge him with two murders. Is that correct?"

"Yes. A Miss Elsie Brown and a Mr Jack Ralph."

"Mm. Your case against Mr Furlong for the Elsie Brown murder is that he was spotted driving past her house in two directions minutes before she was killed. Is that correct?"

"At that point, yes."

"And the identification was made using a new computer system developed by your Technical Support team?"

Yes. It's a really very clever piece of kit. Even a few months ago we wouldn't have managed an ID."

"Quite so." Cedric placed rimless reading glasses on the tip of his nose as he studied one of the documents in the file. He spent several seconds reading before looking up and removing his glasses as he delivered his bombshell.

"Unfortunately, this new software system has not been approved for use in the courts and as such is inadmissible. No judge would allow a jury to hear or see any identification that came from this source."

Steve knew Terry's system wasn't approved.

"Listen Mr Spindle, I've had cases, where the prosecution have found ways of giving the jury information they perhaps shouldn't have had. A barrister worth his fee could get this identification read into the trial even if the judge gives him a reprimand."

"I am aware such tricks are played in court, but you are seeking an opinion and my opinion is that this identification cannot stand." Cedric Spindle was clearly standing his ground.

Steve knew this was not the time nor the place to argue. "What about the rest of the evidence?"

"It's all circumstantial. The fact this man uses a cosh and it's likely this was the weapon used helps but unless you can put the cosh in his hand inside the victim's house, it's pure speculation. I'm afraid your case, even with the identification evidence being permitted, looks weak. You don't have any physical evidence linking back to the victim."

Steve was about to answer when one of the canteen ladies arrived with coffee and biscuits. The interruption allowed the DCI to regroup his thoughts.

Cedric Spindle appeared to relish his drink and certainly didn't hold back on helping himself to the biscuits. Once things had settled down again, the DCI decided to try another approach.

"Look Mr Spindle, we know we have our killer. Surely a simple technicality won't prevent the CPS pursuing this killer and get him off the streets?"

Cedric shrugged and replaced his glasses on the end of his nose. He appeared to glance at the document on top of the file. "I'm sorry DCI Burt; my hands are tied. The identification evidence cannot be used, and without it, as things stand, I do not believe you will get a conviction in the Elsie Brown murder. You need more hard evidence."

Steve didn't dislike this funny looking little man; he knew he was only doing his job and Terry did say the system he'd used wasn't court approved. Steve had a sudden thought.

"It'll take months for any trial to start. What would your position be if we went ahead and charged Furlong now, and before the trial the new system *was* approved for use in court?"

Cedric was quiet and obviously thinking. "Well, I'd have to check on retrospective evidence. The defence would argue that their client was charged using flawed evidentiary techniques that were not approved at the time of his arrest. I'm not sure if a judge would allow the jury to hear the evidence but I'll ask one of my seniors on Monday. It's a nice legal point but I reiterate, my opinion is that even if the ID evidence were allowed, we would struggle to get a conviction. Your case lacks motive, and a jury would need to understand why Furlong killed Elsie Brown."

Steve knew he'd got convictions on less clear evidence but saw where Cedric was coming from.

Cedric once more shuffled his papers. "Now, the second killing, that of Mr Jack Ralph… I believe you may be on firmer ground. You have CCTV of the suspect's vehicle entering and leaving the village of Clare and you can place him at the murder scene at the time of the murder. Is that correct?"

"Yes."

"And you have a witness." Cedric shuffled through his papers looking for the facts he needed. "A Mr Alfred Cook who saw the suspect enter the convenience immediately before the victim was killed."

"Yes." Steve was feeling more positive.

"And you are sure the witness was shown only standard police arrest photographs from which to pick out your suspect?"

"Yes."

"And your witness is sure he saw the person entering the convenience carrying something wooden that may have been a cosh type weapon and the victim was killed by such a weapon?"

"Yes."

"Well, Mr Burt, it's not perfect and again it's circumstantial and without motive, but I believe based on the evidence in this file, I'd be happier to support a case against Mr Furlong for the murder of Jack Ralph rather than the case you mentioned for Elsie Brown. However, my considered opinion is that you do not proceed against Mr Furlong on either murder until you have a clear motive and some physical evidence."

The DCI sat back in a state of shock. He knew he had a case and evidence that a clever prosecution barrister could use to get a conviction, but he conceded that deep down he wasn't 100% sure of his ground and that's why he'd asked for a CPS opinion. Nonetheless he was disappointed and hadn't expected his case to so brutally pulled apart.

"Well Mr Spindle, it's not the opinion I was hoping for, but I hear what you say."

Steve was clearly indicating the meeting was over. Cedric Spindle fussed over his papers and took his time placing the file back into his new briefcase. He rose slowly and offered his hand to both Steve and Poppy.

"I'm sorry Mr Burt. I would have loved to tell you to crack on and take this murderer off the streets, but we're confined by the law. We don't want a verdict overturned on appeal because a clever prosecution barrister using insufficient evidence-based facts succeeds in getting a conviction."

After Cedric left, Steve and Poppy sat in silence.

"What are you going to do, sir?"

"I'm going to think, Poppy. We know Furlong is guilty and the CPS doesn't know about the link to the Nelson killing eleven years ago. That has to be the motive, but Furlong didn't kill Mrs Nelson." Steve was silent. Poppy, realising she couldn't add anything to the debate, left to return to her desk grateful Steve had allowed her to sit in on the CPS meeting.

After ten minutes of mental and ethical gymnastics, Steve phoned Matt Conway. He explained his meeting with Mr Cedric Spindle of the CPS.

"His advice is to gather more evidence before we arrest Furlong."

"Hell Steve, we have him bang to rights. These bloody lawyers know nothing about how we gather evidence. I'm sure we've got our man." Matt was clearly annoyed.

"I agree Matt but so far the ID evidence we've used on the Elsie Brown killing won't stand but I'll talk with Terry on Monday and see if he can get it approved quickly."

"That might help but what do we do on Monday. I hope I'm not sitting up here in Norwich for nothing."

"Mm." The DCI was deep in thought. After a long five seconds of silence, he was back talking into his phone. "We know we're light on physical evidence but the best way to get any is to search Furlong's house. To do that, we either need a search warrant that we probably won't get without admissible ID evidence, or we arrest him for Jack Ralph's murder and search his house that way."

Matt sounded concerned. "I'm keen to get a result but after what the CPS guy said, are you sure we should go near Furlong just now?"

"No, I'm not, Matt, but if we wait any longer, any evidence we might get could be lost." The DCI arrived at a decision. "Let's do it Matt. Bring Furlong in for questioning about the Ralph murder. Get a search warrant; Rory Gillen should get that. Give Furlong a knock at six a.m. on Monday as we said. Life's too short not to do what you think is right."

"Right, sir, consider it done. I'll see you later Monday morning at the Yard. I'm glad it's your decision and not mine but I'll back it all the way."

Steve sat back thinking, if this goes wrong he'd be lucky to keep his existing job, never mind promotion to Norfolk. He smiled and shrugged as he told himself the die was cast. He'd have to live with the consequences.

He headed out the door telling Poppy to enjoy the rest of the weekend. The look of concern on her face told the DCI she'd once again listened in on his conversations. The fact she didn't comment told Steve she was learning. He'd spend a relaxing family weekend and not worry about anything else until the following Monday.

Chapter Eighteen

The DCI had succeeded in enjoying the rest of his weekend. He'd arrived home to find Alison and Rosie dressed and ready for their picnic in the park. Saturday had been warm, and Steve and his family relaxed sitting on a travelling rug that he had pegged out on the grass. Rosie was now at the curious stage and had tried on a few occasions to crawl towards something of interest. Both Steve and Alison took great delight in her antics. She couldn't quite crawl and grew frustrated a few times and letting her parents know by letting out an ear-shattering yell.

Saturday evening in the Burt household involved sitting in front of the TV and not watching what was on. Armed with a glass of wine each, the DCI and his wife were content just to sit holding each other like newlyweds occasionally watching the TV screen and listening out for their daughter to declare her sleep was over. On this Saturday night, Rosie Burt slept right through the night.

Sunday saw Steve rise early at the insistence of his daughter who knew when it was time to eat. He enjoyed feeding Rosie and giving Alison a chance of an extra half hour in bed. He'd promised the previous evening to paint the hallway and knew he had no way out of it, so Sunday was spent putting paint on the walls and almost as much on himself.

Over an early breakfast on Monday morning, Alison touched on the subject of the job in Norfolk.

"I'm not sure. Everyone I've spoken to says it's a great opportunity and it is; it's just a big move to a strange place."

Alison secretly didn't want to move but she kept her feelings from her husband. She'd told herself several times that if he wanted to take the job, she would make the most of it.

"It's your decision, darling. You know I'll support you whatever you decide."

Steve rose from the breakfast bar, kissed Rosie, who was in her bouncer chair, on top of the head and having put his jacket on, kissed his wife and headed out for a week like no other.

The weekend weather had been fine but Monday, September the 25th was the opposite. Rain blew through on a strong northerly wind and fierce-looking dark clouds promised more rain to come. Steve took his car and for once used his reserved parking space in the garage below New Scotland Yard. It was 07.43 a.m. when Steve left his car and hurried to his office. As soon as he entered, his mobile rang.

"It's Matt, sir. We've got Neil Furlong. He wasn't very cooperative and isn't happy but he's in the back of a Suffolk patrol car. We're setting off now."

"Good man, Matt but I thought you were going in at six?"

Matt chuckled. "So did I but the minibus carrying the uniforms wouldn't start so we were late out of the blocks. No harm done. Also, I wanted a word with the CSIs to make sure they knew what we were looking for. The lead technician, a woman called Carol, seems pretty switched on. She's promised to let me have a preliminary ASAP." Matt was about to end the call. "Oh! By the way, Inspector Gillen was given a real roasting by his boss for allowing us to remove the suspect to the Met. Seems Rory knew it would be a problem, so he didn't tell him until he called him at home at seven this morning."

"I knew I liked that DI. Where is he now?"

"He's supervising the forensic and search teams. He's on the ball. Do you want him to do anything else?"

"No. Just say thanks and to keep in touch."

"Will do. Right, I'm off for a long drive south with a foul-mouthed brute in the back of the car. He didn't understand he was being taken in for questioning so I arrested him for driving a car with false licence plates. He's screaming lawyer."

The line went dead, and Steve calculated Matt should arrive with their suspect around noon. He decided to use the peace and quiet to gather his thoughts. Seated behind his desk, he allowed himself to randomly consider the implications of his recent decisions. He was ploughing ahead with the theory that Neil Furlong was guilty of killing both Elsie Brown and Jack Ralph despite the warning from the CPS. He knew this was a risky strategy, but he convinced himself that once he had Furlong in front of him, he would somehow get him to talk.

Steve thought about the events of eleven years ago and this bloke Andy strangling Tracy Nelson and disappearing back to London. He saw Elsie Brown hell-bent on solving the case and her boss, Jack Ralph, being bribed to make a murder charge go away, but who had bribed him? Steve assumed it was this Andy, but no one had checked. He wrote himself a note to have the source of the bribes checked again.

He envisioned Elsie somehow finding the missing witness statement and calling out Neil Furlong. But why? Furlong had nothing to do with Mrs Nelson's killing, but he had called this Andy after Elsie phoned, so it was possible that the London gangster had ordered Furlong to kill both Elsie and Jack Ralph. Whatever Elsie had discovered had clearly spooked Andy. Again, Steve asked himself the question: Why did Elsie phone Furlong about the eleven-year-old murder?

Then this headless corpse case; he felt he was somehow off the pace of the enquiry. Poppy had done her best to keep him up to date and Peter Jones was going through the motions, but Steve was unhappy about the slow pace of the investigation. There was clearly a Mafia connection and they'd identified both girls as daughters of Mafia gang members, but apart from identifying this Luigi, who hadn't left Sicily, and the German Gunther Schmitt, who may have nothing to do with the case, little positive progress had been made. Steve made another note to get himself fully briefed on the enquiry once he'd finished with Neil Furlong.

As always, the spectre of a possible move to Norfolk returned. He knew he wanted to take the job but something deep down was warning him off. Alfie was all for him taking it and Steve had to admit Callum Robertson, despite his reputation as a reformer, seemed to be an OK bloke. He knew he had to decide but not today. Today he had to get to grips with the Norfolk cases and hope his decision to proceed wouldn't backfire.

The DCI heard movement in the outer office and shook himself. The day was beginning.

His first visitor was Inspector Terry Harvey. Terry had stuck his head in just to say he was passing. Poppy was always glad to see her uncle and after an exchange of family gossip, Terry took the chair in front of Steve's desk.

"Nothing special, just passing. Thought I'd see how Norwich was."

Steve filled Terry in on his dilemma with the CPS and his decision to go it alone.

Terry was concerned. "I've seen officers do the same thing in the past Steve. In a few cases it didn't work out too well. Are you sure Furlong is your man?"

"I'm convinced of it." The DCI went on to explain what Cedric Spindle of the CPS had said about the Jack Ralph case and how the case against Furlong was stronger.

"But not strong enough?" Terry finished Steve's statement.

Both men sat in silence. Steve was sure Terry hadn't just popped in for a chat. He always had a reason for his actions. The DCI allowed the silence to linger, waiting for Terry to speak. Eventually he drew a deep breath and casually announced, "We've set the date for the wedding. You'll get your invitation but it's to be November the 10th."

Steve nodded. "About bloody time. I'll look forward to the stag do before the wedding."

"Yeah. There's something else." Terry seemed a little embarrassed. "What have you got Flo working on?"

The question came out of the blue. Steve had almost forgotten he'd asked Flo AKA Twiggy to look into the Italian company who used the same bird logo found tattooed on the two dead Italian girls.

"Oh, it's only background. Remember you found that Italian company that had the bird logo as its corporate sign. I only asked Twiggy to look into it."

"Well, she certainly is. She was at it all weekend. I hardly saw her. I think she's onto something, but she wouldn't tell me what. I think you'll get a visit later so be prepared. You know what she's like if she gets her teeth into something."

"Yes Terry, I do."

Terry Harvey stood to leave but hesitated at the office door.

"Go carefully with this Norfolk thing, Steve. It might bite you in an unpleasant place."

Detective Inspector Peter Jones and DC Mary Dougan were Steve's next callers. They at least had brought coffee. All three sat round Steve's small conference table.

"Peter, I'm still up to my neck in the Norfolk and Suffolk killings but I need to better understand where we are with the two Italian girls' murders."

Inspector Peter Jones clearly wasn't comfortable acting as SIO on these cases. He was doing his best but lacked experience and was young for his rank. Steve had no doubt he'd learn but he needed results now. On-the-job training for a senior detective wasn't good policy.

Peter took out his notebook and Mary already had the file in front of her. Before Peter could speak, Steve said, "Take your time Peter. Let's go over it from the beginning."

"Right. Well, you know the headless body was fished out of the Thames. All we had was a dead female, late twenties or so with a little bird tattooed inside her left arm. At the post-mortem, the pathologist said he thought she was southern European based on her skin tone. He also said he'd had to post another girl with the same skin tone and the same tattoo, six months earlier." Peter went on to explain how they'd discovered the identities of the girls. They were Mariola Scala and Sophia Paulo, both from Sicily. "We searched the flat the girls shared and found a postcard from someone called Luigi and traced him through the Italian police to Sicily where we found out that he's a Mafia gang member. An Inspector Alfonso with the sexy voice…" Peter smiled as did Steve knowing Poppy's description of the Italian "… told us this Luigi was best mates with a guy called Antonio Paulo who was a senior Mafia man and their bookkeeper/accountant. Seems the accountant vanished, leaving his family behind. We believe the headless girl is the daughter of this accountant and she came to London looking for her father."

Peter turned a few pages of his notebook before telling Steve that it seems she hadn't found him and was working as a low-rent prostitute presumably to make ends meet. He went on to say a German, called Gunther Schmitt, who was sometimes used by the Sicilian Mafia to trace people they were interested in, had been spotted outside the girls' flat and he had harassed a few pimps in the area asking if they knew Sophia Paulo.

"We have a working theory that the Mafia hired the German to find the girl so they could use her to put pressure on her father to give himself up. Seems the father disappeared about three years or so ago and apart from this Luigi, no one knows where he is. Inspector Alfonso said if it were suspected that Luigi was in contact with Antonio Paulo, he'd be dead meat. We're looking for the German as at least a point of contact with Italy but as far as figuring out why she was killed and had her head removed, we're stumped."

Steve sat back. He'd heard all this before and knew Terry Harvey's input to the case.

"But if they want to use the girl to get to her father, why kill her and why chop her bloody head off, meaning we can't easily identify her?"

"The Italian policeman said the Mafia always does its own killing so it must have been them who killed her. Maybe something went wrong; maybe she doesn't know where her father is. Remember the postcard said her father thought it was too dangerous for him to contact her so I'm presuming he knows where she lived but she didn't know where he was."

Steve was stroking his chin as he usually did when wrestling with a puzzle.

"What if it wasn't the Mafia who had arranged this? What if this girl was killed by a complete stranger? Are we getting too hung up on the Mafia connection?"

Peter Jones said nothing while Mary Dougan had been rearranging the papers in the file to match the summary Peter had just given.

"If it isn't Mafia, could it have been one of her punters? After all she seems to have been working low-rent." Mary looked at her male colleagues.

"It's another angle, Mary. It sounds as though we're at a dead end so let's follow up that thought. Get back out and talk to the pimps and the other working girls. See if any weird type has been around maybe looking for a girl with a sexy Italian accent.

"And what about the other girl? We don't seem to know much about her. Get Poppy to do a background search. She can talk with her Inspector Alfonso again and at the same time she can ask him if he can talk to this Luigi Repucci. I've a feeling we need to find the girl's father and Luigi obviously knows where he is."

All three stood to leave as Poppy appeared in the doorway.

"You don't have to talk about me behind my back, sir." Steve looked up. Poppy was at it again, listening in to his conversations and using "sir" as a defence. He sat back awaiting Poppy's comments.

"I'll call Alfonso, get details on the other girl and ask him to speak with Luigi about where Antonio Paulo is hiding. Is that it?"

"Yes, Poppy, but if Sophia Paulo came to London looking for her father it stands to reason he's somewhere here. Ask your Italian if he has a mugshot of the father. Let's see what he looks like."

Peter and Mary had left and as Poppy turned to go the DCI called out. "Poppy, eavesdropping isn't a nice thing to do."

"I agree, sir, but you learn a lot."

Steve doubted he'd change her, she was unique. Sitting by himself the DCI knew he would have to take over this Mafia case from his DI, *but* not yet. Neil Furlong was first.

***

Andrew Black had had a rough weekend. As Poppy was telephoning Italy, Andrew was drinking a health drink that was supposed to ease hangovers. He and David had been impressed by how quickly the drug dealers and distributors had accepted the new arrangements and the switch to tablets. The ones the brothers had met were all on board and based on the evidence of only one day, sales were up, and product was finding its way into even more venues. Despite his headache, Andrew was pleased and, as Chairman, could take credit for the apparent success.

He was sitting at his kitchen table in what he thought of as his grand manor. To the outside world it looked more like a garish pile of bricks built to the worst possible design. Andrew had designed it himself to look like the American White House. In this part of Essex such buildings weren't uncommon although Andrew's edifice was either on or very near the top of the list for bad taste. The reason for his bad head was that the pimps they were using had gone rogue and thought they could just take over the brothers' skin business when they'd learned the brothers were moving upmarket and getting into escort services. Some had tried to break away and run the girls for their own profit. Andrew looked at his red, sore-looking knuckles.

He and David had needed to pull these guys back into line and this meant a certain level of violence and, despite trying to keep it to a minimum, David had hospitalised two now former employees. Andrew, as Chairman, had decided to continue running his lower-end stable of girls whilst working with Jean Franco bringing in high-class escorts.

As he massaged his knuckles, he thought about his empire. The drugs and protection parts were going well, and he'd bring the pimps into line. He told himself he had to expect a few bumps along the road to expansion. This thought brought back the memory of Quentin Somersby and the way he had spoken to Andrew. Quentin was probably well connected but according to Jean Franco, he was only the marketing man whose job it was to maintain a steady supply of wealthy punters. Andrew and David were now the real power just as Jean Franco had said. Quentin Somersby had said he worked for the guy Antonio who was at their meeting in Amsterdam, but in Andrew's eyes, this man was insignificant. He hadn't contributed much to the meeting and Andrew was convinced he was a nobody who seemed only to look after the accounts.

He contemplated his health drink and tried to cancel out the drumming in his ears and head. As always after a good punch-up, his adrenaline level had spiked, and this meant he needed alcohol to calm himself down. He'd returned home in the early hours to find his wife waiting up and not in a good mood. The usual marital shouting match followed by something being thrown, and Andrew sleeping on the couch in the living room. It was now ten a.m. and his wife hadn't appeared.

The question of how to handle Quentin Somersby still weighed on his mind. He decided to talk to a couple of heavies he knew, who were ex-IRA. He was sure for five hundred quid they'd hurt him badly enough so he would know not to talk to Andrew, the Chairman, that way again.

David Black appeared at the back door and after a wave and a sympathetic smile, he helped himself to coffee and sat down. There was money to be counted today and this was always a pleasure for David.

Chapter Nineteen

Matt Conway made good time getting to New Scotland Yard at 11.53 a.m. Once he'd handed over his suspect for processing into the system and thanked his colleagues from Suffolk for their help, he made his way to the office of Special Resolutions on the eighth floor.

Poppy was busy typing but stopped to say hello and Matt tapped on Steve's inner office door frame and entered. He sat opposite his boss with a cheeky grin.

"That Neil Furlong's a piece of work. He asked me how much it would cost for me to make whatever we wanted him for to go away. The amounts he was talking about were like telephone numbers."

"Welcome to the real world of crime. I hope you said no?" Steve smiled and Matt shook his head.

"Our man's being processed, and I've told the desk sergeant to move him to the interview suites once he's finished. Should take about half an hour. I've also said to feed him before we start. An hour should do it."

"Good. Let's go and grab a bite in the canteen. We can talk tactics over a plate of grease and cholesterol, and I'll pay."

An hour later, Steve and Matt were sitting opposite Neil Furlong in interview room one. All six rooms were identical with a steel table bolted to the floor, four basic lightweight plastic chairs positioned two each side of the table and a heavy industrial twin recording machine fixed to the table. The walls were painted in a gloss cream colour and a mirror that allowed interested parties to view proceedings from a connected viewing room made up the fittings and fixtures of the room.

On entry Steve was surprised how dishevelled Furlong looked. The DCI had envisaged interviewing a smarter-looking character, but Furlong was far from elegant. His face was lean, sporting a few days' heavy beard growth; his dark thinning hair wasn't combed and looked dirty and greasy, while his shirt and jacket were badly creased as though he had slept in them for many nights.

After the usual preliminaries, and confirmation that he didn't want a solicitor present, the DCI began.

"Neil. Where were you on Monday the 11th of September between nine a.m. and eleven a.m.?

"Can't remember."

"Try. It's important. We're you near Elsie Brown's house in Stone for example?"

"Can't remember but I don't know an Elsie Brown so probably not."

Steve and Matt in their strategy session had decided to concentrate on Elsie's killing first.

"You're lying, Neil. That's not smart so I'll ask you again: where were you on the morning of Monday September 11?"

"Can't remember."

"And you claim you don't know an Elsie Brown?"

"That's what I said." Neil Furlong was looking smug, so the DCI changed tack.

"Neil, tell us how you killed Elsie Brown and Jack Ralph?"

Steve and Matt had decided if they were stonewalled by Furlong, then Steve would go straight in, all guns blazing. Matt had told Steve his impression of Furlong was that he wasn't too bright. Definitely a doer rather than a thinker.

"I never killed nobody. You can't prove a thing."

"Well, you see, Neil, I believe we can. We have you on CCTV."

"Rubbish. You've got nothing."

Steve, remembering the CPS' warning, had discussed with Matt over lunch how he was proposing to use the inadmissible evidence supplied by Terry Harvey. Steve explained that it might backfire in court, and if Matt weren't comfortable, he could excuse himself. The fact that Matt was here was Steve's answer.

"You own a white Land Rover Discovery?"

"Yep. So what?"

"A white Land Rover Discovery was seen at the time of both murders. Was it yours?"

"No and you can't prove it. I bet the number plates don't match mine 'cause I wasn't there."

"Well, you're right about the first killing because you stole a set of plates from a Ford Ka parked in Ipswich, but you got careless with Jack Ralph. You forgot to put the stolen plates back on."

Neil Furlong looked shocked. All he could say was, "No comment." He needed time to think.

"Not a very smart reply, Neil. Now I'm going to help you." Steve glanced at Matt who nodded.

"This is a picture of you driving your Land Rover Discovery passing Elsie Brown's house minutes before she was killed. If you look closely, you'll see there is no doubt that the driver is you." Steve knew showing Furlong this with a view to getting a confession on the strength of it was dodgy. He had made sure the recording machine wasn't switched on, based on Neil Furlong only helping with enquiries and so far, not being interviewed under caution. Furlong not requesting a solicitor had helped but the DCI knew his approach could end his career if it went wrong. Terry Harvey had told him the method used to get the picture wasn't approved for court use but Neil Furlong minus a solicitor didn't know that.

Furlong spluttered, "It's not me, it only looks like me."

"No Neil, it's you. You see we have some very clever kit these days. It's called photo recognition and believe me, this kit recognised you from this picture."

"So what? I'm only driving. I could be on my way to church for all you know."

"True. But we also have the lower part of your body stepping onto Elsie's path to her front door."

"You really are clutching at straws, aren't you, copper? Now you're saying you can identify me from my legs." Furlong laughed. "You're crazy."

The DCI knew he was fishing and understood why Cedric Spindle of the CPS had warned against this interview, but Steve knew he could get something out of this career criminal although it wouldn't be straightforward.

"Well Neil, we can tell the shoe size from the image, and we know you take the same size."

Matt Conway moved in his chair surprised by this statement that he knew wasn't true. They didn't know Furlong's shoe size nor the shoe size in the picture.

"Stand up please Neil."

Neil Furlong shrugged his shoulders and reluctantly complied. He was confused.

The DCI took the photograph of the lower body image caught on the CCTV and walked round the table. He examined the picture comparing it to the footwear Neil Furlong was wearing now. Given his appearance, Steve hoped he didn't change his attire very often and that might include his shoes.

Furlong was wearing black Nike trainers with white soles. The image on the photograph was an exact match.

The DCI gave a silent prayer as he said, "DC Conway, would you look at Neil's shoes and the photograph and tell me if they are identical?"

Steve knew none of this would stand up in court and that he was fishing, but it was possible that this image of a lower body belonged to Furlong.

"Well so what? This guy has the same good taste in trainers as I do. It still doesn't prove anything."

Steve was disappointed. He and Matt had hoped the image of him driving past Elsie's house would be enough to persuade him they had a case and allow them to move Furlong onto the identity of Andy and the nature of the calls from Elsie to him. They'd agreed not to touch this subject until they had Furlong on the defensive.

"Neil, you're not getting it. We can place you outside Elsie Brown's house just before she was murdered. We've got you driving by, and we have your legs going up her path. That's enough for any jury to convict." Steve was putting himself way out on a limb.

Surprisingly, Neil Furlong appeared to be weakening. He didn't immediately respond. Steve felt emboldened and, casting a glance at Matt, once more changed tack.

In an attempt to show Furlong they knew more than they actually did, Steve deviated from the strategy he'd agreed with Matt. "What did you and Elsie talk about on Friday the 8th of September? You had a lot to say based on the length of the call."

Neil Furlong looked surprised and without thinking blurted out "How did you know about…?" He stopped realising he'd said too much.

Steve ploughed on. "Neil, you didn't listen. We've got enough to charge you, but we want to give you a chance." The DCI continued to lie. "We know about the call you got from Andy the night before you killed Elsie when you were ordered to kill her and Jack Ralph. You see, Neil, we know you were working on Andy's instructions." Steve was using his friendly voice, the one that said 'I'm your new best friend; you can trust me'. He hoped Furlong was sufficiently confused as to believe the police knew everything.

Once more Furlong opened his mouth to speak. "But you can't know…" He fell silent, looking sorry for himself, clearly worried and confused.

Steve wanted to get this interview finished. He needed to formalise these proceedings and get everything back to a properly conducted interrogation. He couldn't afford to continue operating so far off the grid because he knew it could be professional suicide, but he needed Neil Furlong to cooperate. Looking at the suspect, Steve knew he had succeeded in getting Furlong to confess. He was elated and knew this was why he had overridden the advice from the CPS. The only way to break a case was by individual contact and that didn't always meet the criteria of the lawyers.

"Neil, thank you for being so forthright with us and putting your hands up for these murders."

For the second time during this interview, Matt Conway looked at his boss. Unless he had been listening to another interview, Matt hadn't heard Neil Furlong say anything of the kind. Matt remained silent hoping Steve knew what he was doing.

The DCI carried on. "We're going to formally arrest you and DS Conway here will read you your rights. Remember you can have a lawyer if you wish."

Steve prayed Furlong would stick to his not needing a lawyer strategy.

"Then we'll have a break and a nice cup of tea and after that we'll switch on the recording machine and start all over again, right from the beginning as though you hadn't already confessed. We'll ask you questions, and you'll give the answers. You know we have you bang to rights so there's no point in lying. Do you understand?"

"If I cooperate what happens to me?" Furlong looked a defeated man.

"That depends, Neil. We have a lot of questions for you. If you're honest and really cooperate, I'll have a word. Maybe get a few years shaved off your sentence but you did kill a copper, so it won't be easy."

"Yeah, but I had to kill the old witch, she—"

Steve raised his hand. "Not now Neil, after we've had our tea. OK?"

Neil Furlong sat back, defeated. Steve rose to leave and nodded to Matt who leaned forward and started to read Neil Furlong his rights. The uniformed officer who'd been standing inside the door was dispatched to get the prisoner a cup of tea. Steve and Matt headed back to the office.

"That was one gamble you took in there, Steve. If any of what went on gets out, we'd both be back directing traffic."

"You don't have to worry, Matt. If anything hits the fan, it's all down to me, as I said. Sometimes we have to bend the rules to get a result and once we get Furlong formally on tape then what just took place never happened."

The DCI smiled at his junior officer. "Now, let's get a coffee, to hell with tea. I need a caffeine shot."

***

Antonio Conti, having returned from his earlier board meeting, and having accomplished his resolution to take control of East Asian ventures with Tommy Lesson's assistance, was now sitting in his plush suite with Quentin Somersby. The pair were enjoying a beautiful cup of Asian tea that was specially blended for the Italian. Quentin Somersby was now dressed like the city gent he purported to be. His gay ensemble was reserved for his other, darker life that he tried to keep secret even from Antonio.

"So you met our new partners." Antonio was curious to learn what his right-hand man thought of his new colleagues.

"Yes. Where the hell did you get them?"

"Nothing to do with me. Jean Franco picked them. He thinks he can control them, meaning I'll have to take them in hand if they step out of line, but they'll stay loyal while the money suits them."

Quentin knew something of Antonio's long-term plans to oust Jean Franco.

"How do they fit with your plans?"

"They don't. They'll suffice as fall guys if anything goes wrong, and we can use them to help expand the skin business. We can step into their drug business at any time but let's leave them to get on with things just now. Once we're ready, we'll take them out."

"Right but why do we really need them?"

Antonio looked at Quentin as though he had asked a dumbest question for the tenth time. He sighed. "It's all about moving the money; it's an old Mafia trick. Most police forces believe if they follow the cash, they'll get to the people they are after. We keep the cash moving from hand to hand. Because it's cash it makes it almost impossible to follow. The more hands it goes through, the harder it is to trace."

"Yes." Quentin sat more upright. "I see." The pair sat enjoying their tea. Quentin eventually asked, "Where are you with the takeover?"

"It's progressing. I need to restructure a bit of the UK, but the basics are in place. You and I control the top holding company and all sixteen subsidiaries are now legally part of the top company. Jean Franco knows nothing about this. Of the sixteen, eight are just to clean up the money. The others are running legitimately and should make profit although we'll pass some currency through them as well. The only concern is the dilution we're taking on the cash. The UK tax system is vile. We're giving away almost 50% in taxes and fees to get the cash cleaned up."

Quentin Somersby laughed. "Don't tell me. I'm paying a fortune to HMRC on my declared income."

Both men chatted amiably on a variety of topics until Antonio brought them back to the brothers.

"They're supposed to be collecting and receiving money today. Go and check on them. Make sure they're not having difficulties. Your man should've picked up the cash from them by now. He has the pay-in details. He knows which accounts to pay into?"

"Yes, don't worry. You give me the pay-in schedule, and I get my guys to collect and pay in, no problems."

Antonio knew Quentin employed several couriers to keep the money moving and had devised a system where each Monday, Quentin received a printout of the companies under Antonio's control that were to receive large sums of money paid into their corporate accounts that week. Antonio spread the payments between his companies so as not to draw attention to any one in particular. So far it had worked well.

Quentin left and Antonio picked up the morning's newspaper to read while he finished his delicious tea. He scanned the front page and passed over a report in the lower right-hand corner, *HEADLESS GIRL'S BODY THOUGHT TO BE ITALIAN*.

***

Steve and Matt reconvened in interview room one. Neil Furlong had not only been given a cup of tea but a ham sandwich. To Steve's eyes he looked a defeated man who now realised his time was up. He was slouched in his chair and remained silent when the two officers entered and explained the procedure of how the interview would be conducted, why it was necessary to record everything that was said from now on. He continued to say nothing when asked again if he wanted a solicitor.

Steve was concerned that Furlong may be in some kind of shock but once the recording machine gave out a loud 'bleep' he seemed to come to and roused himself. Matt, once more for the tape, read him his rights and Furlong grudgingly acknowledged he understood.

The DCI sighed in relief. They were about to start what should be a standard interrogation and the events earlier could be forgotten.

Steve started slowly and professionally, ensuring standard procedure was followed and protocols were observed. He asked Furlong once more if he wanted a solicitor and again Furlong said no. Steve first took his suspect through the events leading up to Elsie Brown's murder. Steve had a burning question he wanted to put to Furlong but knew it had to wait.

"Now Neil, you are admitting you killed Miss Elsie Brown on Monday the 11th of September. Is that correct?"

At first Furlong seemed reluctant to answer and Steve left the question hanging in the air. The silence was intense as no one spoke. Eventually Neil Furlong from his slouched position in his chair shook himself, sat more upright and to the DCI's delight admitted he'd killed Elsie Brown.

"Why did Elsie call you on Friday September the 8th, and what did you talk about?"

Furlong was clearly trying to recall the conversation. His face contorted with the effort of trying to get his memory banks into gear.

"She phoned me out of the blue, said she was a copper investigating the killing of Tracy Nelson in Norfolk eleven years ago. She said I knew something about it."

Neil paused still obviously struggling to get his story into some sort of order. "I told her she was wrong, but she said she'd found evidence linking me to somebody called Andy. I knew she was fishing so I stonewalled her. Told her I knew nothing, and she should get lost. The old witch carried on though, saying she had proof that I'd helped Andy get away from the scene; she even told me the registration number of my car."

Steve interrupted Neil. "This Andy, he's the person who killed Tracy Nelson?"

"Yeah, I was with them and Andy's brother. We was having a good time, you know, a bit of booze and a bit of smack. Tracy was a real looker and liked to have horizontal fun if you know what I mean, especially after she'd smuggled some powder in from one of her trips for Andy. She was an air hostess you know."

"What happened?"

"Well, it was me, David—that's Andy's brother, Andy and Tracy. As I said, we were stoned and drunk. Andy persuaded Tracy to go back to her place and told me to drive them. David was gone and he passed out, so it was only me to drive. I was told to wait while Andy and Tracy went upstairs. I suppose it was an hour or so later that Andy came to the car asking me to go upstairs with him; he said there'd been an accident. I found Tracy dead on the floor. Andy had strangled her; he said it must have been an accident and he couldn't remember doing it. He was in a bit of a state so I got him fully dressed, moved the body onto the bed and wiped as many surfaces as I could to try to get Andy's prints off anything he'd touched. I took him back to the pub he'd been staying at, checked him out and drove him to London."

"What about his brother?"

"As I said, he'd passed out earlier, and I think he must have gone to his room 'cause he wasn't in the lounge when I took Andy back. I suppose he must have come to and figured his brother had left him to sleep it off."

"OK. So Elsie phoned you. Did she say she knew all of this?"

"No. She said she knew I was involved though."

"Neil, before we go on, who is Andy?"

Furlong suddenly looked uncomfortable. Steve saw he was hesitant so went on, "Neil, if I'm going to tell the judge you cooperated fully, I need you to tell me everything."

Neil blurted out, "Andrew and David Black, they're brothers. They run a drugs racket, out of London. Back then they were small-time thugs making a bit by selling drugs but now they have a proper big drugs thing in London."

Steve saw Matt making notes.

"How did Elsie Brown know you were connected to these brothers?"

"I don't know but she was a cop. I think she said she'd spent years matching up every Andy who was around Norwich at the time of the murder with what she called local villains. Maybe she knew I hung out with them when they came up to collect the drugs from Tracy. We'd have been pretty obvious back then, you know, getting stoned in public and Tracy got a lot of attention everywhere we went."

Steve wanted to move on. "Tell me about the call you made to Andy the night before you murdered Elsie."

Neil Furlong was again hesitant. He obviously didn't want to grass up the brothers, but the DCI had put him in a position where he had no choice. Steve was about to remind him that he had to tell everything when Furlong started to talk.

"The old witch called me that Sunday and said she could prove Andy had killed Tracy Nelson and I'd helped him. She said she had proof Andy had bribed a cop to get rid of some evidence and she was taking everything she knew to her bosses on the Monday."

Neil Furlong was clearly uncomfortable, and Steve noticed he had a tear in his eye as he told his tale.

"I phoned Andy and told him what she'd said. He told me to get rid of her and the DI he'd bribed. He said he was too busy to do it himself and it sounded urgent."

"And you just did what you were told?"

"More or less. You've got to understand I'm a junkie. I rely on Andy and David for my stuff and the stuff I sell to make a few bob. They've sort of looked after me over the years so yeah, I killed the two of them."

Over the next hour, Steve coaxed the full story out of Neil Furlong. How he had coshed Elsie in her home and Jack Ralph in the pub toilet. He admitted the brothers had paid him two thousand pounds for doing their dirty work. In the end, Neil Furlong bared his soul and confessed to the murders and had given a plausible theory as to how Elsie Brown had found him and put two and two together. This was the burning question Steve wanted to ask but Neil Furlong had answered it without being asked.

Once the interrogation was over, Neil Furlong was charged and processed. He would have a court appearance in the morning and be bound over. Matt made the arrangements and half an hour after charging their suspect, Matt was back in Steve's office.

"Good work, Steve. Looks like we've solved the current cases but also an eleven-year-old cold case. I suppose we're going to pick up this Andrew Black character?"

"Yes, but let's get Furlong tidied up first." Just as Steve said this his mobile rang. It was DI Rory Gillen from Suffolk Constabulary.

"We've got him, sir." Rory sounded on a high. "We found two wooden coshes in Furlong's house. Both have hair, skin and blood on them. The search team found them straight away, first thing this morning. I got them over to our lab with a hurry-up notice. They've just come back. They found tissue from both Elsie Brown and Jack Ralph on them. Looks like he used a different cosh on each of them. His fingerprints are also on both. Looks like physical evidence to me."

"Good work Rory. We've also got a confession and we've charged him. Can you get the coshes down here and file the report? It looks like it's over now."

"Will do and sir, bloody well done. That's a rapid result no matter how you tell it."

"Thanks Rory but it was teamwork."

Steve and Matt looked at each other and smiled.

"Good job boss but how do you think Elsie put it together?"

"I don't know Matt. We'll never know where she found that witness statement that DI Jack Ralph buried and according to Furlong, she said she'd tracked every Andy in Norwich on the date in question. I suppose she went for known associates living in Norwich and settled on Andy Black and Neil Furlong as a likely combination. Furlong did say back then that they had a high enough profile to stand out." The DCI shrugged. "I'm not sure we'll ever understand it, but Elsie Brown was a standout detective whose persistence got her killed."

Both men shook their heads in agreement and sat in silence for a few seconds almost as a mark of respect to the late Detective Sergeant Elsie Brown.

Steve broke the spell by saying, "We should arrange a bit of a party to celebrate once things settle down."

"Good idea."

"But before we do that, we'd better get this tidied up." Steve called for Poppy to come in.

"Poppy. Get the tape from our interview with Neil Furlong transcribed and into the file. Then send a copy to the CPS and the DPP plus the Heads of CID at both Norfolk and Suffolk Constabularies but wait until DI Gillen from Suffolk sends over his report on the murder weapons they found in Furlong's house."

Poppy stood with her hands on her hips looking directly at Steve. "It's all done, sir, everything's ready. I was just waiting for your order. The stuff from Rory Gillen came in as you were speaking to him."

Once again, Steve marvelled at how efficient Poppy was. He resolved to talk with her about becoming operational. She was certainly good enough.

Chapter Twenty

Steve looked at his watch after telling Matt Conway to have an early night. It was 4.42 p.m. but Steve felt it should be nearer nine p.m. He sat at his desk contemplating whether to get involved in the next case on his agenda, that of the two dead Italian girls.

Just as he'd decided to call it a day, Twiggy, as predicted by Terry Harvey, appeared at his door carrying a large bundle of papers.

"Right, DCI Burt, I hope you've had plenty of coffee because this is going to take time."

The DCI groaned inwardly knowing Twiggy would not give up. Terry had told him she'd worked on something for him all weekend and Steve knew he'd asked her to look into the Italian company with the little bird logo that matched the dead girls' tattoos.

As Steve stood up, he noticed a figure lurking behind Twiggy. Seeing he'd been spotted he worked his way around Twiggy and her large bundle of papers and entered Steve's office. Twiggy placed her papers on the office conference table before introducing the stranger.

"Steve, this is Rupert Carey. He's my boss over at Treasury."

Twiggy had been recruited into the Financial Crimes area and she had become a civil servant working for and trained by HMRC. She was on permanent secondment to the Met's Financial Crimes section, but Steve assumed she still had to report to the Treasury from time to time.

Mr Carey held out his hand and after a brief introduction, Steve asked his guests to be seated. He had no idea why Mr Carey was here nor what his role at Treasury was. He saw a man in his mid-thirties with an air of natural authority that usually came from having had a privileged upbringing. He was dressed in the civil service uniform of dark suit, white shirt and, in his case, a tie that Steve thought represented one of the Cambridge colleges. He was of average height and had a full head of dark hair that was turning grey at the temples. The DCI decided not to be too inquisitive at this stage and let Twiggy do her thing. Having been briefed by Twiggy many times in the past, Steve knew she loved to drag out a story and was inwardly afraid he wouldn't get home any time soon.

He couldn't have known how right he was.

***

Andrew Black looked up at the large clock hanging from the wall of the pub he and David were sitting in. Quentin Somersby had asked for a meeting and wanted to see the figures for the cash that had been either delivered to or collected by the brothers. He had chosen this downmarket drinking pub and at five p.m. exactly, he arrived standing in front of the brothers dressed like a regular businessman.

"Have you got the numbers?"

David Black, keen to be seen to be efficient, produced a ledger from his briefcase and opened it at the correct page. It showed receipts from the drugs business on one half of the left-hand page and receipts from the escort business on the other half. Quentin quickly scanned the numbers already knowing what the totals should be. He was surprised to note in both columns the numbers were higher.

"Good. And one of my associates has called on you and collected the cash?"

David acknowledged he had.

"Very good. This is a promising start, boys; keep this up and you'll both be very wealthy."

Andrew had already calculated their commission at 10% which was stored in their safe, and knew Quentin Somersby was correct about their upcoming wealth. What neither Quentin nor David knew was that Andrew had already put a contract out on Quentin Somersby with the ex-IRA soldiers. Their instructions were to seriously hurt this rude lackey. Andrew had developed a pathological hatred of Quentin and stared at the man with unconcealed loathing. He wouldn't talk to Andrew in such terms again. Andrew continued to sit in silence laughing inwardly at the image of Quentin maybe not being able to talk ever again.

"This is a good start, but don't forget, you have to keep pushing the pills. The first of the girls will be here in ten days; have you got accommodation sorted out?"

"Yes, Quentin." David realised Andrew was in a sulk and he had to do all the talking. "We've got six upmarket apartments ready. The girls will be OK in these places."

"Good, keep it up." Andrew thought Quentin was acting like a superior businessman and he didn't like it; *he* was the chairman. He remained silent showing his disdain for Quentin Somersby.

Quentin carried on. "I'll report back to Antonio that you're fully on board and up to speed. Have a drink tonight and celebrate your first payday." Quentin, who hadn't sat down in the pub, turned and walked away.

Andrew followed him with his eyes wondering when the IRA thugs would strike.

***

At exactly the same time Quentin Somersby arrived at the pub to meet the brothers, Twiggy started her explanation as to why she and Rupert Carey were in Steve's office. Rupert had given Steve one of his business cards. It showed Rupert was Head of Money Laundering and Investigations at the Treasury.

"Right Steve, I looked up the company with the little bird logo. It's called Italian Resources but despite the name, its headquarters are in Amsterdam. I couldn't get very much on it, so I checked with Companies House and found Italian Resources is a cover for a UK listed business called Mayflower Contracts Ltd." Twiggy rose and went to Steve's whiteboard. She wrote at the top *Italian Resources* and immediately below this she penned *Mayflower Contracts* and turned to her audience.

"Now, Mayflower is a holding company responsible for sixteen other businesses." Twiggy drew sixteen lines fanning out from the second company on the board, Mayflower Contracts. At the end of each line, she drew a box.

Rupert Carey saw the confused expression on Steve's face. "We realise, DCI Burt, that this has nothing to do with any cases you may be working on, but Florance thought as you'd introduced this to us there maybe something to be learned by us giving you this briefing."

"Yes, I see. It's true in the past Twiggy... I mean Florance, has helped with our cases when there has been a financial element we didn't understand, so I appreciate the input." Steve turned in his seat. "Poppy?"

Steve knew Poppy would be in the outer office listening to everything and decided as she knew more than most about the Italian girls' murder cases, she should sit in. Steve introduced her and she took a seat at the head of the table just as before. Again, Steve inwardly laughed. Poppy was some girl.

Twiggy reviewed her earlier comments to bring Poppy up to speed, then carried on.

"Mayflower was set up around three years ago and seems to have been funded through the top company, Italian Resources, but here's the thing, the directors and beneficial owners of Mayflower appear to have nothing to do with Italian Resources and the funds seem to have come from a few dubious sources in the Caribbean, Panama and Cyprus. It's as though the two businesses exist independently but the money comes from the top company and a lot of it."

Twiggy walked away from the whiteboard and pulled several copies of a document from one of her files. She retained them in her hand as she once more stepped towards the board.

"The guy who's the CEO and the main shareholder in Mayflower is called Antonio Conti; he seems to be Italian. The only other director is someone called Quentin Somersby who is a Brit."

Twiggy paused to gather her thoughts. "The strange thing is," She held up the document, "this is a list of sixteen companies this guy Conti has either bought a majority stake in, or businesses he's set up from scratch in the last three years. Eight are pure start-ups and each one was making significant profits from day one. I'm not talking a few thousand pounds. These companies were immediately generating millions in turnover and in profits."

Rupert Carey interjected. His clipped and well-toned voice was a pleasure to hear; a wonderful speaking voice. Steve noted Poppy was impressed given that she fluttered her eyelids every time the man from the Treasury looked in her direction.

"You see Mr Burt; most new start-ups take a while to get going. It's almost unheard of for any new business to generate the size of profits these companies did in their first year unless not everything is above board. One of them, called East Coast Silks Ltd, turned over sixty million pounds and declared a profit of 27 million in its first year. It has increased these numbers in each of the following two years. They're quoted as producing silk ties from a factory in Aberdeen. That's a lot of ties."

Twiggy wrote *East Coast Silks* at the end of one of her sixteen lines. She took up where her boss had finished. "Another new start-up, Theatre Hotels Group, has posted full occupancy rates on each of its ten hotels. It's amazing because no hotel chain we know of operates at 100% capacity. This group, right from the start, has been showing well over five million pounds a month in receipts and declaring just over one million in profits."

Twiggy wrote the hotel business at the end of another leg of the fan stemming from Mayflower Contracts. She continued once she saw everyone appeared to understand. "We haven't had a chance to look at every start-up other than a quick glance at what's been filed. All eight start-ups report on time, file their returns on time, and pay their not inconsiderable tax bills, on time. On paper, all eight are perfect, well-run businesses, until you look a bit deeper. The only other start-up I've looked at is called Stringer Health Clubs. It started doing business two years ago. In their accounts, they show twenty-five sites all running at capacity and each site is turning over £4 million a month and generating profits of over one and a half million a month. Like the others, their Companies House file is clean, everything in order."

Twiggy gave one of her smiles, lighting up her face. "That is, until this morning, when I did a search with the Land Registry and checked the locations of these clubs. I called Burnley Local Authority to see if the planning had been approved and was all above board. The Burnley club was the latest one to open. It seems Mr Conti bought an old mill for cash two years ago and hasn't applied to do anything with it. The registration is in the name of Mayflower and according to Companies House, the Burnley club is the best yet. It's running at a weekly profit of just over one million pounds."

Steve started to stroke his chin and Twiggy knew he was seeing something in his mind's eye.

"So you're saying an old mill is filing accounts showing weekly profits of over a million?"

"Yes, and before you ask, it's not possible. I took a look at the accounts for this one club and their banking is in order and their cash deposits are made regularly twice a week, but guess what?" Twiggy didn't wait for a reply. "The cash is always paid into a London branch of NatWest."

"And you're thinking it should be paid into the Bolton branch?" Steve was fully alert.

"Yes."

"I can see there's something hooky about these start-ups but what about the existing businesses you say they have bought into?"

"Ah, that's not so straightforward, Mr Burt." Rupert Carey had taken up Twiggy's narrative. "From what little time Florance has had to check, it seems every business Mr Conti has invested in has flourished." Rupert sat back and placed his palms on the table and with a wide grin, started another tale.

"He bought into a second-division football club eighteen months ago. Florance checked the accounts, and they were struggling, losing over four thousand pounds a week. Since Mayflower bought the club, the gate receipts have multiplied three hundredfold; the club accounts show they are making handsome profits, but they are still in division two despite on paper buying overseas players for millions. Their gate receipts are the same as Manchester United although their ground is only licensed to hold five thousand."

Steve sat back. "Well Mr Carey, it does seem a bit odd."

"To say the least, but it doesn't end there. Conti has bought into some of our biggest companies but not as Mayflower but as himself. He's the largest shareholder in the Hazel Group. You know, Thomas Lesson's company, but we got a quick look at all of Conti's businesses, and it looks like he's recruiting respectable public figures onto the boards of his more dubious companies. Remember we haven't had long and Florance has been at it all weekend and today, but Thomas Lesson is a director of a company called East Asian Ventures. We haven't had time to do any real digging, but it seems our Mr Conti is trying to present an even more respectable front."

"Since he bought into Tommy Lesson's business, what's happened to their profits?" Steve knew of Tommy Lesson as a man of the people and a friend and confidant to senior politicians. It was rumoured he was the biggest contributor to the governing party."

"We don't know yet."

Twiggy had been sitting listening to her boss and the DCI. "Steve, it looks as though this Antonio Conti is up to his neck in dirty money. He's clearly money laundering but in great lumps. His Mayflower business is the biggest privately owned company in the country. If he went public, it would go straight into the Top 100 companies. We've a lot of work to do but we wanted to let you know we'll be on Conti's case and didn't want to cut across anything you were investigating that might touch Conti."

As Twiggy finished talking, Poppy abruptly stood and left. Twiggy looked at Steve with a quizzical look that said *was it something I said?*

"I'm not sure anything you've told me moves our murder cases forward. We have two dead Italian girls that both have that small bird tattooed on their inner arm. Apart from the fact that your Mr Conti is Italian, and this is the logo they use for their businesses, I don't see any connection."

The debate about the logo, the girls and how Mayflower had managed to grow so quickly ran on for half an hour. They all agreed there was a link, but no one could understand how things fitted except that Rupert and Twiggy had a definite case to work on.

Rupert Carey was about to say something when Poppy breezed in and took her seat. Without any preamble she launched into what she had to say.

"I'm sorry sir, but you're wrong. Remember one of the girl's father, was a Mafia accountant and he'd run off about five years ago?"

Steve looked curious. "Yes."

"And remember he was called Antonio but not Conti, he was called Paulo?

Steve wondered where Poppy was going with this. "Yes."

"I've just checked with Inspector Alfonso. He checked with the Italian National Register. No Antonio Conti left Italy five years ago who has not returned, but an Antonio Paulo did leave and has not returned.

Alfonso is sending a picture of Antonio Paulo and I've been on the police only immigration site and called up a picture of Antonio Conti. What if they match? What if Antonio Conti is the missing mafia accountant Antonio Paulo?"

The three other people round the table looked at Poppy in silence.

Steve leaned forward. "If the pictures match, Rupert, then we do have an interest in this case."

It was now 7.48 p.m. and the DCI had had enough for the day. Poppy looked as fresh as ever and suggested to Twiggy they might go for a drink. Twiggy apologised saying she had wedding plans to make. As Poppy looked at Rupert he said, "Yes, a drink or even dinner would be in order. It looks as though our departments may be working closely in the next few days."

Poppy was beaming as she and Rupert left. Twiggy walked with Steve to the main entrance and as they went their separate ways, they promised to touch base in the morning.

Chapter Twenty-One

Tuesday September the 26th started with high winds and driving rain. As the DCI sat in his kitchen looking out at the weather, he reflected it matched his mood. He'd arrived home late yesterday evening hoping for a quiet night and an early bed. His brain was swirling like a carnival ride, and he needed space to think through the conversation with Twiggy and her boss, plus he would have to decide what to do about Andy Black and the eleven-year-old murder in Norwich. Alison had his evening meal prepared and as he ate, she asked if he'd decided to take the Norfolk job.

In the years they'd been married, Steve could not recall them ever having any serious domestic tiffs but last night had proven too much. He explained that he was too busy to think about the Norfolk job and he had a few things like murder and money laundering to deal with. Alison said she needed to know what he was going to do as she had plans to make; he'd replied he didn't know, and the conversation quickly led to stony silences all round and a frosty 'good night'.

This morning Alison was feeding their daughter, but an air of silence and petulance could be felt between the pair. Steve had tried to repair things by saying they'd discuss it tonight, but this peace offering was met by a cold stare and a shrug that said, 'If you like'.

A despondent DCI set off for his office. He drove this time because of the weather and arrived early only to find Poppy was already at her desk. Steve tried to put his domestic issue behind him but found he couldn't settle. He'd never had harsh words with Alison and vowed to get things back to how they had been before the question of promotion to Norfolk came up.

Poppy was bouncing. She was dressed in a new trouser suit and she'd somehow managed to do her hair so it looked as though she had come straight from the hairdresser.

"I have news." She flourished a piece of paper. "First, Alfonso in Italy spoke to this bloke Luigi; he's the friend of the Mafia accountant who did a runner." Poppy looked at Steve before continuing. "Luigi refused to say where Antonio Paulo was. He said it was too dangerous for Antonio and for himself, so we won't get any information from that quarter."

Steve sat wondering how much more Poppy had to tell him. "I've got the picture from Italy of Antonio Paulo and the Immigration shot of Antonio Conti." Poppy laid them side by side on Steve's desk. "It's the same man, boss; we've found the dead girl's father." Poppy was obviously jubilant. Steve examined the grainy photographs and had to agree. Antonio Conti was the Mafia accountant who was on the run.

"Good work, Poppy. The others should be in soon. Why not get four coffees and we'll catch up on these Italian murders? Matt won't be in for a while. He's in court looking after Furlong's arraignment."

"Will do." Poppy skipped off, obviously happy. Steve speculated about her dinner date last night with Rupert Carey but decided not to pry. He needed his brain concentrating on the matters at hand.

Although it was only 8.33 a.m., Steve called Twiggy who answered on the first ring.

"Can you come to a briefing at nine this morning in my office?"

"Of course. I've got a few bits following last night to look at but sure, I'll be there."

The pair talked about domestic matters for a few minutes before they hung up.

Steve had his A4 pad in front of him and he doodled trying to arrange his thoughts in some sort of order. He started with the Neil Furlong case. He wrote the name, put a line through it and told himself that was finished. Elsie Brown and Jack Ralph's killings were solved.

Below Furlong's name he wrote *Andy Black* and *Tracy Nelson*. Steve spoke to himself out loud. "We think Black killed Nelson eleven years ago and we have Furlong's testimony."

Beside Black's name he once more wrote *Brown* and *Ralph*. "We know Andy Black ordered the hit."

As the DCI sat back, Poppy appeared with the coffee. Steve sipped it slowly and wrote *ARREST ANDY BLACK FOR NELSON MURDER AND CONSPIRACY IN BROWN AND RALPH CASES*. He saw the connection and felt he could make a case against Black but first he had to understand where the Mafia and the dead Italian girls fitted into the puzzle. Was it just a coincidence and the Mafia had nothing to do with the murders?

Steve started doodling again. He wrote *Mariola Scala*, the first Italian girl. He remembered he'd asked for a background check. "Poppy, did you get anything back on Mariola Scala, the first Italian girl?"

Predictably, Poppy instantly appeared in the doorway. "Yes and no. I'm waiting for a call from the Italian Embassy. All I've got is she arrived here from Italy over a year or so ago. She had no criminal convictions, never been in trouble but strangely she doesn't have a National Insurance number here and doesn't seem to have had a job. I've got a general appeal for information circulating all the temp agencies in case she was working cash in hand, but the landlord confirmed both girls paid their rent on time, so money was coming from somewhere. Remember we don't think the other one started selling her body until after her flatmate was murdered."

"So you think Mariola had money from somewhere that supported both girls and when she disappeared the other one, Sophia, needed money and started on the game?"

"Looks that way but I'll chase up the Italian Embassy."

Steve could hear his team arriving in the outer office and stopped his scribbling. He knew anything he deduced by scribbling on his pad would also come out during the meeting.

Twiggy arrived carrying her usual bundle of papers and sat at Steve's conference table beside Mary Dougan. Peter Jones sat opposite Mary, and Poppy placed herself without ceremony once more at the head of the table. She had her laptop opened and was keying something into it before looking up and sitting with a look of anticipation on her face. Steve took a chair at the opposite end of the table from Poppy so as to appear that he was running the meeting. It also put him nearer the whiteboard.

"OK, folks, let's get started. We have the dead girl who was decapitated and found in the Thames. We now know she was Sophia Paulo and that she was Italian. We also think she arrived in the UK over twelve months ago to look for her father who we now know is using the name Antonio Conti. His real name is Antonio Paulo and he's on the run from the Sicilian Mafia. He was the mob's accountant and according to the Italian police, he may have absconded with Mafia secrets, and they want to find him.

We believe a German private detective called Gunther Schmitt may have been hired by the Mafia to find Antonio's daughter as a way of getting to him. We know he has been rousting pimps in the area she seems to have plied her trade in, so we assume this German knew she was working as a prostitute." Steve stopped to draw breath and think of his conclusions.

"Do we think the Mafia killed this girl if the German found her?" He left the question dangling, expecting answers from around the table.

DI Peter Jones was first to answer. "It's a possibility. Mary and I spent most of yesterday chasing up the pimps in the area and none of them claimed to know this Italian girl but confirmed the German had been asking about her. The thing that doesn't make sense is why behead her if the killing was designed to draw the father out of hiding? If we couldn't identify her then he wouldn't know the body was his daughter."

Poppy, from the opposite end of the table, chipped in. "We know from Inspector Alfonso of the Italian police that the Mafia never subcontract their killings. They like to do it themselves. We've checked out Mafia activity in London and the Crime Coordination Unit have no record of any extra Mafia activity in London so it's likely she wasn't killed by them."

Steve enjoyed Poppy's summary and was about to say so when Twiggy began. "You've tracked down the father Antonio Conti to London but he's not hiding. All he's done is change his name. We believe he's involved in a huge money laundering business and from what we've discovered so far, he's using Mafia tactics to launder millions from criminal activities. As the Mafia's accountant, he'd know exactly what to do but if you found him then so could the Mafia. Why haven't they and if they have, why kill his daughter and not him?"

Steve stepped in. "Let's not get too complicated. From what we know I think it's likely whoever killed Sophia Paulo wasn't mob connected so we're looking elsewhere for her killer. But where?"

Mary Dougan spoke up. "Her lifestyle as a cheap prostitute would have left her open to all sorts of weirdos. We checked the local pubs to see if anyone recognised her but again, we drew a blank. However, she was getting her punters she wasn't circulating in normal places. She must have been a street corner hooker meaning anyone she went with could have killed her."

The DCI had a sudden flash. "Hold on Mary, that's very good. We haven't looked at street CCTV. If she was finding johns on street corners, maybe we can get her on CCTV. Poppy, get Terry to check out all CCTVs that look onto streets where working girls are known to look for trade. We might get lucky."

Poppy typed into her laptop and after a few minutes looked up. "Done. I've sent him an e-mail."

Twiggy started to recount some of the discussions she'd had the previous evening and explained how Antonio Conti appeared to be running a multimillion-pound money laundering business. "I don't see how this is connected other than he's the dead girl's father, especially if you don't see a Mafia connection."

"Not at the moment, but we know from experience there's no such thing as a coincidence. We must keep an open mind. Now what about the other girl, Mariola Scala; do we think the murders are connected?"

No one spoke. Everyone round the table looked to be in deep thought.

"The killings were different. The only thing connecting them is they were both Italian and had the same tattoo." Once again Mary Dougan spoke up, but as she spoke, she realised her words wouldn't move the case forward.

Peter Jones was next. "We think the tattoo is a Mafia symbol, but we don't have a connection with this killing to the Mafia."

"No, we don't. Poppy get back to your Italian policeman. See what he can tell you about Mariola Scala."

"I already have. It's in the file, boss." Poppy was showing a cheeky grin. "He told me, her family are middle ranking and would only just qualify for the little bird tattoo. She left Sicily at the same time as the other victim without her family's blessing. Her father is an enforcer and a good Mafioso. Seems it had been arranged for her to marry the son of a senior gang member, but she didn't like the idea. If she had her father would have moved up the rankings."

Poppy stopped talking and from her expression it was obvious that she'd had a thought. "Don't the Mafia have an honour thing? You know, save face at all costs. Suppose the fact that Mariola ran instead of marrying this son was reason enough for them to take revenge?"

"It's an idea, Poppy, and a good one, but it doesn't connect the two murders."

The DCI knew they were getting nowhere. He realised he needed a break in the cases but couldn't see where it might come from. "All we have is that both girls were from Italian Mafia families; they arrived together and shared a flat. The fact that both have been murdered cannot be a coincidence." With an air of frustration Steve stated the obvious. "We must be looking for the same killer. Peter, look into Mariola Scala's background again. Where and if she worked, who her friends were, bank account and credit cards, holidays, hobbies, the works. She was the first victim so she may hold the key."

Peter Jones made notes and nodded.

"Right. Let's finish there. Poppy, you've got your tasks and follow up on your idea. It's a long shot but check with Immigration. see if any Italians arrived from Sicily the week before Mariola Scala was killed. Peter, you and Mary check in with Terry Harvey once he's got any CCTV footage. You know what Sophia Paulo looks like so you may spot her. Let's meet again tonight at five to see where we are."

Everyone filed out except Twiggy.

Twiggy was playing with the ribbon that was keeping one of her files together. "Do you think this Antonio Conti's involved in your murder cases?"

The DCI sat back almost lounging in his chair. He tried to relax by placing his hands behind his head. "I don't know, Twiggy. This whole thing's a mystery but it looks like we've given you enough work."

Twiggy smiled at her old boss. "No kidding. From what I've seen this could be one of the biggest money laundering operations in Europe. One of my team has picked up another dodgy looking set of accounts and…"

Steve laughed. "Listen to you, Miss Florance Rough. One of my team. You've come a long way, Twiggy, in the past three years."

Twiggy paused to reflect and allowed herself to become nostalgic. "Yes. I suppose I have but it's all thanks to you. If you hadn't solved that first impossible case, we were all out on our ears. I sometimes think back to that case and remember it as one of the best times of my life as a police officer. I remember you treated me like a real cop."

Steve was feeling relaxed and decided to confide in Twiggy. "Twiggy, keep this to yourself but I've had an offer to become head of Norfolk CID, but I'm not sure."

Twiggy's mouth opened. It took a few seconds for any kind of sound to appear. "That must be a Chief Super's rank. What's to think about?"

"I know, everyone tells me I should take it. You know the usual once-in-a-lifetime opportunity and so on, but I'm happy here and Alison has her medical practice."

Twiggy became serious. "You deserve this. You have the skills to be great head of CID. Listen Steve, you've seen other people move on and up. Look at Andy Miller. He's now a DI with the National Crime Agency. When you got him he was a fairly useless individual, but you helped him find his feet. Look at me with my staff. If you hadn't mentored me, I'd be nowhere." Twiggy was getting into her stride. "The Cap is happy in his own little corner of the Force." Twiggy giggled. "I'm not sure what he's doing but you found him a home that suited him."

Steve thought back to DI Abul Ishmal. He was one of the original officers assigned to the Special Resolutions Unit that Steve had headed up since its inception. The DCI had christened him 'The Cap' due to his surname being similar to the Ishmael in Moby Dick. He recalled the joking Abul with fond memories but equally remembered he was prone to being lazy and a bit slipshod. Once the 12th floor had suggested he might be better redeployed, Steve hadn't objected.

"Yes, you're right of course and I know I'd be a fool not to take it. Thanks Twiggy, I appreciate your thoughts. Now..." Steve pulled himself up in his chair. "What about this case? I suppose I can't see us having a role. I can't see Antonio Conti killing his own daughter and if Poppy's right about the other victim being a Mafia killing, well..."

The phone on the DCI's desk rang. He stood to answer it, listened and replaced the receiver. "You and I are summoned to the twelfth floor. Alfie Brooks wants to see us both."

***

In a plush wood-panelled room on the first floor of the Treasury Building in Whitehall, an unlikely gathering was meeting, just as Steve and Twiggy arrived in the office of Commander Alfie Brooks. It was 09.57 a.m. on Tuesday September the 26th.

Stephanie Clarkson, a senior civil servant with over twenty years' service, had called the meeting. Everyone invited to attend was senior to her, but she knew they would come. She had been instrumental in providing them with wealth way beyond their expectations. Stephanie was the first to arrive and helped herself to coffee and a biscuit. Miss Clarkson was an attractive woman in her early fifties with what could still be described as an hourglass figure. She didn't work out, drank little, didn't smoke, and only ate healthy meals. She was a career civil servant having been recruited straight from university. Initially her career had followed a predictable path with regular promotions and as she approached her mid-thirties, she was the most senior woman in the Service running her own department. She was seen as bright, competent and not short of solutions to problems.

However, her career had faltered, and she now knew that she had reached her level of seniority. She had been married twice but on both occasions her desire for promotion and the long working hours necessary had taken their toll. Her second marriage only lasted nine months. Although her career had stalled, she was still sought out by her more senior colleagues for her opinions and suggestions, most of which they used when briefing government ministers and claiming her insights as their own. She ruefully thought that no major government financial event that had taken place over the past ten years had been made without some input from her.

Stephanie had been approached by Antonio Conti five years earlier, shortly after he had disappeared from Sicily and before he had met Jean Franco. As an ex-Mafia money man, he knew the importance of having someone on the inside of government financial institutions. Stephanie had been willing to act as an unofficial consultant on a generous retainer that was paid in cash into a Gibraltar bank that Antonio had set up for her. Although nothing was said that could be construed as illegal,

Stephanie knew she was expected to protect Antonio and his businesses. As far as she was concerned, she was simply building her pension pot to give her a more luxurious retirement in the Caribbean.

She knew such an arrangement wasn't allowed but decided the rewards outweighed the risks and as a senior member of the Treasury, she was well equipped to advise Antonio without drawing attention to herself. She had deliberately set up a series of junior members of the service to pass on gossip and rumour to her in order that she might know if anything was festering that might affect her arrangement with Antonio. It was such a piece of gossip that had led to her calling this meeting.

As she sat at the conference table, two men arrived at the same time. One was Sir Pollock Hargreaves, Senior Private Secretary to the Chancellor of the Exchequer. The other was Sir Brandon Lamping, in charge of the department responsible for ensuring that the taxable income going into the Exchequer was maximised. Both men had joined the service at the same time and were friends. They were also powerful Whitehall mandarins.

"What's this all about Steph?" Sir Pollock didn't look happy. "I'm a busy man and can't be called to meetings like this at the drop of a hat."

Sir Brandon, having spotted the coffee, poured two cups and joined his colleagues at the table.

"Don't worry, Brandon. All will become clear. We're only waiting for one more member."

Sir Brandon made a face as he tasted the coffee. It wasn't very good. "Look Steph, we need to get on and I for one can't spend time on something I know nothing about."

"If you just hang on all will be clear."

As Miss Clarkson finished talking, a tall figure in police uniform entered. Both knighted civil servants recognised him instantly as Assistant Commissioner Hayden Giles of the Metropolitan Police Force. He refused the offer of coffee and, with obvious irritation, took a chair at the table. He too was busy and said he should be somewhere else. Stephanie Clarkson sat back examining her male colleagues. She had no papers in front of her and stated before she opened the meeting that no notes or minutes would be taken. As she hesitated, looking at the door, another figure appeared that once more everyone recognised. He was

Darius Hackney-Law, and he was a senior member of the ruling party and the party's treasurer.

Once again, the new arrival stated he was too busy to deal with any nonsense Stephanie might want to talk about but took a chair.

Stephanie noted that all four of her male colleagues had claimed pressure of work but surprisingly, they had all turned up. She allowed herself a sly smile.

She began. "Over the past few years, all four of you have benefitted in some way from the generosity of my benefactor, a Mr Antonio Conti. Pollock, you receive a generous allowance each month to support your wildlife charity and we know most of the money is spent upkeeping that great pile of bricks you call a stately home."

Sir Pollock spluttered in disbelief. "Now hang on Steph, that is confidential, and it was you who arranged Mr Conti's donation. It was never stipulated that everything should be spent on the charity."

"Agreed. But three million pounds over two years is a lot of nature watch."

Sir Pollock was about to launch into a defence before Stephanie raised her had. "It's of no consequence, Pollock. I am simply reminding you, as I am reminding Brendan, that the interest-free loan he was given eighteen months ago to buy his monster property in Kensington is not required to be paid back." Stephanie leant forward. "How much was it, Brendan?"

A sheepish Sir Brendan Lamping stared at the tabletop. "I can't remember, but where are you going with this Steph? This is all confidential."

"It was eleven million pounds, and it is confidential. Anyone looking will have a hard time finding where the funds came from. I'm simply setting the scene for what's to come."

Steph turned to the man in uniform who had suddenly shrunk in stature. "And you Hayden. How is your villa in Portugal that Antonio Conti bought for you last year? I believe it cost the equivalent of three million pounds at the then exchange rate, and you, Darius, not only six million into party funds of which you have only admitted to receiving half. The other half hasn't been declared officially so someone at party headquarters must be having a ball. Plus, you have that nice new sailboat in Poole Harbour for the weekend family getaways."

Stephanie Clarkson carried on, "You see, gentlemen, you are all heavily indebted to Mr Conti. When we first met to discuss his generosity, I don't recall any of you refusing to take advantage of his money. My instructions were to find people of influence who were greedy and wouldn't ask too many questions in return for being able to help in the event that there was trouble later on. Well, look at you. I'd say I fulfilled my brief as far as influence and greed goes, so now it's your turn to provide the influence when Antonio Conti may need your help. Nothing too serious, but something that must be nipped in the bud before it becomes a problem."

The men at the table bristled with this description of themselves and but for the truth of Stephanie's statement, each might have taken exception. The only one to react was the Assistant Commissioner.

Hayden Giles stood up with a force that sent his chair skidding backwards. "Are you blackmailing us because if you are you can go to hell!"

Stephanie looked at the policeman with a slight pitiful smile. "Sit down Hayden; don't get so excited. No one's talking blackmail although if things don't get resolved it's always a possibility." She left the threat hanging in the room.

Sir Pollock Hargreaves spoke up. "Let's not argue. We take your point, Steph, but just tell us what's going on and what you want."

Stephanie was pleased to see Sir Pollock was being pragmatic. Like his colleagues present, he knew he would have to cooperate to keep his involvement with Antonio Conti a secret. Sir Pollock was simultaneously recalling how clever Stephanie Clarkson was when she had introduced him to Conti.

Stephanie placed the tips of her fingers together and rested them on her chin. "As you know, my position in the Treasury has somewhat diminished over the years and that has allowed me to get closer to the troops on the ground. My relationship with Mr Conti has developed to a point that he trusts me to look after his best interests. So, I pay certain junior colleagues to bring me bits of gossip and rumour. One such snippet I received on Monday morning involves Antonio Conti's business,

Mayflower Contracts Ltd. I hear some nosey copper has raised the profile of this company and now Treasury investigators together with the Met's Financial Crimes Unit may be about to start an investigation. Clearly this is not in our interests."

Everyone round the table sat in silence, each rapidly trying to analyse what impact an investigation might have on them individually. Sir Brendan Lamping was the first to speak up. "I don't follow. If there's an investigation it will run its course. Nothing to do with us."

Stephanie sighed and looked at Brendan as a mother looks at her child who cannot do his homework. "Brendan, you personally are in Conti's pocket for a lot of money, but apart from that, do you know how much tax Mayflower Contracts paid last year?"

"Well, no."

"It was in the billions. You should know, being responsible for the country's taxes. Mayflower pay as much tax as any one of the Top 100 registered companies on the Footsie."

Sir Brendon was a bit slow to follow Stephanie's remarks, but Sir Pollock Hargreaves was not. "You mean we're back into 'too big to fail' territory?"

"Precisely. Everyone round this table knows how Antonio Conti makes his money but to the outside world, he's a successful but reclusive businessman who donates to charities, supports good causes and is a friend of the rich and powerful, including yourselves. The fact he trades in some products we don't like doesn't mean he's a bad man. He just has a different set of morals to most of us." Steph Clarkson saw her words weren't getting through, so she banged her hand on the table and raised her voice in order to try to get a reaction from what in her opinion were her semi-comatose colleagues. "Hell! In other countries drugs and prostitution are legal."

Stephanie's outburst at least got a reaction from Darius Hackney-Law. Strangely for a politician, he had been very quiet, and Steph put it down to his lack of experience when dealing with the likes of the two knights of the realm and a senior police officer. Darius gave a slight cough in order to attract attention to himself.

"It seems to me we are all in this together. We all thought we could enjoy something for nothing but as my father said there's no such thing as a free lunch. From what Miss Clarkson has told us, the situation hasn't escalated to a point where any of us need to wield whatever influence we have to make any investigation go away. We don't even know if there will be an investigation and if there is, we have sufficient seniority around the table to crush it." The party treasurer was talking as he reasoned what they had in front of them. "I understand none of us want to be seen as the one blocking any investigation but surely a way can be found to keep us all away from the sharp end."

"How do you propose to do that? The only way I can see is if I walk into New Scotland Yard tomorrow and tell the head of Financial Crimes to stop investigating Mayflower Contracts, and I'm not about to do that." The Assistant Commissioner sat back and crossed his arms in a gesture that said, 'Don't look to me for help'.

Darius ploughed on. "No Hayden, but suppose we could somehow buy someone off?" He raised his eyebrows in a way that suggested he had a plan. "Who's likely to be running the investigation?" This was directed at Stephanie.

"I'm told the whole thing was started by a DCI Steve Burt and he's involved a Miss Florance Rough who's seconded from Treasury to the Financial Crimes Unit at the Yard."

"And that's all we know?"

"Yes."

"What about you, Hayden. Any inside information?"

AC Hayden Giles made a great show of interrogating his memory banks before speaking. "I've heard of this DCI Burt. From what I know you won't bribe him."

"What about his superior?"

"Oh! Old Alfie Brooks. He's a Commander and the unit this DCI Burt heads up reports directly to him. I think Alfie's due to retire at Christmas."

"Ah! Maybe we have our solution. I'm sure even a commander's pension could benefit from a boost of cash. Say one million to tell his subordinate to look the other way?"

The solution hung over the table like a blessing from above.

"Do you think it's possible, Hayden?" Sir Brendan Lamping was smiling a sly smile as he addressed the Assistant Commissioner.

"Anything's possible. I don't know anything about the Commander but saying that, I haven't heard anything bad said against him. He's an old-time copper so I suppose it's worth a try."

Stephanie was keen to move things on. "Right. If we all think this might work, who's going to approach this Commander Brooks?"

Sir Pollock Hargreaves wasn't totally convinced. As he spoke, he appeared to get more agitated. "Aren't we getting ahead of ourselves? All Steph has is a rumour from yesterday. Shouldn't we wait until we know there is going to be an investigation before we show our hand and presumably ask Conti to stump up a million to buy off this old policeman?"

Silence descended before Stephanie Clarkson took charge. "You're right, Pollock. Leave it with me to monitor the situation. I'll alert Antonio to the possibility of an investigation, but I'll assure him we can take care of it. I don't think the odd million should faze him."

No one spoke as the meeting broke up. They all had a lot to worry about.

Chapter Twenty-Two

Andrew Black had had another late night and decided to take his time getting up. He looked at the bedside clock and saw it read in three lines one above the other.
TUESDAY
26 SEPTEMBER
09.53 a.m.

Dressed in vest and boxer shorts, he took his great bulk downstairs to the kitchen half expecting to see his wife as usual sitting at the table drinking tea and smoking her tenth cigarette before ten a.m. As he opened the kitchen door, he was relieved find his wife had already left for her part-time job at the local garage.

Sitting with a cup of strong tea and his first cigarette of the day, Andrew's eyes settled on the tin where he had stored the envelope he'd been handed by Jean Franco. For some reason he couldn't explain to himself, he was desperate to open it but so far had taken his brother's advice to do as Jean Franco had instructed. "Only open it if you are in trouble." He walked over to the tin and took out the envelope.

He felt as though he had lost control and was no longer his own boss, but he knew their association with Jean Franco was good for them and by selling tablets instead of powder, their business was expanding. The idea of wholesaling the drugs and having dealers as agents seemed to be working. After all, every pusher had signed the contracts although some had needed a bit of persuasion. He stared at the unopened envelope as he played with it in his large hands. He thought back to their meeting in Amsterdam only nine days previously. A lot had happened and there was no doubt their business was more secure with the new high-class escorts coming plus the twenty who were already working, Andrew admitted things were on the up. But still he felt depressed.

He liked Jean Franco and thought he was a smart bloke. Andy had even started modelling himself on the Amsterdam crime boss. He told himself that Antonio Conti, the bean counter, was a nobody, and Jean Franco was the real deal. He convinced himself it was only a matter of time before Antonio Conti would be replaced, and gave a large smile that distorted his face. The cigarette hanging from the corner of his mouth and the saliva dripping over his chin wasn't a pretty picture. He scratched his oversized stomach and envisaged Conti's puppet, Quentin Somersby, bleeding from more than one wound on his body, but the Irish IRA pair hadn't yet carried out their task and he'd no idea what they were planning.

Maybe it was the fact that Quentin Somersby was still around that was causing his depressed mood. He couldn't think of anything else and determined to speak to the Irishmen to find out what their plans were. Not for the first time he realised he really didn't like Quentin Somersby and once more grinned at the thought that the latter would never again talk without respect to Andrew, the Chairman..

The envelope was still in his hands. He wished he could see through the paper and even considered using steam from the kettle to open the flap so his brother wouldn't know he had opened it. With a sigh, he realised David would be there shortly and he'd better get dressed, so he reluctantly returned the envelope to the tin box and put it back on the shelf.

The day ahead had been allocated to visiting estate agents and rental agents looking for the next high-quality rentals that would be necessary to house future escorts.

As he stood up and once more scratched his oversized stomach, he told himself this was Quentin Somersby's job and after he was out of hospital, Andrew would take great delight in telling him so.

***

Antonio Conti had just showered after having a late continental breakfast. His valet had laid out his business suit for the day and as he dressed, he thought about his upcoming schedule. There was nothing too onerous and after his early call to Jean Franco, he felt relieved that the rest of his morning was free. Jean Franco didn't fully understand that the one-hour time difference between London and Amsterdam meant

Antonio had to be prepared one hour earlier than his colleague. To make matters worse, Jean Franco insisted they speak at seven a.m. his time, but that was six a.m. London time. This was one of the many reasons Antonio didn't want to extend his relationship with the man in Amsterdam any longer than he had to, but he also realised timing was everything.

This telephone call was for Jean Franco's benefit. Antonio, as always, had given him the recent cash take from drugs and prostitution in London and in turn Jean Franco gave Antonio the same data from his EU operation. As predicted, the pair argued that the take from Europe was too small given the size of the population and Antonio was yet again forced to listen to Jean Franco talk about opportunity. Such regular debates were helping Antonio prepare his ground. "Listen Jean, I've told you before. The EU is too big to manage from one central spot. You're losing up to 25% of your Colombian to high-jackings and with open borders, you've no chance of finding the thieves. Each country is running its own drugs and flesh operations and breaking into those with no on-street presence is impossible plus the prices are too low due to competition. There are too many little gangs selling."

Antonio carried on making his case that the UK was easier to operate in due to its small size and rich population. "Look at the numbers, Jean. The UK is doing as much business as the whole of the other twenty-seven countries. If you want to grow mainland Europe you need a plan."

The Italian knew the mention of a plan would bring the conversation to an end. Jean Franco was frightened of the word and relied on Antonio to advise him. Antonio smirked to himself. He was advising the gangster but not in the direction Jean Franco necessarily wanted to travel. Jean Franco hung up at 06.41 a.m. London time.

Antonio's first meeting wasn't until early afternoon, so as he usually did after exercising in his private gym, showering and dressing, he sat and relaxed with the morning's *Financial Times* and a pot of delicious Colombian coffee as a companion. There was nothing in the paper to interest him and as he sat holding his coffee cup, he smiled to himself about the success of his UK operations.

Despite his misgivings about the Black brothers, the younger one, David, was showing himself to be competent and willing. Quentin Somersby had reported that the elder brother, for some unknown reason, appeared to be loyal to Jean Franco despite only having met him once. Andrew Black was also the least able of the brothers and according to Quentin, a bit stupid. Antonio had taken on board Quentin's assessment of the pair and had made a note to replace Andrew Black as soon as he could.

He thought about the arrangements he had made a few years ago to aid his takeover of Jean Franco's UK business and the steps he still had to take. One evening soon after he had arrived in London on Jean Franco's business, he had gone to a performance of *Tosca* at the Royal Opera House in Covent Garden. Fate had decreed he was seated next to a not unpleasant looking woman wearing a purple evening dress who smiled sweetly at him and accepted the offer of a drink at the interval. She told him her name was Stephanie Clarkson and she was a civil servant. They exchanged phone numbers and a few nights later, Stephanie had spent the night with Antonio at his rented flat.

Antonio smiled as he recalled how willing this woman had been to please him. As time moved on and Antonio became more established and ambitious and his plans to oust Jean Franco became more urgent, he realised this casual acquaintance from a chance meeting at the opera might be useful to him. As a Mafia man born and bred, he still adopted their tried and tested principles. One of which was to ensure enough people of influence were in your debt in case you needed their leverage should problems occur in the future.

It was common practice to put such a network of usually greedy public servants in place as they were best placed to assist in removing bureaucratic roadblocks. As Antonio developed his plan to take over the UK operation from Jean Franco, he saw Stephanie Clarkson as an ideal liaison. She had grabbed the opportunity of becoming a consultant and Antonio suspected she loved him deeply. She'd been complaining that her career had stalled, and she felt she was not getting recognition for the work she was doing. She was clearly frustrated and in Antonio's mind a perfect candidate. He had been proven correct and she had become an effective partner, recruiting several influential individuals, all of whom were happy to receive Antonio's bribes. Stephanie herself had become very wealthy and apart from the cash in her offshore bank accounts, she now owned a large villa in Antigua that no one knew about. If the money wasn't enough and in order to keep her loyal to him, Antonio wined, dined and bedded her once a month. He smiled as he thought that overall, it was not an unpleasant experience.

He helped himself to more coffee and as he did so, he told himself that at Stephanie's level everything was fine, and he felt protected, although he had never met any of her recruits. Using Mafia protocols, Antonio had put in place a further level of protection outside Stephanie's circle. He had recruited three very powerful men who could, if required, bring pressure to bear even on Stephanie's circle of contacts. Also, at the beginning of his time in London working for Jean Franco, he had made it his business to get himself invited to almost every dinner, social event or party on the London scene in order to circulate with the type of individuals he was seeking. In true Mafia fashion he had bought his way into society.

The Mafia knew the benefits of always having another more senior protective layer above the working one, but equally understood the importance of keeping your most senior — and therefore your most valuable — assets separate. If these senior members of industry, the government or society were to function successfully when required to act, it was always vital they didn't know that each was working separately for the Mafia or in this instance, Antonio Conti. It was also vital that the second-string assets recruited by Stephanie Clarkson didn't know of the existence of these more powerful people. These men could do things including collapsing murder trials, making fraud charges disappear and generally keeping Antonio and his associates out of prison no matter their crime, in the event that Stephanie's circle failed. He hoped never to call on their services and although each had been paid handsomely for nothing, they represented a significant insurance policy.

Thinking of Jean Franco handing the envelope to Andrew Black brought a frown to Antonio's face. It contained the names of all three of Antonio's senior men any one of whom he would look to in the event that he was in serious trouble. Jean Franco had given away a priceless piece of information and Antonio didn't think Andrew Black would respect it. If he opened the envelope and read the names, Antonio had no idea what the consequences might be. He sat up sharply realising he was working himself into a nervous state. Jean Franco had been playing the big gang boss when he handed the brothers the envelope and had no idea how valuable those names were, nor how much Antonio had invested in these men. Giving that envelope to Andrew Black was a big mistake. A mistake Antonio would have to correct. And soon.

***

Steve and Twiggy arrived in Commander Alfie Brooks' office at exactly 09.57 a.m. to find Twiggy's boss and Poppy's date from last night, Rupert Carey, sitting with Alfie at his conference table. Like the gentleman he undoubtedly was, Rupert stood as Twiggy entered, said hello and shook Steve's hand. Alfie remained seated. As Steve took a chair opposite Rupert, he turned to see a young man sitting in one of Alfie's comfortable chairs typing furiously onto a laptop. There was a pile of papers scattered at his feet and he didn't appear to notice the new arrivals.

As everyone got comfortable, Twiggy, seeing Steve's confusion, pointed to the young man. "That's Philip. He's one of mine and the best analyst I have." She looked quizzically at her boss.

"He's following up on one of Mayflower's companies. It's the one you suggested. I thought if we could get the information for this meeting, we'd make more progress. I brought Philip along to speed things up. I think we can do a physical audit, but it depends on the validity numbers."

Twiggy nodded and could hardly object to one of her staff being kidnapped by her boss to try to prove one of her ideas. Twiggy once more saw confusion on Steve's face. She glanced at Alfie who looked as though he had been briefed. "It's a way of rapidly spotting a problem."

Steve nodded and leant forward. Philip was still banging keys and the sound was annoying the DCI. Twiggy continued. "We take one of Conti's businesses that hopefully involves people. You know, like a cinema or a pub. Something where we can count people going in. If we know the average spend of an average person on an average night we can calculate the likely takings, give or take. Unfortunately, Mayflower only report company numbers so we're drilling down looking for one of their businesses that would be easy to follow but first we have to verify that all the branches they claim are making money actually exist."

The DCI was impressed and a glance at Alfie confirmed there was more to this meeting than a lesson in forensic accounting techniques.

Rupert Carey cleared his throat just as the room went quiet. Philip had stopped punishing the laptop keyboard.

"I've been discussing our various options with the Commander. It seems, DCI Burt, that you may have an interest in Mayflower, something to do with the daughter of the owner being murdered?"

"Yes."

"I understand you don't think the CEO, Mr Antonio Conti, is involved?"

Steve looked at Twiggy. "We don't believe so, Mr Carey, but at this stage we're not ruling anything out."

Alfie adjusted himself in his chair. "What Rupert and I have decided is we'll run a mini joint operation until you have ruled Conti out as a suspect. Miss Rough's team will handle the financial investigations and your unit, Steve, will take care of any heavy lifting arrest-wise if you find Conti's involved in the murders. As soon as you've eliminated him, you'll back off and let Financial Crimes take over. I think Miss Rough would appreciate your help even in the short term."

Rupert Carey took up where Alfie left off. Whereas Alfie had addressed Steve, Rupert was addressing Twiggy. "Flo, you know this has the potential to be the biggest case of your career and I'm happy to let you run it but if there is any chance of capital charges being raised against Conti, I want the Met in there. This thing will run for years. The numbers are huge and I'm sure as we get into it we'll get a few surprises. We don't want any crossed wires in case our case is compromised by over-exuberant police work so you two must liaise closely and tell each other your moves. Once the Met are satisfied the only crimes being committed are financial, it's all yours."

The DCI and Twiggy sat back and laughed at each other. "Just like old times, sir." Twiggy hadn't called Steve "sir" for a long time. It took them back to their first meeting.

"Are you both clear on this?" Rupert Carey was a typical anxious civil servant and needed reassurance.

Steve decided the time was right to say his piece. "Yes Rupert, I think it's a good plan and we'll all get on like a house on fire."

A degree of impatience entered Steve's voice. From the corner of his eye, he could see Alfie squirming in his chair obviously fearful of what Steve would say next.

"Conti has to be considered a suspect until we prove otherwise. I really don't think he killed his daughter, but we never barge in and alert suspects, no matter their alleged crime. My understanding is these businesses are laundering money, but the money comes from crimes. Our Drugs Squad and Vice Squad will be interested, and I don't see you keeping them at arm's length while you slowly build a money laundering case."

"Steve, it's not your concern. Once you're satisfied, another meeting like this will be held with Drugs and Vice." Alfie looked relieved that the DCI had bitten his tongue.

Steve liked the look of Rupert Carey but could see the civil servant in him rising to the fore with this plan.

Philip appeared at the table unannounced and with a flourish allowed his pile of papers to slide from his arms and scatter over the table and the floor. Twiggy stood and scooped up most of the documents and told Philip not to be overly concerned. "Just sit down and set up your laptop."

Steve was pleased to see how Twiggy was dealing with her awkward colleague. Philip looked to be about sixteen but was probably mid-twenties. He reminded Steve of one of his previous officers who was equally clumsy and shy but turned out to be an exceptional officer. Both men even dressed the same. Philip was wearing a long-sleeved shirt that had once been white but was now grey, what looked like an old secondary school tie that was covered in stains and which Philip obviously never unknotted and a multicoloured knitted, sleeveless top that didn't quite meet his waist. He was tall at over six foot, thin and was wearing brown corduroy trousers and heavy brown shoes. He wore rimless glasses and had a mop of unruly brown hair that looked as though it was a stranger to a comb.

"Are you ready, Philip?"

"Yes Flo." Philip didn't look ready but the expectant silence around the table seemed to spur him on. "Can I use the whiteboard?"

Alfie had a whiteboard attached to the far wall of his office. To the best of Steve's knowledge, it had never been written on. On a nod from Alfie, Philip stood and approached the board.

Without looking at his audience and finding something interesting on the floor to look at, Philip began.

"You remember you told me to look for an easy check and I might try clubs or gaming places?" The question was addressed to Twiggy.

"Yes."

"Well, I took one of the companies called Rainbow Caves Ltd. It has nine branches of gay clubs around the country and one of them is in London so a count in should be easy." Philip wrote the company name at the top of the board. "As I said, there are nine branches." The shy analyst started to write the branch locations one under the other and spoke as he wrote.

"The first to open was in Canary Wharf. That was two years ago, then eighteen months ago, they opened in Brighton, then Weston-Super-Mare, and Henley. Fifteen months ago, they set up in Sheffield, Newcastle and York. A year ago, they opened in Manchester and Birmingham." Philip stood back admiring his work. All nine locations were neatly penned and precisely under each other.

"I've checked the accounts for Rainbow Caves and of course they file consolidated versions, but I found an appendix that listed the branches and gave their individual turnover and profit figures. I worked these back to the submitted accounts and everything tallied. I've split the turnover down to average monthly amounts."

Although Philip was not a great orator, he held his audience spellbound with his precise and matter-of-fact delivery of the salient points. He notated the profit and loss figure against each branch as he spoke.

"I checked the bank details and the total turnover figures matched almost exactly the amount paid into Rainbow Caves' bank account. All the money was paid into NatWest in London."

Philip was completing his work on the board and in an extravagant gesture that Steve thought was not normal for this tall, shy man, he opened his arms wide with a theatrical flair to reveal the whiteboard.

It was neatly written and appeared easy to understand. Those sitting around the table examined Philip's work.

CANARY WHARF. TURNOVER 2 MILLION. PROFIT 1.1 MILLION.
BRIGHTON. TURNOVER 2 MILLION. PROFIT 1.1 MILLION.
WESTON. S.M. TURNOVER 2 MILLION. PROFIT 1.1 MILLION.
HENLEY. TURNOVER 2 MILLION. PROFIT 1.1 MILLION.
SHEFFIELD. TURNOVER 2 MILLION. PROFIT 1.1 MILLION.
NEWCASTLE. TURNOVER 2 MILLION. PROFIT 1.1 MILLION.
YORK. TURNOVER 2 MILLION. PROFIT 1.1 MILLION.
MANCHESTER. TURNOVER 2 MILLION. PROFIT 1.1 MILLION.
BIRMINGHAM. TURNOVER 2 MILLION. PROFIT 1.1 MILLION.

Philip cleverly let his audience digest the significance of what was on the board. "You'll see this is impossible. No business can have nine branches and each branch produces exactly the same turnover and profit figure."

No one spoke, not even Twiggy. Steve surmised she wanted to give Philip time to complete his briefing before asking questions.

"Now, I've checked with the Land Registry and Companies House and apart from the unrealistic numbers, there's more that's odd. Canary Wharf exists and is trading as is Brighton. All the others are either shells of buildings that Mayflower have bought or in the case of Henley, Newcastle and York, the business addresses just don't exist. Seven out of nine branches that have submitted accounts don't exist."

Philip replaced the marker pen he'd been twiddling in his hands and sat down without any final remarks.

"Philip, these declared numbers, you said they're averaged out monthly numbers?" Twiggy was scribbling on her notepad as she asked her question.

"Yes. It works out based on a thirty-day month each branch is taking approximately £67,000 a day."

"Agreed. So that's our test figure. If we can't prove sixty-seven grand a day then we have an investigation on our hands."

Rupert Carey seemed almost overjoyed. "OK, Flo, what do you need?"

Before Twiggy could answer, Steve spoke up. "Are you saying this Antonio Conti has set up Rainbow Caves to deliberately pay taxes even though seven of his places don't exist?"

"Yes." Twiggy looked at Steve. "It's money laundering, Steve." She took a new page on her pad and wrote as she spoke. "Look. Say Conti gets no business through any of these clubs but on paper he reports a turnover of two million a month, that's 24 million a year and he has nine of them, so that's 216 million a year he is telling us these clubs have earned. In reality, the money is all cash and comes from his illegal activities. By declaring these results and a profit of 117 million, he'll pay around 25 million in tax on his turnover of 216 million, but the rest of the money is now clean, and he can use it without questions being asked."

The DCI looked at Alfie Brooks. "Bloody hell Alfie, it's a different world."

The Commander nodded but said nothing. He clearly wasn't happy being in the presence of these bean counters.

Philip raised his hand. "I think they've produced one set of accounts and used them nine times just changing the name at the top."

Twiggy decided to take charge. "Right. If DCI Burt agrees, I think this is what we need. I'll get two investigators from Treasury to stake out the Canary Wharf place tonight. They'll do the counting, see how many punters actually go into the place. I'll get one of them to visit as soon as it opens and check out prices, drinks, food and so on just to get an idea of what can be spent legitimately by one punter. It'll be a long night. I don't suppose it closes until the wee hours. Steve, can you provide some backup just in case?"

The DCI couldn't see why it was necessary but knew Alfie had a stake in this operation. "Yes, I can get Matt Conway and a couple of uniform officers to sit behind your lads' car. They'll love the overtime."

"Good. My men will be on site from four when it opens. I don't think Matt needs to be present before say eight o'clock."

"Works for me." Steve knew Matt wouldn't be happy.

Rupert Carey summarised as only a lifelong civil servant could.

"So Philip has shown that the Canary Wharf club should be taking in around sixty-seven thousand a night. Our investigators will confirm the spend potential and count the clients to determine if the number of clients times the average spend comes anywhere near this figure. The surveillance will commence at four p.m. DCI Burt, on behalf of the Metropolitan Police, will provide a CID officer and two uniformed constables as backup support in the event of any trouble. The Met surveillance will commence at eight p.m. All counts and findings will be reported before the Treasury investigators finish their shift in order Treasury and Metropolitan Police Financial Crimes Units can assess the situation tomorrow morning. Is that about it?"

Rupert Carey was looking smug. The DCI decided to burst his bubble of smugness.

"In the interests of cooperation and liaison, Mr Carey, I'd just like to inform you," Steve paused and looked in Twiggy's direction, "and of course Miss Rough, that I shall be visiting Mr Conti this afternoon."

Rupert Carey almost choked and coughed several times trying to regain his equilibrium. "But you can't. You'll alert him we are about to investigate him."

"Mr Carey, his daughter has been murdered and he has yet to be informed. It would be stranger still if the police didn't call on him. Even the worst criminal needs to know if his daughter has been killed."

Rupert Carey sat back, defeated.

Commander Alfie Brooks stood with a beaming smile stupidly stuck to his face. "Well, that all seems satisfactory."

The smile said 'Well done, Steve, for getting the last word'. "Steve, better keep me posted on these murders now Treasury are involved."

Everyone was now standing. The DCI looked at his watch. It read 11.54 a.m. Twiggy caught sight of Steve and mouthed a "see you later" message before everyone disappeared, leaving Alfie to consider what had just happened. He told himself he must be getting old because sitting outside a gay club, counting people going in, wasn't his idea of policing.

Chapter Twenty-Three

Steve, having gone via the canteen to collect four coffees, arrived in his office to find DS Matt Conway frantically writing in his notebook. This was not a good sign. Matt looked up and stopped writing, eyeing the cardboard tray with the coffees. Steve knew the signs and walked into his inner office calling for Matt to join him. Matt was clearly flustered about something.

Once both men had their cups in their hands, Matt spoke up. "We had a bit of a problem earlier, Steve, with Neil Furlong, at his arraignment hearing."

"Oh yeah?"

Matt nodded. "Yeah. He found a lawyer from somewhere and told him about our — let's say — *unofficial* interrogation—"

Steve interrupted. "*My* unofficial interrogation, Matt, not yours."

"Yes, well, I was there and could have said something." A silence descended before the DS carried on. "Anyway, this brief wanted to know if it was true. I pleaded no knowledge and asked if his client could elaborate because all we had was the official tape of the interview and his client's confession. He rabbited on about unlawful interrogations and unsound confessions. He said he'd advised Furlong to change his plea to not guilty and he'd get the confession thrown out."

"Christ's sake, Matt, you should have called me." Steve was concerned.

"Oh! I thought about it, but I took this lawyer to one side, reminded him his saintly client had bashed two people over the head and one was a serving cop and the other a retired cop. I told him his client was mistaken and we hadn't interrogated him, simply asked him to help us with our enquiries, and while he was helping, he volunteered a few facts that allowed us to put two and two together before we formally interviewed him under caution."

"And he bought it?"

Matt laughed. "Well not at first. He said he'd have to seek a meeting with the CPS and the DPP to report our irregularities. I told him again how bad that would look, keeping an obvious killer off the streets, and sometimes things had to be done for the greater good, but at no time did we coerce or trick a confession from his client. I told him if he'd listened to the official tape, he'd hear everything was done by the book." Matt stopped and drained his coffee.

The DCI was listening and beginning to feel a void in his stomach opening up. He regretted his actions but once more told himself it was necessary.

Matt Conway seemed relaxed, so Steve hoped he had sorted everything out. He listened intently as Matt continued

"Then I hit him with the forensics the Suffolk lads got from Furlong's house. The two coshes with brain matter still attached. Not only found in his house but his fingerprints all over them. It only took a few minutes for this lawyer to see we didn't need the confession. I think he knew we'd played close to the edge and made a decent but not perfect job of hiding our tracks, but knew his client was guilty. Luckily, I think this bloke had been round the block and knew how things worked. He wasn't one of those 'the law's the law' types. I think he was more practical."

"And that was that?" Steve started a second cup and handed one to Matt.

"Pretty much. The lawyer agreed to talk to Furlong and explain things to him. Furlong was called and pleaded guilty. He's in the system now so we won't hear much from him until his trial. We opposed bail and it wasn't granted. The question of the first unrecorded interview didn't come up."

The DCI joked, "A bit of a narrow squeak, Detective Sergeant." Steve used a stern voice. "Just shows you should do everything by the book." Feeling mightily relieved, he smiled. "Well done, Matt, sounds like you saved the day."

DS Matt Conway complained he now had a lot of notes to write up just in case this raised its head at Furlong's trial.

"Thanks Matt. Now, as a reward for handling the Furlong court hearing as well as you did, I have an easy job for you and a load of overtime."

Steve explained about the operation at the Rainbow Cave Club and said that Matt and two uniformed officers should provide backup. He tried to explain the accounting side of the operation but found he only confused himself.

Matt sat back. "You mean Treasury run cases by sitting outside bars and clubs and counting people? I'm in the wrong branch."

Steve once more tried to repeat some of his earlier meeting. "Seems they call themselves investigators, not cops. They use accountants to ferret through paperwork and build their cases based on paper trails. It's what they call evidence, but they don't go getting their faces bashed in; they leave that to us. That's why you're getting all the overtime tonight."

"Great. Overtime and boredom all at the same time." The DS smiled.

"That's for later. We'll go and see Antonio Conti this afternoon and tell him about his daughter. Get a pool car out and I'll meet you in the garage at two p.m. Ask Poppy for his business address. We'll see him there. I'm interested to see what a major-league criminal looks like close up."

"Right you are, Steve. What about this Andrew Black? If we're right he's implicated in the Furlong killings and the eleven-year-old case that Elsie Brown was chasing down, should we not at least bring him in?"

"Yes. You're right but let's leave him till tomorrow. I don't think he's going anywhere."

"Fair enough," Matt rose, "back to my notes."

Steve was considering getting a sandwich from the canteen when Poppy appeared. In an unusual move, she closed the office door and stood with her hands on her hips facing her boss. She was looking fierce, and the DCI didn't like this version of his admin assistant.

"Are you leaving?" Poppy didn't bother with any preamble. Despite her insubordinate tone she had not used her lifeboat of adding the word "sir".

Steve was taken aback by the direct approach and stuttered, "I-I beg your pardon, Detective Constable?"

Poppy stood her ground. "Are you leaving?" This was said in a gentler tone, but Poppy did not change her stance.

"Sit down Poppy." Steve adopted his fatherly pose. "I don't know where you got this from, but as of right now, I am not leaving. I may be leaving in the future and if I am I will inform the team together at the appropriate time. Do you understand?"

From her chair Poppy nodded but needed reassurance. "I heard you telling Twiggy that you might be going to Norfolk as Head of CID, so I know you're thinking of leaving." Despite Poppy's attempt at being tough, Steve saw the beginning of a tear well up in her left eye. "I don't want you to leave. You said I'd be operational, but a new guy may not move me over. I like working here but it won't be the same without you. Please don't leave, Steve."

Poppy was struggling to maintain her composure. She clearly felt deeply about working for the DCI.

With the kindest voice he could muster, Steve told Poppy. "Listening at doors doesn't always do you any good, does it, but I really don't know if I'm leaving. The Commander doesn't know; hell, Poppy, even my wife doesn't know, so believe me, nothing has been decided."

Poppy was looking at her lap and raised her eyes to meet Steve's. Steve thought she looked like a sixteen-year-old schoolgirl who was in trouble with her headmistress. "Yeah, but you will do, won't you?"

Steve sighed. "Poppy, when I know, the team will know. Now no more of this. Keep this to yourself. I don't want any distractions while we have cases ongoing, and don't worry. We'll talk about your future soon, I promise."

A reluctant Poppy stood up, wiped her eye and smiled weakly. "Peter wants you in the viewing room. I've been sent to get an enlarged photo of Sophia Paulo. I think Uncle Terry's got something from the CCTV."

***

Antonio Conti had arrived at the comfortable offices of Mayflower Contracts Ltd in time to attend his first meeting of the day at twelve fifteen p.m. The offices were located on the third floor of a glass-and-steel modern building located behind Holborn tube station. Antonio didn't believe in the need to expend money on flashy offices. He preferred quality and practical surroundings that told the outside world Mayflower was a conservative upright company with no need for flashy premises. He did not believe in drawing attention to himself or his business unnecessarily and flashy offices were always a magnet for inquisitive people.

The first meeting was simply to consider whether Mayflower should buy a legitimate engineering business that needed capital to expand. As always, Antonio surrounded himself with established and honest City advisors who knew nothing of where Antonio's wealth really came from.

Although he got a buzz out of investing in legitimate businesses, he bored very quickly with all the rules and regulations involved. He preferred the darker world of crime where the strongest made the rules. Antonio knew he was strong, and he liked playing by his rules.

Mayflower only rented half of the third floor which was divided into a reasonably sized conference room and three smaller individual offices. Two were each occupied by a clerk. One who looked after all the banking activities for Antonio's criminal business and the other the accounts for Antonio's legitimate businesses. The third was the domain of Antonio's secretary who also doubled up as his companion on those evenings he needed a diversion.

The accommodations were completed by Antonio's office, the largest of the rooms. It was furnished comfortably with a neat looking desk, several cabinets, a drinks cabinet and four tub chairs positioned around a low coffee table, itself positioned by the large single-pane window that looked out over other buildings and rear gardens.

Antonio entered his office to find Quentin Somersby, dressed in his city business suit, sitting in one of the tub chairs reading the morning's newspaper. On seeing Antonio, he folded the paper and placed it on the coffee table. "I've ordered sandwiches for lunch, just the usual."

Antonio acknowledged Quentin's presence and sat behind his desk. "My next meeting isn't until four, thank goodness. How do last night's figures look?"

Quentin reeled off a string of numbers that sounded indecipherable but both men understood their meaning. The report showed another good day, and the escort business was going well. "When are the new girls arriving? We can certainly use them."

"I'll double check with Jean Franco but maybe at the weekend. Are you sure those idiot brothers have got the accommodations sorted out?"

"Looks like it. I've checked out the first six and they look fine."

"Good. I'll let you know…" Antonio's phone rang. Surprisingly, it was Stephanie Clarkson. She never rang Antonio at his office.

"Hello darling, are you missing me?" The voice on the other end of the phone was sheer treacle. Antonio squirmed.

"No, I'm not missing you and I'm very busy. What do you want?"

Stephanie hadn't expected such a hostile reception but made allowances knowing Antonio was in his office and must be busy. "I just wanted to let you know that you may be about to be investigated by the police's Financial Crimes Unit and the Treasury."

Antonio's initial reaction was one of disbelief. "Are you sure, and why?"

"It's very early and only a bit of gossip, but I thought I'd better tell you."

Steph explained about her meeting with the people who were indebted to Antonio and the proposal that that in order to kill it before it even started, they would bribe a senior commander at the Yard.

"The whole thing seems to have started with a DCI Steve Burt. According to our sources, he's pretty much untouchable. You know the type, too honest for their own good. The financial side would be led by a Florance Rough. She has a reputation of being very good at her job and incorruptible."

Miss Clarkson went on to describe the meeting and finished by saying, "We think this DCI's boss, Commander Brooks, might be the key to making it go away before it starts but it'll cost you a million."

Antonio didn't like this news, but realised Stephanie appeared to have matters in hand. "Do what you think best and keep me informed."

"I could give you a personal briefing tonight?" The treacle was back in Stephanie's voice.

Antonio rolled his eyes. "All right, come to the hotel around seven."

Quentin was looking quizzically at Antonio as he replaced the receiver. "Seems some policeman has been asking questions about the business. Stephanie's on it but it's a worry. I wonder what made him look at us?" Both men were quiet as their sandwiches and coffee were delivered.

***

The DCI followed Poppy as they made their way to the highly technical viewing room Inspector Terry Harvey had somehow managed to have installed at a time when Metropolitan Police budgets were tight. Every time Steve entered this mini cinema, he was struck by the blinking lights and high-tech gizmos together with the plush surroundings. He spotted DI Peter Jones and DC Mary Dougan sitting beside each other on the front row of the three-row cinema. Terry Harvey was talking to a technician seated at a panel of impressive-looking instruments and two what looked to be computer screens.

Poppy danced over to Peter Jones and handed him the enlarged photograph of their headless victim. The DCI gave a silent prayer, "Thank goodness for Immigration and passport photos."

On seeing the DCI Terry broke off his conversation. "Ah! DCI Burt, you've arrived in time for the good bit."

Steve looked at Peter Jones who was grinning like a Cheshire cat. Clearly, they had found something. Poppy left to man the office while Steve took a seat on the second row. Terry went to work pacing in front of the huge TV screen mounted on the wall above his head.

"You suggested we look at CCTV images around the areas we know where low end prostitutes ply their trade." This was directed at Steve. "Well, there are a lot of them and normally it would be a waste of time, but we got lucky." Looking at the technician sitting in front of the impressive bank of dials, Terry nodded. "Play camera 47."

A grainy image and a series of horizontal wavy lines appeared on the large TV screen. There was no sound and it took several seconds for the image to settle down.

"This is from a fixed traffic camera at the junction of Baden Road and Jinks Lane. The camera is angled to catch cars not stopping at the intersection. You'll see there's a railway bridge that runs over the intersection. I had to get the information from Vice, and they say this is a popular spot because the bridge gives the tarts shelter from the rain. Also, any john who's on the pull can stop at the kerb off the main road." Terry paused and looked directly at Steve. "You see DCI Burt the amount of research we do for you."

As Terry smiled Steve said, "Just so long as you don't sample any for research. I know a financial analyst who wouldn't understand it was in the line of duty." The whole room sniggered before Terry, still standing under the TV screen, carried on.

"Right." Using a remote-control Terry fast-forwarded the images. "This is from the night the post-mortem suggests our girl was murdered on September 18." Terry waved a hand in the direction of the top left-hand corner of the screen. "See, the date and time."

He fast forwarded the images until the time showed 9.17 p.m. then slowed the frames to one each five seconds. "Now look, watch the bottom right." The images slowly moved forward until Terry clicked to freeze the image and shouted. "There, see that!"

Steve leaned forward straining his eyes to see but the image was too small and blurred. "Sorry Terry, I don't get it."

"No worries." Terry clicked a few more frames forward until he could see the image more clearly. It was a girl. He scrolled further up, but returned to this image, as this was the one frame she was caught looking in the direction of the camera. "Any better?"

"Not really." Steve felt Terry was playing with him.

Terry turned to his technician. "Enhance and enlarge please."

The screen went blank for several seconds whilst the technician hit computer keys. Eventually the screen burst into life and a fuller picture of a girl, clearly crossing the road and checking for traffic appeared. The image wasn't sharp, but it was good enough to identify the girl. To be sure Terry held the picture Poppy had delivered beside the image on the screen. "Bingo, that's Sophia Paulo, the headless corpse."

Terry took the plaudits he so richly deserved but the DCI didn't see an end point. He thought Peter Jones as SIO should have picked up on this.

"Terry, you must have something else. All this tells us is our victim was out working the night she was killed."

Terry sighed. "Always impatient you CID lot. Patience Steve, all will be revealed." Terry, using his remote controller, reset the system and allowed the images to roll forward, and stopped it when the time clock read 10.33 p.m. Again, he slowed the images right down and stopped the system when a car appeared at the kerb side. "Now pay attention. You see the car?" Steve could just about make out the shape of a dark-coloured saloon. Given the location of the camera, only about a quarter of the car was visible and the lighting was poor.

Terry moved each frame forward individually. "See, the girls all charge towards the car but the driver clearly only wants one specific one."

As the frames jerked forward, a girl appeared from the crowd and got in the car. Once more Terry turned to his technician and said, "Enhance and enlarge please."

As before, the system went blank but burst into life showing a girl getting into this car. The image wasn't as good as previously due to the poor light, but it was obvious that the girl was Sophia Paulo.

The room was silent for a few long seconds.

"I don't suppose you got the registration number of the car?" Steve knew he was pushing his luck.

"Not quite but we got the first two letters. They are 'MA', and I can tell you it's an Audi. Look." Terry reset the system and rolled the images forward. Each frame showed the car in the bottom right-hand corner but only its back-left quarter moving away from the kerb. The rest of the car was outside the viewing field of the camera. Terry stopped at a frame that showed the two letters from the registration number and a part image of the badge on the boot lid that could only be Audi.

"Good work Terry. So we know the victim was alive at 10.33 p.m. on the night she was murdered, and that she went off with a punter in an Audi car with the first two letters of the registration being 'MA'. I suppose our theory has to be that the driver of that car killed her." Steve leaned back and looking at his watch realised he had to leave to meet Matt in the garage.

"Peter, you and Mary follow this up. I'll be back later, and we can debrief then." Peter Jones, having turned in his cinema style chair to watch his boss, nodded.

"Well done, Terry. We'll touch base later." The DCI waved and rushed out of the viewing room.

Twenty-Four

Steve and Matt Conway arrived at the offices of Mayflower Contracts Ltd at 2.31 p.m. They were shown into the presence of the CEO, Mr Antonio Conti, by one of the clerks whose office was nearest to the exit from the lift.

Antonio Conti, on seeing the police officers entering, chose to return to his desk and stood awaiting his visitors to walk towards him. He eyed them suspiciously especially upon hearing one of them introduce himself as DCI Burt. Antonio quickly thought Stephanie Clarkson may have some explaining to do.

After showing their warrant cards and completing the introductions, Steve looked towards Quentin Somersby who had remained. "I think it would be better if we discussed our reason for being here in private, sir."

Seated behind his desk Antonio signalled for the officers to take the upright chairs in front of him as he waved a hand vaguely towards Quentin. "Mr Somersby is a partner in the firm, gentlemen. I have no secrets from him."

"This has nothing to do with your business sir, it's a personal matter." Steve was sure he saw Antonio Conti visibly relax.

"No matter. Quentin remains."

Steve took a deep breath. "Very well. Can you please confirm your real name is in fact Antonio Paulo from Sicily?"

Antonio immediately became angry. "That is no concern of the British Police. I am known as Conti in this country and pay my taxes as such."

"Quite so, sir, but we need to establish if you are the same Antonio Paulo who is the father of Sophia Paulo."

Antonio calmed down and, staring at Steve, held his breath. Eventually he exhaled and nodded, still holding Steve's gaze with something that carried menace.

"Can you please confirm, sir, that you have a daughter named Sophia?"

Reluctantly Antonio answered. "Yes."

"And she is in London. Is that correct?"

"I do not know where my daughter is, Inspector."

The DCI knew this was a lie and wondered why a father would lie about the whereabouts of his daughter. He felt conflict in the air and realised this was not the usual way of informing a relative that someone was dead. Steve decided to come from another direction and seek conflict. He knew this man was a crook and felt little sympathy for him anyway.

"Mr Paulo." The DCI knew the use of Antonio's given name would cause an issue. "You're lying. We have a postcard from a friend of yours in Sicily addressed to your daughter telling her you will be in touch with her soon. That suggests you have her address."

Antonio's temper flared again but he quickly brought it under control. He realised this policeman was no fool.

"Very well. Yes, I have her address, but I have never visited, nor have I sought her out. But why are you so interested."

Steve produced a picture of the bird tattoo. "Does your daughter have this tattoo on her left inner arm?"

Antonio studied the image. "Yes."

Steve didn't like this part of the job and softened his approach. "Mr Conti, I'm afraid the body of a young woman was recovered from the Thames some days ago and we have reason to believe it is that of your daughter, Sophia."

Antonio didn't blink. "Do you not have a photograph?"

"No sir, I'm afraid the body was badly mutilated, and the head is missing."

"So apart from this tattoo, what makes you think it's my daughter?"

"By a process of elimination and searching her flat we believe the body is that of your daughter sir, but just to be certain we'd like you to provide a DNA swab. I'm really sorry, sir." Steve used his most sincere voice but knowing how this man made his money his sympathy was limited.

"Yes of course." Antonio appeared to be thinking fast and was deep in thought. He was not outwardly upset by the news and appeared in control. Matt cracked the DNA swab kit and collected the sample from inside Antonio's mouth.

Both detectives having delivered the news and secured the DNA sample made to leave, when Quentin Somersby chipped in. "Do you know who did it?"

"We're following up several lines of enquiry but are not ready to make an arrest." This was the Metropolitan Police's standard reply to such questions.

"How did it happen?" Quentin persisted.

"Again sir, we cannot comment." Steve led the way to the door.

"But you must know something?" Quentin persisted but Steve ignored him choosing to address his next comment to Antonio. "Once we have DNA confirmation sir, we'll be in touch."

Antonio, still deep in thought and possibly suffering from mild shock, simply waved the officers out of his office.

Quentin sat looking at his business colleague knowing he personally had done well out of his association with this man.

"I'm sorry about your daughter Antonio and I'd no idea about your connections."

Antonio Conti moved slowly to sit beside Quentin. He was clearly shocked and looked a grey colour. After a few minutes he looked up at Quentin and told him the whole story. How he had been born into the Mafia and the training he'd been given. He explained about the constant need to prove you were a good member by being present at some brutal and horrific executions.

"I stuck it for years but six years ago I'd had enough and started to plan to escape. I copied all the incriminating financial files I could as a defence and five years ago I took my chance. I left behind my family, changed my name and have been hiding in plain sight since."

He explained how he'd met Jean Franco three years earlier and how he had become involved with the business, helping Jean Franco grow his empire.

"A friend in Sicily told me where Sophia was living in London, but I couldn't take the risk of seeing her. The Mafia have a long reach and I didn't want to put her in danger." Antonio paused before standing up suddenly. "And now this. Who'd kill my little girl?"

"Do you think the Mafia found her?"

Antonio sat down again. "No. If they had they'd have found a way of letting me know. They may not know who I am now, but they'll know I still have friends in Sicily." Antonio was silent.

"No, this is something else. Put feelers out among your low-life contacts, Quentin. Throw money around. I want to know who did this and I want to get to them before the police. Whoever did this is going to suffer a long, slow, agonising death."

***

Steve and Matt stood outside the office block. Steve spotted something that got his mind revolving. He had to get back to the office. On the way and with Matt driving he brought his DS up to speed on the CCTV evidence Terry Harvey had unearthed.

"So we have an image of the dead girl getting into this car on the night she was killed?"

"That's about it, but we don't know who was driving. If we find the driver, I'm pretty sure we'll find our killer."

Both men were silent for the rest of the journey with the DCI's brain seeking answers in areas that no one had yet gone. Steve told Matt to knock off and get ready for his shift helping Twiggy's investigators to count the customers visiting the Rainbow Cave Club in Canary Wharf. "You have everything set up I hope?"

"Yes. I'm picking up the two uniformed officers here at seven thirty p.m. and we'll head over to the club."

"Good. You can have a late start tomorrow. I won't expect you till lunchtime."

"Thanks boss, I think I'll need the extra sleep."

***

As Matt disappeared in the car, Steve made his way to his office. He noticed it was all very quiet with only Poppy at her desk. As she saw Steve arrive, she held up her hand.

"Peter and Mary have only just gone to the canteen; I'll call them back." Poppy seemed a bit flustered as though she were hiding something.

Steve decided to probe. "Go on Poppy. What's up?"

"Nothing really. It's just Peter isn't sure how to follow up on the CCTV images and Mary doesn't seem to be able to help him."

The DCI didn't like the sound of this explanation. He was relying on DI Peter Jones as his second in command to show some initiative and leadership. "Fine, Poppy. Call them back and then get onto DVLA. Find out how many cars are owned and registered to Mayflower Contracts."

As Poppy called her two colleagues, Steve sat behind his desk. What he'd spotted outside Mayflower Contracts' offices troubled him. He looked at his watch. It was 3.33 p.m. and he hoped Peter Jones would have enough sense to bring coffee back with him. He did.

The three detectives sat round Steve's conference table. Still absorbing Poppy's comments on his DI, Steve decided to take things slowly.

"Right Peter. What have you got?"

"Not much, Steve." The DI looked upset. "We have the CCTV images of our victim getting into that Audi but that's it. I'm not sure we know much more."

Steve inwardly sighed and reflected once more that some of his role appeared to be that of a training officer, babysitting graduate entrants.

"Look at what we have, Peter. Our victim getting into an Audi with the first two letters of the registration shown as 'MA'. Have you followed anything up with DVLA?"

"Er, no sir. I should have thought of that."

Steve made no comment and right on cue Poppy appeared waving a piece of paper. As usual she didn't knock nor wait to be heard. "I've got it, boss. Mayflower has three cars registered in its name. All Audis and all with private plates."

Steve was grinning despite having his teaching session with his DI interrupted. "And all starting with 'MA'?"

Poppy immediately saw the connection. "Yes. They're MAY 04, MAY 05 and MAY 06."

"And they're all dark-coloured. I saw two of them this afternoon."

Poppy remained standing as a contemplative silence hung over the room. Mary Dougan was the first to speak.

"We have CCTV of the victim getting into a dark Audi with the first two letters of the registration as 'MA'. We now know Mayflower Contracts runs three dark Audis with the first two letters 'MA' and Mayflower is run by the victim's father."

"Yes, Mary, but what you and Peter don't know is that her father — who now calls himself Antonio Conti — is in fact on the run from the Italian Mafia and is involved in drugs and prostitution big time here in London. Financial Crimes are looking at him for money laundering and we have a brief to provide backup while Antonio Conti is a person of interest in his daughter's murder."

Poppy chipped in. "I suppose these cars make him a possible suspect?"

"Could be, Poppy. Either him or one of his employees with access to one of those cars."

"What do we do next, Steve?" Peter Jones didn't look comfortable, but Steve decided he didn't have time to talk to his DI.

"Let's get a warrant to search those cars. If Sophia Paulo was in one of them, she must have left trace evidence. Then tonight, Peter, you and Mary get out to that crossroads where the CCTV picked up our victim. Talk to the girls, it must be their regular spot so they could have seen who was driving the car. Splash the cash if you have to but…"

Terry Harvey walked into Steve's office and stood behind his niece. He had what was clearly an enlarged photograph in his hand. "I think you'll want to see this."

The DCI's heart missed a beat. Terry Harvey only brought evidence pertinent to Steve's cases and usually what he brought was significant. Without standing on ceremony, Terry placed the photograph on the table and took a chair facing Steve.

Steve examined the image but was immediately disappointed. He couldn't see anything unusual. The picture was obviously taken by the same CCTV camera that captured Sophia Paulo getting into the Audi. It showed a few girls standing around but nothing else that was obvious.

"Bottom right-hand corner." Terry was sitting forward directing the detectives to what he wanted them to see.

"Sorry Terry. I'm not seeing it."

Inspector Harvey produced a Sherlock Holmes style magnifying glass and passed it to the DCI. "Bottom right. It's a bit faint but it's there."

Steve examined the bottom corner through the magnifying glass. After a few seconds he looked up. "Bloody hell, Terry, that's our German!" Steve laid the picture and glass down and pushed them in the direction of Peter Jones. "What was that German man's name Poppy? The one we have an all-ports out on. The one we think was hired by the Mafia to find Sophia Paulo?"

Poppy thought for a split second before almost shouting, "Gunther Schmitt but we've not had any sightings."

"So Terry, this image was taken when?"

"It's seven frames after your victim got in the car. He was there at the same time."

Steve suddenly became more animated. "Right Peter, you and Mary get out there tonight. Show the photograph we have of Gunther from his passport, and check if any of the girls saw our victim get into the car and maybe even who was driving. I'm convinced the driver is our killer."

With a positive instruction Peter Jones looked happier. "Right Steve. Come on Mary, let's get organised."

As Peter and Mary left, Poppy remained standing. "Poppy, get that warrant sorted. I want to check those cars. If we find any evidence that Sophia Paulo was in the front seat of any of those cars, I think we'll have our killer."

Poppy left in a rush.

Just as Terry was about to follow his niece, his fiancée in the shape of Florance Rough arrived carrying her usual pile of files. Steve had often asked what was in the files because he'd never seen her refer to them apart from the odd top one. The couple were too professional for any intimate exchanges and after a few comments Terry declared, "Well I'll be off and leave you two to solve crimes."

***

As Terry Harvey left Steve and his fiancée to deliberate about their joint venture, Twiggy's investigators were parking up in a side street in Canary Wharf with a perfect view of the entrance to the Rainbow Cave Club. One of the investigators who happened to be the younger of the two exited the car and set off on his snooping trip to try to establish how much an average clubber could spend in an evening in the Rainbow.

It had just turned four p.m. and the club was officially opened but there was no sign of anyone around. As Twiggy's agent entered, he noticed a sign that read *"OPEN TO NON-MEMBERS. ENTRANCE £50."*

This gave the snooper his first figure. Seeing no one, he moved deeper into the badly lit space that opened out to be a bar area. On the counter was a list of drink prices. He noted it was £10 for a bottle of beer and £30 for a gin and tonic. All other drinks including fancy cocktails seemed to range up to £50. Twiggy's man stood and mentally calculated that, based on the gin and tonic price, the punter out on a good night might drink six gin and tonics. He calculated this could work out at £180 for alcohol plus the entrance fee meaning the likely spend so far to be £250. As he scanned the area beyond the bar, he noticed booths whose seats were covered in rich velvet and some booths had a curtain that could obviously be pulled around to give the occupants complete privacy. There were two walls of these booths and a series of small round tables in the middle of what could be a dance floor. The usual large glass ball was suspended from the ceiling and combined with coloured discs obviously enhanced the mood when everything was on.

There was a small round table beside the bar. He picked up one of the leaflets neatly laid out on its glass top. The leaflet explained that to hire a booth was £200 an hour with a minimum of two hours. Below these tariffs was another section that said if a club host was being entertained then it was an additional £150 with again a two-hour minimum boking. The investigator calculated, that if a punter used this facility, then it would cost another £700 plus the entrance and drinks budget. He decided a nice round £1,000 a night could be spent in this club that he could not wait to leave. Giving the place another look, he thought he had enough and was pleased not to have been challenged by anyone. He had a cover story but preferred not to use it.

He returned to the car to find his partner lazing back in the driver's seat. "I reckon a grand should do it."

"Bloody hell. These guys must be made of money." His older partner was surprised by the amount.

"I don't know what goes on in there, but they must think thirty quid for a gin and tonic is worth it."

Both men settled down for a long evening. The older observer said, "Once the boys in blue get here, we'll leave them to count and go get a bar meal in a decent pub. Even the cops can't screw up counting people in."

***

Steve and Twiggy were sitting opposite each other, and once Terry had departed, Twiggy looked at Steve with what he took to be sympathy, but he didn't know why.

"I hope you didn't mind my asking for your involvement in this, Steve."

"I didn't know you had but what I don't understand is, why all this counting people into the club? Surely you've got enough with the non-existent clubs and the false accounts?"

"You'd think so, and in your world, you'd be right in there, size tens all over the place, but with us it's different. We investigate white-collar crimes whereas you simply solve crimes. All our evidence is in front of us. Financial crooks deal in numbers, and we work with those numbers. We don't have to go searching for evidence, the evidence is in front of us, we just have to understand it."

Steve was impressed by Twiggy and again told himself she had come a long way since their first meeting. "So why this counting?"

Twiggy sat back. "Think about it. Antonio Conti has set up fictitious branches but he's declaring income and paying tax into the Exchequer. What crime has he committed apart from a dodgy set of accounts? You could argue he's doing the country a favour by paying tax. The issue is where does he get his money from. We need to show that as far as his declaration for Rainbow Caves is concerned, the money does not come from income. Tonight should hopefully show that. Then we move on to looking for his real source of income. This whole case is going to take months if not years to get over the line. We have sixteen businesses to examine in fine detail. No doubt the Vice and Drugs Squads will be involved but we'll keep the lead. As soon as you say you're finished with Conti, you won't hear about this again."

"It's a feather in your cap though, Twiggy. A high-profile case like this, it can't do your career any harm?"

Twiggy almost blushed. "Rupert Carey is very good at stealing the limelight. You know, loves the camera, but I'll elbow my way in." She laughed. "After all, I haven't lost so much weight, I can't pack a punch."

Twiggy stood to go. "Everything laid on for tonight?"

"Yes. Matt Conway drew the short straw. He'll be there by eight with two uniforms. I think it's a waste of space but anything to help an old colleague." The DCI smiled.

"Thanks Steve. We usually have uniformed backup on a job like this. Having Matt is a bit of insurance. After all, you started this thing."

Twiggy picked up her pile of papers and with a 'see you', she was gone.

Steve saw it was approaching five p.m. and decided to call it a day. He had to talk with his wife tonight about his future and where they, as a family, would live.

He arrived home at 5.39 p.m. expecting a frosty reception given how he had left things with Alison in the morning. As he walked in his wife greeted him with a light kiss on his lips and an instruction to open a bottle of wine. Rosie their daughter was sleeping soundly in her pink, padded rocker and the smell of Chinese food made Steve's mouth water.

"Let's eat and then you can tell me where we'll be living this time next year." Alison was upbeat and Steve was relieved he didn't have to say too much.

Alison continued, "I got a bundle of properties for sale around Norwich this morning. An estate agent said Callum Robertson had asked them to send a selection." Alison was fussing in the kitchen dishing up the takeaway. "The places look great, and the prices are half what you would pay in London. We'll have a look after we've eaten."

Steve was slightly taken aback. Alison seemed nervous and very rarely spoke so quickly. The DCI wasn't sure where his wife was taking the conversation, but he was happy to let her take the lead.

Once their meal was finished and their daughter had been put to bed for the night, the couple settled down on their sofa. Alison lay her head on Steve's shoulder. "I've been thinking, darling. Maybe moving to Norfolk wouldn't be such a bad thing. It's a big promotion for you and I know you love your job. The timing is right for Rosie, and you know I'd like to go back into NHS practice. The houses from the estate agent are stunning and I think you're right. We can have more open space and maybe it's a better environment to bring up Rosie."

Steve looked down at his wife. "Are you saying you'd move to Norfolk?"

"Yes, darling, I think I am if you want to go."

Chapter Twenty-Five

After a relaxing evening spent with his wife reviewing properties in Norfolk, Steve set out for his office with an unusual spring in his step. Had he known what this Wednesday September the 27th had in store for him, his step may not have been so spritely.

He arrived at New Scotland Yard at 07.57 a.m. to find DS Matt Conway slumped in the chair behind his desk, snoring gently. Steve was initially taken aback by this sight and considered leaving him to sleep but instead gently nudged him awake. Matt came to with a start, obviously disorientated and grasping to understand his immediate situation. After a few seconds he became fully conscious and stretched his frame while sitting in his chair.

"Good morning; have you been here all night?"

"Er. Yes boss, we had a bit of an incident at the club, and I've got a couple of characters downstairs I think you'll want to talk to." Matt broke off to stretch his arms over his head and yawned deeply.

"Look Matt, you go and get yourself tidied up. Have a shower and sort yourself out, and I'll see you in the canteen in half an hour. You can fill me in over breakfast, and I'll buy, full English I suppose?"

Matt Conway nodded and left quickly anticipating his fried breakfast.

Poppy was next to arrive, bringing him a coffee. As there was no one about, she lingered at Steve's door and gradually worked her way into his office before sitting down. He noted she was still dressing more conservatively these days but decided not to comment.

"I've got Uncle Terry tied up in knots just now." Poppy just blurted out this statement.

Steve could believe Poppy could easily twist Inspector Terry Harvey around her little finger but didn't understand what she meant.

"How so Poppy?" Steve sipped his coffee and although Poppy was a distraction, his mind kept wandering back to what Matt Conway had to tell him.

"Remember I suggested we look for Italians arriving from Palermo just before the first victim, Mariola Scala, was killed? Well Terry has been running a programme he's written just for the job. He's been at it for over a day."

Steve had a vague recollection of his conversation with Poppy but thought the idea of identifying Mafia killers arriving in the UK to knock off an Italian girl was an impossible task. Poppy had clearly thought otherwise and had asked her uncle to try to solve the problem.

"Well, no doubt he'll tell us when he has anything."

Poppy was sensitive enough to see her boss had things on his mind. "I'll get started then. I think Peter and Mary were out late last night following up with the girls under the rail bridge. I'm not sure when they'll be in."

Steve finished his coffee and set out for the canteen. He found a corner table, ordered a tea for himself and coffee for Matt plus his full English breakfast. Matt appeared just as Steve sat down. He looked fresher although his shirt and suit were in a sorry looking state being full of creases.

The pair sat while the drinks were delivered. "Right Matt, from the top. How come you pulled an all-night stint?"

Matt drank his coffee. "You know I was helping the finance guys stake out the Rainbow Caves Club last night?"

"Yes."

"Well, me and two uniformed lads got there about eight p.m. as planned. First thing the two so-called investigators say is can we count anybody going in. They're off for a pub meal. They got back about nine and nothing had happened. I left the two uniforms and sat with the finance guys until ten. Still nothing was happening. Not a soul had even tried to enter the club. I went back to our own car and then about quarter past ten, this guy turns up, dressed in bright colours and wearing a huge hat. One of the uniforms pointed out a couple of rough-looking individuals who turned up and seemed to be following the bloke in the bright colours. We kept an eye on them but all they did was stand in a doorway and smoke."

Matt broke off as his cooked breakfast arrived. In between mouthfuls he continued with his report.

"At 1.33 a.m., this colourful figure came out of the club and turned in the direction of the two guys in the doorway. As soon as he was level with them, they struck out and started to beat the living daylights out of him. We ran across the road and managed to pull the two thugs off and got them cuffed. The bloke on the ground was in a bad way so I called an ambulance and arrested the two tearaways." Matt wiped his plate with a piece of bread.

"Then what, you didn't stay here all night just because you arrested someone for affray?"

Pushing his plate away the detective sergeant gave a satisfied smile and drained his coffee. He signalled for a refill.

"I took them to central booking, but they wanted to talk, as I did, because I recognised the victim." Matt paused, building up the suspense.

Steve took the bait. "Well?"

"It was that guy we met yesterday with Antonio Conti, the one who sat in the corner, Quentin Somersby."

Matt sat back with a glow on his face while Steve tried to understand the significance of this information.

"You're sure it's him? He didn't look like a guy who would frequent a place like that and certainly not in bright clothes."

"It's him, Steve. That's why I was up most of the night. After we got the heavies into processing, I went to A and E. Quentin is in a bad way with internal injuries, broken bones and ribs and a fractured skull. These two knew what they were doing."

"Sounds like it." Steve was trying to work out the puzzle. "But what does it all mean?"

Matt sat forward. "I had the two brutes transferred to the holding cells downstairs and had an informal chat. Nothing official and nothing expected. They were happy to talk. They were keen to put a certain Andrew Black in the frame, said he'd paid them to teach Quentin Somersby a lesson. They wanted a deal and were happy to cooperate.

They said they were ex-IRA and hired themselves out for what they called security jobs."

Steve called for another two coffees. He decided he needed the caffeine buzz he didn't get from tea. "So you're saying our prime suspect in the Tracy Nelson murder eleven years ago and the bloke we've linked to the killings of Elsie Brown and Jack Ralph ordered Quentin Somersby to be beaten up and Quentin Somersby works with Antonio Conti, the headless girl's father who is also old Mafia?" Steve leaned forward and drew a deep breath. "Bloody hell Matt, what have we got here?"

"A puzzle Steve, but an interesting one, don't you think?"

"Is this telling us there's a connection between Antonio Conti and Andrew Black?"

"Well Quentin Somersby seems to be an associate of Antonio Conti so why would a low life like Andrew Black want to hurt Quentin unless he knew Antonio?"

"I need to think about this. Can you take statements from the two you arrested last night but do it by the book, no slip ups? It may be that Treasury will need this to help make their case, then you can knock off. I'll see you tomorrow."

"I'd rather hang around, Steve. I know you intend to lift this Black character today and in light of last night, I'd like to be around. This guy has some serious questions to answer."

"If you're sure." Smiling, Steve added, "Just don't fall asleep during the interview."

Matt finished his third cup of coffee and set off to interview the two ex-IRA men while the DCI went in search of answers.

***

Commander Alfie Brooks arrived at his office just as Matt Conway was finishing his third cup of coffee. His secretary-cum- gatekeeper hadn't arrived, so Alfie pushed open the door to his office to find a strange woman seated in one of his comfortable armchairs. A surprised Alfie didn't say anything but looked at this not unattractive woman who sat very primly, obviously awaiting the arrival of the commander. Alfie had always been susceptible to a shapely leg and a pretty face, and this visitor certainly caught his attention.

"Can I help you?"

The woman smiled and still sitting, offered her hand in such a way that Alfie didn't know whether to shake it or kiss it. He decided to shake it.

"I'm Stephanie Clarkson. I'm with the Treasury."

Alfie was curious and sat opposite his visitor. "Why are you here so early in the morning, Miss Clarkson?"

Stephanie gave a shy smile and almost fluttered her eyelids. "Please, call me Steph, all my friends do."

Alfie appreciated the vibrations coming from this woman but had no idea why she was here.

"OK Steph, but why are you here?"

Stephanie gave Alfie another long look. "I like that, Alfie." Steph was playing the role of sex queen very well. "Straight to the point. I can see we'll get on very well."

Alfie, taken aback as he was by this woman's presence in his office but enjoying the moment, was still none the wiser as to why she was there.

"Yes, that's as may be, but why are you here?"

"Oh, why does business always get in the way of making new friends, Alfie?" Steph gave a theatrical sigh before becoming more serious. "We understand you are in charge of an investigation into a company in which we have an interest."

"Oh, yes?"

"Yes, Mayflower Contracts run by a businessman called Antonio Conti."

"You know I can't comment on investigations."

"Not really." Stephanie became suddenly harder. Her facial features became less attractive. "You see Alfie, we need you to call off the investigation. In return we'll improve your pension pot by one million pounds. You'll be able to live well with that kind of cash and no one will ever know."

During his career Alfie had been offered bribes but never this amount of money. "Who is this 'we'?"

"Let's just say a group of people who have an interest in seeing any investigation into Mayflower Contracts ending before it begins."

"I think you overestimate my role here. As I understand it, any investigation will be handled by your own Treasury Department, and our role, if we have one, will be very minimal."

"But it was your DCI Burt who initiated the enquiry, and he reports to you. If you call your boy off then the whole thing will go away."

Alfie wasn't fully up to speed on Steve and Twiggy's joint task force, but it was clear this woman had heard something.

"Miss Clarkson, I'm going to do you a favour. I'm going to forget you were here and say nothing to my superiors."

Steph became angry and again her demeanour changed from sweet to hostile.

"Commander, you are a fool! All you have to do is call your boy off and get a million for doing almost nothing. If you don't cooperate, there are ways of letting it be known you are on the take." Stephanie Clarkson's voice had acquired a harsh, grating tone. "We can leak bank details with your name showing you have received money. If we did your career would be finished and your retirement would be a very poor one."

She stood up and looked down at Alfie. "Think about it, Alfie. A simple order from you to DCI Burt and a happy prosperous retirement or disgrace and no pension at all." Steph produced a business card and laid it down. "My number's on the card. You have forty-eight hours to agree or we release bank account details showing you're on the take."

What had at first been seen as a very attractive lady was leaving as a hard-nosed corrupt bitch who could ruin Alfie's career. He sat speechless and picked up Stephanie's card.

***

On his return to his office, Steve noted Peter and Mary were at their desks and Poppy was, as usual, typing away furiously. A quizzical look from Steve confirmed she was processing Matt's notes from last night into the electronic file.

As Steve passed her desk Poppy stopped her frenzied typing and announced, "We have the warrant to search the cars at Mayflower Contracts."

"Good. Mary, get a forensic team together and serve the warrant. We have the registration numbers of the three cars. If they're not all at the offices find them but get forensics to go over them with a fine-tooth comb. If Sophia Paulo was in the front seat of any of those cars, there will be trace evidence. Stay with them till they're finished."

DC Mary Dougan was surprised by this sudden injection of activity but gladly leapt to her feet, took the warrant from Poppy and rushed out the door.

Steve and Peter Jones sat around Steve's conference table. Steve hadn't had time to consider how the events of last night fitted into his theory that Andrew Black was involved in three murders. As the pair sat Peter waited for his boss to start the conversation.

"Have you heard about last night's events, Peter?"

"Only vaguely. I hear Matt had a late night."

"Yes, he did. Andrew Black, our main suspect in the Tracy Nelson murder eleven years ago, and the guy who ordered the killings of Elsie Brown and Jack Ralph, may be involved with Antonio Conti. Seems he paid two Irish heavies to seriously hurt Conti's partner."

Steve lapsed into deep thought and started talking to himself. "Now why would he do that? Unless he's working with Conti, and Quentin Somersby just got in the way. But what would a low life like Black have to do with Conti?" Steve shook his head. "Peter, let's bring Andrew Black in. We've got enough on him to arrest him for involvement in the three murders. If we can get him to talk maybe we'll learn why he had Somersby beaten up. Get a warrant and a search team together. Let's lift him at home. See what nasty secrets he has hidden away. Do it now, Peter. We'll squeeze him this afternoon."

Peter Jones looked pleased to have something positive to do at last but as he was leaving the DCI remembered what he'd been tasked with last night. "Did you get anywhere with the girls under the bridge last night?"

"Not really, Steve. One or two said they'd seen our victim and one even remembered the car. A bit flash for their normal punters was the expression but apart from that we drew a blank."

"OK Peter. Make sure you write it up and get Poppy to transpose it."

Peter Jones grinned. "Already done, boss."

Steve was about to move to his desk when Twiggy appeared carrying her usual bundle of papers. She let them fall from her grasp and took a seat opposite the DCI.

"And good morning to you Miss Rough."

Twiggy didn't blink. "Is it. I've been at it since the small hours. I hear you had a bit of excitement last night."

Steve brought his former colleague up to speed.

"But I don't understand where this Andrew Black fits in with Antonio Conti." Steve's tone was pleading.

"Ah! DCI Burt, our time together is paying off." Twiggy was laughing. Steve couldn't help but smile, despite his frustrations.

"You told me, back in the day the Black brothers were small-time drugs dealers. I think you said the murder victim was cabin crew flying out of Norwich and you thought she was a mule bringing in product for the brothers."

"Yes. I did say that."

"Well, once a drug dealer, always a drug dealer. Remember, we believe Conti makes his money from drugs and prostitution. It's not a big leap to see the brothers working for Conti. Maybe that's your connection."

Steve sat back and ran a few possibilities through his head. "You could be right Twiggy. Maybe that is the connection. Have you established where Conti gets his money?"

"No. It's early days but a word with the Drug Squad may not be a bad idea. I'll bet they have the Black brothers on their radar."

The DCI was silent. "Good idea but it's taking us into unknown territory. My focus is the murders and this Mafia thing's a distraction. I need to charge Andrew Black with three murders. Once I've done that all that's outstanding are the two Italian girls and I'm fairly sure Antonio Conti isn't involved. No father would kill his daughter and saw off her head. It's unthinkable."

"I agree, so what do you have?"

"A partial plate from an Audi. Mary Dougan is with a forensic team searching the Mayflower Contract cars. They all have private plates starting with the two registration letters 'MA' and their Audi is very similar to the one on the CCTV."

"So you think Antonio Conti didn't kill his daughter but one of his employees did?"

"It's possible but let's wait for Forensics."

"Does this mean you're still in this case for the time being?"

"I suppose so, but I don't want to get involved with vice, drugs or money laundering, just the murders."

Twiggy smiled a knowing smile. "If you say so, Steve. Right, I'd better bring you up to speed."

The DCI groaned. "If you must."

"Yes DCI Burt, I must." Twiggy made herself more comfortable in her chair. "We counted only sixteen punters going into the Rainbow Caves Club, so we are certain the monies being recorded as revenue aren't from takings. The money they claim to take as a result of trading must be dirty and coming from illegal sources."

"I'd have thought that was obvious given what your man Philip told us yesterday."

"You're right but as I said, in my world we move more slowly, but now we can carry out a full forensic examination of these clubs accounts. Remember it's only one of sixteen companies we have to check. We won't move until we have a watertight case. Juries don't usually understand financial trials, so we need everything in order. When Conti comes to court the trial could last two years."

Steve sat back and put his hands behind his head. "Rather you than me. I wouldn't have the patience."

"You will when you're Head of CID in Norfolk."

Steve gave Twiggy a withering look before he smiled. "We'll see. Now unless there's anything else, I need to think."

Twiggy collected her bundle of papers and left saying she'd keep in touch.

Steve looked at his watch. It was 10.59 a.m. "Poppy, do me a favour and get me a tea and something for yourself."

Poppy complied, saying as she left, "Frontline detectives don't get sent for tea and coffee."

Chapter Twenty-Six

As Steve finished his tea, Matt Conway appeared. "That's those two all taken care of. They admit the beating and confirm Andrew Black paid them five hundred quid to do it. They told me Black had insisted on them really hurting Quentin Somersby. 'Put him in hospital' was what one of them said Black told him."

Matt sat down as Steve sat back. "What's the connection? Why would Andrew Black want to hurt this Quentin Somersby character, and how do they know each other?"

"All good questions, boss, but there's clearly a connection."

Steve suddenly stood up. "Come on, let's pay Antonio Conti a visit. Mary and the forensic team should just about be done with the cars. Maybe they've got something for us."

As they left, Steve asked Poppy to have someone from the Intelligence Unit call him on his mobile. He wanted to talk to someone about the drugs trade in London. As Matt drove the pair to the offices of Mayflower Contracts, Steve's mobile rang.

"DCI Burt? This is DS Simon Spooner of Intelligence. I hear you want a word."

"Yes, DS Spooner. Thanks for calling." Steve looked at his watch. It was only fifteen minutes since he had asked Poppy to arrange this call. "I'm wondering what you have on a guy called Andrew Black."

Over the connection the DCI was sure he felt a sharp intake of breath and was surprised by the enthusiastic response he received. "Ah! The Black brothers, nasty types and the biggest drug dealers in the city."

"Apart from that have you anything on them?"

"No. They're slippery but I tell you one thing and it's strange really. They seem to have suddenly become organised. They were pushing Colombian white to anyone who'd buy but now they seem to be running a business, plus they're not selling powder any more but tablets. Looks like in the past few weeks they've become more sophisticated. Someone even reported they were wholesaling the tabs and expecting the pushers to place orders. If it's true it's an escalation to a proper business but what I know of the Blacks, it seems obvious that someone's put them up to it. We don't know where the tabs are being produced but they obviously do. I'd say they have a partner."

"Were they big in drugs before this move into tablets?"

"Oh yes. They weren't so well organised, but they did control most of the distribution. If anyone tried to set up in competition, one of the brothers would pay them a visit and suddenly the competition would disappear. The Drug Squad has been after them for years but so far haven't laid a finger on them."

Steve sat watching the traffic. "Interesting. Thank you, DS Spooner. Just so you know, Andrew Black has been arrested on murder charges so this background will help."

"Really? Well good luck, sir. He's a slippery one."

As Steve hung up, he turned to Matt who had heard the entire conversation over the car's hands-free system. "Any thoughts?"

Matt, concentrating on the traffic, which was typically congested for London, drew a deep breath. "I suppose if the Blacks were already big in drugs in London, is it possible Antonio Conti moved in and somehow persuaded them to work for him. He seems to run a proper business model with corporate offices and the like. The DS from Intelligence said the brothers were now better organised and running a business. Maybe that's the connection and how Andrew Black knows Quentin Somersby. They're all working together, and Conti is supplying these tablets."

"Yes. It makes sense, Matt. Let's ask Mr Conti."

As the two detectives exited their car, having parked it in a space marked for visitors in Mayflower Contracts carpark, DC Mary Dougal approached.

"No luck, boss. Forensics say all three cars are clean. Our victim wasn't in any of these cars."

The DCI was crestfallen. He had felt one of these cars was the one seen on the CCTV and that perhaps his visit now might have been to arrest a suspect. "Bugger. I'd hoped they would have found something. OK Mary, stand the team down."

"What do you want me to do?"

"Go back to the office." Steve was literally thinking on his feet as he stood opposite his detective constable. "I was so sure it was one of these cars I didn't ask for a full DVLA search of similar vehicles. Get Poppy to search for any dark-coloured Audi with the first two letters of the registration 'MA'. Tell her to only look inside the M25. We'll be finished here shortly so should be back within the hour."

Mary set off to stand down Forensics as Steve and Matt once again made their way to the office of Antonio Conti.

As they entered his office, they could see that the Italian was upset. Before Steve could say anything, Conti launched into a tirade of abuse and questions. He was clearly unhappy about having his cars searched and was demanding an explanation. "That woman detective you sent wouldn't tell me anything. All she gave me was this piece of paper called a warrant." Antonio marched to his desk and brandished the warrant. "What is going on Detective Chief Inspector? My staff are very concerned."

Steve and Matt let Antonio rant on until he ran out of steam. Steve decided as one father to another he should probably be more sympathetic towards Conti despite his criminal involvement in drugs and other illegal activities.

"I'm sorry if you are upset, sir. Please sit down and I'll tell you what I can."

Antonio Conti, having used his energy blowing off steam, sat quietly behind his desk. Steve and Matt sat opposite.

"We have CCTV of your daughter getting into an Audi similar to your company cars downstairs. We couldn't see the driver and only got a partial number plate. The first two index letters were 'MA', just like your car's downstairs, sir. You can see why we had to search them in case one of those cars was used in the murder of your daughter."

Antonio who looked to be in shock asked. "And?"

"We didn't find any evidence your daughter had been inside any of those vehicles."

Suddenly Antonio Conti sat up and became more animated. "You say my daughter got into an Audi similar to mine downstairs and it had 'MA' as the first two letters of the numberplate?"

"Yes sir." Steve could see Antonio had worked something out. "Does it mean anything to you?"

Antonio tried to cover up his obvious realisation as to who may have killed his daughter. He wasn't a very good actor and Steve knew he had worked something out.

"No, nothing Inspector. I'm not surprised you found nothing. Those cars are used by my staff and none of them would harm my little bird."

As Antonio talked, the DCI became convinced he knew something, but it was obvious he wasn't about to share anything with the police. Steve changed tack.

"I have to inform you, sir, that last night a serious incident took place involving your associate, Quentin Somersby. Mr Somersby was badly beaten and is in intensive care in St Thomas' Hospital. He is in a coma."

Antonio looked shocked. He was clearly trying to absorb this information. Almost to himself and in a quiet unbelieving voice he said, "What's going on, DCI Burt? First my daughter and now my partner. Suddenly I feel vulnerable. Is someone out to get me?"

"I don't know, sir. It may be just coincidence. I wanted to let you know about Mr Somersby." The two detectives stood to leave. Antonio was sitting behind his desk looking stunned. The swashbuckling angry individual who had greeted Steve and Matt five minutes ago was now missing to be replaced by what appeared to be a very puzzled man.

Steve recalling Antonio's reaction to the CCTV news prodded again. "You're sure, sir, that you don't know anything about an Audi similar to your own?"

Antonio was drifting into his own world but roused himself to answer. "No, Inspector, nothing."

He stood as the detectives made for the door. "Just one more thing, sir. Do you know a man called Andrew Black?"

Antonio was caught off guard and answered too quickly. "Oh no. Never heard of him. Why?"

Steve saw Conti was lying. "No reason. His name came up in our enquiries."

"Does he have anything to do with what happened to Quentin?"

Steve was diplomatic. "As I said, sir, it's just a name that came up."

Outside Steve pulled Matt's elbow as both officers came to a stop beside their car. "He's lying and I think he knows who killed his daughter. When I told him about the CCTV did you see how his whole body language, changed? His facial expression hardened, and you could almost see a light in his eyes. He's figured something out, but I don't know what it is. I just hope we can get to the killer before Antonio Conti does. The look in his eyes was pure evil."

"Do you want him watched?"

"No. We don't have enough. It's only my gut feeling but I'm sure I'm right. Antonio Conti knows who killed his daughter and we'd better find out who before he takes matters into his own hands."

***

Commander Alfie Brooks had spent most of the morning reviewing his conversation with Miss Clarkson. One moment he was telling himself to forget it as she obviously didn't know how little Steve and his team were involved in investigating Antonio Conti. The next moment, he was wondering how serious she was about setting up a false bank account in order to compromise him and potentially leave a nasty taste that he might be on the take. After deliberating his options, he made an appointment to see Assistant Commissioner Hayden Giles and to seek his advice.

At 12 noon exactly, Alfie entered the large modern office of the Assistant Commissioner. Hayden Giles was, as always, dressed immaculately and didn't appear to have a hair out of place.

The Commander was treated to coffee and biscuits and seated himself in one of the four red leather armchairs surrounding a coffee table. Alfie glibly thought that all senior officers' offices looked alike.

"Now Alfie, what can I do for you? You don't normally come round this way."

"Er. No sir, I've come about a Stephanie Clarkson. She—"

"Stop right there, Commander. Whatever you have come to allege you'd better have all the facts and watertight evidence. My relationship with Miss Clarkson is purely professional."

Alfie was stunned. This was not the reaction he was expecting. He had no idea why the AC was acting like this but the old cop in him told him to stay quiet. Something wasn't right here. As Alfie said nothing but pulled an inquisitive face, the AC felt obliged to continue.

"What have you heard, Commander, because whatever it is you'll never prove it."

Alfie saw beads of sweat appear on Hayden Giles' top lip. He wasn't a very good poker player.

Alfie decided to push his luck. The AC was obviously a worried man, and the name Stephanie Clarkson was clearly known to him.

"How do you know Miss Clarkson, sir?"

"As I said, professionally. She's a senior civil servant at Treasury and our paths have crossed once or twice. I think she does some ex-gratia consultancy work for a national company, and I seem to remember she asked my advice on security."

Alfie's policeman's instinct kicked in. He'd maybe ridden a desk for years but his nose for lies was still as sharp. He needed time to think why the AC had become so abrasive and defensive at the mention of Stephanie Clarkson's name. He didn't want to push his luck but wanted more from this senior officer who clearly had something to hide.

"She came to see me this morning, sir."

Hayden moved around in his chair, obviously uncomfortable. "Yes. What about?"

Alfie had to make a decision. He'd no idea what the AC was into, but his policeman's brain was shouting CORRUPTION. Alfie thought, *Why else would this senior officer be so nervous on hearing this woman's name?*

"She offered me a one-million-pound bribe to turn off an enquiry we are running."

The AC visibly relaxed and he smiled. "Is that it? I thought you were here for a different reason. I know about the approach Alfie. I hope you said yes; much easier for everyone."

Alfie couldn't believe what he was hearing. The Assistant Commissioner of the Metropolitan Police Force was encouraging an officer to accept a bribe! Commander Alfie Brooks had stumbled on something that needed careful thought and discussion with other officers. He needed to tease a few more details out of the AC before taking his leave.

"What did you have to do for your money, sir?"

"Now Alfie, we don't wash our dirty linen among ourselves. Suffice to say myself and a few others are expected to perform certain tasks to protect a certain businessman when asked to do so. We discussed how best to proceed in this case and thought a substantial payment towards your retirement might persuade you to call DCI Burt off."

Alfie saw how things were developing. "And the businessman in question is one Antonio Conti?"

Hayden Giles suddenly became wary of Alfie.

Alfie picked up on the change of mood and realised he had pushed too hard. "Well, sir, thank you for seeing me, it has been very informative and helped me make a decision."

Hayden wasn't sure whether he had blown his cover or whether Commander Brooks was now one of Miss Clarkson's team. "Any time Alfie, take my advice. Take the money and retire in luxury. Call off your man Burt; no one will be any wiser."

Alfie left, his head spinning. Having arrived to tell all about his bribe he was leaving being persuaded to take it. Assistant Commissioner Hayden Giles was obviously involved in some corrupt activity involving Stephanie Clarkson and Antonio Conti. But what? Alfie had to speak to Steve and Twiggy.

Chapter Twenty-Seven

Steve and Matt arrived back at New Scotland Yard just after one p.m. Matt went to the canteen to buy sandwiches for himself and his boss while Steve went straight to his office. There was an air of excitement and a buzz about the place. Peter, Mary and Poppy were all there chatting in an animated way Steve hadn't seen before.

"Good, everyone's here. Come on in. I want a debrief on where we are."

Matt arrived with the food and coffee as Steve's entire team settled in around his small conference table.

"Right. You first, Peter. What have you got?"

DI Peter Jones didn't refer to any notes. "We arrested Andrew Black on murder charges as instructed at 09.49 this morning. He was in his residence and wasn't happy. At one point he had to be restrained by two uniformed officers. He did a lot of shouting about his rights and got his wife to call a solicitor. He seemed to calm down after I showed him the search warrant."

Peter broke off his narrative to look directly at Steve. "Here's the thing, Steve. He calmed down and sat in the kitchen while we organised transport. One of the uniforms saw him remove an envelope from a tin on a shelf and stuff it into his pocket, obviously hoping no one would notice."

"Strange. Did you challenge him?"

"No. I knew we'd find it once he was booked. Anyway, we got him to central booking and when he had to empty his pockets, he kicked off again and again had to be restrained. I think it was only his lawyer turning up that calmed him down, but he was going on about the envelope, saying it belonged to him…" Peter paused. "You know the thing. He knows his rights, etc. Eventually we got him processed and I arranged to have him transferred to our cells in the basement. He's there now with his lawyer."

"Good work, Peter. What's so important about this envelope do you think?"

"I don't know." Peter fished inside his jacket and produced a plastic evidence bag, "I have it here. It's obviously important to him." Peter handed the evidence bag to his boss.

The DCI examined it, noted the envelope was sealed and wondered what it contained. He wanted to move on, so put the plastic bag to one side. "Matt and I will interview Mr Black later this afternoon."

"Mary, still nothing from forensics and the cars?"

"No, sorry boss. All three cars were clean."

Steve explained to his team about his discussion with Antonio Conti and his belief Conti knew who killed his daughter.

"I must have fed him something that I didn't know I had. I saw his whole being change when I mentioned the cars and then he blanked me, but it has to be something." Steve was obviously concerned. "Come on folks, help me out. What was it I told Conti?"

The table was silent. Mary offered a view that maybe the DCI had misread Antonio Conti's reaction. "Maybe he was just shocked. His daughter's been murdered, and we were as good as accusing him or a member of his staff of killing her."

"It's possible Mary but I know I saw something in his eyes. I gave him the missing piece, but I don't know what it is."

No one offered an explanation and Steve was about to wrap the meeting up when two things happened almost at once. First, he had a call from Commander Alfie Brooks ordering him to a meeting with Alfie at three p.m. and as soon as he had hung up, Inspector Terry Harvey arrived.

With his head spinning trying to recall exactly what he'd said to Antonio Conti, Steve motioned Terry to be seated. Steve knew Terry didn't waste anyone's time. He was here because he had something.

Terry Harvey had a buff-coloured file with him that he placed on the table in front of him. He looked at the sea of expectant faces and hoped his presentation skills were up to it. This looked like an audience hungry for information.

"I've spent a lot of computer time chasing up an idea DC Cooper there had." Terry nodded in Poppy's direction. She was used to being referred to as Poppy, but Terry, as her uncle, was conscious people didn't always remember her given name. "Poppy suggested we look at all Italians entering the UK just before the first Italian girl…" Terry paused to look at his notes, "… Mariola Scala, was murdered. It was one big task and to my surprise we found something."

Steve sat up while Poppy took on a look of self-satisfied pride.

"We found a Reggio Scala arriving from Palermo into Stanstead on the 4th of April, a week before the murder. I got his picture from Immigration and circulated it to Interpol and the Italian police. A policeman other than Poppy's dishy Inspector Alfonso," Mary sniggered at this remark, "came back to me, a Captain Tarragona. He's with the anti-Mafia squad on Sicily itself. Seems Reggio Scala is Mafia muscle, and his daughter did disappear from the family home to go to London. He confirmed she was due to marry another Mafia bloke but didn't fancy the idea. Captain Tarragona told me it is an honour thing. If your offspring is betrothed to the son or daughter of another member and doesn't go through with it, then it's all about honour. The offending family is ostracised until revenge has been taken."

Steve was interested but wished Terry would get to the punchline. "What form of revenge?"

Terry looked solemn as he replied "Death. In Captain Tarragona's opinion the girl's family would only be accepted back into the fold if she were killed."

"Bloody hell! That's a bit barbaric, isn't it?" Matt looked shocked.

Terry just shrugged. "I'm only the messenger but apart from the father being on the flight, there were two other Mafia members who, according to Captain Tarragona, would have been more than capable of carrying out the killing. His theory is that the father met with his daughter here one last time and the two thugs killed her after the father said goodbye to his daughter.

"Reggio Scala left Gatwick for Palermo two days after he arrived. The two thugs left the same day the girl's body was found. Captain Tarragona has their names and says he'll bring them in and sweat them but he's not hopeful of getting anything. He says if it's an honour killing then from our standpoint we may as well close the case. We'll never get a conviction."

Steve sat back. "Thanks Terry. So our first murder looks like a Mafia honour killing and that's that."

"Sorry Steve but it looks like it."

Matt Conway spoke up. "We've no forensics sir and the pathologist who raised this one with us said there was nothing on the body. Inspector Harvey's suggestion seems to fit. If the killers have gone back to Sicily and we've no evidence to get them back here, we should maybe let the Italians handle it."

With a huge sigh Steve stood up clearly disappointed that Matt was right. They'd nothing on the Mariola Scala killing. "You're right Matt. We've got enough going on without interfering in a Mafia killing."

As he walked towards his desk, his team stood ready to leave. "Matt, we'll take Andrew Black after I've seen the Commander. Peter and Mary write up your notes and give them to Poppy for the file."

Steve held up the envelope inside the plastic bag. "I wonder why this is so important to Andrew Black?" The DCI locked it in the top drawer of his desk before leaving to meet Commander Alfie Brooks.

***

It was exactly 2.56 p.m. when Steve was ushered into Alfie's office by his secretary. As he entered, he was surprised to see Twiggy deep in conversation with the elderly policeman.

"Ah! Steve come and join us. Miss Rough has been filling me in on her case. All very complicated, but it sounds fascinating." Alfie seemed in a jovial mood but that was about to change. No coffee was offered, and once Steve sat down Alfie launched into his pre-prepared speech.

"What I'm about to say goes no further than this room." Alfie didn't wait for an acknowledgement. "Have you come across a Stephanie Clarkson in any of your investigations involving this Antonio Conti character?"

Steve and Twiggy looked at each other and shrugged a no.

Alfie had a thin file in front of him. He removed the two sheets of A4 paper the file contained and left them on top of the file.

"It seems someone doesn't want Antonio Conti investigated. This Stephanie Clarkson mistakenly thought I could influence both your investigations and offered me one million pounds to order you, Steve, to drop any enquiries into Mayflower Contracts and Antonio Conti. She was quite insistent and even threatened me with a stitch-up showing I had been on the take if I didn't agree to her demands."

Steve let out a whistle. "Wow! Alfie. Where does she come from?"

"That's the point. She's a senior civil servant in the Treasury. You're sure you haven't come across her, Miss Rough?"

"No, I think I'd remember."

Alfie lifted the papers but didn't pass them around. "This is a record of my conversation with this Stephanie written immediately after she left. I want you to witness my signature and each keep a copy in a safe place in case she follows up on her threat." Alfie signed each page and passed over the papers to be countersigned. Steve and Twiggy retained their copies.

"Christ Alfie, this sounds serious. If this woman spreads rumours about you it could lead to an enquiry."

Alfie grinned. "Don't worry, Steve. I've been at this a long time but keep that paper safe just in case."

Everyone was silent.

"Now for something really spooky." Alfie explained his conversation with Assistant Commissioner Hayden Giles and how he went to talk over the bribe but ended up being encouraged to accept it. "Giles has to be on the take but how do we prove it? I'm reluctant to go to Professional Standards in case I am wrong. He is after all a very senior officer. I don't suppose his name has cropped up in your enquiries?"

Twiggy answered. "No sir. Do you want me to take a look at his financials? I could see if anything looks odd. If there is, it may be enough to take it to Professional Standards."

"Could you do it without him or anyone else knowing?"

Twiggy laughed. "Don't worry sir, I'm famous for not leaving a trail."

"OK but unofficially and only discuss this with me or Steve."

"No problem. Now if you'll excuse me, I have a mountain of work and you've just added to it, sir." Twiggy stood as did Steve. She rushed ahead of him, and as she left, she waved Alfie's piece of paper behind her. "Don't worry about this. It's safe with me." In a flash Twiggy was gone.

Steve was slower to exit.

"How's the case coming?" Alfie was looking happier than he had a few minutes earlier.

"Looks like the first Italian killing was a Mafia thing, an honour killing. We think we've identified the killers but they're back in Italy. The Italian cops will sweat them but we've no forensic or evidence of any kind so it's not looking like we'll get a result."

Steve went on to explain his suspect in the eleven-year-old Norfolk murder, and the recent killings he'd gone to Norwich to investigate, appeared to be involved with Antonio Conti and had ordered the beating of Conti's number two. The DCI didn't confide in his senior officer the fact he believed Antonio Conti knew the identity of his daughter's killer.

"Well, if you need any help let me know. It sounds like you have enough on your plate."

With a nod of agreement, Steve returned to his own office where Matt Conway was waiting.

"Boss, that lawyer Andrew Black has is screaming blue murder. He says his client has been held for seven hours and hasn't been seen by a single CID officer. He's threatening to put in a complaint."

"All right Matt. Give me five and we'll make a start. Pull all the files. I'll lead but you back me up."

As Matt Conway went to retrieve the hard copy files, Poppy appeared and was in an even more excited state than usual. "Sir, we've found the German."

Steve stared in disbelief. "What, Gunther Schmitt?"

"The very one. Uniform picked him up on Kensington High Street. Seems he was window shopping and didn't know we were looking for him. He's downstairs in interview room three."

Steve took a deep breath. Everything was happening at once and he had to prioritise. He called out for Peter Jones and Matt. "Peter, you go with Matt and start with Andrew Black. Start interviewing him but only on the old case from Norwich, just stick to that. It's all in the file and Matt is more or less up to speed. Witness statements, DNA, proof he was in Norwich the day of the killing. Everything you'll need to get him to talk. I'll get to him when I can. Mary and I need to talk to this German. Can you do this?"

Peter Jones looked nervous but pluckily said he could. Matt Conway just stood with a neutral look covering his features, but his eyes said something different. He shrugged and nodded. All four officers headed to the interview suite below New Scotland Yard. The DCI's head was spinning but he felt alive and could feel the adrenaline rush. He was looking forward to the next few hours and felt something was about to break.

Steve and Mary entered the interview room housing Gunther Schmitt. He was seated behind the standard table screwed to the floor and Steve thought perhaps this wasn't the best environment for this interview. A softer atmosphere would have been better, since, after all, Gunther wasn't a suspect. Steve and Mary sat opposite the German. Steve had a slim file he placed in front of him.

Gunther was what most people thought a German looked like. He had a beer belly that must have taken some filling over the years, he was tall but overweight, had the red-veined nose of a drinker and the complexion of someone who spent time outdoors.

"Mr Schmitt, thank you for agreeing to this interview."

"I had little choice. Two policemen approached me and asked my name. Next thing I'm in a police car being driven here. Can you please inform me why I am here?"

Gunther spoke perfect English, slightly accented the way American actors portray German soldiers in World War Two movies.

"We believe you can help us with our enquiries into the death of a Miss Sophia Paulo."

Gunther moved his bulk uncomfortably in his cheap plastic chair. "Ah! I see."

"Can you tell us what your involvement with Miss Paulo was?"

"I didn't have any involvement." Gunther smiled a weak smile and was obviously considering how to answer. In the end he decided to tell all. "Inspector, I am a private enquiry agent and it just happens I do a lot of missing persons work for an organisation based in Sicily." Gunther tilted his head. "You'll understand I cannot say who my client is?"

The DCI nodded. "Please carry on."

"I was given a commission to find a lady called Sophia Paulo. I was told she was living in London and all I had to do was discover where she was living and pass the address on to my client. That's it, Inspector, nothing more than a missing persons case."

Steve noticed Mary was taking notes. Gunther was here as a witness, so the recording machine was not switched on. Steve analysed Gunther's statement.

"And did you find her?"

"Yes, eventually. At first all I could discover was that she was working as a prostitute. I went around all the places such people hang out with their pimps and eventually met the lady."

Steve remembered Gunther had been reported as harassing pimps, so his story stood up to scrutiny. Steve remained silent allowing Gunther to carry on.

"She didn't want to give me her address but after a few false starts I eventually followed her home and passed the address to my client. That done, my contract was finished. I received my fee and have been having a few days' holiday seeing the sights of London."

This sounded plausible but Steve wasn't convinced Herr Schmitt was being totally truthful. He took a few seconds before deciding to carry on. He produced the CCTV picture of Gunther watching Sophia Paulo get into the Audi. The picture was slid across the table.

"I don't think that's totally correct is it sir? That photograph shows you spying on the victim after you had discovered where she lived. Can you explain it?"

Gunther wasn't fazed. He looked at the picture. "Yes, my client wanted me to keep an eye on the lady to ensure she didn't leave London. Also, he wanted me to report if she met a man who wasn't a customer and if she did, I was to follow the man and report his address. This picture is of me keeping her under surveillance, nothing more."

Steve had to admit Gunther Schmitt was an impressive witness. Being caught lying didn't upset him. He just changed his narrative to make it sound convincing.

"And did she meet any men who weren't clients?"

"Not that I saw."

Steve was beginning to wonder if Gunther had anything useful to offer. He seemed to be what they thought he was. Someone paid by the Mafia to find Antonio Conti's daughter in the hope she would lead them to her father.

Steve didn't see any advantage in continuing to interview Gunther until Mary Dougan asked, "From your position in the photograph, sir, it looks like you had a view of the driver of the Audi car our victim is getting into. Did you see the driver?"

The DCI was annoyed with himself. He should have thought of that. He silently thanked Mary.

"No, I didn't have a view of the driver."

"Did you see anything, sir? Was he a big or small man, was he black or white; what was the colour of his hair? Anything you can recall sir will be a help." Mary had become excited by her own sudden thoughts regarding this interview.

"I'm sorry miss, but as I said I didn't see the driver, but you are wrong in one aspect. The driver wasn't a man. It was definitely a woman driving that car."

Both Steve and Mary looked at each other completely taken aback. Both blurted out simultaneously, "A *woman*!?"

Gunther gave a satisfied grin. "Yes. All I can tell you is that the car was parked with the passenger door on the kerb side so Miss Paulo could walk straight into the car. The driver leant over, and the passenger door window was obviously down so she could talk to Miss Paulo before she got into the car. The lighting was poor, but I could make out a white woman with fair longish hair as she stretched across to speak with Miss Paulo."

The DCI sat back trying to work out what this meant. The working theory was that whoever killed Sophia Paulo was the driver of the Audi and that he was almost certainly a punter who used low rent prostitutes, but this revelation changed everything.

Steve stood followed by Mary. "Mr Schmitt you have been very helpful. If I can ask you to write what you have told us down as a statement, a constable will give you pen and paper and no doubt a cup of coffee. If you put your address in Germany on your statement and a contact number, we'd be grateful. Once you've finished, we will have a car take you anywhere you need to be in London."

Mary hurried off to arrange things and Gunther stood and shook Steve's hand. It had all been very civilised and very revealing, but Steve had no idea what this evidence did to his case.

Chapter Twenty-Eight

The DCI got back to his office to find Twiggy talking to Poppy. He looked at the clock; it was 4.27 p.m. As soon as she spotted her old boss, Twiggy immediately stood and followed Steve into his office.

"You look terrible."

"Well thanks for that warm greeting, Miss Rough. In fact, I may look bad, but I feel fine. I'm living on caffeine and adrenaline at the moment." He told Twiggy what Gunther Schmitt had just told him. Looking puzzled Steve asked, "Have you got any woman in the frame on the accounting side? The only one I've got is Conti's secretary. She has access to the cars so it could have been her, but the cars are all clean."

Twiggy thought. "No, there are no female players in the Mayflower business I can think of, unless you include the escorts."

Steve's mind was spinning but he knew from previous experience not to push too hard for an answer. One would come.

"Anyway Twiggy, what have you got?"

"Not much, but I wanted you to know we've traced the money back to a company in Amsterdam called Italian Resources. It's run by a character called Jean Franco. But here's the thing. It was set up three years ago and the second name on the registration is Antonio Conti. Most of the money used to set up Mayflower seems to have come from Amsterdam, but get this, Jean Franco's not on any of the documents for Mayflower. It looks like Conti used the money from Italian Resources to set up his own business. I just wondered if the killing of his daughter might be some form of revenge attack for cutting Franco out of the London deal?"

"It's possible but it doesn't sit right. If it was revenge then why sever the head and make it almost impossible to identify the body. Surely revenge means I'm telling you what I've done."

"Good point Steve. Ah well, it was just a thought. I'm off to spend the next few hours with Philip going over another of Conti's fictitious companies. Wish me luck."

Twiggy was gone and before Steve could draw breath Peter and Matt entered. Steve could tell by their body language that they hadn't got very far with Andrew Black.

"Nothing but a string of no comments. Every bloody question, and that solicitor is a waste of space. He's happy to sit there and smile at his client." Matt Conway was stomping around. Steve thought if he had a cat then Matt would be kicking it all over the office.

Peter Jones took a seat and held up his hands. "Sorry Steve. We tried everything but he's saying nothing. Maybe you should have a go at him."

Mary Dougan arrived next carrying a tray of coffees and Steve's team assembled in his office with their coffee. Poppy, without being invited, joined them and as before took the seat at the head of the table. Steve was looking perplexed and decided to try to tease out what the team knew.

"We've got two cases running in parallel. The Sophia Paulo murder that seems to be linked to her father's illegal empire and the eleven-year-old Norwich murder of Tracy Nelson that's linked to the more recent murders of Elsie Brown and Jack Ralph. We're nowhere on the first case. We have the killer of the second downstairs but he's not talking. Also, there's a suspicion that the man downstairs is somehow tied up with the second victim's father." He looked around the table and once more asked for ideas.

Poppy was the first to speak up. "Can either of the cases wait? I mean shouldn't we concentrate on the easiest one first?"

"We could try to crack Andrew Black. He's downstairs and we have the evidence. We just need to get to him." Mary Dougal was grinning at Poppy.

"Not a bad idea, unless we have anything concrete on the Sophia Paulo killing. Our new evidence doesn't take us very far and we're now looking for a woman but have no idea who she might be."

"Sounds like a plan, boss. Let's leave the Conti killing for now and concentrate on getting a result on the other case." Matt looked tired but still seemed alert. Steve remembered his DS hadn't had more than four hours' sleep last night and that was in an uncomfortable office chair.

The DCI made a decision. "Right, Matt, you and I will have a go at Andrew Black. Peter, you and Mary go through everything we have on Antonio Conti and the murder notes. Check to see if any women appear that we've overlooked. Poppy, chase up DVLA again. Let's get a list of Audis with the first two registration characters 'MA'." He scanned the table. "Got it?"

With fresh enthusiasm the team left to do their bit and Steve and Matt walked down to the interview suite below New Scotland Yard.

Andrew Black looked exactly as Steve had envisioned him, big, fat and ugly. He noticed the size of his hands and thought he'd never seen bigger hands on a human being. After the formalities, Matt switched on the mandated twin tape deck, Steve and Matt introduced themselves to the tape and the DCI began.

"Now Andy, my sergeant here tells me you've not been very cooperative." Steve looked at his suspect with a cold stare. He recalled practising this look in his bathroom mirror and hoped it would have the desired effect on Andrew Black. It certainly scared Steve looking in his mirror.

"That's always a mistake, Andy. You see, if you talk to us we can help you see how impossible your position is. It will also help us to understand if we are wrong about anything. Who knows? You might be able to explain away all of our evidence and you can leave a free man." Steve paused and continued with his stare. "Of course if you don't talk to us we'll draw our own conclusions and charge you with three murders. Then it's up to the cou—"

"Three murders! Where the hell do you get that from?" *Now* Andy Black was talking.

"There you are, Andy. I was just about to say if you don't talk to us it'll be up to the courts to decide on your guilt based on the evidence, but you've found your tongue."

Steve switched from his practiced look to applying his more friendly 'I'm your new best friend' look.

"Tell us about Tracy Nelson Andy?"

"Who? Never heard of her."

Steve tutted. "Andy, if you're going to talk to us at least make it the truth. You knew Tracy Nelson. She was an air hostess who flew out of Norwich Airport and brought in your drugs from Amsterdam." Steve kept his voice light. "You should remember, you strangled her eleven years ago with those great big hands of yours."

"You've got no proof."

"Ah Andy. It's good we're talking because I can show you why we think you're guilty of this murder. It may be that we have no proof but let's get started, shall we?"

Andy Black made no comment as Steve opened his file and continued in his new-best-friend mode. Pretending to be ill-prepared, Steve took a few minutes to find what in fact was always the first report in the file.

"Ah! Here it is. You and your brother stayed at the Horse and Crown in Norwich the night before and after Tracy Nelson's murder. That was in 2010. Is that correct?"

"Could have been but it was a long time ago."

"Yes, of course. You were seen with Tracy on the day of her murder going into her flat by a neighbour. She reported you were both in a drunken state and you were rude to this neighbour."

"I don't remember, anyway I thought that had bee—"

Steve smirked. Andrew Black had made his first mistake. "You thought that report had been lost. You thought DI Jack Ralph had buried it in exchange for bribe money."

Andy looked shocked and like all crooks of limited intelligence, he couldn't multitask using his limited number of brain cells. The DCI knew if he kept changing the subject matter, Andy would slip up.

"How could you know about that?" Andy looked at his lawyer who shifted uncomfortably in his seat. He was experienced enough to see the police had a case against his client.

"You see, Andy, we know everything. But let's not dwell on that; after all, we're having a chat and I'm telling you why we think you killed Tracy Nelson." Steve turned over another page in his file.

"We know you were in Tracy's bedroom, and you had sex with her. Your DNA was all over the place. Our forensic team was impressed by the places where they found your semen. I think the word they used was 'athletic'." Steve tried to look envious. "Now surely you're not going to deny having sex with Tracy on the day she was killed?"

Steve was sure he saw Andy's chest swell at being told his sexual prowess was athletic.

"Well, no, I gave her a good time all right."

"So you're now saying you knew Tracy Nelson?"

"Well yeah but I never killed her. We might have fooled around a bit but that was all."

"You see Andy how smart you are to talk to us. We thought you'd killed her after you'd had sex with her but here you are setting us straight."

Andrew Black sat up at Steve's words almost proud that he'd found a way out of a tight hole.

Steve continued. "So your fingerprints being all over the bedroom are to be expected given you've admitted to being there, and also your DNA, as you've explained?"

Again, Andy sat up straight. "Of course, you can't have one without the other." He was smiling and even looked like he was enjoying himself.

His solicitor could see the traps and knew Steve was no fool. He tried to caution his client to go back to 'no comment' answers but Andrew now mentally back as the Chairman told his brief to be quiet. He was handling things.

Steve was inwardly delighted by Andy's attitude. He turned another page in the file.

"We'll take a cast of your hands later, but I'll bet the bruising on Tracy's neck where her killer held her and strangled her will match the spread of those enormous hands of yours, Andy. Our pathologist thought the killer had to have a long spread with his fingers and must have had overly large hands. Did you know we can match hands to bruises where a victim has been manually strangled, Andy?"

The Chairman wasn't looking so confident now. He said nothing but his gaze dropped to the table. Steve ploughed on. "Do you know a man called Neil Furlong, Andy?"

"No." Andy was looking less than comfortable.

"Now Andy, what did we say about talking and lying?" Steve was still being Andy's best friend. "You see, we have Furlong on a double murder charge, and he told us you called him after you'd killed Tracy Nelson and he tidied up before he got you out of the flat and back to London. Now Furlong has no need to make up such a story Andy. His statement together with the evidence we have and your confirmation you were there makes for a pretty watertight case, I'd say."

Turning to Andy's solicitor, Steve carried on, "Wouldn't you agree your client appears to be bang to rights?"

The lawyer made no comment but whispered in Andy's ear. After a few seconds of urgent whispering, the lawyer asked to be left alone with his client. Matt spoke for the tape suspending the interview at 5.43 p.m. on Wednesday the 27th of September.

***

Matt and Steve returned to the office to find Poppy keying away furiously on her keyboard. Peter and Mary had obviously decided the search for a woman somewhere in the murder notes was a waste of time and had closed all the files. No one said anything as the pair arrived back.

"Why so gloomy?" Steve's remark was addressed to Mary.

She shrugged her shoulders. "There's no unknown woman anywhere in these files, boss. We haven't missed anybody."

Poppy's phone rang and Steve, still standing in his outer office, heard her side of the conversation. The part that spiked his interest was Poppy saying, "He's still here," and, "I don't know but he seems OK."

As Poppy replaced the receiver she looked shyly at Steve. "That was Inspector Harvey sir. He's coming over."

Steve in turn looked quizzically at his admin assistant. Knowing Poppy was up to speed on most things that happened he was surprised she wasn't more forthcoming and also very formal calling her uncle by his rank.

Steve and Matt went into Steve's inner office and sat at his conference table awaiting Terry Harvey. "Matt, no offence but you look like you're doubling as a scarecrow. You're in the same gear you arrived in yesterday morning, and you've only had a few hours' sleep. Call it a day and don't come in tomorrow. You've earned a rest."

"Thanks Steve, but I get a feeling we're zeroing in on something." Matt shrugged. "If I don't fall asleep, I'd like to hang around. I'll bet our man downstairs coughs to the Tracy Nelson murder and then we'll have him for conspiracy, at least on the other two. By the way, the way you handled the interview was brilliant. I didn't know you were such a good actor."

Before Steve could comment, Terry Harvey appeared at the office door, tapped gently and walked in with his niece in tow. Without being invited both Terry and Poppy sat down. Both looked crestfallen and Steve wondered what was coming.

"Steve. I'm sorry but we screwed up. Poppy asked me to do a DVLA search for cars owned by Mayflower Contracts."

Steve wasn't in the mood for more of Poppy's delegations. "I told *you* to do that, Poppy."

Terry Harvey held up his hand. "Look Steve. She asked and I have more horsepower to do that kind of search than she does. Roast her later if you want but please hear me out."

Steve had never seen Terry like this before, so he backed off and let his friend carry on.

"As you know we got three hits, and all had the prefix letters 'MA'."

"Yes, but they were all clean."

"Well, I missed a fourth."

"What!" The DCI was incredulous. "How! Why!"

"Mayflower contracts bought four identical Audis, and each had a private plate starting with 'MA'. Three stayed with the company but the fourth was gifted by Antonio Conti to someone else, I presume his girlfriend."

Both Steve and Matt sat forward hanging on Terry's every word. "Go on."

"The car was being transferred to the new keeper and that's how we missed it. It was a timing thing. If our search had been fifteen minutes later, we'd have found it."

Steve was having palpitations. The build-up to Terry's reveal was too much to take. "Just give us the name Terry."

"The fourth car was transferred to a Miss Stephanie Clarkson."

The DCI sat back. He could hardly believe it but slowly all the pieces fell into place. This was the woman who had tried to bribe Alfie Brooks to persuade him make any investigation into Antonio Conti go away. She had a similar car as had been seen on the CCTV, and the German Gunther said it was a woman driving the car that picked up Conti's daughter the night she was murdered.

Silence descended on the table. Slowly Steve's breathing returned to normal. He looked deliberately at Poppy.

"Get Stephanie Clarkson's address and get a warrant to search her premises and her car."

Steve looked at his watch. It was 6.44 p.m. He called out to Mary and Peter, "Peter, get a forensic search team on the go. Poppy will give you the address. I want you and them there at seven thirty tonight. I think we may have our killer.

"Mary get down to the interview suite and have Andrew Black held overnight. This now has priority. We'll pick up with him again tomorrow. Matt if you're up to it, you come with me, and we'll see what Miss Clarkson has to say for herself."

"You really think this woman could be the killer?" Matt was standing up and tying his tie back into his creased collar.

Steve surmised, that if she were brazen enough to bribe a Metropolitan Police Commander, she could easily be capable of murder. Steve paused to think, but why? Why would a senior civil servant decapitate the daughter of the man who presumably was more than just a friend?

"I think it's possible Matt but let's go and find out. Right troops, we'll leave from the garage at seven p.m. sharp."

Terry Harvey stood. "Sorry Steve, I should have looked."

The DCI playfully punched the Inspector's shoulder. He smiled as he said "Yes, you should but no harm done. Who knows, you may have just solved our case."

***

Stephanie Clarkson had been surprised and delighted to get Antonio's phone call telling her he would visit her tonight and that he was taking her out for an elegant meal. Steph was excited as Antonio had proven to be a man of fixed habits and her enjoyment of him had been restricted to a once-a-month dinner, followed by passionate and athletic sex. For him to call out of his normal routine must mean something and she hoped he had at last seen the sense of formalising their relationship with marriage.

She had spent hours on her hair, her make-up, her dress selection and most importantly, her underwear. She had decided to give Antonio the full Stephanie Clarkson treatment in the hope her fantasy of marriage might come to pass.

Antonio entered Stephanie's apartment in fashionable Knightsbridge at exactly the time DCI Burt and his team were leaving the underground garage at New Scotland Yard heading for the same apartment. It was seven p.m. exactly.

Antonio, dressed in a smart dinner jacket, was carrying a large bunch of roses that he handed to Stephanie as he lightly kissed her on both cheeks. Antonio had never brought flowers before, and Stephanie's heart missed a beat hoping this signified her wildest dreams might come true.

"I have wine chilling, darling. Help yourself while I put these lovely roses in water." Steph headed for the kitchen as she spoke. "I'll leave them in water in the sink and get a vase later. They really are beautiful."

She returned from the kitchen to find Antonio had poured two glasses of white wine, but she was disappointed to see he had seated himself in a single armchair and not the oversized sofa that dominated the elegant room. Steph took her glass from the table and sat down on the sofa. She had hoped for something more intimate but thought things would change as the evening wore on.

"Well, this is an unexpected pleasure, darling. Are we celebrating something special?"

Antonio sipped his wine and stared at his girlfriend. He said nothing.

Steph tried again. "Where are we going, darling? Somewhere horribly expensive?"

Antonio placed his wine on a side table beside his chair. "I know exactly where you are going, DARLING" The emphasis on the word and the venom that was evident in Antonio's voice startled Stephanie. She wasn't sure how to react but pretended not to notice a chilling of the atmosphere.

"What do you mean, Antonio? You know exactly where I'm going; surely we're going together."

Antonio Conti allowed himself a sarcastic smile. "You may be right but I'm not going just yet, but you my DARLING," the menace that came with this word was there again, "are headed there very soon."

Stephanie was becoming nervous. "Stop talking in riddles. Where am I going? Is it a holiday?"

She was suddenly very uncomfortable and nervous. She was talking purely to settle her nerves.

Antonio stood and looked down at this glamorous lady seated on the elegant sofa. "You my dear are going to hell; I may well follow you but not tonight."

She cowered back into the corner of the sofa. Her glass of wine spilt onto her elegant and expensive gown. "I don't understand. What is going on, Antonio?"

Antonio's words were said slowly to emphasise the venom they held. "You killed my little bird, my beautiful Sophia."

Steph suddenly jerked back further into the corner. "No, no Antonio, I didn't! How could you think such a thing? I love you; I'd never do anything to hurt you."

"The police came to see me earlier. They said they had CCTV of one of my cars picking up Sophia the night she was killed."

In a panic Steph blurted out, "But what makes you think it was me? Anyone in the office could have used the car?"

Antonio drew a knife from his inside pocket. It was an evil-looking weapon that he now caressed running his thumb over the sharp blade.

"Unfortunately for you my dear, the British police are smart and searched the three cars at the office. They didn't find any evidence of Sophia having been in any of them. Of course I don't think they know about your car. I bet, if they search your car, they will find traces of my little bird." Antonio continued to play with the knife and saw Stephanie's eyes were glued to it. She was staring at it almost mesmerised.

"But you don't know it was me!" Stephanie was shouting and had begun to cry.

"The police knew the registration started with 'MA'. I know it was you. All I need you to tell me is why." Antonio's voice was calm and measured. He was choosing his words carefully.

Steph was now crying uncontrollably. She decided to tell Antonio everything. In between sobs and deep uncontrollable breaths, she started to explain, to show she had done it for him.

"You told me your daughter was living in London, but you couldn't see her because it wasn't safe. I love you Antonio and will do anything for you, so I decided to find your daughter." An uncontrollable bout of sobbing delayed Steph's story for a few minutes. Antonio waited. Eventually she carried on.

"I found her and realised she was a prostitute. She would have blackened your family name and I knew that she would bring trouble to us after we were married. I had hoped to persuade her to give up her way of life and told her we were to be married." More sobs and tears before Steph gathered herself and continued. "She threw me out and told me not to come back. It was obvious she didn't want to be part of your new family and I knew she would always be a problem."

Antonio still stroked the blade of his knife. Stephanie, on seeing this, thought she was persuading him she had acted in his best interests.

"I went to the place I knew she worked from and told her you wanted to see her. I brought her here and ran a bath. She was stinking of sweat and sex, it was horrible. I don't know how it happened, but I saw her clothes on the bathroom floor all cheap and nasty and something snapped. I knew our only chance of happiness was if this creature were not part of our lives." Stephanie once more broke down and cried uncontrollably. Her expensive make-up was running down her face in rivers as she wiped her eyes with the back of her hand.

"I'm so sorry, Antonio. I grabbed her hair from behind while she was in the bath. I don't remember how it got there but I had a kitchen knife in my hand, and I just slashed away at her throat. I don't remember but I must have kept slashing because the next thing I knew I was holding her head by her hair."

Stephanie Clarkson had just admitted killing Antonio's daughter. She was pleading for her life. Antonio knelt in front of her as though he were about to propose.

***

The DCI accompanied by Matt Conway and two uniformed officers approached the door to Stephanie Clarkson's flat, having been given access to the building by the porter on duty. As Steve was about to knock on the door, they heard a loud scream. Looking anxiously at Matt and on hearing further loud cries the DCI nodded to the bigger of the uniformed officers to break down the door, having tried the handle and found the door locked. After three attempts, the officer succeeded in splintering the door frame allowing Steve to enter, followed by Matt and the uniformed officers.

"Good evening, Inspector." Antonio Conti was kneeling in front of Stephanie who had blood on her cheek and her throat. Antonio was holding the knife in his right hand and Steve noticed there was already blood on the blade. Antonio continued. "You are just in time to witness an act of revenge. This lady has admitted to killing my little bird and now you will see the price she must pay for such an act." Antonio moved the knife closer to his girlfriend's throat.

"Hold on sir, we know this woman killed your daughter, that's why we are here. We have the evidence, and the courts will convict her. What you're doing isn't justice, it's murder."

Antonio appeared to be thinking about the DCI's plea. "You are, of course, right but I'm afraid revenge has to be mine. British justice must come second."

Steve moved a pace forward wondering if he could rush Antonio and take the knife from him. He calculated he couldn't. The knife point was too close to the woman's throat, and it looked as though Antonio had already cut her cheek and throat. He was clearly intent on using the knife. Steve tried again.

"Listen sir. We have the evidence. She'll go away for a very long time but if you carry on, you'll go to prison. Please put down the knife and let us arrest her."

Steve took another step forward, but Antonio raised his free hand. "That's far enough Mr Burt. I know you mean well but my code of honour demands I do this."

Stephanie was sobbing and almost paralysed with fear. She was crouching in the corner of the sofa; her face was a mixture of congealed blood and black make-up that had run with her tears. She just sat and sobbed.

Antonio, seeing Steve was ready to pounce, decided he had to act. Before any of the policemen could react, he lowered the hand holding the knife, removing it from Stephanie's throat. He held it with the handle firmly placed against his heart and the blade pointing away from his body. In one swift move, he lunged towards Stephanie. The knife penetrated her heart and with Antonio's weight behind it, the blade sawed through other vital organs. Stephanie Clarkson died instantly.

Steve saw Antonio fall on top of the woman, but it took several seconds for him to realise what had just happened. Antonio remained lying on top of Stephanie after the knife did its job. The room was silent as Steve and Matt slowly moved forward. Steve touched Antonio's shoulder and the Italian rose from his kneeling position to face the policeman.

"I had to do it; she killed my little girl." Antonio just stood, arms by his side and a satisfied smile on his face. In his mind he had avenged his daughter and nothing else mattered.

"Matt, read him his rights and get him over to central." Steve noticed Matt was now looking all-in. "No, instead, wait for Peter to get here. He can process him, and you can get off home. Get one of the uniforms to take you. You're in no fit state to drive."

Matt slowly read Antonio Conti his rights, cuffed him and sat him in the chair he had first used on his arrival.

Peter Jones arrived in a flourish accompanied by white-suited forensic technicians. He came to a sudden halt as he saw the scene in front of him.

Steve approached Peter. "Take him in and get him processed at central. The charge is murder. Arrange for him to be moved to our interview suite tomorrow around lunchtime. Matt's exhausted, he's going home now. I'll hold on here with the forensics guys and get the body collected. It's pretty straightforward. We witnessed the killing so it's open and shut. I'll call Mary in a moment and get her over here to help out."

"Right you are, sir. Does that mean the headless girl murder is solved?"

Steve made allowances for the fact Peter may not be totally up to speed, but he was surprised by the naivety of the question. With a heartfelt sigh the DCI said. "Yes Peter, I believe it does."

Chapter Twenty-Nine

The DCI spent most of the evening organising the cumbersome wheels of justice and evidence gathering that was inevitable at a murder scene. After Peter Jones and Matt had left, he'd called in a pathology team, and requested an evidence and exhibits officer to attend. Mary Dougan arrived thirty minutes after her two male colleagues had departed.

He was surprised how long it took the pathologist to agree to moving the body. In Steve's mind it was straightforward. Stephanie Clarkson had been murdered by Antonio Conti who had used a knife that was still in the victim. Steve paced the apartment being careful not to touch anything without wearing his blue plastic gloves. He had instructed the exhibits officer to start on Stephanie's study. He had spotted various files and wanted to view them more out of curiosity than anything pertinent to his case. He recalled this was the lady who had tried to bribe Alfie Brooks and wondered if there might be evidence that compromised Alfie even though he had rejected the overture.

Just after quarter to ten the body of Stephanie Clarkson was eventually removed. Mary was asking the forensic team questions, and several sealed evidence bags of ledgers had been removed from Stephanie's study. He left the crime scene at 11.06 p.m.

As had become his custom, he slept in his armchair so as not to disturb his wife and he knew he wanted an early start. He set his phone alarm for six a.m. and when it blared into life, he struggled to silence it. He saw the time and registered the fact today was Thursday September the 28th.

Alison was standing in front of him in her pink dressing gown. She was tutting at the sight of her husband, telling him he should have come to bed and not sleep in his chair.

"I'll make you some breakfast, go and have a shower. You can tell me why you stayed out late after you smell better."

Right from the beginning of their marriage, Dr Alison Mills had accepted Steve was a policeman and didn't work regular hours. She kissed him lightly on the lips and pushed him towards their bathroom.

After a shower and breakfast, Steve felt almost human and as he left, he promised his wife he would not be late home. They kissed and embraced by the front door of their house and Steve set off for his office in New Scotland Yard. The early morning was dark, and a fresh breeze kept the temperature down, but the DCI thought it a perfect morning to walk to work and for thinking. He knew today would be difficult. He had a lot of loose ends to tie up and he would have to brief Alfie Brooks. With a sigh, he walked on, telling himself days like today didn't come along very often.

As he expected no one was in the office; it was 07.34 a.m. On his desk was a box containing the various ledgers and books he had spotted in Stephanie Clarkson's study. He hoped they might contain information that could be pertinent to either Twiggy or Alfie. Each book or ledger had been fingerprinted, catalogued and entered into an exhibits' register. The DCI was now clear to examine them at his leisure.

He retrieved a red, leather-covered file that had been split by cardboard dividers allowing five separate sections. On the edge of each section was a name. The name that caught Steve's eye was that of Hayden Giles. The DCI recalled Alfie's comment that when he went to report the offer of a bribe, the Assistant Commissioner had suggested he take it. Steve scanned the notes in Giles' file and had a summary glance at the other four names.

The canteen wasn't open this early, so he set to dictating his statement following last night's events. Once he'd finished, he placed the small battery-powered dictating machine on his desk. He pulled his A4-sized notepad towards him and started to doodle. He knew the headless body case was over. Sophia Paulo could be buried with her name on her headstone. Steve's mind turned to Antonio Conti, Sophia's father and reputed ex-Mafia money man. He would serve life for the killing of Stephanie Clarkson and Steve surmised they'd never know the relationship between the pair although from the data in the box on Steve's desk, Stephanie was more than Antonio's lover. She appeared to exert some control over parts of his empire, and not always the nicest parts.

The DCI wondered how Conti's arrest would affect Twiggy's case. He made a note to call her.

His mind turned to his outstanding interview with Andrew Black and the Norwich murders. Technically the case was closed. Neil Furlong had confessed and was awaiting trial. Steve allowed himself to consider the killing of Tracy Nelson, eleven years ago. That was still an active case, and he knew Andrew Black had killed her. He just needed a confession. He made another note.

As he wrote he scribbled *Elsie Brown* and *Jack Ralph*. He wrote against this *Case closed* but drew a series of question marks. He needed to get Andrew Black to admit that he gave the order to kill the Norwich pair. As he sat back, he knew this was for his own satisfaction and that the real killer of Elsie Brown and Jack Ralph was actually Andrew Black. He realised he could close the case allowing Furlong to take the fall by himself but to Steve, this didn't seem fair. He wrote in bold letters *Black — Conspiracy*.

Poppy appeared bearing coffee and looked as though she wanted to chat about her future.

"Poppy, leave it just now. We had a hard night last night and there'll be a lot of tidying up to do today. I promise we'll sit and talk about it but not at the moment."

Poppy who hadn't expected more, nonetheless pulled a pouting theatrical face showing her disappointment. "OK, but you won't forget?"

Steve handed her the tape from his dictating machine. "Set up a file for the murder of Stephanie Clarkson; that's my statement. You'll get the post-mortem report later today and Matt, Peter and Mary will give you their statements."

"Right." Poppy, forever nosey, asked, "What's in the box?"

"Just evidence from last night's killing. I want to go through it to see if it'll help Twiggy."

Poppy shrugged and left.

Sipping his coffee, Steve dialled Twiggy's number. She answered on the first ring. He explained about the killing of Stephanie Clarkson, her apparent part in helping to carry out Antonio Conti's dirty work and the fact he had several ledgers that appeared to show illegal payments to prominent citizens.

"Oh goody. I like getting the dirt on the great and the good especially if it's someone I don't like." Twiggy was jubilant. "The fact that you have Conti for murder might not help our case but on the other hand we don't have to pussyfoot around in case we spook him. I can get warrants for all his businesses, and we can move in mob-handed. It sounds like a good night's work, Steve." Twiggy carried on, "When can I get those ledgers?"

"Later today; I'll call you."

Steve called out to Poppy, "Poppy, check that Antonio Conti is being brought over here later this morning from Central. Try to get a time. Also check that Andrew Black had a good night in the holding cell downstairs and tell them to have him in an interview room at ten a.m."

The DCI was draining his coffee as he noticed a figure appear in his doorway. Pitching the cardboard receptacle into a bin Steve examined the newcomer without successfully identifying him.

He sat and looked at the little man then realised this was Andrew Black's lawyer. "Can I help you?"

"Er. Yes, I hope you can." The man introduced himself as Mr Humphrey, Mr Black's solicitor.

Steve thought this was very formal but knew solicitors came in all shapes and sizes and some were formal to the point of stupidity. He put Mr Humphrey in the latter category. The DCI gestured for the solicitor to take a seat which he did. He sat upright on Steve's chair and sat, still dressed in an unsuitable raincoat and gripping his briefcase on his lap.

"I had a word with my client after you left last night, Mr Burt. He wants to talk to you today but without my being present. I believe you have enough evidence to obtain a conviction for the murder of Mrs Nelson, and I told him so." Mr Humphrey gave a weak smile. "My client has asked me to retrieve an envelope he had in his possession when he was arrested. He claims it is his personal property and nothing to do with the charges. If you could arrange for me to have it, I'll deliver it to Mr Black."

At first Steve could not think what this lawyer was talking about but suddenly he remembered the envelope still in its evidence bag that was locked in the top drawer of his desk. He unlocked the drawer and produced the plastic bag.

"Did your client say why he wants this envelope?"

"No. I just got the impression it is very important to him."

"Mm. As you can see Mr Humphrey it is evidence. We haven't opened it yet but I'm afraid your client cannot have it unless he tells me what it contains."

Mr Humphrey looked disappointed. "You could open it in my presence and if you decide it is innocent, then I could deliver it as my client has requested."

Steve broke the seal on the evidence bag and extracted the envelope. It had already been dusted for fingerprints, but he handled it carefully placing a pair of blue plastic gloves on his hands. As a precaution, he used his phone to photograph the envelope before opening it. He carefully slit along the top edge and took out a single sheet of flimsy paper. He unfolded it and laid it flat smoothing out the creases from the folds. Again, Steve used his phone to photograph the sheet of paper. Satisfied he had followed protocols, he carefully picked it up and read the contents.

There were three names and against each a mobile phone number. The first name was Thomas Lesson. Steve vaguely recalled this was some big-time businessman who was always on the news talking about government and industrial cooperation. The other two names the DCI recognised at once as being very powerful individuals and certainly names he would not expect to come across in his daily duties.

Something lit up inside Steve's brain and he quickly replaced the paper in its envelope. "I'm sorry Mr Humphrey but I cannot give you this envelope. It is evidence in a murder enquiry."

Steve hurriedly put the evidence bag and the envelope back in his drawer.

"Oh well. I said I would ask, and I have. I hope you find my client cooperative later this morning, DCI Burt. I have explained everything to him."

The little lawyer stood and left. Steve wondered why he was wearing a raincoat when it wasn't raining. He let the thought go as he retrieved the envelope and again looked at the names and the phone numbers. The DCI didn't know if this paper meant anything, but he felt it was significant. After debating with himself for several minutes, he left to seek out Inspector Terry Harvey of Technical Support.

He found Terry in his office as usual poring over computer printouts while the entire office was one mass of computers, screens and printers. Terry seeing Steve approach pushed the printout away from him and beckoned his friend in.

"I've got something, and I need your very discreet help." Steve had photocopied the piece of paper from the envelope and passed the copy to Terry. The Inspector examined it and looked up.

"Some high-powered names here, Steve. I hope you're not thinking of going after any of them. That could be a real career ender."

"Well not today." Steve smiled. "Any thoughts on those phone numbers?"

"No. Not until I test them."

"What does that mean?"

"I can run them through a test programme that will confirm if they're still active. We can send a silent pulse and if it returns, the phone is good. Then we can search the numbers for the owners, but you look as though you already know who they are. We can see if they're registered but short of dialling the number, I'm not sure what else I can do."

Steve stood up. "Do what you can Terry but keep it hush-hush. I've a feeling that piece of paper is important."

***

Back in his office Steve was feeling the benefit of his early start. It was only 9.03 a.m. and he felt he had achieved a lot in a short space of time. As he was about to ask Poppy to get a round of coffee, Peter Jones appeared in the outer office and simultaneously Steve's phone rang. It was Commander Brooks with one his summonses. "My office now."

Steve hurried up to the twelfth floor and took the red leather-bound file he'd been looking at earlier in the morning. He walked into Alfie's office to find Alfie talking to Assistant Commissioner Hayden Giles.

As usual, the AC was dressed in his immaculately tailored uniform and looked scrubbed. His cheeks were bright, and his hair was neatly cut and combed. As he saw Steve, he almost rushed towards him, his right hand extended for Steve to shake it.

"My dear DCI Burt, brilliant police work yesterday. I understand you solved a most perplexing murder case that our murder squad had given up on, plus you have a murderer already charged for a killing that only happened last night. I must say such activity does our crime figures and clear-up rates the world of good. I just wanted to meet you and congratulate you."

Steve shook the senior officer's hand and mumbled a thank you.

Alfie stood apart with a serious look on his face. Steve was recalling the last conversation he had with the Commander and the letter he was keeping safely on Alfie's behalf. A letter that more or less accused this senior officer of being corrupt. The devil got into Steve. It may have been the early start or perhaps he was high on caffeine and adrenaline.

"The lady who was killed last night, sir, was called Stephanie Clarkson. I believe you knew her?"

Hayden Giles tried to cover up his shock at hearing Steph's name. Steve thought he made a reasonable job of it, but it wasn't good enough.

"No, no, I don't recall the name. Why do you ask?"

Steve didn't reply directly to the question. "She was a senior civil servant but was associated with a crime boss called Antonio Conti. She did a lot of his less-savoury errands, such as bribing senior figures."

The DCI knew Hayden Giles must have read the overnight reports and knew perfectly well the identities of last night's murder victim and the killer. His being here to congratulate the DCI was proof enough. AC Hayden Giles had made a mistake.

"I just wondered, sir, how she came to have your name in this book." Steve held up the red leather-bound book in order for both senior officers to see it.

Alfie was glaring at the DCI trying to telepathically tell him not to go any further. With Stephanie Clarkson dead, the bribery allegation was also dead. Alfie didn't want to pursue Hayden Giles, but he couldn't stop his DCI.

"I'm sorry DCI Burt but I have no idea." Hayden turned to go. "Again, well done on last night. I must be off." As the AC turned to leave,

Alfie hurried forward in an attempt to get him out of the office before Steve started up again.

"Are you spending much time in your villa in Portugal these days, sir?" Steve had raised his voice slightly. Hayden Giles stopped dead in his tracks causing Alfie's guiding hand to slide down his back.

"What did you say, Mr Burt?"

"I was just wondering how much time you spend in your villa in Portugal which, it appears, Antonio Conti paid for."

"Now just remember who you are talking to, DCI Burt. That is a very serious accusation, and you'd better have proof. Otherwise, your career will be over."

Steve took out photocopies of the pages that were in the section of the book marked 'Hayden Giles'. He handed them to Alfie who scanned them and reluctantly passed them over to the AC.

"You'll see there are copies of minutes of meetings you had with Miss Clarkson together with bank statements, bank transfer slips and copies of title deeds showing Miss Clarkson funded the purchase of a villa on the Algarve and transferred it to your ownership. If you read the notes, you'll see she has commented it was for future favours unspecified."

"Where did you get this?" Hayden Giles was both angry and crestfallen. He pulled a chair out from Alfie's conference table and sat down.

"Our forensic team searched Miss Clarkson's flat, and this book was discovered. If it's of any consolation, sir there are a number of files detailing other influential people whom she also bribed on behalf of Antonio Conti. You are not alone."

The AC sat looking at the floor holding the records in his hands. "What are you going to do?"

"At the moment, nothing. I'm trying to tidy up my outstanding caseload, but this book and others will be handed over to the appropriate authorities both internal and external early next week. What you decide to do in the meantime is up to you, sir."

Assistant Commissioner Hayden Giles stood. He looked grey and knew he had been caught out. He was disappointed, believing the killing of Stephanie Clarkson and the arrest of Antonio Conti should have severed all ties between them and his corruption would be buried with Stephanie. "I suppose I should thank you for buying me a little time, Steve. I'm not going to try to justify myself except to say she never asked me to do anything illegal or anything that would have influenced any of our cases until the other day and your investigation into Mayflower. She referred to us as Antonio Conti's insurance. I have been stupid and now I'll have to face the music."

Hayden Giles left, still upright and looking smart in his uniform. He looked like the public's idea of what a senior Metropolitan Police Officer should look like.

Alfie sat in one of his armchairs. "That was a bit brutal, Steve. I know I told you I suspected he was bent but you might have let him down a bit more gently. I suppose those records are accurate?"

"I'll have Miss Rough verify everything before going forward but yes, I think they're real and he didn't deny any of it."

"No, he didn't, did he? Thank you, Steve. It seems my concerns about being stitched up are unfounded."

"I had a good look, Alfie. Your name didn't appear in any of the documents I saw, except this one." The DCI produced a one-page document he'd removed from another ledger found in Stephanie's apartment. It was a note of her conversation with Alfie saying she'd offered him the bribe to put a stop to the investigation into Mayflower Contracts Ltd. He handed it to the Commander. "I never saw that sir, if I were you, I'd shred it."

Alfie looked stunned and grateful.

Before he could say anything, the DCI carried on. "I need to bring you up to speed on the investigations.

"We now have confirmation that an eleven-year-old murder has led us to a criminal gang involved in money laundering, drugs and prostitution. As you know, the company involved had been thought legitimate as it paid its taxes and was a large contributor to the sitting government party. Plus, as you have just witnessed, evidence of corruption among the highest in the land has been discovered."

He explained how the headless corpse had led to Antonio Conti through a tattoo and how Andrew Black's ham-fisted contract to beat up Quentin Somersby had connected him to the same criminal gang. For reasons Steve couldn't explain to himself he didn't tell Alfie about the three names and the envelope.

"I've finished the murder enquiries and that was my job. But now I've got all these loose ends to tie up. Twiggy wants to get her teeth into this Mayflower business but with Conti charged with murder, I'm not sure where she can take it."

"Leave it with me, Steve. I don't know how you can keep all of that in your head."

Steve turned to leave and heard a weak voice behind him as Alfie mumbled a thank you. It was 09.41 a.m., and he had an appointment with Andrew Black at ten.

**

Terry was waiting for Steve as he walked into his office. He replaced the red book in its evidence bag, noted he'd removed it and the time he'd returned it. He placed the book back in the cardboard box with the other evidence he wanted to review.

"I've checked those numbers, Steve. They're all pay-as-you-go burner phones." Terry looked confused. "Why would these three upstanding pillars of the community have burner phones but not any burner phones? I traced them back. They all went live on the same day at more or less the same time. I'd say someone bought them, activated them and then passed them on. From the phone evidence, these three are involved in something."

"Well, I think that what are we seeing here is three very important individuals involved with Antonio Conti. Conti pays a fortune in taxes to clean up his dirty money, and his girlfriend seems to have gone round bribing anyone she thought might help her man in the future." Steve stopped to think. "I don't suppose you can link the phones to Antonio Conti?"

"No. Sorry Steve, I'm good but not that good."

"Yeah well, thanks Terry. We'll just have to see where we go."

Peter Jones and Mary were sitting at their desks writing up their statements from last night. Mary looked tired and Steve made a note to tell her to leave at lunchtime.

"Peter, you're with me. Let's try to close this other case." As the DCI was leaving, he turned to Mary. "Get a warrant to search Andrew Black's office. Let's see what secrets he's keeping there. Don't wait for me. Get a search team and you and Poppy get along there."

Poppy stopped typing. She looked up. "Really, boss? I get to go on a real case?"

"Yes, Poppy, I did promise."

***

Andrew Black had been brought from his holding cell and looked fresh after his night in the cell. He was sitting behind the table and appeared to be unconcerned by his situation. As soon as Steve and Peter sat down and Peter had activated the double tape deck, Andrew Black spoke up.

"My lawyer tells me I'm not getting my envelope. If I don't get it, I'm saying nothing more."

Steve hadn't expected this response. "Why is the envelope so important Andy? It only has a slip of paper in it."

"You've opened it!" Andy Black almost jumped from his chair.

Steve was playing the calm, considerate friendly policeman. "Yes, it's standard procedure with evidence."

"But that's not evidence, it's my personal property. You had no right to open it."

"Well Andy, that genie is out of the bottle. We *did* open it. What do you want to tell us about it? How does it fit in with the murder of Tracy Nelson and the two killings Neil Furlong carried out on your order?"

The DCI had set a trap and hoped Andrew Black wouldn't notice. He'd linked the murders and if Black didn't differentiate them, then by default he was admitting to them.

"The envelope has nothing to do with any of that."

Steve wasn't sure whether to pursue the killings or the source of the envelope. In the end Andrew Black solved his problem.

"Look Mr Burt, if I tell you what you want to know will you give me the envelope?"

Clearly the sheet of paper with the names meant more to Andrew Black than the DCI could imagine. He appeared to be prepared to tell all in exchange for the names. Steve thought about it for a few minutes and in the end he decided.

"OK Andy, tell us what happened, and I'll give you back the envelope."

Andrew Black smiled a sly smile. Jean Franco had told him if he were in serious trouble, he should call one of the three names inside the envelope. Andy had considered his position overnight and decided he could tell the police everything provided he could call one of the names. If Jean Franco were right, any of the three names should get him off anything he'd got mixed up in. Even with his limited IQ, Andy saw this strategy as his only way out. His lawyer had advised him to plead guilty to all the charges but if he had his get out of jail card in the shape of a friend in high places, he'd nothing to lose.

Silence hung in the air before Steve broke it by asking Andy. "Tell us about the killing of Tracy Nelson."

Andrew Black recounted the events that led up to his strangling Tracy. His account almost matched exactly that of Neil Furlong who had helped him clean up and escape back to London. Andy filled in the events of the actual murder.

"See, we'd just had a romp for the second time, and she wanted to smoke more weed. I'd had more than her and told her she didn't need it, but she got angry. Started screaming I was no good, said I didn't pay her enough for the chances she took bringing in the dope, said she'd go to the police and tell them everything. She was off her head. I tried to calm her down but somehow, I strangled her. I don't remember doing it, but I do remember phoning Neil." Andrew was emotional and a small tear trickled down his cheek. For such a big man he suddenly looked a character to be pitied. "It was an accident Mr Burt; I didn't mean to do it."

"So you are admitting to killing Tracy Nelson in her flat in Norwich eleven years ago. Is that correct?"

A sullen Andrew who was no longer playing the part of the Chairman, nodded. "Yes, I suppose so, but it was an accident."

Steve looked at Peter who had taken on a self-satisfied look.

"Now Andy, tell us why you asked Neil Furlong to kill the other two."

Once more a subdued Andy started to explain how Furlong had phoned him and told him Elsie Brown was claiming she had evidence that her boss had deliberately lost a witness statement that would prove he had killed Tracy and how she knew he had bribed Jack Ralph. "Well, I couldn't let that get out, so I told Neil to take care of them."

"Did you pay Furlong, and did you tell him specifically to murder them?"

"I threw a few grand Neil's way, but I never said kill them. As I said, I only told him to take care of them. It was his interpretation to kill them."

"Just to be clear Andy. You told Neil Furlong to take care of a problem caused by Elsie Brown uncovering your involvement in the killing of Tracy Nelson and you specifically mentioned Elsie and Jack Ralph?"

"Yes."

"Surely you knew such a phrase as 'take care of them' meant you expected them to be silenced and killed?"

"Well, I suppose so, but I never said kill them."

Steve sat back. He had enough to charge Andrew Black with conspiracy in the murders of Elsie Brown and Jack Ralph. That was all he wanted. He felt satisfied that Elsie had not died for nothing. Her years of work uncovering evidence against Andrew Black were now justified and Steve determined to try to get her the recognition she deserved.

As he sat looking at Andy Black, Steve decided to go deeper. "Where did you get the envelope, Andy?"

This sudden change in direction appeared to throw Andrew Black off balance.

"Ah! Er... what do you mean?"

"Simple question Andy. Who gave you the envelope?"

"That's my business."

"Does your business involve a Quentin Somersby?"

Andy looked flushed and confused. The DCI knew such sudden changes in questions often caught suspects off balance and could lead to interesting replies.

"I don't know anybody called Quentin anything."

"Now Andrew, and we were getting on so well. You've told the truth and you're helping yourself, but now you're lying. You see, we have the two Irish thugs you hired to hurt your friend Quentin and they've told us everything. Even how much you paid them."

Andy Black looked angry. His emotions were being stretched by the DCI and he found he couldn't concentrate on the answers he was giving. He needed time to think so he folded his arms over his chest and sat back. "I'm saying nothing."

Steve was still being Andrew's new best friend. "Look Andy, you've admitted to the more serious crimes. Arranging to have someone beaten up is less serious but you'd get everything out in the open and make a clean breast of things. We know you paid these guys to do it, but we don't know why."

Still sitting back, frustration got to Andy and he decided to throw caution to the wind. It didn't matter what he said. The envelope would save him.

"All right, I didn't like the bloke. He was odd. He tried to tell me what to do. Me and my brother were the new rulers and this bloke said we weren't. He said we worked for him, and some Italian called Conti. I couldn't let him get away with being disrespectful to me and my brother, so I had him taught a lesson."

Steve couldn't believe what he'd just been told. This would-be gangster had just admitted a link to Antonio Conti and his criminal empire! A sudden thought came to the DCI.

"Did Antonio Conti give you the envelope?"

Without thinking Andy Black blurted out. "No." With obvious pride he carried on. "I got it from the real boss in Amsterdam. That Conti guy's just the hired help. Jean Franco's the main man and me and my brother are his right-hand men in London."

Things were unfolding too quickly for Steve. He could follow this up later if he had to. He needed to consider everything Andrew Black had said. He turned to Peter but spoke to his prisoner.

"Andrew Black, you will be charged with the murder of Tracy Nelson, conspiracy in the murders of Elsie Brown and Jack Ralph, plus conspiracy in the attack on Quentin Somersby. Detective Inspector Jones will read you your rights now and accompany you to central booking where you will be formally charged awaiting a court appearance. Do you understand?"

Andy simply nodded. "Can I have my envelope now?"

"I'll arrange for it to be delivered to you after you have been processed."

***

Steve left Peter to take care of everything and returned to his office. It was 11.39 a.m. He pondered his early start and the morning spent tidying up the loose ends. He felt drained and concluded it wasn't such a good idea to start so early. He acknowledged to himself everything he was doing was necessary but questioned whether any of it helped his cases. After all, he had concluded his investigations and apart from the murder of Stephanie Clarkson, his caseload was empty. As he slowly trudged upstairs from the basement interview suite, the DCI started to analyse what he knew and wondered how any of it impacted on his cases.

Chapter Thirty

DC Mary Dougan and DC Amelia Cooper, AKA Poppy, together with a forensic search team, entered the not-so-palatial offices of the Black brothers. David Black was sitting on an old floral-patterned chair, that should have been placed in a skip years earlier. He was reading a newspaper and his legs were dangling over one of the arms of the chair. On seeing the two policewomen enter, he jumped up looking both over with a lustful eye.

"Yes girls, have you come for a job?"

From his expression Mary realised what kind of job he was offering. She produced her warrant card, introduced herself and Poppy and presented the search warrant to David. He was taken aback but appeared to control himself.

"Help yourself. What are you looking for?"

Mary, as the more experienced officer, took the lead by not answering David's question.

"We have a team of forensic officers who will be here presently. We would appreciate your cooperation sir."

David Black, apparently unfazed by this invasion, sat back down in his chair and appeared to admire the two shapely women police officers. It was clear from his leer that he liked what he saw. As he sat, he wondered what they were looking for. He was worried. He hadn't heard from his elder brother and knew no one had been to collect the two days' cash takings that were in the large safe in the corner of the room. He tried to calculate how much there was and arrived at a figure of around one hundred thousand. He started to sweat a little as he realised he couldn't allow the police to see inside the safe.

After half an hour or so the white-suited technicians had bagged several ledgers that Andrew kept in his desk and two mobile phones that David knew nothing about. Then Mary approached the seated David.

"Can you open the safe please, sir?"

David had pre-armed himself with a ready reply. "I'm sorry officer, I don't have the key. My brother always keeps it." David lied and felt the key heavy inside his trouser pocket.

"Mr Black, please don't piss us about. Your brother is at this moment in custody on multiple murder charges and he had no key that might open that safe on him." Mary pointed to the safe.

The news of Andrew's arrest was unexpected. "For murder you say? But how?"

"I'm not at liberty to say, sir but I do need the key to that safe."

David was thinking hard and fast. He loved his brother but knew he often sailed close to the wind, and he didn't like the arrangement with Jean Franco. He'd get more details later but for now he had to keep the contents of the safe secret.

"Sorry love, I can't help you. If he doesn't have it on him and it's not here, he must have left it at home."

One of the forensic technicians examined the safe and shook his head in a gesture that said he couldn't open it. Mary had one of the technicians seal all sides of the door with police tape. "That safe is now sealed into evidence sir. It is a criminal offence if you tamper with it or break the seal. Do you understand?"

"Yes. I suppose so but as I said, I don't have the key."

Poppy had for once remained silent. She knew nothing of this world and wanted to learn. She knew she was close to persuading the DCI to let her back to operational duties and didn't want to spoil her chances. She observed the technicians at work and as she did so, she remembered her previous boss telling her she was being moved out of uniform to CID as a non-operational officer because she was too frivolous to be taken seriously as a beat officer and because she was not too hard on the eye, male officers were fighting over the opportunity to partner her on her beat. Poppy was determined to grab whatever benefit there was to being one of Steve's officers.

Mary was continuing to talk to David Black. "We'll be back tomorrow with either the key or a locksmith." Mary pointed a finger as a schoolteacher might when telling off a naughty schoolboy. "Do not touch that safe. Are we clear?"

"Oh yes, love; will you and your friend be here again tomorrow? If you came around lunchtime maybe we could have a pub lunch." The grin on David's face told Mary he had more than lunch in mind.

Once the police had left, David opened the safe and removed the cash. He counted one hundred and ninety-five grand. There had been no pickup of money since Tuesday. David knew that was unusual but thought Andrew having been arrested might have something to do with it. He had estimated the drug and prostitution money came to around two hundred grand for the two days. He was spot on. The rest of the money was his and Andrew's commission that Andrew had let build up over the past week plus the money from their other illegal activities. This other amount of money looked to be the same again.

David Black sat in the middle of the floor surrounded by money. He knew he had over two hundred thousand in his bank account at Lloyds and thought how best to get out of this nightmare Andrew had got them into. In the safe was over a million pounds worth of tabs that could be sold anywhere. David knew drugs were a transferable commodity. He supposed Andrew would walk away from the murder charges because he had the envelope, but he equally knew their days as London's representatives for Jean Franco and Antonio Conti would be over.

***

As Mary and Poppy were leaving David Black, Steve walked into his office and was surprised to see Matt Conway. He had told his sergeant to take the day off but here he was, sitting behind his desk obviously writing up his notes from last night. The DCI said nothing as he walked past except, "You look better than you did last night."

The phone on Steve's desk rang. It was Alfie Brooks. "Steve, I've called a meeting for two o'clock. I'm getting everybody together. This Conti thing seems to be getting out of hand and we need to involve Vice and the drug squad plus of course Financial Crimes. Bring your files. I want to hand as much over to the specialists as I can. Our part is done. You've solved the murders so it's time to move on."

"You know sir, I was just thinking the same thing."

"Good and by the way, I shredded that piece of paper."

"What piece of paper sir?" The DCI paused. "I'll see you at two." The line went dead. Steve noted it was 11.55 a.m. With a groan, he lifted himself from his chair and walked into the outer office. "Matt, as you're here you may as well sit in on the Antonio Conti interview."

***

The interview with Antonio shouldn't take long. At least that's what Steve told himself, but he knew he wanted answers to things outside the murder of Stephanie Clarkson. Antonio Conti was seated as the pair of detectives arrived. He looked fresh and alert and smiled at his interrogators.

After Matt had followed procedure and switched on the tape, Steve sat back and let silence fill the air. It wasn't that he needed to get under Antonio's skin and make him uncomfortable, it was simply that he wasn't sure where to start. Eventually he spoke.

"We know why you killed Stephanie Clarkson but why did she kill your daughter?"

Antonio looked calm and comfortable. "She had a mad idea that we would get married and live happily ever after. I think she was obsessed by the idea. She thought she could bring Sophia back to me, and I'd be grateful enough to go along with her happy families plan. Oh, I admit I used her, but I'd never have married her. I think she thought it was a certainty if she could reunite me and Sophia.

"She didn't understand I couldn't risk approaching Sophia for fear her life might be put in danger. She said when she saw the squalor my little bird was living in, and the fact she was a prostitute and a low-end one at that, her dream of us living as one big happy family wouldn't work. I think she said Sophia would be an embarrassment to the family. She said she offered Sophia a bath but snapped. She admitted killing my little girl. You must understand, Detective Chief Inspector, where I come from you must take personal revenge against anyone who hurts your family." Antonio Conti told his story without emotion.

"You mean the Mafia?"

"Yes."

"What did Stephanie do for you exactly?"

"She looked after my back. She knew my business wasn't strictly legal, but I always fronted it as though it was. I paid my taxes and washed my illegal earnings such that dirty money became clean money. Steph's position in the Treasury gave me an early warning if anything was suspicious concerning my business. She set up what she called a committee of influential people who could help if things got seriously difficult. She used my money to bribe them. This was my first line of defence."

"Do you know who they are?"

"No. It was better I didn't know; they were at arm's length from me. I have my own second line of defence." Antonio was looking smug.

Steve thought back to the red leather-bound book with the dividers. He correctly assumed this book contained the names of Antonio's first line of defence. The DCI made a mental note.

Antonio continued, "You see Mr Burt, I'm happy to confess to killing Stephanie Clarkson. I could hardly deny it with you as a witness, but my chances of going to prison are remote. I have paid a lot of money to cope with a situation just like this."

Steve thought back to Andrew Black's insistence that he be given the envelope with the three names inside. This thought opened up another line of questioning. "Do you know an Andrew Black?"

Antonio looked startled but recovered. "Yes. He is a horribly uncouth man, but he serves a purpose. Why do you ask?"

Steve ignored the question. He had just made a huge mental leap and hoped he was correct. "Did you give him an envelope containing the names of three influential people here in London?"

For the first time, Antonio Conti looked concerned. He remembered not being happy that Jean Franco had given the names to the Black brothers. These names were for *his* escape plans, not the Black brothers'. Antonio had to think quickly.

"No Inspector, I didn't give that man anything."

Steve noticed a slight tic in Antonio's left eye. He pushed on. "Strange. He seems to think, like you, that he'll escape punishment simply because he has an envelope he was given in Amsterdam."

Antonio said nothing but wondered if the police knew the identities of the people whose names were inside the envelope. He shrugged and remained silent.

Steve changed tack. "We found several ledgers in your apartment. They were in your safe. Our financial boys say they are old records in Italian. We also understand from the Italian police that you are on the run from the Mafia and that you were their accountant. Is that correct, sir?"

"No comment."

"Is this the reason you couldn't risk meeting your daughter, for fear you were being followed by Mafia killers?"

"No comment."

Steve looked at Matt who nodded. "This interview is terminated at 01.17 p.m. Detective Sergeant Conway here will read you your rights and you will be charged with the murder of Stephanie Clarkson." Steve turned to his DS. "Matt, do the honours." The DCI left Matt reading Antonio his rights and headed straight to his office.

**

Poppy and Mary had returned. Poppy was excited and was furiously typing away at her keyboard inputting her statement onto the file. Mary was writing her statement and looked up on seeing the DCI enter.

"Hi boss."

"How did you get on at Black's office?"

"You mean apart from being propositioned by his brother?" Mary squinted her eyes. "No chance. He's a deadbeat."

Steve heard Poppy giggle behind him.

"No, Mary. How did the search go?"

"We found a load of ledgers that seem to show money coming in, a lot of money. We found papers referring to the supply contracts for narcotics and something about high-class escorts arriving next week from Amsterdam. Forensics have it for processing, but we should get it all before close of play today."

"Good. Anything else?"

"Yes. There's a big bloody safe we couldn't get into. The brother says Andrew has the key but I'm not sure I believe him. We tagged it and I'll go back tomorrow with a locksmith."

"Mm. If you think it can wait?"

"Should be OK, sir. I don't think David Black is the running type."

The DCI adjourned to his office and started to think through recent events. After a fruitless five minutes of confusing thoughts, he called out, "Poppy, I need all the files you have on the Neil Furlong case, the Andrew Black case and the Antonio Conti case. Plus, all the financial stuff that has still to go to Florance Rough. I've got a meeting upstairs in ten minutes so now would be good."

Within minutes, Poppy was standing in front of Steve's desk. She dumped a stack of files on it. "Each file is labelled, and there's a reference to the electronic file. That's the lot."

"Keep our cases back—that's the murders but leave the rest."

Poppy looked puzzled but did as Steve had requested.

***

At the same time Steve was asking Poppy for the files, two well-dressed men sat down to enjoy a glass of wine at the Hounds Club in Pall Mall. One was the newly appointed Director of Public Prosecutions, Mr Sebastian Low-Clifford, and the other was a very senior government minister. The pair exchanged pleasantries as the Minister reminded the head of the DPP how much he owed his appointment to the patronage of the Minister.

Both men had known each other for several years and despite moving in different circles, they got on well.

"Now Sebastian, I wanted to meet you because we have a small problem. One of our leading contributors to party funds finds himself in a bit of bother with the boys in blue."

"What kind of bother?"

"Oh, something and nothing, I'm sure. But the thing is, not only is he our biggest donor, but his company pays a fortune in taxes. It's been said if he were a public company, he'd easily be in the top ten by turnover." The politician drew breath before continuing. "However, his business isn't what you or I would call mainstream."

"How so?"

"Well. Not to put too fine a point on it, he's heavily into drugs and prostitution. So far this has been kept away from prying eyes, but recent events mean this is likely to come to the attention of the public. You can see the headlines…" The government minister expanded his arms suggesting a banner headline. "'GOVERNMENT TAKE MONEY FROM DRUGS AND PROSTITUTION KING'."

Sebastian sat back and whistled. "I see the problem but how can I help?"

"Well, you are the Director of Public Prosecutions. If, let's say, you took a view that this fellow should not stand trial in the public interest then we'd have a good chance of keeping everything under wraps."

"What's the charge?"

"It appears he killed his girlfriend last night but only because she had earlier murdered his daughter."

"Christ, I can't cover that up!"

The politician sat back and examined the Head of the DPP. He tutted. "My dear Sebastian, you can do anything you like. Just don't draw attention to yourself and don't get caught. Look, you can claim it's not in the public interest and I promise our friend will not be a problem going forward. He's ex-Italian Mafia and they are looking for him. A word in the right ear and we won't have to worry about him."

Sebastian Low-Clifford didn't know how to react. He felt he was being placed in an impossible position.

"I'm sorry but I can't do it."

"My dear old fellow, remember where you were six months ago. In a dead-end job in dead-end chambers taking any cases bankrupt solicitors threw your way. Remember who interviewed you and gave you your chance. I also remember a promise of 'if I can ever do anything for you…', but do *you* remember?"

"Well yes, but that's something people say. I didn't mean it."

"No, I see that now, but, my friend, what can be given can be taken away. I'm sure you don't want to go down in history as the shortest-serving head of the DPP?"

Sebastian swallowed hard. "You wouldn't. You couldn't!"

The smooth-talking politician who had not changed his silky delivery throughout the meeting simply smiled. "Are you brave enough to put it to the test? A simple public interest ruling, and we carry on as normal."

Sebastian looked crestfallen. He realised he was between a rock and a hard place.

"What's the name of the prisoner?"

"That's the spirit. He's called Antonio Conti. You'll probably get the file from the Met by Friday. The SIO is a DCI Steve Burt. If you publish the public interest notice, say Friday afternoon, our man can be released Friday evening and you won't hear any more about it. A grateful Government may, however, find a knighthood for you in the New Year's list. You never know."

The government minister rose and rang a bell. A tall well-built man dressed in a lightweight suit entered. The minister introduced him to Sebastian. "This gentleman is with the security service. He will meet Mr Conti on his release and take care of everything." The politician nodded to the newcomer who nodded back and left.

What Sebastian Low-Clifford didn't know was that the minister was the second name on the list Steve had extracted from the envelope Andrew Black was so keen to have returned.

***

At 2.03 p.m., Steve entered Commander Alfie Brooks' office. He saw a conference table full of plain-clothes officers, most of whom he recognised. He saw Twiggy and her boss Rupert Carey sitting together deep in conversation and studying a thick computer printout. He also recognised the chief superintendents responsible for the Vice and Drug squads. He nodded a hello to them. As he made his way further into Alfie's office, he saw the chief superintendent from Professional Standards. Steve couldn't remember her name but knew she had a fearsome reputation. There was another woman present that the DCI didn't know and as he started to look for a seat, she broke away from her conversation with Alfie and approached Steve. Alfie followed.

"DCI Burt, I'm Pauline Roberts. I've just been appointed to head up the new Anti-Corruption Unit. I understand this grand meeting today is all down to you?"

Steve shook her hand and with some embarrassment mumbled, "Nice to meet you but I hope this is not for my benefit."

Alfie arrived. "Ah! You've met. Good."

He turned to the room, clapped his hands and ordered everyone to sit. Alfie took the seat at the head of the table and instructed Steve to sit at the opposite end. Twiggy was seated next to him.

Alfie began. "Thank you all for coming at short notice but we have a situation that is pressing. Before asking DCI Burt to explain his recent investigations…" Steve's heart sank, and he said a mental 'Thank you Alfie' on hearing he was to be the star turn. "… I want to record the work DCI Burt has done in exposing corruption within our force and the extent of criminal activity surrounding a well-organised gang."

Alfie sat back and held his hand out to Steve. "Carry on, Steve."

Without any pre-prepared notes Steve started by letting his audience know Alfie had dropped him in it. This got the expected laughter and helped break the ice. The DCI once more explained how an old murder in Norfolk had led him to Mayflower Contracts and Antonio Conti. He tried to simplify his explanation as to how various seemingly unconnected strands all led to Conti. He explained how the Black brothers fitted in and the connection to Amsterdam. After thirty minutes of mental juggling, the DCI felt he'd explained everything as best he could.

Finally, he patted the files in front of him. "I have completed my investigations into the murders, and we have the culprits in custody. In these files are the non-murder items that are outside my brief. I presume the Commander has called this meeting for me to pass these files over to the appropriate departments. I know Miss Rough has started her investigation into Conti's companies, but I do not believe how he earned his money has yet been investigated."

Steve sat back and looked towards the other end of the table and Alfie Brooks. Everyone around the table was quick to congratulate Steve on a remarkable job.

Alfie knocked on the table to bring the meeting to order. "I have reported all this to the Commissioner who has instructed that I set up an inter-departmental task force to pull all the different elements of DCI Burt's investigation together. Mr Carey from Treasury will coordinate the activities of the task force while Miss Rough will lead the investigation into the financial side, money laundering and the like. I will oversee the operation and each of you will concentrate on your individual areas of expertise." Alfie paused.

"I think you've all met DCI Pauline Roberts. She's heading up the new Anti-Corruption Unit and will work alongside Financial Crimes. We have a big job to do, and it will get complicated, but I don't want any inter-departmental rivalry. You will work as a team, and I want daily briefings at least, until I'm satisfied we've broken the back of this thing. Any questions?"

No one said anything until Twiggy spoke up. "It's not a question sir but everyone should know Mayflower Contracts comprises sixteen separate companies, some of which are legitimate, but most are dummies created to launder money. From our investigations so far, we haven't been able to find the source of the money, but we have it traced to individual company bank accounts. I'll let everyone have a detailed printout of our findings, as this might help."

"Thank you, Florance. Right, everyone, to work. First briefing tomorrow, here at four p.m."

Alfie stood, indicating the meeting was over.

As everyone was drifting off to their own offices, Steve, knowing he no longer had a part to play in the investigation, took Twiggy's arm.

"The key to all this is Quentin Somersby. Get to him first. I hear he's out of the coma and talking. I'd get to him this afternoon."

Twiggy saw a glint in the DCI'S eye and understood he was right.

"Thanks Steve, I'm on it."

Chapter Thirty-One

Steve was in his office reviewing the exhibits from Stephanie Clarkson's house. Despite having handed the enquiry over to Alfie's task force, Steve knew he would continue to be involved if only because he knew more about the case than anyone on the task force including Twiggy. He didn't feel under any pressure to be an active member but decided to review the exhibits when it suited him. Leafing through the red-leather book he realised that, apart from Assistant Commissioner Giles, the other three names were equally corrupt, but none were serving police officers. He surmised this was the reason Pauline Roberts' Anti-Corruption unit had been set up, to go after officials who might normally be too important to challenge. The DCI decided he would pass on the red book tomorrow.

DI Peter Jones tapped lightly on the door frame and walked in. "Our man Andy Black is now well and truly in the system. He's screaming for the envelope you promised him."

Steve smiled and removed the envelope from his desk drawer. He removed the piece of paper and handed Peter the empty envelope. "Get that over to him and tell him I've kept my part of the bargain."

Peter Jones laughed. "You cunning devil, he'll go ballistic. He's expecting the contents. I think he thinks it will give him a free pass on the murder charges."

Steve wasn't sure why he was determined to keep the names secret for now and didn't comment on his DI's assumption. There was something telling the DCI to be very careful with these names. He knew Antonio Conti had bribed a lot of senior officials but any suggestion that the names on the list had been bribed was almost unbelievable. He remembered Twiggy had told him Thomas Lesson was involved with Conti and sat on the boards of some of his scam companies. Steve suspected it would be easy to out Lesson and would talk to DCI Pauline Roberts of the new Anti-Corruption Unit on Monday, but the other two names, if they got out, would cause a major political firestorm.

On reflection, Steve thought he would keep the names secret for now. He smiled to himself, thinking *You never know when this information might be needed*. It was obvious both names had been bought and paid for by Antonio Conti. He would look at the documents taken from Conti's flat for evidence of corruption and hold on to everything until the time was right.

Steve decided to stand down his entire team until Monday, feeling they all deserved the long weekend. Everything was finished. Poppy had received the only outstanding item, the post-mortem results on Stephanie Clarkson. It was all straightforward, so she had completed the file and forwarded it to the Crown Prosecution Service and the DPP. The CPS had already confirmed all Steve's murder cases against Antonio Conti, Andrew Black and Neil Furlong were solid and almost certain to lead to convictions.

As the DCI contemplated the events of the past two weeks, his mind turned to Norfolk and the people he'd met, especially Chief Superintendent Emily Channel, head of Norfolk CID. He recalled her initial reaction to the DCI being brought in to oversee the Elsie Brown murder and her total loyalty to her team most of whom were being pensioned off. Without thinking why, he dialled Norfolk Headquarters and spoke to the Chief Superintendent.

"I just thought you should know Ma'am that it looks like Neil Furlong is going down for both murders of Elsie Brown and Jack Ralph. The CPS are sure of a result."

Emily Channel wasn't by nature a sentimental woman, but this news brought a slight tear to her eye. "Thank you for telling me, Steve. It was very thoughtful."

"I just thought you'd like to know. I never met Elsie, but she was tenacious in her pursuit of Tracy Nelson's killer. It was that that got her killed. She must have been an exceptional police officer."

"She was, and at least we know she got her man even from the grave." The Chief Superintendent paused to wipe away a tear. "Steve? I don't want to know whether you're coming here or not but if you do, I'll retire happy knowing Norfolk CID will be in good hands." Suddenly the line went dead.

Steve sat for several minutes his mind completely blank. Eventually and after much sighing, his thoughts turned to his team. He knew there would be changes regardless of whether he went to Norfolk or not. Poppy deserved her chance to become operational; Matt Conway had developed into a first-class officer and deserved Steve's support when it came to promotion. He wondered about Mary Dougan who as a graduate entrant would be moved on in a few months anyway and then his thoughts turned to Peter Jones. The DCI knew Peter wasn't cut out for CID. He was bright enough but lacked imagination. Steve knew he would have to have words but as he yawned and stretched, he told himself everything could wait until Monday.

Everyone was at their desks in the outer office. He told them all about the stand down and a happy but tired bunch of CID officers left to enjoy their weekend knowing their job was done. Poppy and Mary held back.

"We've got a locksmith booked for tomorrow to open the safe at the brothers' office."

"Ah. Yes, sorry. If you can just attend and then knock off as soon as you can. Make sure you have a forensic team with you but I'm sure everything can wait until Monday."

***

At the time Steve was standing down his team, a man whose passport said his name was David Grove was enjoying a glass of wine in the British Airways executive lounge at Heathrow Airport. He was dressed as any ordinary tourist and didn't stand out except for the size of his backpack. It was larger than normal but because he was travelling Club Class, he surmised correctly he would be allowed to be take this into the cabin. He had put a large suitcase in the hold and that contained the tablets he'd taken from the safe. The money was stuffed in his backpack. David Black was booked on the late afternoon flight to Malaga in the Costa del Sol, Spain and what he hoped was the start of a new but still criminal life away from his brother.

***

Heathrow Airport was busy and while David Black waited for his flight, another British Airways flight from Amsterdam was disgorging its passengers at the arrivals section of terminal five. Among the passengers were two evil-looking men who worked for Jean Franco in Europe. Jean Franco had become aware of Antonio Conti's and Andrew Black's arrests. He had tried to call David Black, but he wasn't answering his phone.

Realising things weren't right, he had dispatched these two thugs to pick up the pieces and ensure Jean Franco's empire carried on. The two were trusted lieutenants of Jean Franco and knew how he operated. Jean didn't understand Antonio's contracts system and had instructed the new heads of his London operation to revert back to the old ways. London was about to become a more violent place.

Both men had been briefed and knew enough to quickly put the operation back together again, but in Jean Franco's way. Their presence confirmed that organised crime would carry on no matter how successful DCI Burt and his colleagues were in rooting it out.

***

An Alitalia flight from Palermo also arrived at Heathrow the same afternoon. On board were two well-dressed Italian Mafia members who had been sent by their boss to attend to Antonio Paulo. A call had been made from London telling the man in Sicily that Antonio Paulo had been identified and that a member of a secret government organisation would deliver him to them tomorrow, Friday September the 29th. This cooperation proved that the reach of the Mafia and their ability to buy information was still a weapon in their armoury. No one should write them off. The two men knew exactly what they had to do.

***

Friday morning the 29th of September was wet, windy and cold. The weather matched the mood of the Head of the DPP, Sebastian Low-Clifford. He had had the Conti file on his desk for several hours and had been staring at it for over an hour, trying to get up the courage to tell his sponsor he was not going to roll over and free Conti.

Eventually he signed the document that declared prosecuting Antonio Paulo AKA Conti would not be in the public interest. He cited various obscure statutes and reasons as justification for his actions and had the document circulated as was standard practice. He knew various people would scream that this was not the correct decision, but he had been promised the support of the senior government figure who'd instructed him to take this course of action. He'd been told the furore would die down after a few days and be forgotten about within a month.

Antonio Conti walked out of Central Holding at 2.33 p.m. on Friday to be met by a man in a lightweight grey suit. He was accompanied by two well-dressed Italians and all four men got into a dark-coloured Mercedes car.

***

The DCI rose late on this wild and wet Friday oblivious of what the day would bring. He was determined to enjoy his long weekend. After breakfast, he had a long talk with his wife and explained that this was the day he had to decide about the job offer in Norfolk. Dr Alison Mills had a full surgery and didn't have time to discuss anything. She was running late and holding a piece of toast, kissed their daughter on the forehead and told her husband he had to decide. Whatever he did was fine by her.

Steve, with Rosie on his knee, knew he had to decide but instead of concentrating on the job offer, he decided to take his daughter for a walk despite the weather. He enjoyed pushing Rosie in her pram and it gave him time to think.

Antonio Conti's tortured body was found in Epping Forest the following day, Saturday September the 30th. He had clearly suffered a slow, painful death.

THE END

If you enjoyed reading *The Norwich Murders* then look out for the next novel in the DCI Steve Burt Murder Mystery series.

The Abduction

A soldier retires from the army and is recruited into a mysterious government unit, and a young woman is abducted and murdered. These completely separate events become central to DCI Steve Burt´s latest and most devastating case.

DCI Steve Burt, whose Special Resolutions Unit is under threat of closure by his new boss, is reluctantly given the abduction case, which soon becomes a murder investigation.

The abducted girl is the daughter of a high court judge, who is told his daughter will be returned if he finds the defendant in his current trial not guilty, but Steve thinks the man on trial isn't important enough to have a judge's daughter kidnapped. Something isn't right, but what?

The young woman's death takes the DCI on a journey involving murder and corruption and the team begin to unearth apparently unrelated events that, when put together, draw them back to a previous investigation.

Meanwhile one of Steve's officers feels there is a different side to the investigation and decides to follow her own course of action without supervision, with disastrous consequences.